ABOUT THE AUTHOR

D0189351

Syd Moore lives in Essex where the Rosie Strange novels are set. Previously to writing, she was a lecturer and a presenter on *Pulp*, the Channel 4 books programme. She is the author of the mystery novels *The Drowning Pool* and *Witch Hunt*. *Strange Sight* is the second novel in the Essex Witch Museum Series. The first book in the series is *Strange Magic* and the next instalment, *Strange Fascination*, will be published in 2018.

STRANGE
SIGHT

SYD MOORE

**POINT
BLANK**

A Point Blank Book

First published in the United Kingdom, United States and Australia by
Point Blank, an imprint of Oneworld Publications, 2017

ISBN 978-1-78607-205-4
ISBN 978-1-78607-206-1 (ebook)

Typeset by Fakenham Prepress Solutions, Fakenham, Norfolk NR21 8NN
Printed and bound in Great Britain by Clays Ltd, St Ives plc

Oneworld Publications
10 Bloomsbury Street
London WC1B 3SR
England

Stay up to date with the latest books,
special offers, and exclusive content from
Oneworld with our monthly newsletter

Sign up on our website
oneworld-publications.com

[definition] Strange /streɪn(d)ʒ/

Adjective: strange
1. Unusual or surprising; difficult to understand or explain.

Comparative adjective: stranger; *superlative adjective*: strangest

Synonyms: Odd, curious, peculiar, funny, bizarre, weird, uncanny, queer, unexpected, unfamiliar, abnormal, atypical, anomalous, different, out of the ordinary, out of the way, extraordinary, remarkable, puzzling, mystifying, mysterious, perplexing, baffling, unaccountable, inexplicable, incongruous, uncommon, irregular, singular, deviant, aberrant, freak, freakish, surreal, alien.

PROLOGUE

The rat sniffed a discarded crisp packet then, finding it empty, turned its attention to the central rail.

This was the time they tended to come out, when the crowds were thinning post-pub, and Saturday night revellers were either calling it a night, splashing out on a cab, maybe bracing the horrors of the night bus, or forgetting about Sunday and going on to a club.

Not that anywhere in London ever really 'thinned' out. Though the Square Mile, home to the financial district, or the City of London as it liked to crown itself, was quieter than anywhere else. At the weekend anyway. The nine-to-fivers hotfooted it from work on a Friday afternoon and stayed away from the place as long as they possibly could or till their alarms rudely ordered them back on Monday morning. Hardly anyone actually lived in the City any more. The few that could afford the stratospheric rents swanned up west at weekends in pursuit of bright lights and glamour, dancing, dining, drugs or drinks. Or a combination thereof.

Mary wondered if she would ever get to join the ranks of these elusive types – people who got weekends. That magical formula of two consecutive days with no interruptions or demands from work. What bliss, she sighed. It was the first thing to go if you went into the catering business. A mild twang of envy resounded within as her mind spewed an unbidden image of herself and Tom sitting at a circular table in a bijou little café bar. She caught a gleaming tablecloth. Tasteful and expensive. A fresh white. The opposite of the on-trend maroon efforts that the interior designer had chosen for La Fleur where she was the restaurant manager. No, this fantasy table that existed in another life was set against a classy background, simply furnished. Laid for dinner. And across it she imagined Tom's arm entwined with hers as they sipped each other's cocktail glasses.

That'd be nice, she thought.

One day.

Maybe.

Out of the corner of her eye, she saw the furry blackness appear before the rail and scurry towards the platform.

A middle-aged man, who was standing a few feet away swaying, coughed and made a retching noise.

Mary leant over the Tube track and watched as the rat stopped stock-still. It sniffed the air, then suddenly powered up its haunches and darted into a crumbling hole.

The action reminded her of the rodent that had made a similarly speedy, though wholly unexpected, appearance in La Fleur's dining room just eight weeks ago.

What a fiasco that had been. They'd had a couple of regular customers in too. Big spenders. And that woman who looked like a hairdresser but actually reviewed restaurants for some 'city-living' blog. Because of her, Ratty's debut had been extremely well publicised. In the following month's bookings had taken a real hammering. It was only in the past week that they'd managed to reach the level of custom they needed to break even. Which is why today had been so devastating. At about noon she'd received a blistering phone call from one of their best customers, an American businessman wooing China, who was threatening to sue. He was so wound up she'd called in her dad and he was not best pleased. Had to stop what he was doing and go and see the guy in person. But there was nothing else for it. These were exceptional circumstances: last night the customer had spent an absolute fortune on La Fleur, ordering up the finest wines, arranging for Seth, the chef, to create a particular Chinese starter that he believed would impress the delegation and seal his big deal. Those who had partaken of that oriental delicacy, it turned out, had all gone down with food poisoning. Mary seriously felt sick herself when she got off the end of that phone call.

'Did they also have the fish?' she'd asked and then cringed and slapped her forehead, grateful that there was no one else in the office to hear. She shouldn't have said that. Her father told her never to admit liability. 'Let them prove it,' was his motto. But she'd not been able to stop herself blurting it out. Not that it mattered. One had gone for guinea fowl, another had indeed consumed the sea bass, but then two of the others who had also become ill were vegetarian.

It was the second irate call of the evening. She'd managed to deal with the first without seeking help from Dad. That had been from a young man who she'd never seen before. His date had ordered the sea bass and started chucking up in the taxi home. Very embarrassing for all parties and yes they'd pay the cleaning bills.

It didn't make sense. Four different dishes, same symptoms. It had to be a hygiene issue, not food poisoning. Which was worse, really.

She shuddered and looked at the rail again. It was vibrating. A train was on its way. She'd have to have that conversation with Seth on Monday, before her dad got to him. He could be quite formidable. But then again, this kind of thing was the death kiss to restaurants and, as chef, Seth really should be taking responsibility for standards in his kitchen. They certainly paid him enough and she couldn't have eyes and ears everywhere, all the time.

The thought of the inevitable confrontation made her feel totally and utterly fatigued.

Like most good chefs, Seth was talented, imaginative and a total prima donna. There would be tantrums and swear words, denials and counter-accusations. Plates might even be broken. But it would have to be done.

She was just relieved that she hadn't had to face him tonight. She'd been slightly cowardly and left a note on his workstation telling him they needed to speak when the restaurant reopened Monday morning.

That meant, she thought, as the train trundled out of the tunnel and along the platform, she had thirty-four whole hours to spend with Tom. She didn't want to be thinking about Seth now. She wanted to be thinking about Tom and how his face was going to light up when she showed him the beautiful cashmere jumper she had bought to celebrate their twelve-week anniversary. He'd tell her she shouldn't have, but she'd tell him he deserved it and that she'd taken note when he'd muttered about being cold in her flat and moaned that he didn't fit into any of her fleeces.

It was so soft that she just couldn't resist it and of a pale blue that reminded her of duck down, and spring, and, if she were being totally honest, her boyfriend's eyes. Though she wasn't sure if she'd tell him that. Might save it for a few months. He could get awfully squeamish about that sort of thing.

As the train slowed to a stop she reached down to her side to pat the paper bag which held the gift, wrapped in silver tissue paper and tied with grey ribbon.

Her fingers slipped through the air.

'No!' She looked down. Not there.

How could it not be there?

She almost stamped her feet as, to her great frustration, she remembered stopping in the kitchen to write Seth's note. She had put it down. *Dammit.*

That was just before she left for the night.

Bugger.

Had she left Tom's jumper on the food prep area?

She might have done.

It certainly wasn't here with her now, was it?

Damn, damn, damn.

The restaurant was closed tomorrow and she wasn't sure when she was seeing Tom after tonight.

There was nothing else for it – she'd have to go back.

Blast.

That meant she'd miss the last Tube as well and have to get a cab.

A typically stupid ending to a hellishly bad day.

She let a bald man in a denim jacket get off ahead of her, cursed silently, then turned and followed him out the exit.

The night was getting cold as the midnight hour progressed.

Mary wrapped her arms around herself and stepped into the near-empty streets.

Round this way, hard, shiny office blocks, bullies of the landscape, were springing up everywhere. She marvelled at the way they built themselves up and up, looking like they were sending a one-fingered salute to the sky. Sexy and sleek, they were so very unlike the mostly glum minions who filled them. But as smart and as modern as these structures might try to appear, they simply couldn't shake off their old neighbours – squat Tudor guildhalls, Victorian thoroughfares, medieval church ruins and other lopsided survivors that let down the neighbourhood. Inconveniently historic. Stupidly listed. Retrogressively protected.

It was these little nooks, crannies and courts down which she skittered to and from work that Mary both loved and hated in equal measure.

During the day she couldn't shift the feeling that they were watching her with interest and benevolence, like impassive stone observers who, she fancied, might one day tell the story of their lives and feature her as a heroine. But at night those personas vanished. Overwhelmed by shadows they seemed to transform into dark and jealous sentries who kept guard over the ancient secrets.

Silly, of course, on lots of levels. Not least the fact that most of London's secrets were completely out now, paraded and picked over for the delectation and prurience of native and international tourists. Millions and millions each year.

She didn't really like knowing about the furtive, squalid aspect of her city – the dark side. But it wasn't easy to ignore. You overheard and saw things: snatches of talks from well-informed guides, plaques that piqued your interest and prompted a quick google, customers who showed off their local knowledge to gossip-hungry waiting staff. It seeped in. It laid eggs. It hatched troubling visions.

She was unaccountably aware for instance that the road down which she presently trod had at one time been a bear-baiting circus; that its adjoining Fetter Lane had once swarmed with beggars, vagrants, vagabonds, thieves; that in among this distinctive throng the ladies of the night had sallied and swung their hips; that one of them, Mary Ann Nichols, or Polly as she liked to be called, was born on a street of cottages underneath the foundations of the upmarket fast-food outlet that she was passing now. And she also sadly knew that this woman, this Polly, had, in the early hours of August 1888, stumbled into the waiting arms of Jack the Ripper to become his very first victim. You couldn't *not* know that round here. It was where one of the London ghost tours began each day, except for bank holidays, at seven o'clock on the dot. She'd done it with her dad when they first started looking at restaurants in the area. He'd thought it was fun. It had given Mary the creeps.

The shadows grew deeper.

Mary hunched her shoulders and increased her speed, checking her reflection in the mirror of a neighbouring barbers, the bitterly ironic Sweeney Todd's, named after the local killer who had set up his business but a stone's throw away.

It was no wonder her imagination went into overdrive sometimes.

She straightened her shoulders against these imagined ghosts of the past and noticed, in the halos around the street lights, moisture was forming into droplets – a fog was descending. She quickened her pace, listening to the echo of her solitary footsteps click-clacking over the pavement towards Fleur de Lis Court, from which the restaurant took its name. But as she turned the corner into the court something made her pause.

She wasn't conscious of exactly what that might be but she had the distinct notion that something was different. Though the street looked as it always did on late spring nights – a narrow cul-de-sac, bordered with high buildings that kept it perpetually dim, archaic in parts with its cobbled forecourt fighting for space among the elegant and modern glass fronts and revolving doors. Tonight, however, the cobbles were already shiny and damp. Fog had slithered through the narrow court like a snake. She heard the *drip drip* as it met with cold stone and began to melt against it. But there was no obvious change she could put her finger on.

Maybe she'd picked up on a subtle difference in the atmospheric pressure about the narrow row of buildings? Or perhaps she'd subconsciously detected a faint cry, the shriek of a fox, a variation in the light?

A moment passed as she watched her quick breaths make clouds in the air and, out of nowhere, a shudder ran down her back.

Suddenly she was overcome with a feeling of intense dread.

'For God's sake, Mary,' she whispered aloud. She really needed to get a grip. What the blimmin' heck was she doing, standing here like a lost lemon? She should get out of the dampness ASAP and on with her business.

Hurrying over to the door she brought her handbag up to her chest and peered into its dark interior. It was so hard to see. Why did they have black linings in handbags? She supposed it was to hide the dirt – crusty chocolate and toffees stuck to the internal fabric, smears of lipstick, grubby-looking fingerprints, fluff and such. It was practical, yes, but also exceedingly annoying at times like this, when the light was bad. It was always bad. She could never see properly these days. That was half the problem, she thought wryly.

Her hand felt past her inhaler, lipstick, comb, gum till her fingers closed on four sharp prongs – one key for the office and three for the front door. It was London after all. With a grunt she heaved open the glass doors and went to dismantle the alarm only to find it hadn't yet been set.

Now that was peculiar: everyone was usually well away by now on a Saturday.

But as she made her way across the dining-room floor she saw a glimmer of light in the kitchen.

Oh no. Was Seth still here working late on the new menu?

Damn. She really did not want to have *that* conversation now.

She was wondering if she should just cut her losses and turn around when she heard a voice. Or were they voices? Raised.

She pushed open the swing doors and pressed the light switches. They blinked twice and buzzed on.

Yes, she could hear Seth's booming bass tone. It was coming up from the cellar.

There was a sudden loud clang, the noise of a heavy weight hitting the floor. He'd dropped something.

'Hello?' Mary called, directing her voice towards the door to the cellar.

She stood there a good minute, waiting.

No answer.

Maybe he didn't want to talk to her either. Maybe he'd found out about the complaints. Okay, well if that was the case then it served her purpose to be quick. She bent her gaze and inspected the surfaces. All tidy and shiny and clear. Definitely no package there. She crossed the floor to the staff lockers. Nothing there either.

It must be in the office.

She turned towards the room.

Out of habit she had replaced her keys in her bag and spent another half a minute searching and cursing until finally she unlocked the door.

Yes. Eur-bloody-reka! The daintily wrapped package was exactly where she had put it to keep it away from splatters and fat. On top of the filing cabinet. Unable to resist a quick peak at the cashmere nestled in its tissues, she unwrapped it, touched the softness and then swiftly did it up again. It was perfect. Tom would love it.

Right, now home. She snuck the package firmly under her arm and bolted from the office, accidentally slamming the door in her haste.

Oh no. That would alert Seth, for sure.

Best be super quick.

She was locking the office when she heard something that stilled her.

A groan.

A not nice groan. A man's possibly. Dozy, sluggish but distressed. Torn-sounding.

She swivelled her eyes over to the cellar from whence it had come.

Something down there made a scraping squeaking noise.

That didn't sound good.

Drawing a deep emboldening breath, Mary began to move across the kitchen floor towards it.

A horrible gurgling noise issued from the cellar. This time it was higher, more panicked, scratchy, reminding her of a promo one of their suppliers had sent about humanely slaughtering pigs.

Ugh.

She was about to move closer still, to take the top steps, when all at once the cellar door was thrown wide open.

She clutched Tom's package to her breast and froze.

Above her the fluorescent lights fizzed and flickered.

There was someone there.

Mary squinted, aware of her pulse accelerating.

This wasn't Seth.

This person was odd – flimsy, amorphous, vague as if waving in a breeze that wasn't there, for the air was still inside the kitchen. Very still.

Mary was so taken aback that she forgot to be afraid and squinted to determine the outline – tall, thin and diaphanous. With something on her head. A wide-brimmed hat, so curiously anachronistic, was held to the apparition's hair.

Mary narrowed her eyes again and the figure grew more blurry, less substantial, though she thought saw the bodice flutter, as if there was movement there. The long skirt moved similarly. Gossamer-touched, wispy, the woman looked for all the world like she had walked straight out of the eighteenth century.

'Oh God,' Mary muttered. Not again. Not now.

She blinked to get rid of the vision but when her eyes opened she saw there, still, the woman in white, dress shifting …

Though now she spotted something else too – something awful that made her stomach lurch: down by the woman's sides there was blood, blood all over her hands.

Mary paused, and for one paralysing moment thought the spectre was going to come straight for her. But she didn't, she straightened her bonnet, set a course for the door, walked over, through it and out.

Oh – my – god.

Mary stood, stuck fast to the spot, her heart battering

against her ribcage. Everyone, the whole neighbourhood, must be able to hear it, she thought.

She was going mad. Totally insane. She would have to get an appointment at the doctor's. She would have to …

A weak rattle echoed up from the cellar.

Her gaze snapped to the stairs.

Christ.

What was going on?

What was real?

What had the ghost done? Was it a ghost or a hallucination? And why had it got blood on its hands?

A hundred million horrible thoughts churned through Mary's mind, as she attempted to impose some order – she needed help – maybe her dad or Tom? Or should she phone 999? What to report? A ghost? Don't be silly. A break-in? Was it? What was happening?

There was another sound, something like a guttural sigh. Something that sounded like surrender and blood.

Someone was still down there.

Oh crap. She'd have to go down. She had to.

Forcing herself to walk across the floor she reached the steep staircase that led down to the basement room. Yep, the light was on but she couldn't see any further than the bottom of the stairs. Gingerly sliding her back against the wall she took them one trembling step at a time and descended into the bowels of the cellar.

It had never had a particularly pleasant atmosphere.

But now it looked odd. Different.

She couldn't work it out first of all.

The cellar wasn't like the cellar. It had been painted a different colour: white. Or was that new carpet on the floor? Why on earth would there be a new carpet in the cellar? And a white one at that. Except right there, in the middle, it wasn't white at all.

Her eyes travelled up from the thickening stain and took in the sight.

Seth was standing there in some weird ballerina pose – his hands clasped up above his head, fastened to the meat hook, legs bent at the knee – looking like he was about to pirouette off to the left. *Why is he doing that?* she wondered. *If this is a joke* ... But then she saw something else: something dark was crawling over his chest. Something that was writhing and wriggling down the front of him, puddling, collecting itself on the floor, trying to rise.

'Seth?' she cried. 'Oh god, are you okay?'

It was a stupid question for when she reached the bottom of the stairs the full horror of his state became clear.

It wasn't a creature that was wriggling down the front. It was Seth's insides. Someone had sliced his throat and belly and a gallon and a half of blood and gut was dripping out of him.

His eyelids flickered.

Mary screamed, a long sustained howl, then collapsed to the floor with a thump.

CHAPTER ONE

'No blood.'

'No blood?'

'None, thank you.'

'Is that an order?'

'Can I give you an order?'

'I don't think so. Technically I am the owner of the museum. That's got to trump curator, I'm afraid.'

'Has it indeed? Well, still I maintain don't squirt the blood on. Please.'

'Why not?'

'It's tacky. Vulgar.'

'Yeah, but probably anatomically correct: the noose was likely to have broken the skin when it drew tight around her neck.'

Sam opened his mouth to speak and then shut it again.

'What?' I asked and gave him a shrug. 'People like a bit of sensationalism, don't they? You told me that. That ye olde granddaddy Septimus thought you had to take that line to get punters into the place. Because that's what they're really after, isn't it? The thrill of the darkness, the nastiness, the safe horror. Don't you want the museum to flourish?'

'Did you know, Rosie, they've taken the word "lurid" out of the dictionary?'

'Have they?' I asked. Seemed a bit odd but whatever rocked your boat.

'Rosie Strange,' Sam sighed. 'If I didn't know you better I might think that you were winding me up.' The gold in his eyes glinted.

'*Moi*?' I said. He'd caught me fair and square, I supposed, so I fluttered my new eyelashes at him. They were a recent gift from my auntie Babs who ran a salon not far from here. Then I added, 'As if.'

Sam stepped away from the exhibit – a replica of a sixteenth-century gibbet with a decomposing waxwork woman encased inside it – and frowned.

'Actually,' I said, giving the gibbet a poke, 'if I'm being honest, I reckon we should get rid of this altogether. There's something kind of weird about having it here. It's like violence porn or something. Ursula Cadence went through enough in her lifetime, we should restore some dignity to her.'

Sam raised his eyebrows. 'Really?'

I did another quick flutter, then said, 'Let's just have a simple grave with a cross on it. She hasn't got one, so we can commemorate her here. That feels better, doesn't it? Then we can use the end panel to tell the story about what happened to her, you know, after she died and that.'

'I thought you were going to sell the museum,' Sam said, a dainty nick of a smile impressing his left cheek.

'Yeah, well …' I trailed off and set the bottle of red ink in the open hand of a nearby witchfinder. He was seated stiffly in a high-backed wooden chair that resembled a throne.

'Don't put it on Darcy,' Sam warned and stepped towards his chair. 'If that stuff spills over him we'll have to source a new jerkin. There's no more in the stock room.'

I snorted and cast a glance at the sedentary lord of the manor. 'Actually, I think we should get rid of him too.' His chubby grinning face was rouged on the cheeks. A dusty handlebar moustache made him look more twentieth century than seventeenth and definitely a little mental. The red dots I had just added to the eyes now also suggested a hint of unnatural evil. A mere hint mind. 'He's the villain of the piece,' I went on. 'Well, one of them. Why don't we recycle him into George Chin?' I was referring to a not very nice man from the crazy chase we had just been on and who had practically set us up. But really I wanted to see if Sam would bite. He had once liked the Chin guy.

'Shh,' Sam hushed and nodded to the mannequin. 'You'll hurt his feelings.'

'Made of wax.' I flicked the witchfinder's forehead. The dummy rocked back, upsetting the bottle and spilling its contents all over his lap.

Sam tutted. 'I could see that coming.'

'All right, Nostradamus, go and make yourself useful. Fetch me a cloth.'

Another tut then Sam turned on his heel and disappeared out the exit leaving me alone with the waxworks.

It was quiet in here but for the slight buzz of the electrics.

Beyond that you couldn't hear any traffic or noise. We were very out of the way. It was so different to my flat in Leytonstone, but not uncomfortable. Not really. At least, I thought, now the roof had been repaired we didn't have to listen to the perpetual drip of water ruining the exhibits.

It dawned on me that I was getting used to this cabinet of curiosities, the Essex Witch Museum. My grandfather Septimus had actually called it the Great Essex Witch Museum, but the 'Great' had fallen off a long time ago and I had no intention of rectifying it. The last thing a footloose and fancy-free gal like me needed was a high-maintenance tourist attraction in deepest darkest Essex that sucked up money like a Dyson. I planned to flog it to some real-estate developer soon. Get the big bucks in. Pay off some of my extortionate London mortgage. Maybe put a down payment on a flat somewhere in Spain. I just hadn't got round to it yet.

To be fair, I'd only inherited the museum a couple of months back and quite a lot had happened in that time to seriously occupy me. Namely the update to the Cadence exhibit, over which the museum's curator, Sam, and I were currently wrangling. Though the background to this had involved a hell of a lot of a traipsing, albeit in a frantic and rather scary manner, around the country to recover the bones of one Ursula Cadence, a woman executed for witchcraft at the hands of Brian Darcy. But that was a whole other story.

'Here you go,' Sam threw a wet J-cloth at me.

I caught it and pretended to give it a sniff, 'Ah, my favourite – mildew with a hint of disinfectant.'

He rolled up his sleeves and set about sponging up the reddening stain. It was dripping on to the floor. Whoopsie.

'I'm wondering if you did that on purpose,' Sam said, and pulled across an abandoned saucepan, once set to catch water from the leaking roof, then dipped his sponge in the gooey liquid it held. I could tell he was trying to sound cross but actually he was grinning.

I liked it when he grinned.

So this was the thing with Sam, right? He really was the most arrogant, irritating and demanding fellow to have about the place, but he knew everything there was to know about Essex witches and had a fairly tight bum to boot. Not literally to boot. Though there were times when I was sorely tempted.

See, I had inherited Sam with the museum. A PhD student-cum-curator/manager/outreach officer, allegedly. Though I still hadn't worked out the details of what he did in practice. Ran the place, I think. Acted like he owned it. But he didn't. I did.

'Why on earth would I wreck my own stock, eh?' I asked, all innocence, widening my eyes and again batting the lashes.

'It's nothing to do with the fact you don't want the witch-finders in here?'

'I never said that.'

'You did. Last night.'

I couldn't remember doing so but then again, we'd shared a couple of bottles of red and I was a little cloudy on details. Having said that, he was to some extent right. I didn't like the idea that we had a few nasty witchfinders represented in here. 'Well, it's the Essex *Witch* Museum. There's a reason

Septimus had that emphasis, right? The museum belongs to the witches not the witchfinders. Actually, that's not true – it belongs to me.' The ink had soaked through the Darcy dummy's puffball skirt or shorts or doublet or whatever it was that was covering his privates. It looked like he'd had a nasty accident down there. Sam was still mopping up the drips on the floor.

Cursorily I moved the J-cloth around Darcy's groin but the damage was clearly done. 'I say we bin him,' I said, and gave the old sod a light kick. 'Or turn him into a witch. There'd be a kind of justice in that. I've got a pair of comedy breasts at home that could help the transgendering.'

Sam finished cleaning and knelt back on his haunches. 'Comedy breasts. Really?'

'Yeah. From my friend Cerise's hen night.'

'I got the impression she was single?' he said, pushing himself up on to his knees.

'Yeah.' I nodded, thinking back to that night. 'She is.'

'I see.' Sam shifted his weight to his calves then caught on to Darcy's throne and levered himself upright.

I put my hand on my hip and watched him tut at my half-hearted attempt at damage limitation. Then, to my great pleasure, the tut changed into a chuckle and he tossed back his head. His hair was tawny, wavy, thick. It rippled now, like a short mane that needed a trim. I thought it gave him a kind of feline appearance. And this was really the most irritating thing about Sam – he was oddly entrancing. Not my usual type at all. Not that I had a type. I was generally pretty much attracted to people who expressed an interest in me. Which sounds a bit pathetic, I know, but it isn't because, well, tall, dark and handsome went a long way too. And Sam was. In spades. Dangerously so. And he reminded me of cats. Big ones. Sexy ones. Sometimes, not often, but on a couple of occasions, I'd found a certain kittenish quality lurking beneath the composed exterior. You know, playful. Mostly, however, he prowled around Bagheera-like, watching and thinking, thinking and watching, through dark eyes that switched between umber, coal and amber depending on his mood.

'Come on then,' he said, his eyes amber this time. 'Time to get a move on.' Then he plucked the J-cloth out of my hands and stalked towards the end of the display to where the switchbox was concealed behind a badly stuffed toad. A second later the exhibition was in darkness, our way out illuminated only be the light coming from an emergency exit sign.

I shivered. It was so damp in this wing I could almost taste it when I breathed in.

'No time to dither, Rosie, we have to get our socks on.' Sam was returning to hurry me up. 'Certainly if we want to meet Ray Boundersby on time.'

Ah yes. Our appointment. It was a bit of a liberty if you asked me. Boundersby had been meant to meet us yesterday but cancelled at the last minute because of 'work issues', which I thought highly improbable on a Saturday afternoon when Tottenham was playing Villa. Now, however, he was demanding we went up and meet him at his restaurant. Personally I thought doing business on a Sunday was a massive imposition but this Boundersby bloke was not only a friend of my auntie Babs but also, allegedly, an ex-con to whom you didn't say no. If you wanted to keep your kneecaps. Plus, he had sounded quite frantic when I listened to his message on the phone. And it helped that he was offering substantial payment. 'All right,' I conceded. I would have preferred to go for a Sunday lunch at the Seven Stars down the road. We'd dutifully agreed to give it a rain check.

I could see Sam a few feet in front of me prowling towards the exit. He was wearing a black long-sleeved T-shirt with a helpfully fluorescent pattern that was glowing in the dark. The tee was slightly on the small side, but the tightness on the shoulders highlighted his muscle tone in quite an admirable style. For a second, I wondered if he'd chosen it for that reason. Which meant he might just have selected it for my appreciation. That thought triggered a little flush of chemicals in my stomach, which I tried immediately to counter. Though we'd had a couple of 'moments', nothing thus far had developed into fully fledged touching. 'Boundersby didn't give you many details, did he?' he asked over his shoulder.

'Not really,' I said, mentally focusing on Ray Boundersby who, I imagined, was far less attractive than my curator. The bloke had only phoned half an hour before he was meant to be here and had rearranged for today. No details, no questions. Apparently it was all 'need to know'.

Sam pulled back the curtain that partitioned off the Cadence wing from the main body of the Museum. I ducked through and closed it.

'Well, best not to be tardy, Rosie – that man sounds like

someone I should not like to disappoint. Didn't your aunt say that you let him down on pain of death?'

'Something like that.'

'Well, come on then.'

The clock on my phone however, suggested it was still early – only half past ten. I figured it would only take about an hour or so to get there from Essex, and we didn't have to be in town till one o'clock. Most of the traffic would be coming out of London, not going in.

'Relax,' I told him. 'We've got plenty of time.' But he was already round the corner and out of sight.

I sighed and followed him from the Cadence wing and up the corridor to the main reception. Last night Sam had wanted to show me some of the rooms on the floor above this end of the museum. I hadn't been there yet but he said he'd got some ideas to renovate them. One of them was apparently my dad's old bedroom. It seemed kind of odd, as I really couldn't sense much of Ted Strange in the museum at all. He had hotfooted it out of Adder's Fork, as soon as he came of age and took up a position in a Chelmsford accountancy firm, later moving further south when he met Mum.

Anyway, like I said, I'd brought down a couple of bottles of El Plonko and in the end we hadn't budged from the living room. Till we went to bed. Separately.

When I visited the museum I slept in my grandfather's old bedroom. Despite its old-fashioned décor and sparse furnishings, it boasted a luxurious four-poster with a soft mattress and duck-down pillows. Sam used a spare room that came off the living quarters. It was currently stuffed with redundant dummies that doubled as coat stands and tooth-brush holders. I couldn't work out how he could sleep in there – the waxworks gave me the shivers. I'd suggested we moved them all to the storage area on the ground floor. 'Perhaps next weekend,' he'd said, then snuck off to bed, leaving his door half ajar.

I was never sure if that was an invitation or not.

In fact, I was in such deep contemplation of this conundrum that I didn't notice Sam had stopped up ahead and walked right into him, squashing my breasts against his chest *completely accidentally*. Honest.

'Sorry,' he said, and swallowed loudly, backing on to the wall and knocking one of Septimus's paintings askew. This one looked to be a witches' sabbath by some woman called Paula according to the label below.

I switched back on to Sam and sent him a brazen smile. 'Yes?'

He wiped his hair back and apologised again, then said, 'I suppose we're, er, taking your car, are we?'

Recollections of the curator's yellow rust bucket caused an impromptu shudder.

'Well, I'm not going in yours. These boots are new. Look at them, even the gold is leather. Golden leather. Leather gold.' I sighed to express my quantum of bliss. 'Not forgetting the jeans which are £120 worth of lift and shape that are no way touching your passenger seat unless you put a towel down. Potentially several.'

Sam emitted an audible huff and let his eyes rove down

my torso to my hips (any excuse). 'Hope they didn't come out of our last fee?'

'What?' I said, threading outrage through my voice but keeping my eyes down on the boots so that he couldn't read me. Sometimes with Sam, I just couldn't obfuscate. 'No way!' I said, loudly. They had. 'How dare you? I work for a living remember. Very hard too, unlike some I might choose to mention, who lounge around reading books and stuff.'

'Okay, okay,' I heard him say, and was mightily pleased he couldn't see my face. 'All right, fine. Just saying. We need to be careful with money. Well, we'll take your car then, shall we? But on one condition: that I drive. Please. Just this once.'

I considered this for a moment. The insurance I had for work might be stretched to cover him. And certainly he was an extremely exasperating back-seat driver. Maybe if he had the driving wheel it might shut him up. 'Okay,' I told him. 'We can try. Just this once. Do we have to take any equipment or anything?'

When I looked up again I saw he had an amused little half-grin playing on his lips. 'What sort of equipment are you talking about?'

I knew for a fact that in the office, behind reception, there was a cupboard full of electronic devices, the function of which I wasn't yet privy to.

'Don't know,' I said. 'That's your department, isn't it? I'm just coming along to bring the common-sense element to all of this malarkey.'

Sam laughed. His eyes sparkled.

We fell into step as we continued down the corridor.

'I mean,' I went on, 'aren't we meant to be checking out Boundersby's place to see if there's anything, you know, a bit spooky going on? He gabbled something about a ghost.'

'Rosie,' Sam said. He was looking down at me, as he spoke, a good half-foot taller. 'We're not ghostbusters. As far as I'm aware there aren't any proton packs or giga-meters lying about the Folk Magic section.'

'Mmm.' I narrowed my eyes. 'You seem to know an awful lot of detail about that film.'

'Childhood favourite,' he said, and looked away. His fringe flopped forwards. 'I've got a couple of video cameras and tripods that we could fix up. We can pack my automatic recording device for potential EVP. Tripwires etc. Talc. The usual.' He pushed his hair back again with the hand that was still clutching the sponge. It left a streak of red paint down the right-hand side of his face. I didn't tell him.

'So,' I went on, 'what's EVP when it's at home in the Witch Museum?'

'Electronic voice phenomenon,' he said. 'Sounds on electronic recordings. They're often interpreted as spirit voices that have been either unintentionally recorded or intentionally requested and recorded.'

'Thank you, Wikipedia.' This is what he was like.

Then he winked and nudged me in the ribs. 'Though there are others who regard it as a form of auditory pareidolia.'

I jumped at his touch and took a few strides to regain myself. 'Pareidolia? Not that old chestnut?'

He let out a chortle and I joined in.

'Not sure that there's anything in EVP personally,' he went on once we'd stopped giggling at each other. 'But we may as well add it all to our bag of tricks – the gentleman's offering a very healthy fee.'

Two months ago if someone had said I would be able to joke, albeit weakly, about pareidolia I would have dialled them a taxi for the funny farm. On me. Now, it was like water and ducks.

I'd only known Sam for a couple of weeks, but they had been intense weeks and I'd experienced strange goings-on and learnt a lot about phenomena and conditions that I had previously no inkling even existed. At least they'd not come up on any staff development training in my day job investigating benefit fraud.

Pareidolia, for instance, I now knew, was the condition in which people can perceive human features in something that is not human at all. Not even usually animate: faces in clouds, human profiles in rock formations or leaf patterns, Mother Teresa in a cheese toastie. That kind of stuff.

Sam had explained it to me once and then just days later I experienced it myself. That is, I'd seen something like a woman's face in a cloud of dust. Sam, of course, wasn't convinced by my explanation. He was a sceptic, sure, but he was more of your *X-Files* Mulder type – he *wanted* to believe.

Personally I took more of a Scully line.

Oh, yes, and I'd found out we had one of those over here too. An X-Files. Well, a British one. Part of MI5 or MI6, allegedly. I didn't know what they were actually called but I'd met one of their operatives. Though I'm sure this is all a bit much to take on board. It was for me. So I'll go back to the part where we were walking through the museum.

Well, by the time we finished chuckling we had reached the lobby. It wasn't a big space but still managed to squeeze in a ticket office and an 'Inquisition' exhibit which was terrible. Though when I say 'terrible' I don't mean frightening. Originally my grandfather must have hoped it would incite large amounts of fear and trembling but now the waxworks were so ropy and caked in dust, the exhibit looked like an advert for S & M granddads. Three waxworks figured in the dungeon scene. One scrawny prisoner in nothing but a tiny sackcloth tunic was suspended from the wall in chains. Before him stood a dark-robed figure. He had his back to the prisoner on the wall and was grimacing with wicked intent through a dusty beard. His hand rested on a wooden lever. If the exhibition had been on, he would have jerked it back and forth mirroring the actions of a crescent blade, which threatened to slice into another prisoner fastened to a rack. Only it was Sunday and the museum was closed, so the three dummies were taking a break from their sixteenth-century torture regime, to dangle limply in their skimpy shorts and sacks. We really needed to replace that with something else. Or would do, if I was going to keep the place. But I wasn't.

We passed the main entrance to the museum's interior – a padded leather-look door that was usually lit by a green backlight and announced by a deep recorded voice: 'Abandon hope all ye who enter here.' Cheesy, I know. It had Granddad's name all over it.

Beyond it were sections that Sam had commandeered and overhauled: display cabinets crammed full of folkloric objects and neatly labelled artefacts. On the walls beside them educational quizzes for kids. In another section, there were rows and rows of conscientiously displayed botanicals. But for the most part, waxworks pouted and creaked doing their best to look ghastly. The whole place needed a facelift.

Sam unlocked the door to the ticket office and we squeezed past the till, turning a corner into a large office – the nerve centre of the operation – which would have looked a bit like a cross between a library and a junk shop if it weren't for the long wooden table positioned in the middle, which appeared to be perpetually laid for tea.

'Damn,' said Sam. 'I need talc.'

'Planning to get sweaty?' I couldn't help it. There was something about Sam that made me want to wind him up all the time. Well, most of the time. There were moments when I wanted to do other things to him.

He smiled wryly and said, 'There will be some in the girls' room.'

I stopped fiddling with the tablecloth and said, 'What girls' room?' This was a new one on me.

'The attic,' he explained. 'Where all your aunt and grandmother's stuff is stored.'

'Ah, right,' I said. I knew there was an attic. I just hadn't been in it yet and didn't know what it contained. 'You'll have to show it to me sometime. When we get back, yeah?'

'Of course,' he said, and then ducked out of the room.

I fed Hecate, the museum cat, black of course, then cleared the table and washed the cups in the sink.

Sam came downstairs with a battered suitcase, which he filled with wires, screens, cameras and other stuff that I didn't recognise at all.

'Mmm,' he said thoughtfully as he snapped the suitcase shut. 'Better pack some extra undies?'

'Why?' I asked. 'Are you planning to soil the ones you've got on?'

He rolled his eyes and picked up the case. 'In case we have to stay up there.'

'Ah, come on.' I gave Hecate a rub behind her ears. 'We just have to get in there, look around, set up some of this equipment and then leave. It'll be flying visit, won't it? Ghosts don't exist, after all.'

The cat changed position. Now she was stretching, no, not stretching, but backing away from me. She twitched her head, padded over to Sam and meowed loudly.

'I know,' he said to her. 'And I'll be there when she does. Come on then,' he continued his conversation with the museum's furry resident as she waved her tail in my direction dismissively. 'And you don't mind if I leave the place in your capable paws, do you, dear H?'

The cat meowed again then they both disappeared into the ticket office.

This place was seriously nuts.

An afternoon in a swanky modern restaurant was going to be just the tonic.

CHAPTER TWO

The dark pines that bordered the perimeter of the Witch Museum glittered wetly as clouds departed the sun and allowed it to shine for just a moment on our little patch of Essex. I sent a farewell nod to the museum, a lumpy white building that looked uncannily like a skull, then jumped in the car and strapped myself in next to Sam.

It felt slightly odd to be in the passenger seat but I had decided to make an effort not to nag while he drove. It wouldn't help. And, actually, as he eased my silver Mercedes out of the car park I was relieved to see him executing safe and competent manoeuvres. I liked a man who could control his gearstick.

'I've driven this make a few times,' he explained as he changed gear. 'My father had one.'

He'd never mentioned his parents before and I found myself surprised to learn he had them at all. Sometimes I imagined that he had sprung fully grown from a giant egg or something. But he was just as human as the rest of us, it seemed. 'Are they, you know, still around?' I asked.

He began to brake and started looking left and right as we approached the main road. 'No.'

'Oh, I'm sorry.'

A little smile cracked his furrowed expression. 'They're in America. Mum's a professor at the University of California.'

'Oh,' I said. That rather stumped me. 'And do you have siblings?'

'An older sister, Sybil.'

I banished Prunella Scales from my mind. 'Does she still live over here?'

'No, she's in Ibiza.'

Why all of this shocked me into silence is anybody's guess. I suppose I had lumped the curator into the 'orphaned loner' category, though I wasn't sure why. After all, he was confident (possibly to the point of arrogance), and didn't seem to shun society (mostly), though I knew he also enjoyed his semi-solitude at the museum. Even so the associations with California and Ibiza were unexpected. These were hip, cool-sounding places. And although Sam was by no means square he paid only a cursory nod to passing trends. I knew he took care of himself though – he had a muscular frame that had been worked on, I was sure. I snuck a quick glance at his thighs – just to check. He'd got chinos on today and, instead of his usual denim jacket or parka, had put on a classic herring-bone suit jacket which he'd done up over his T-shirt. Along with the high cheekbones and excellent teeth, which a posh person might assume to be a sign of good breeding, I reckon he might pass for a preppy American.

My guess was that he was intending to make a positive impression on Mr Boundersby, who was a wealthy man and therefore also a potential Witch Museum benefactor. I'd thought about that too and had swapped my regular boots for the new black-and-gold leathers that made me feel breathy and a little too excited. Teamed with my silky bomber jacket I knew I looked a class act. 'Course, I was wearing jeans but like I said, they were designer. I figured you could tell.

Sam had stopped the car at the exit and put the handbrake on, which I thought was a little bit over-cautious. Though when I looked over his way, I saw the reason why loom into view.

Beyond Sam, a tatty grey face was scowling into the car. It was Audrey, our resident protester. With her protruding red nose and wild wiry hair she looked more like a witch than anyone else in the museum, animate or otherwise. Generally, I was aware, she tended to take up residence on the pavement outside along with her placards and a table dispensing leaflets whenever she got bored of the Christian fellowship club and WI.

I heard Sam sigh as she rapped on the car roof and made a rotating gesture for him to wind the window down. Behind her fog-drenched bulk I could see one of her hand-made posters propped against the museum's sign. It had a picture of Jesus on the Mount defying a reddish devil figure. Except, no, he wasn't on the Mount. He was on a photocopied picture of the Witch Museum. Coming out of its door were myself, Sam and Bronson, our handyman-cum-caretaker. We all appeared to have grown horns. Underneath she'd written: *Woe unto them that call evil good, and good evil. Isaiah 5:20, 21*. Nice.

'Oi, you,' Audrey poked a bony finger in my direction.

Dishevelled hair fell across her face as she spoke. Though it was April she had on thick woolly fingerless gloves. I caught a whiff of damp, cat wee and lily-of-the-valley and tried not to gag. 'You there,' she said again. 'Spawn of the Strange.'

I leant forwards to meet her gaze. 'You called? Well, good morning, Audrey. Weather looks like it might turn. Let's hope spring's on its way, at last. It's been a rainy few days, hasn't it?'

She pursed her lips. A thousand wrinkles deepened around them. 'You said you were going to sell the damn hellhole. Haven't seen any for-sale signs going up.' It was an accusation filled with ragged disappointment.

I nodded. 'There will be soon. All in good time.'

Audrey narrowed her eyes and spent some time staring hard at me while Sam drummed his fingers on the steering wheel.

'All right,' she said slowly, beginning to withdraw her head. 'You make sure you get on with it.' She sniffed and straightened and started to back away then as an after-thought looked back in and spat, 'Satan's whore.'

Sam checked his right mirror. 'Twinned with Adder's Fork,' he muttered under his breath, then focusing on something beyond me he nodded respectfully, 'Morning Mr de Vere.'

I followed his gaze and saw a very old man wheeling a bicycle. He stopped and lifted a sopping panama hat in greeting.

'Who's that?' I asked Sam.

'Edward de Vere,' he whispered. 'Lord of the manor and

local patron of the village's minimal artistic community. He painted the Strange family portrait I showed you when you first came down.'

'Oh, yeah,' I said, thinking back to the huge picture which dominated Septimus's living room. It featured my granddad in a grey silk suit, nicely accessorised by a triangle of white handkerchief in his breast pocket – upright and firm. Next to him his wife, Ethel-Rose, smiled lusciously, almost coquettish if I'm honest, a coil of raven hair wound down her neck practically pointing to her full creamy bosom. Strawberry cheeks and alabaster skin suggested the artist had enjoyed painting this particular subject. In her arms my grandmother cradled baby Celeste, my dead auntie, all wrapped up in christening clothes. By her side a small boy in a sailor suit, my dad, scowled.

'Didn't you say that was painted around 1952?' I ventured. Despite the ruddy complexion and kinky white hair the cyclist looked surprisingly agile. 'How old is he?'

'In his nineties.'

'Wow,' I said. 'What's his secret?'

'Never worked a day in his life.'

'Ah, that'll do it,' I said.

As Sam turned into the road, the old man's eyes caught mine. For a moment we smiled at each other.

When we finally accelerated into the lane, I caught a glimpse of him in the rear mirror. He was still staring at me. Despite myself I felt an odd flutter of adrenalin run though my body. I didn't know why or how that might be.

CHAPTER THREE

'Stop! Stop! You're going to kill us.' Pause. Breathe. 'But I'm not going to bloody let that happen. Stop. Stop right now.'

'What?' Sam's eyes were wide. Though he wasn't letting on, I could tell he was kind of flustered. And so should he be too. 'What? It's not my fault – I'm driving by the rules.'

'That's the problem,' I said. 'You can't do that in London. We're too late now. Get out. Out of the car!'

I opened the door and stood on the pavement somewhere in Whitechapel, instantly creating a bottleneck of traffic and attracting several honks and a barrage of assorted death threats.

It was true Sam was driving by the Highway Code, but no one else was and his style was causing some serious issues with other drivers.

I plonked my hands firmly on my hips, removing my right only to flick a V in the direction of a crimson-faced lorry driver who looked a bit like Pete Postlethwaite if he'd taken too many steroids.

Sam was still in the car.

For god's sake.

I stomped around the bonnet and opened the driver's door. 'I am not going to sit there like a moron while you play grown-up bumper cars on the streets of London in *my* car. You may have a death wish, but I would like to see the sunset if that's all right with you?'

His face was pinched and whiter than usual. 'You were the one who said I could drive!'

'Yes, but that was to shut you up so you'd stop calling out every single friggin' road sign that we pass. And we're late now, and you yourself said we shouldn't irritate someone like Ray Boundersby.'

He was pig-headedly standing his ground. 'Look, Rosie just get in, will you? You're stopping traffic.'

'I'm not getting in there with you! You get out. I'm driving. It's my car.' I folded my arms.

He opened his mouth, thought better of it, and snapped it shut. I saw his head bob as he breathed out then he squeezed across the handbrake on to the passenger seat.

I whizzed in.

Now defeated, he was beginning to seethe. 'You really are something else, you know that, don't you?'

'Yes, I do,' I said, and pulled off into the middle lane. 'One of a kind. Aren't you lucky?'

We managed a terse quarter of an hour of silent fuming before we got into the City of London proper.

Despite thick patches of grey, the sun was trying to pop out. It managed ten minutes as we headed west to Embankment. A view of the Thames and the elegant tree-lined boulevards briefly raised my spirits and made me forget about our recent fracas. Things had been going okay before that, we'd hardly argued at all. Oh well, a timely reminder that he was not Mr Perfect, I rued, and let my eyes trail the classic tourist postcard vista: the dark rippling mirror of river that reflected back whatever you felt, riverboats and clippers, the bankside grand buildings, courts with ancient 'temple' names, excited tourists and dolphin-wrapped lamp posts.

I wound the window down to let in some fresh air but got a lungful of fumes, despite the fact the roads were clearer than during the week, so wound it up again while Sam directed me, through gritted teeth, to the car park of a new hotel. Here, according to a text, Ray Boundersby had organised a parking space for us. The hotel was an impressive-looking place with a little courtyard and a handy subterranean car park.

Once we'd sorted out the details with the receptionist we weaved our way on foot through the narrow backstreets and alleys until we popped out on to Fleet Street.

I didn't know this part of the City very well. I'd once had a temp job further east, in Leadenhall Market, a tiny but well-preserved Victorian arcade made famous by various films. But it hadn't lasted long. The market was always chock-full of suits and Harry Potter tourists seeking out Diagon Alley. I didn't mind either group particularly, it was just they took up so much room. Every day walking from the Tube to work you had to jostle with other pedestrians for foot space. Then every time you walked back you had to keep your place in the herd or get trampled underfoot. At least that was what it felt like.

Thank goodness today was fairly calm. We passed a walking group. Their tour guide was pointing west towards a needle-shaped monolith with a dragon on the top, Temple Bar, explaining that it commemorated the old entrance to the City of London. The gate itself, I overheard the guide saying, had been on a bit of a journey and now resided in Paternoster Square where they were off to next. A blond-haired young man with dreadlocks stopped in front of us, took a gigantic camera out of his backpack and started clicking.

Sam and I politely waited for him to finish, apologised, then crossed the street.

'Weird, isn't it?' said Sam, as we scampered to the middle. 'To think that this was once the headquarters of the British newspaper industry.'

I dashed across the second lane and on to the pavement. 'In a few years' time people will think it's weird that there were ever newspapers at all.'

'That's rather pessimistic,' said Sam catching up with me. 'You don't believe that they'll endure?'

'No,' I said. 'They're on the brink of extinction. News is a minute-by-minute phenomenon now. Daily papers can't keep up with that. They'll have to go online or become history.'

'Do you mind that?' Sam asked. I shot him a quick look to check his mood. But it was too quick – we were in the middle of the road after all. I only clocked his decisive jaw. I liked it. Always looked like he meant business. And his thrust. See, there was a power to both his frame and IQ that was impressive and at the same time unnerving to see in an academic. His convictions were the only thing about him that were a bit baggy. Some of them anyway. Personally I preferred things firm – black and white. Sam and the museum though, they were full of shifting grey shadows. In fact, I had to say, they'd inspired a few contradictions to sprout within myself. The bugger was I couldn't nip down the salon and have them lasered off.

'I mean,' said Sam, bringing me out of my brief contemplation. 'Would it bother you if that whole industry disappeared?'

'Doesn't matter if I mind or not. It's going to happen,' I said, glimpsing my reflection in a shop window. 'Evolution.' I flicked the bottom section of my hair, the blonde part, over my shoulders. It looked neater like that. The ends were getting way too dry and frazzled. This dip dye was going to have to get the chop too. I might go for a swingy bob. Summer wasn't far off and I didn't fancy spending hours every morning defrizzing and straightening as was my current custom. Enough with the faffiness, it was time for a change.

I became aware of Sam's eyes on me again.

'What?' I said, acutely aware of my split ends. 'Why are you looking at me like that?'

He shrugged. 'I was thinking about how reductive you are.'

'Reductive,' I said finally. 'Is that a good thing or a bad thing?'

His eyes widened ever so slightly. 'You simplify everything into binary context when, in fact, the situation is often much more complex.'

'Yep. It's a gift,' I said, pleased.

A kind of snorty noise came out of Sam's mouth. 'I bet your job has had a lot to do with that,' he muttered. 'Septimus was quite the opposite, he understood intricacy.'

I wasn't sure whether to get shirty about that last statement or not. 'Well, certainly, in my given occupation you have to make difficult decisions. I don't make the rules. I enforce them. Simple as that.' I sniffed. 'And secondly, I do understand intricacy. I've watched *Black Swan*. Twice. And get it: it was in her head, and that. And anyway, I didn't really have much to do with my granddad. I told you before. I can't even remember the last time I saw him. Not really. I never saw enough of him to understand his version of intricacy. And that's not my fault.' The words came out without the correct intonation or pitch and sounded way too plaintive. I hadn't meant it to leak out like that. Not really.

I saw Sam swallow. 'But given all that, it's strange that he left you the museum, isn't it?'

Now, this made me sigh. And I didn't bother keeping that in. We'd been here before. I wondered again if he was asking out of petulance, because he had expected the museum to be left to him. A kink of anger fired up inside. 'He bequeathed it to me, Sam. Me. I'm the eldest. John, my brother, is younger. And more than a little lazy. And, I know, you've done a lot for him and helped him with the museum and I'm really grateful for that, honest. But you're not family, are you?'

The muscles in his cheek contracted. 'I didn't mean that, Rosie. I'm not challenging his decision. I was merely alluding to the fact Septimus didn't leave it to your father. His surviving heir.'

I laughed. 'Dad would have just put it straight on the market without so much as visiting the pl—' I stopped mid-sentence.

Sam had halted. 'Precisely,' he said. His eyes were intense and dancing. Amber flints whirred within.

'Oh,' I said, and shook my head. 'How could he have possibly known that I'd even come down and see it? Meet you and Bronson?' I shrugged and started off again. 'I'm still selling it,' I said, and tried to make it sound firm.

'And yet here you are,' Sam said softly beside me. 'Ghost-hunting in London on behalf of the museum. Like Audrey said, you've still not even got a valuation.'

'I – I – we've been busy.' I protested.

'That's right,' he said. 'We have. You have indeed. Seeking out the bones of a woman executed for witchcraft and, I suspect, sabotaging the witchfinder effigies within the museum. I told you it would weave its magic over you. I know you didn't believe me but look at the evidence. You'll see. Oh, left here. We need to turn into Fetter Lane.'

I opened my mouth to protest but decided against it. There was some truth in what he said. I had prevaricated for sure. But that was because I'd been sidetracked by other things. Other things which promised income. Other capers that indeed *had* borne fruit. My brand new boots were testament to that.

Besides, I thought as we went up the road, Septimus had left a house in Devon to my father and money to my brother.

He was sensitive to Ted's aversion to all things witchy and aware of John's propensity for idleness. If anything, I'd probably got the crappy end of the deal. After all there was a lot of work that needed to be done to the witch museum to bring it up to modern standards to get a top-end evaluation. Sam was simply doing his best to woo me into keeping it. It was his bread and butter after all. And a goldmine of research for his PhD thesis – the definitive book on witchcraft in Essex. Or something like that. One had to admire his dedication. He never stopped trying to persuade me, the silver-tongued charmer.

'Rosie! Stop dithering,' he yapped. 'Come on, we're late. Keep up, old girl.'

Charming. 'Less of the old, thank you.'

He threw me a fulsome smile. 'You're only two years older.'

'Thanks for reminding me,' I said, and ducked out the way to avoid a homeless woman with two shopping trolleys.

The lane was wider than was usual in the City of London – a one-way street that comprised three lanes of traffic. Although located in a very old part of town, six- and seven-storey offices towered over us, evidence of 1980s construction sprees. Not the greatest architectural era for London, it had to be said.

Sam was squinting at a map he'd printed last night. 'It should be a clean turn-off here on the right.' He waved his arm north and gestured for us to cross.

I spotted the cut leading off after a chain pub. However, I could also see the outline of a chubby chick standing at the front. With her hands loosely held behind her back, feet rooted to the ground, bowler-style hat and red-and-white-checked cravat even from this distance I could tell she was City of London police.

'Oo-er,' I said as we approached. 'Looks like there's something going on.'

'There's always something going on in London,' Sam grumbled. 'Too many people, not enough space.'

'You sure you're in your thirties?' I eyed him, though privately I agreed.

'Indeed.'

'You have a lot in common with my dad.'

'I'm sure Edward Strange is a charming man so I'll choose to take that as a compliment.'

'Suit yourself.' I became aware of the policewoman eying us. She was chewing gum and had a 'Sandra face' on. This was an expression used by my team in Leytonstone to describe someone of either sex whose job it was to be a bureaucratic obstacle. When this Sandra locked eyes on me, her mouth hunkered down so that she resembled, if I might be permitted to use my dad's favourite idiom, a bulldog chewing a wasp. Behind her blue-and-white tape cordoned off the small road.

'Hello?' I said. It wasn't worth smiling. This one was clearly inured against charm.

She had a mushroom-like pallor, that could have done with a bit of bronzer to liven it up, and recessed eyes. The lips twitched like they wanted to squeeze together and spit out Mr Waspy but good training prevailed. It was too close to call whether she was by nature miserable or if this was some Sandra-faced attitude required by her job.

'We have an appointment. Through there.' I pointed over her shoulder into the alley beyond.

Suspicious brown eyes roamed over the pair of us, taking in Sam's battered old suitcase. I registered a prickle of disapproval and fleeting interest in our pairing. Sam, I imagined, looked out of place by my side. In pre-Internet days he could have passed for an *Encyclopaedia Britannica* salesman.

'You have an appointment? With whom?' The policewoman took her eyes off the suitcase and gave my boots a good look. I couldn't blame her – they were bloody gorgeous. An ugly line nicked her forehead. Probably jealous: not everyone could rock this look, it was true.

I watched the policewoman's eyes flick up to my face and saw dark circles beneath them that might be easily reduced with a lighter foundation. That was pure laziness. Or maybe exhaustion. A long shift no doubt. On a Sunday too. A spasm of sympathy passed through me.

'We've come to see Ray Boundersby,' Sam was saying. 'And we're rather late, I'm afraid. Would you mind letting us through?'

The policewoman stood her ground and uptilted her chin. 'What's the nature of your business?'

'He'd like us to, er, inspect the restaurant.'

This clearly seemed absurd to the woman. 'Oh, yeah, really? Names?'

'Sam Stone and Rosie Strange,' I told her.

She smiled to herself. It wasn't a comforting sight. It was the smile that presaged the Sandra-face triumph – dismissal. 'Let's see, shall we?' Then she tucked her chin down towards the radio on her chest and announced us to whoever was on the other end.

We waited a long moment, while Sandra switched between glaring and gloating, until the tinny radio responded. The Sandra face fell. Reluctantly she 'over and outed' then lifted the tape for us to pass through. 'Report to the officer outside La Fleur.'

'Why?' I asked. 'What's going on?'

But she merely sent us a smirk, her parting gift, then turned her back on us.

We marched over cobbles till we reached the tight, glossy entrance and were ushered in by the uniformed officer who continued to escort us to the far side of the restaurant where we were instructed to take a seat at the table and wait.

'I'll start with a prawn cocktail, thanks,' I said to the police guy but he didn't laugh.

I could see now that the narrow exterior façade was rather misleading, for the restaurant interior was huge. Truly Tardis-like. At least it certainly seemed that way – for the ceilings were enormously high. The architect had knocked through part of the first floor so the height at the front was at least twenty foot. The windows weren't opaque, blacked-out, as I'd supposed on my way in, but actually drew in the light from the court outside.

The effect was sexy and rich and opulent.

'Wow,' said Sam, taking in his surroundings and obviously coming to the same conclusion as me. 'Very nouveau.'

I frowned. 'Cuisine?'

'Riche,' he replied.

'Sam, you're such a snob.'

'Just joshing.' He laughed at my expression. 'I knew you'd take the bait.'

Seriously, compared to the Witch Museum, or the Benefit Fraud offices this was a whole different galaxy. Where the first floor would have been, a huge contemporary chandelier dangled down. Ostentatious and glitzy, it made a statement, and that statement was *I'm expensive*. It was the perfect place for city ladies and gents to show off the size of their disposal income. Or the disposable income of their companies. I mean, with that ceiling height, the proprietors were clearly not worried about heating bills. And that was going to filter through to the price you paid for a meal.

Beyond the chandelier a sweeping glass staircase led to a mezzanine level. Unlike the ground floor, which was tiled with granite slabs, up there it looked to be carpeted in lush black. Baroque frames displaying contemporary art graced ebony walls. It all gave the restaurant a nocturnal, clubby atmosphere.

About us everywhere objects glittered gold and shiny: vases, cutlery, clean-line candlesticks.

They presented quite a contrast to the mucky footprints all over the floor. It was a pretty curious scene, to be honest.

Sam wasn't looking at floor though; he was sitting back at the table taking in the height of the place. 'Hard to tell when it dates back to. This part of the city has been built upon multiple times. The current structure is maybe Georgian. Lower rooms earlier than that in all probability.'

His eyes were quick and darting, zipping round the room,

exploring tiny architectural details that hadn't been blasted away by interior designers. He noticed my gaze and turned. 'You're going to say something smart-arse, aren't you?'

I wasn't. In reality I was admiring his jawline again. It looked good, though I suspected the lighting had been designed to flatter everyone in here.

'No,' I returned, 'I'm not that predictable actually,' and started ad-libbing. 'I was wondering if there were witches here. In London.' My eyes caught the urbane chandelier. 'I suppose they're mostly in rural settings – cottages or caves or forests, stirring cauldrons under the new moon. You know, places that are a bit more herbal.'

Sam had removed his phone from his pocket and was jabbing at a compass app. 'Mmm,' he said, head bent to it. 'Margaret Jourdemayne was executed just up the road at Smithfield. It's a meat market now but it was once an execution site. The Witch of Eye, I believe she was called. Got caught up in court affairs, tried to help a noblewoman conceive. Burnt at the stake.'

'Here?'

Sam swapped seats so he had a better view into the space. 'A place called the Elms in Smithfield,' he squinted into the middle distance. 'I think, if memory bears me right.' He looked back at the app and jiggled it around. 'It's slightly north of St Bartholomew the Great.' He pointed in the direction of the kitchens.

'Is that relevant?' I said.

'Well, we don't know yet, do we? Right now, we have to keep an open mind—'

'And a healthy scepticism,' I finished his sentence. It was his motto, I had learnt.

'Indeed,' he added. 'Especially as it looks like something quite serious has happened. There's a sizeable police presence.' He leant his forearms across the table. 'Through that hatch.' Once more he jabbed his finger at the rear of the restaurant. 'There're wombles in the kitchen.'

'You're hallucinating, dear boy. The excitement must be getting to you.' But I could hear plenty of sounds coming from that direction – muffled footsteps, murmured conversations, the odd radio beeping.

'Forensics,' he explained. 'You know – the policemen in white jumpsuits who analyse the crime scene.'

'Or women,' I added.

'Yes,' he said. 'Them. They're in the kitchen. I just saw one pass by that open hatch. And that guy over there,' he directed my gaze to the double swing doors where another uniformed policeman stood to attention. 'Is he on guard or something?'

It was all very intriguing indeed. 'Break-in?' I suggested.

Sam shrugged. 'Do you think we'll still be required?'

I had no chance to reply because at that moment the kitchen doors swung open, almost knocking the uniform to the floor, and a man in a light grey suit appeared. His eyes swept the restaurant floor, then, when they settled on us, he hustled over swiftly.

'Detective Sergeant Jason Edwards,' the bloke announced, before he was anywhere near the table.

'Hello,' said Sam.

I nodded.

The cop had some height on him and was dark and lean. He was also trying his damn best to look unharassed and in control. Only there was a vein pumping quickly above his eye, which suggested otherwise. He too, like the police-woman, was dog-tired, but seemed way more stressed, full of prickly energy. When he took a seat I noticed his shoulders were almost touching his ears.

Detective Sergeant Jason Edwards stifled a yawn then leant back and stretched his spine along the back of the chair. He blinked several times, rubbed his eyes then removed a notebook from his inside jacket pocket and tossed it on the table.

'So exactly what have you come to inspect, Mr Strange, Miss Stone?' he asked, clasping his hands on his lap. There was a hint of south London accent there. His voice was deep but strained-sounding like he was forcing himself through the motions, fighting off the exhaustion with only willpower. And he was dropping consonants left right and centre, which, I thought, probably signified approaching stupor – he certainly wasn't drunk and was sharp enough to clock the lack of wedding ring on my fingers and address me accordingly. Though I preferred Ms.

'Other way round,' I said, lifting my chin up and smiling. 'I'm Strange. He's Stone.'

'So you are,' he said. The whites of his unblinking eyes were tinged with dark red veins. A cutting intelligence lurked behind them. Despite the outward signs of intense fatigue, the guy knew what he was doing. He was checking we were telling the truth, or had well-rehearsed fake names. I wouldn't fake mine though, would I?

He breathed in again, shaking his head out, as if he were shrugging off an unwelcome thought, then abruptly stopped and eyeballed us. 'As you were saying?'

Sam put his elbows on the table. 'Possible supernatural phenomenon,' he said.

I prepared to cringe and colour at the detective's reaction. However to my utter amazement DS Edwards didn't gasp or laugh. He dipped his head as if we'd answered the question correctly, his face expressionless.

'Is that … a … fact?' The words came out gradually.

I nodded again.

'How timely,' he said, and made a point of staring but not speaking for a full minute.

It was rather uncomfortable. I darted a glance at Sam who shrugged.

Edwards waited another moment more, then repeated Sam's answer: '"Possible – supernatural – phenomenon."' This time he fully articulated all vowels and consonants. Like he was testing the words out. Like they struck a chord inside that big old brain of his.

'That's right,' said Sam, a little hesitant.

'And you've come all the way up from?'

'Essex,' said Sam.

Edwards looked at me and smiled slyly. 'It's the only way …'

I clenched my jaw and prepared to propel myself across the floor. This sort of talk touched a nerve, you might say.

Having been born and spent most of my life in the county, when I arrived in Leytonstone, aged fourteen, a prepubescent girl from just over the border in Essex, I found that I was unwittingly relieving Stinky-touch Simon of the mantle of class joke. Which was ridiculous as, my mum had told me, Leytonstone used to be in Essex anyway. But kids, well they'll pick on anyone who's different, won't they? Just as folk did with the witches, actually, which is maybe why I seemed to have developed some sympathy with them. For four years, the stereotype was projected upon me relentlessly, converting faltering answers into hysteria-inducing howlers – evidence of my geographically accorded stupidity. The toe-testing of relationships became a clear indication that, true to form, I was indeed an Essex slag. And of course I became the unwilling butt of a seemingly endless supply of jokes like, 'What's the difference between an Essex Girl and a computer?' 'You only need to punch information into a computer once.'

Difficult to know what to do with that when you're fourteen.

As an adult I decided I wasn't taking this crap any more.

'Essex Girls indeed!' I said, not trying to conceal my outrage. 'What's bloody wrong with them anyway? That you cling on to the stereotype is more offensive than any so-called "Essex Girl". Are you really telling me no one else in the country has sex before they're married or enjoys a drink or three at the weekend?'

Detective Edwards stared.

'And the "thick" thing?' I went on, not giving an inch. 'Well, people are just as stupid in London, I can testify, but you never hear anything about a "London Girl", do you? Oh no.'

Sam was biting his lip and shaking his head ever so slightly. But he wasn't stepping in.

I filled my lungs so I could deliver my punchline in one go. 'The Essex Girl, Detective Edwards, is a dated 1980s concept that should have been laid to rest along with Cabbage Patch Kids and He-Man. The fact that people still mention it is testament to how dull and uninventive they are.'

Sam let out a hefty sigh and looked up at the ceiling.

I stood my ground and waited to see if I'd got through.

But Edwards merely yawned and rubbed his eyes, though truth be told, under his nose I could see the smallest kink on his mouth. 'Oh yeah? You're probably right.' Then abruptly he sat up straight and pointed. 'What's in the suitcase then?'

That wrong-footed me. Usually I readied myself for at least a little bit of argy-bargy. The fact that he didn't engage left me with my mouth open but nothing to say.

Sam cleared his throat and tapped the case. 'Equipment – Go-Pro mounted cameras, infrared cameras, IR lights, audio and video recording devices. Also motion sensors and a pair of Tri-Field meters. There's a Spirit Box, in there somewhere too. An SB-11.'

'A Spirit Box?' DS Edwards repeated.

'Yes, it's basically a radio frequency scanner that some people believe allows the voices of discarnate entities to manifest in between the static. Other investigators sometimes use Rem Pods. I don't. I do, however, keep a few thermometers about the place, both probe and IR types.'

'Is that so?' asked Edwards and stood up.

'And talc,' I added.

Sam just shot me daggers and waited for the detective to respond.

When he did it was to smooth down the creases on his suit trousers. They disappeared quickly which suggested the weaves weren't compressed. The suit was new. 'You don't mind then if I have a look?' he said gesturing to the case.

It wasn't a question.

'Be my guest,' said Sam and heaved it on to the table. Edwards ever so slightly nudged him out of his way with a deft movement of his hip. Alpha male, I thought, as he centred himself over the handles.

With two clicks the lid sprang open and he plunged his hands into the box, beginning to rummage and thus giving me the opportunity I had been waiting for to survey him for clues.

I liked the fact that he had chosen not to rise to my Essex Girl rant. It was refreshingly different. He was different. And still unfazed. He'd moved on to the next subject so rapidly, I found that my adrenalin was still buzzing round my body, all dressed up with nowhere to go.

I decided to trot out a little huff and then channel my energy into interpreting the detective's unconscious signals: I was guessing the recently acquired suit meant either a formal occasion had been attended or that he'd invested in some new clothes because he'd come into some money. The suit was slate-grey, so non-funerary. Did people wear grey suits to weddings? Possibly. Though this was a very standard style – nothing flamboyant or showy. Definitely more suitable for workwear. If I had to pick a background story I'd plump for a recent promotion. He obviously wanted to look good. And yet he had stubble. Not a designer type. It was more randomly located. Which meant he'd probably been up a long while and hadn't had a chance to shave.

'What's this?' the detective said, unsheathing a rectangular object with a rainbow of lights at one end. He held it as far away from himself as he possibly could, almost as if he thought he'd catch something off it.

'An EMF meter. Please allow me demonstrate.' Sam plucked it out of his hands and pressed a red button on the side. 'This one is sensitive. Not cheap.' The rainbow lights flicked on. 'It measures changes and fluctuations in nearby electromagnetic fields.'

'Uh-huh,' said DS Edwards. 'Are ghosts made of electricity then?'

'There are many explanations for phenomena that seem on first inspection to be extraordinary,' Sam began.

But Edwards wasn't listening to him. He'd moved on to something else – a silver video camera.

'Ooh,' said Sam. 'Be careful.' Tiny beads of sweat appeared on his upper lip. He ran a finger round his shirt collar to loosen it. 'That's quite fragile. It's a—'

'I can see what it is, thank you,' he squinted down one end and tried a button. A side compartment popped out at his touch. 'You're still using tape? How quaint.'

'We can't afford to keep updating the kit.' Sam pouted. 'Not constantly. Though that one,' he gestured to a small boxy camera mounted on a handle which Edwards immediately seized and turned over in his hands. 'That's thermal imaging,' he announced proudly. Then unable to resist any longer, he reached over to relieve the detective of it. 'Very delicate. And quite pricey too.'

'So,' said Edwards straightening his tie. 'Who asked you to come and look at La Fleur?'

Sam stroked the camera and swaddled it in bubble wrap, then with very great care, like it was a little baby, he tucked it back into the suitcase.

When the camera was safe and asleep, he removed his jacket and folded it over the back of his chair. His face suggested he hadn't enjoyed seeing the sergeant's grubby fingers handle his belongings. Or maybe they were 'ours'. I'd have to find out later.

'It was Mr Boundersby who contacted us,' he said finally answering the policeman's question.

I jumped slightly – something had brushed against the back of my calf. A light pressure. Maybe a cat. No, it was too slimy, almost gelatinous. I bent over to look beneath the table. For a second, hanging there upside down, I experienced a slight dizziness and the fleeting notion that down here in this liquidy darkness things curled and slimed as they did in the murky depths of the Thames estuary, or as the day-trippers called it 'the Toilet'. Still, I couldn't see what had brushed me.

I considered the possibilities and unexpectedly let go an 'Ew', which surprised everyone including myself.

'You all right there?' asked Edwards.

'Yes, fine,' I said, breathing slowly and righting myself.

'Something touched me. A cat, maybe.' I could feel the blood pumping at the sides of my forehead. I bet I was unattractively ruddy.

'Yeah?' Edwards shifted in his chair and tried, badly, to conceal a shudder of distaste. 'And? What was it?'

'Only shadows.'

'Mmm,' he said, lip still curled, and cast a couple of quick glances at the floor. 'In this place it's more likely to be a rat.'

My cringe was as involuntary as it was immediate. 'A rat! Why?'

Even Sam started to look shifty and crossed his legs twice.

'I take it you don't read *SquareMileMeal.com*?'

'No?' I raised my feet on to the crossbar between the table legs. 'Why? Should I?'

'Shirl Van Hoeden nearly shut this place down with her "Rat in Mi Kitchen" review. They had a bit of a problem here, I believe.'

I looked uncertainly at the floor again. 'No. Doubt it was a rodent,' I said. 'It was right up the top of my calf, just under my knee. That'd be too big ...' An image flashed across my mental screen – a dog-high rat, rubbing friskily against the back of my leg. 'Wouldn't it?' I trailed off and suppressed the urge to gag.

We all looked around till Edwards said, 'But that's not what you've come to inspect?' He stuck his pen in his mouth and bit it. 'Or is that a sideline?' he added.

'God no,' I said, insulted. I mean, did pest controllers wear Cuban heels? Did they have dip dyes? Regular manis? Well, actually I didn't know. They could well do. I started to give voice to another little huff anyway, but as it was halfway over my lips, it occurred to me that, really, we did kind of deal with pests. Or investigate the symptoms of infestation. Sort of. Well, Sam did. I was only coming along because I was pretty sharp when it came to reading people.

Derek, my line manager at work, reckons I'm the best he's ever met. I don't think that's entirely true but, for sure, I can pick up on other things that people don't generally notice. The way people talk but not with their mouths. The way they move themselves or shape their eyes. Eyes are the main thing though. And eyebrows. They tend to speak volumes. Though odour communicates a lot about a person too – how often they might be washing their clothes, hair, bed sheets; how regularly they vacuum and dust, or how much their household co-workers do. It can tell you about the quality and price of their clothes, which in turn suggests how much importance they place on appearance. Sweat reveals whether they exercise regularly, take drugs, booze, eat curry and that.

I'd already picked up that Edwards' breath was unclean. He had tried, almost successfully, to mask the sulphuric farty smell with a Fisherman's Friend. It had nearly worked, but there were still base notes evident that suggested he hadn't drunk enough water today. Possibly hadn't eaten enough either. Which, summed up, indicated that he had been so caught up in his work he hadn't been conscious of his body's demands. Something big had gone down.

I looked back at Edwards to find him staring at me expect-antly – eyes all round and momentarily goggly.

'Ray Boundersby,' Sam was explaining, 'came to see us. At the museum.'

DS Edwards blinked, brought his peepers back in a bit, edged on to his seat and regarded the pair of us from beneath well-shaped black eyebrows. I think they were natural although he might have gone in for a bit of DIY tweezering.

'When was this?' he asked, relinquishing his gaze to hunch shoulders over his notebook. Here then was the nub: Boundersby.

Sam shot me a quick puzzled shrug and said, 'Yesterday.'

Edwards' pen squeaked slightly on the paper as he wrote He was pressing down on it hard. The bloke was really tense. 'Only yesterday, you say?'

What was with this 'only'? I wondered. I corrected Sam's explanation, 'Mr Boundersby was meant to come down to the museum yesterday but cancelled. My auntie Babs had made the appointment for him the week before.'

He lifted his pen to scratch the stubble on his chin and waited for an explanation. 'Your auntie Babs?' His gaze was continuous and piercing.

I took it and returned it. 'Yes. Babs also lives in High Wigchuff.'

One of the sergeant's eyebrows went up. 'High what?'

'It's where Ray Boundersby lives some of the time,' I explained. 'My uncle Del runs a scaffolding company and had done some work on his country house.'

Opposite me, Sam tutted to himself.

Edwards' eyebrow, meanwhile, lowered itself back down

to a more comfortable height. 'Ah, I see. That's not long ago. Had he made overtures to you before then? Mr Boundersby?'

'We were otherwise engaged for another client,' Sam interjected.

'I work in Benefit Fraud,' I said, though god knows why.

Jason Edwards dutifully wrote it down. 'Benefit Fraud. Is that relevant?' he asked.

I could see Sam rolling his eyes.

'Not really,' I admitted. 'I keep saying it out of habit.'

To my surprise, the sergeant let go a little snicker and nodded. 'Yep, I get that too. When I'm tired. Which is all the time. Occupational hazard.'

He met my eyes again and grinned loosely. *Oo-er*, I thought. He was actually quite attractive.

Sam coughed.

'Sorry,' said the sergeant for no reason and went on. 'So your boyfriend was saying that you couldn't respond to Mr Boundersby earlier than Saturday because you were busy?'

Very quickly, possibly a little too quickly, I answered, 'He's not my boyfriend.'

Sam pushed his chair out so abruptly that it squeaked against the floor. Edwards and I turned to the noise.

'We were on business for the museum,' Sam said, and pursed his lips. 'Both of us.'

'So,' the DS addressed his remarks to him, 'can I just confirm that the earliest that you two,' he looked back at me, with a slight smile on his lips, then returned to the curator, 'could make it was yesterday? Together?'

'Yes, that's right,' Sam nodded. 'Rosie works during the week, as she said.'

But my working hours appeared of no interest to Edwards. 'And you say that Boundersby had highlighted his, er, problems a week ago?'

'Indeed.' I came in again, leaning forwards on to the table, wresting his attention back. 'To my aunt. Babs. Barbara.'

Edwards flashed me a stunning smile – wide and full of strong healthy teeth. 'And what's this, er ... museum that you mention?'

'I'm the owner of the Essex Witch Museum,' I said, with a proud little head wobble. Which was kind of weird, as I hadn't felt particularly delighted about it till now. I think I had literally just realised how impressive it sounded. 'Owner'. Yes, that was nice. 'Sam is my curator,' I continued, then immediately regretted using the possessive pronoun. That was bound to wind him up.

But he didn't flinched or anything, though his mouth had gone kind of tight and narrow and he had begun tapping his fingers on the table. 'Look,' he said, craning his neck towards the back of the restaurant. 'Is Mr Boundersby here? What's happened? Are you going to tell us?'

'The answers to those questions are mostly no,' replied Edwards and closed his notebook. 'Did Boundersby say why he wanted you to come down?'

Sam sighed and inclined his head to me.

'Only that there had been some "incidents" in the restaurant,' I told the detective, 'that he wanted checked out.'

DS Edwards took a breath. His voice became serious. 'Did he say what type of incidents, Miss Strange?'

The tone of his voice made me pause to think back. 'He alluded to supernatural phenomena but said he'd explain more today.'

'But you took those "incidents" to be what?' The detective was at his most alert since we'd sat down.

I shrugged and batted it over to Sam, who said, 'Presumably the usual suspects: demonic possession, poltergeist activity, aural/optical illusion, haunting – that sort of thing.'

DS Jason Edwards stopped writing and put his pen on the table. For a long moment he stared at Sam. 'And that's your regular fare, is it?'

Sam shook his head. 'My day-to-day work is at the museum researching witchcraft. Mostly cases occurring in Essex. There were lots. Most people aren't aware of it, but Essex had more deaths on a single day than the Pendle witch-hunts. Did you know that?'

The detective's face was beginning to screw up. He was going to label us as nuts, have us taken down the station. I really didn't fancy that so decided to distract him by slamming my hand on the table, a little more strongly than I meant to.

Sam jumped. DS Edwards wearily turned his head to me. 'Yes?'

'Now, listen here,' I said, unaccountably wagging my finger. 'We're becoming very late for this appointment. I demand to see Mr Boundersby.'

'Sorry, that won't be possible,' said Edwards. His charming grin had slipped off.

'He's not …' said Sam and looked back at the kitchen hatch. 'Nothing's happened to him, has it?'

'No.' Edwards pushed his chair out. 'But you can't see him, I'm afraid. Right now he happens to be down the station helping us with our enquiries.' He gripped the side of the table and pushed himself off and up. 'Miss Strange, Mr Stone, thank you for your time. I'd be grateful if you could leave your contact details with the constable outside. We will be seeing you presently so don't leave town, as they say.'

I thought he was going to go back into the kitchen but he didn't. He took out his phone and headed for the front door. It was all rather sudden.

'Bloody hell,' I said to Sam. 'I can't believe this.'

He had lifted his suitcase off the table and looked like he was readying to leave. 'What does he mean – "don't leave town"? Ridiculous showmanship.'

I checked the front door through which the sergeant had disappeared. 'I suppose he needs to say that to everyone. You know in case they need more information.'

'But why would they need to talk to us?' Sam shook his head as the constable who'd escorted us in returned to take down our particulars. A joke was on the tip of my tongue but I squashed it. Everyone round here had a humour bypass.

Once the contact details box had been ticked we were quickly and efficiently ejected into the courtyard with assurances someone would be in touch.

As we reached the junction of Fleur de Lis Court and Fetter Lane, the stout policewoman lifted the tape while we scuttled back under, and inspected my boots again. They were rather lovely, it had to be said.

'eBay,' I told her helpfully. 'Pricey though.'

She looked at me, flabby face full of contempt. 'I know,' she said. 'You've got the label hanging off the back.'

She was bloody right too. How had I not seen it? How had Sam not seen it?

'You could have told me,' I raged down the street after him.

As usual he completely disregarded my sartorial faux pas. 'I wonder if it's got anything to do with Boundersby's concerns,' he mused.

I insisted we stopped while I removed the offending boot and bit through the plastic thread. Only once I was satisfied that they were free of any type of marketing paraphenalia did we continue down Fetter Lane.

'Could this be related to the supernatural phenomenon he mentioned?' Sam continued.

I was still grumping. 'Hardly likely as it doesn't exist.'

'But if someone thinks it does—' Sam began but stopped and turned towards the building at our side. I followed his gaze and noticed a shadow had detached itself from the wall of the building to our left and silently slipped into step two or three paces after us.

'You the ghostbusters?' it hissed.

A sliver of a man about twenty years or so, with gelled cropped hair, a large English rose tattoo on his neck and a heavy gold chain slunk close behind. He was smoking a roll-up but removed it from his mouth long enough to whisper, 'Fer fuck sake don't look. Don't let the rozzers see you be talkin' to me.'

I played along snapping my eyes to the road ahead. 'Why not?' I hissed back.

'Me first,' said the shadow. 'You the ghostbusters?'

'No,' said Sam. 'We are most certainly not.'

'Yes, we are,' I called to our trailing shadow. 'Ignore my colleague; he doesn't want to blow our cover. We've got all our equipment in the suitcase. All the giga-meters and electrons, you know.'

My colleague let rip an exasperated sigh. I shouted out extra words that sounded professional to cover it up: 'Phasers and OCD recorders. Scientific stuff.'

A squeak came out through Sam's nose. I didn't look at him. I didn't want to start laughing too.

'Fought you were,' the shade rustled fast behind. 'We need to talk.'

I resisted the urge to turn around and have a good look at the little bloke. 'Who are you?'

'Joel Rogers. Kitchen boy, assistant at La Fleur. For real, you're the ghostbusters?'

'We are,' I said. 'For real.' Sam's face was becoming incredulous. 'Can you tell us what's supposed to have happened at the restaurant? The police won't.'

'Not 'ere,' Joel whistled somewhere around my shoulder blades. 'There's a pub down the road. Turn left, go for two hundred yards or so then turn left again. The Leicester. Meet you in there.'

I gave in to temptation and spun around catching a wisp

of baggy grey sweatshirt and jeans that hung off a very bony behind and exposed a large band of underpants. Above it, as was the custom today, a little nick of bum crack was neatly displayed.

'Why did you say that?' Sam had obviously changed his tune for his voice was now tinged with a heavy dose of annoyance. 'That we're ghostbusters. It's cheapening. And you don't even believe it. It just makes me look like an idiot.'

'The fact he knew what we were here for means he was privy to Ray Boundersby's concerns. He's got inside knowledge. He might be able to tell us what's going on.'

We had reached Fleet Street. Our car was parked to the right, the Joel Rogers assignation was to the left. Sam looked in both directions then turned left.

I followed.

'I'm surprised,' he said as got into his stride. 'You're usually the one who wants rid of trouble.'

'Usually,' I agreed. 'But I've got a feeling, this time, trouble's already found us.'

CHAPTER FOUR

The Leicester was a poky subterranean bar that, despite current legislation, was full of smoke. Its TV, in the main salon, was showing sport and the place was half full of people in storeroom uniforms and tour-bus guides on their lunch hour, who all sat silently watching the screen, nursing pints and chasers.

There were a couple of snugs on each side of the room. It was in one, right at the back of the bar on the way to the toilets and the slot machines, that I spied our wiry shadow friend. Instructing Sam to give me the suitcase and fetch us some stiff drinks, I bumped and squeezed my way through the tables to Joel Rogers.

'Hello?' On closer inspection, I wasn't sure if it was him for a large black baseball hat was now perched on top of his head. It looked several sizes too large and had the effect of making him appear younger and slightly lost within the excess folds of fabric swamping his scrawny frame. He didn't much look like a kitchen boy. More like someone who tried the handles on parked cars for a living. 'Joel?'

Cradling a lit cigarette over a green china ashtray full of

butts, he took his eye off the end long enough to register me. 'A'right,' he said, and squashed a match into the ceramic pot, leant back and stuck his gangly legs out underneath the table. The little bloke, like the big sergeant, was doing his best to look louche and completely unbothered by all the drama.

'Do you want a drink?' I asked. He looked like he needed one. His skin was pasty though there were blotches of red round his eyes that might have been eczema.

'Bud,' he said, and yawned. Inside his mouth he had small sharp teeth.

'Okay.' I caught Sam's eye over at the bar and mimed the drink to him.

'You all right if I sit down?' Always best to be polite.

Joel Rogers looked sideways, as if checking with invisible friends, then shrugged.

I sat down on one of two pew-like seats that faced each other. My boots squeaked against the sticky red vinyl coverings. This wasn't a pub for city slickers unless they had a penchant for an altogether different kind of slick.

'So,' I said. 'You all right?'

He nodded slowly, like a sage about to pronounce a long-deliberated verdict. 'S'pose.' There was a shake to his hands, which he was trying hard to conceal.

'Good,' I said. 'Now how did you know that we were the ghostb—?' I stopped myself. 'The investigators?' Must avoid the G-word. If it stuck, Sam would go nuts. I tried to picture what that might look like but all I could summon was an image of him frowning with a thundercloud over his head.

Joel slid lower down on the bench so that he was almost

horizontal and clasped bony hands over a concave stomach. 'You two look well weird. Suitcase. Tweed. And you with them mad blinging boots.'

'Hey! These are quality, I'll have you know.' But I had to concede the curator and I were an unlikely fit. After all, we had not been drawn together organically. More like I had been thrust upon Sam.

Now there was an image.

Joel shrugged. 'Just sayin', you don't look like police. Don't look like forensics.' His accent was loose and roving, cobbled together from different postcodes, and even countries; for I was sure there was a bit of the US in there probably mimicked from music videos and interviews with urban pop stars. 'They wouldn't let media behind the lines,' he was saying. 'You was out of place but theys let you through anyways. Got to think why – why would they let some fashion bird and a teacher type in? Maybe they experts? The bloke there, he could play it but you don't look no expert in my book. So you must have been coming anyways. They must have wanted to talk to *you*. Not the other way round. So who do I know who is coming to the gaff? Ghostbusters, that's who.'

'Well deduced,' I said, and he half closed his eyes and bobbed his head slowly in a modest show of self-congratulation. 'Who did you hear that from, though? That we were to visit the restaurant?'

'Heard MT gassing to Anita 'bout you.' Joel was sitting up a bit more now but still managing to look untidy.

'Uh-huh,' I said, leaning forwards on my elbows. 'And who is MT?'

He pushed back his cap and rubbed a palm into his eye. The boy would detach a cornea if he kept going like that. It was a temporary condition but one which if untreated could seriously impede your capacity to work. 'Marta Thompson,' he said with what appeared great effort.

I frowned.

'MT is kinda what everyone calls her. She front of house, the hostess. Comes and takes you to yer table.'

The mention of this MT person seemed to inject him with enough energy to push up into a normal sitting position. He jiggled his legs and cleared his throat then stuck his chin out. 'Mr Boundersby calls her the *maître d'hôtel*.'

'Got it,' I said. 'So what did the maître d' say to you?'

He leant forwards. 'Can't remember exactly. Just that she 'eard you was coming up, checking out what's bin going on.' He nodded to himself, again, like he was another person confirming the statement. 'Yeah.'

Someone by the table coughed. We both looked up.

'Yes, I'd like to know about more about that.' Sam crouched over us. 'Nobody's told us a thing. It's about time we learnt what all the fuss is about. What exactly has been going on at La Fleur restaurant?' He deposited the drinks clumsily, slopping brown liquid everywhere. 'Sorry,' he added, not sounding it.

Out of the corner of my eye I saw Joel shrink. At first I thought it was something Sam had said, but then I saw he was gawping at the glasses with horror. I looked at them and saw what the problem was. 'Oh, Sam,' I whined.

Before I could articulate the rest of the sentence Joel had

come in with, 'Coke! Fuckin' soft drinks.' He was practically spitting. 'What's that all about?'

'Well,' Sam said, towering over our table. 'You're driving.' He prodded the air over my head then turned his attention to Joel, who was back down the seat again, slouching moodily. 'He looks underage and I, for one, intend to have my wits about me.'

'I'm nineteen!' Joel bristled. I caught a whiff of Lynx sprayed on top of body odour. He jerked his head at Sam. 'This your dad or somefink?'

'Or something,' I said, smiling fractionally. 'But now you mention it,' I sighed. 'There are similarities.' I'd said I wanted a stiff drink too. What was dear Mr Stone thinking of? Sam rolled his eyes. The wrinkles around them, born no doubt from constant squinting over historic documentation or doing his condescending face too many times, began to recede. He looked younger than his thirty-one years, briefly. 'We'll see. I might get another round in a bit.' He had sat down heavily on the stool at the end of the table then pushed one of the glasses over to Joel who looked epically unimpressed but picked it up anyway and took a sip.

A group of men positioned underneath the TV suddenly started cheering. We all looked over – footballers on the screen were approaching the goal.

'Actually,' I said, bringing the boys back. 'Before we go into what's happened at the restaurant in the past, I'd really like to find out what's going on there right now. What's with all the police?'

Joel's frail body seemed to cave in a bit. 'My sources say it's Seth,' he said finally.

'Who's Seth?' asked Sam and took a notebook out of his jacket.

Joel shook his head slowly from side to side and sucked his teeth. 'Chef. He bin killed.'

I gasped. Blimey. I had no idea it was anything as serious. Joel looked up, his expression startled.

'An accident?' asked Sam.

The kitchen boy's thumbnail crept between his lips. He put it between his teeth and began to bite it so that his features looked like he was snarling. 'Jackson told me. His place backs on to our courtyard out back. Import-export. Fine teas. He's looking after the place while his uncle's away. Overheard the police talkin'. It was on their radios. Seth's throat bin slit. In the old meat and wine cellar.' His voice cracked on the final word.

For a moment I found myself at a loss. It wasn't what I had been expecting. A burglary, perhaps. Maybe a gas leak. But murder?

No wonder the place was crawling with police.

Joel had dropped his eyes to the floor again. Without looking at the glass he reached out and picked it up.

Sam intercepted the young man's arm and patted it. 'I'm going to get you a whisky,' he said to Joel, his voice set just above a whisper but still brisk and businesslike. 'That all right?'

The kitchen boy flinched at his touch. Yet when he looked into Sam's face something there calmed him.

In an instant, I saw the young lad's bravado for what it was – a camouflage for his distress. Good old Sam, I thought.

There had been episodes recently when my colleague had shown a surprising amount of kindness and sensitivity when I myself had been oblivious to any need for compassion. An occupational hazard, I suspected. After all when you were in my line of work you had to keep your wits about you. Give an inch and the real benefit fraudsters would take a blimmin' light year. Which made it kind of weird that when I saw Sam do his stuff, it touched me. Somehow made him stronger. Don't ask me why, I'm not a psychologist.

As Sam got to his feet I saw him smile at Joel; his eyes were in their 'mellow nutmeg' shade, the crinkles around them etched not by what I often perceived as patrician disapproval but right now, right at that moment, real concern.

He glanced over, nodded to me, then left for the bar.

Joel went back to trapping the crisp wrapper with the toe of his trainer. Without Sam the silence between us grew static.

I grimaced, then threw myself into 'nice' mode though it was difficult without a drink in me. 'Are you all right?'

Keeping his eyes on the wrapper, he shrugged, 'Whatever.'

'Well,' I said, determined to emanate Sam's sensitivity. 'I'm only asking because you knew Seth personally, I presume. I mean you've worked with someone, this chef, so you've spent days in the kitchen with him, cooked with him, exchanged banter with him, and now, well, he's been murdered. Brutally too. I mean, his throat slit. Oh, just think of it. How horrible. What a way to go. He must have been surprised or if not he'd have probably fought back. So then he'd be overpowered. I wonder if he felt the knife. The pain of it slicing through the skin? He probably choked on the gushing blood … Not nice, I think you'll agree?'

Joel made a funny noise, then rubbed his hands across his face and groaned into them. 'What you gettin' at? I heard about people like you.'

'Just saying I wouldn't want to go like that.'

Joel jerked himself up. His lips, I saw, were drawn back, eyes narrow with rage, and watery. 'I know your game. I know what you're doin'. Well, it won't work.' Corners of his lips were strung with saliva.

I wasn't completely sure but I starting to think 'nice mode' wasn't working on him.

Joel's index finger jabbed in my direction. 'You're tryin' to work me up so that I confess. I've seen it on TV.' His lips quivered.

'I am not!' I said.

'Well, it won't work!' he thumbed his chest. 'Not on me.'

'Okay, okay,' I put my hands up in mock surrender. 'I was just saying—'

'Weren't me!' Joel repeated then, just as quickly, withdrew back into the folds of his sweatshirt, head retreating like a tortoise. From the depths of jersey fabric he protested, 'I didn't have nuffin to do with it.'

I repressed the urge to point out his double negative, 'Of course not.' No, this was not going as smoothly as planned. Best say nothing and wait for the diplomat of the team to return to the negotiating table.

But after a moment Joel broke the silence. He huffed his arms together and stuck out his chin in a gesture of defiance. 'He was fit, Seth. He worked out. It'd be well hard to kill him. And I got no reason, 'ave I? To knock Seth off? Why would I? Plus, I didn't find him or nuffin neither,' he said, less combatively this time, regarding me with new suspicion from under his sparse brow. 'Mary did, if you want to know.'

'What?' I said in as neutral a tone as I could muster. 'And did this Mary have a motive to kill him?'

'No, no! Fuck's sake!' He was like a tightly coiled spring. Uncoiling. 'Mary *found* him,' he overemphasised the verb so there was no chance of misunderstanding.

'Oh, right,' I said, waiting for him to point out the relevance. 'And?'

'They say don't trust the finder but, in this case, they got that wrong.' He was back up now, hands near the ashtray. 'Mary ain't done nuffin, I can tell you now. None of us done it. We wouldn't. Why would we? He was savin' that place, Seth. No one got reason to do him in. 'Specially not me.'

Did I detect a note of pleading in his tone? I wondered, as Sam's shadow fell over us again.

'That's right,' he said soothingly. Boy, was I glad to see him back. 'Rosie's not accusing you, are you, Rosie?' He sent me a sharp look.

I wondered how much of 'nice mode' he'd overheard.

'No, no.' I smiled but with only half my mouth.

He had brought three tumblers filled, this time, with a couple of inches of yellowish liquid and cubes of ice. 'There you go, Joel. You've had a shock, mate. Drink this.'

I'd never heard him say 'mate' before. It sounded inauthentic but Joel didn't notice. He merely smiled, accepted the glass then took a big gulp of it down. I followed suit. It was hard being nice.

'Now, tell me about Mary,' Sam continued. 'She found the bod— she found Seth, did she?'

Puckering his lips, Joel nodded. He'd completely changed his attitude to Sam. I noted a kind of grudging gratitude. The kid fumbled for a fag.

'She's real nice, Mary. Ray's daughter.' He popped the cigarette in his mouth.

Sam picked up the lighter and lit it. Joel nodded a brief thank you. 'They got her down the nick. Think she's a suspect. But she wouldna done it. Though it's her what's seen most of the funny stuff, true enough.'

I was going to ask him to elaborate but Sam hushed me with a glance. I was guessing he wanted to guide this one.

Sam replaced the lighter on top of the cigarette box. 'What sort of funny stuff are we talking about, Joel?'

Expelling a long lungful of smoke, Joel said, 'Well, we all seen some of it. Things ain't right here. A lot of things ain't right here.' He looked hard at Sam and paused. 'But Mary, she reckons she's seen a woman round the place. Goin' though walls and that. Nasty feel. Not a normal lady but like old-fashioned. With clothes from the olden days.'

Sam nodded. He opened his notebook and began writing. 'Do you know any details of what she looked like?'

Joel shook his head. 'Just that she wasn't from now. She was a – like a ghost.' He brightened suddenly and wagged his cigarette at Sam's notebook. 'But she did say once, she wore a hat.'

He paused to watch Sam note it down.

Part of what he'd said had also caught my attention. I mean, it was one thing, someone saying they could see a ghost, but was Joel suggesting others had witnessed it too? 'But you said you'd *all* seen funny stuff?' I pressed Joel. 'How do you mean?'

He looked at me, his body growing rigid again, features all sulky, and took another glug of whisky. 'This place,' he said, looking back at Sam. 'La Fleur. The restaurant. See, it's cursed.'

'Cursed?' I repeated, unable to hide the disbelief in my voice.

'Is it? How?' Sam interjected, all bassy and serious.

'Different things,' said Joel. He shrugged and rolled the cigarette between his thumb and index finger. 'Lots of 'em. We kept puttin' 'em down to bad luck till one night, back in March, this thing happened.' He took a long drag, brought his shoulders to the table and lowered his voice.

Sam and I responded to his conspiratorial tone by bringing our faces closer in too.

Joel looked from side to side, checking there was no one nearby, then whispered, 'We all thought it was some kind of joke. But now, I dunno. Wasn't very funny. Didn't think so at the time neither.'

'Go on. What happened?' Sam nudged gently.

The kitchen boy wiped his mouth with the cuff of his sweatshirt. 'It was well cold that night.' He bent his shoulders lower over the table. 'Well cold. And misty, you see. Don't know if that had anything to do with it. Kind of unreal though, that night, outside. You could feel something in the air. You know when sometimes you is cruisin', mindin' your own business but you feel like everyone is watching you or like you're in a film or somethink. That's what it was like. But we was busy so when trade started kickin' in you didn't have no time to think about it. Must have been a Friday,' he nodded. 'No. Maybe Thursday. Didn't feel like a Saturday. Wasn't full but was fast enough for us to be sweatin' it in the kitchen.' His eyes darted around the pub.

Sam and I exchanged glances. He had taken something that looked like a Dictaphone out and laid it quietly on the corner of the table. Sam obviously thought this was meaningful. I followed his cue and bent closer to Joel.

The kitchen boy cleared his throat and whispered, 'So I was on the salads, right, shaving the cucumbers.'

I frowned and dismissed the mental image of a salad vegetable in a barber's chair.

'When John comes in all funny,' Joel said. 'Flustered, right. He's one of the waiters. Normally he all useful, solid. You know – Australian. Likes cricket. Goes on all the time about this Gabba thing they got over there. But not tonight. Tonight he is shoutin' for a bucket, right? Honest to god I swear I did a double-take when I first sees him because there's all this dark shit down his shirt.' Joel rubbed his own hand on his sweatshirt to illustrate then gulped down a mouthful of liquor. The memory was clearly disturbing him. 'Thought he bin shanked first off. But he says no, it ain't his blud. Says it's comin' out of the light, spurtin' from the ceiling and I need to get in there and sort it out pronto. 'Cept he didn't say pronto, he said "quick-smart" or somethink. So I races round to the cleanin' store, nabs a mop and soon as I walks out on to the floor, I sees it.' He took a final drag of his ciggy and stubbed it out. 'And it makes me stop dead. Right there, halfway across the floor. Strangest sight I ever did see.' He paused, shook his head and reached into his tracksuit pocket. 'I filmed it. Just a bit. Before I got caught. But I dunno, it looked like somethink out of a horror film.'

He scrolled through his videos then put the phone on the desk and pressed play.

You could make out the dining floor of La Fleur. It was a view from the perspective of the kitchen doors. The mobile operator, Joel, was walking on to the floor. He must have been holding things because the camera work was very unsteady – one-handed. As he progressed into the dining area it became obvious that something shocking was going on. The tables in front of him were empty, half-eaten food had been abandoned, knives and forks scattered across the top, glasses overturned and spilling wine over one of the tablecloths.

He turned slightly to the right and caught a line of startled diners all of whom appeared to be looking in the opposite direction. Joel swung the camera round to focus on whatever was appalling them so, and settled on the chic sweeping chandelier, the statement feature of the room that was suspended over the diners.

This time it didn't look sexy and smart.

It was dark. Not bright and sparkling like it had been this morning. A viscous red liquid was cascading down its crystal beads.

Joel laid both hands on the table. 'It was drippin'. Mucky red stuff. Comin' all down the chains, goin' into the bulbs, slip-sloppin' on to the customers, the tables, the food and all over the floor like some Stephen King waterfall.' He shuddered and shook his head.

I was impressed by the simile. He was right too – it looked like something out of *Carrie*. It must, I reflected, have been a bit of a showstopper in such glitzy surroundings.

Someone off camera shouted, 'Christ mate, you're meant to be cleaning it not filming it. Get on.' And the image froze, then went to black. The film clip ended.

Sam nudged the recorder closer to Joel.

'That was John,' he said. 'I knew I shouldn't have whipped the phone out but you could see what it was like. Got worse too, cos the lights,' he said, 'in the chandelier, they was dimmin', getting sticky with the stuff. Some of them was flickerin'. A couple exploded while I was standin' there moppin' before the customers start freakin'. But that was way too late to clear it up and pretend nuffin had happened – they not stupid or blind. They all seen it. But John goes over and starts explainin' there is a leak. I said maybe there was too. Cos the offices above, they was empty. The landlord was refurbishin' so he could up the rent.'

'Uh-huh, uh-huh,' I said, unable to drag my eyes from the blank phone screen. It had looked very nasty but also mesmerising.

Joel shifted and lit another fag. 'And now the blood that was comin' down, it were getting thicker and faster. And Mary-Jane, she's another waitress, well fit, pretty, you know, I like brunettes. Well, she was comin' over and she says she'll go upstairs and try and sort it. So off she goes and so I get in with the mop proper. But there ain't no mistakin' it, I tell you, it well looked like blood. And it was spreadin' across the floor, big puddles of the shit.'

I looked at Sam. 'Could be rust?'

He nodded and shushed me. 'Go on, Joel.'

'So I'm getting busy with the mop but you can hear, at the tables all around us, the diners they moaning and moaning and one party gets up to leave when just then – bang! All the lights goes out.'

Sam and I stirred and leant away from him.

'They fused?' Sam offered.

'Yeah,' said Joel. ''Cept for the ones on the mezz over the pictures. They on a different circuit. So everywhere, right, is in darkness, 'cept for up on the mezz. And everyone looks up there and then someone starts screamin', "Oh my god!" He shrieked this in a high, camp voice. '"Look! Look!"'

'Why?' I asked. 'What was happening?'

'Because,' Joel knew he held us in his thrall. He paused, looking from me to Sam and back again, 'there was words on the walls.'

Sam stopped writing and gave Joel his full attention. 'Where?'

'At the top of the stairs: they was glowin'.'

'What did they say?' Sam asked.

'I took a photo,' he said with caution. 'Don't tell Ray.'

We both agreed not to.

'But it was so weird. Shiny. Kind of green. Horrible. And the words, they was well creepy.'

Joel scrolled through the phone again till he came to the right image. 'Here,' he said, and showed us.

You couldn't see much. It was dark, but just as Joel had described, there was something up on the walls. Thin yellow-green curves and lines, luminescent. I picked up the screen and made the image bigger so that I was able to read what was written there.

'*Till the blood gushed from her eyes*,' Joel read out. The look on his face mingled horror with triumph, the cat presenting the dead mouse.

Whoa! Nasty. That indeed was quite a story.

I passed the phone back to him. You could certainly see how that might affect the staff. No wonder Boundersby had got in touch.

Sam was staring at Joel, nodding his head slightly up and down. The words had made an impact on him too, you could tell.

When neither of us spoke Joel went on, 'So do you think they was there because—?' He stopped. A hand went to his mouth as something in his head shifted a gear. Darkness passed across his face. 'Oh god.' He rubbed over his face where stubble might have grown. 'Seth! Oh god.' He sat back up again, cheeks paling. 'Do you think it was a warning? The blood?' His hands came down quickly and gripped the table as he tried to master himself.

'It certainly sounds ominous, I give you that,' Sam picked up his glass and took a sip.

Joel released his grip on the wood and drained the final dregs of his drink. 'Mary thought it was for her.' He licked his lips uncertainly. 'From the ghost woman she bin seein'.'

'Mary,' Sam repeated. 'She's the kitchen manager, yes?'

Joel nodded. 'She seen the bitch. We should have got rid of her. Should have.' He shook his head.

'The bitch?' I was getting slightly lost in the narrative.

'Ghost,' he said. 'Wot done it.'

Ah, I thought. *Here we go.* I tried to lock on to his flitting gaze. 'Okay, Joel, it's probably time for us to assure you that there are lots of explanations for ghosts. Striking phenomenon, like this,' I gestured at his phone, 'that at first sight appears to be extraordinary is often something else. Usually something quite mundane.' I looked at Sam meaningfully, wanting him to back me up, but he didn't. He was drumming his fingers against his chin this time and frowning hard.

'Oh, yeah?' Joel's voice was hopeful. He wanted this reassurance.

'Yes,' Sam came in, amusement playing on his lips. 'Do expand, Rosie.'

They were both looking at me, waiting for my pearls.

'Well.' I threw back my shoulders ready to hold this court. 'People often put two and two together and make five. They interpret things differently. All over the world. I mean, the power of suggestion is just that – a power in its own right. It can make people see things that aren't really there. Like, before the incident in the restaurant, Mary had already suggested that the place was haunted, right? So everyone was or might have been a little on edge, watching out for the extraordinary anyway. When it came, that's what they attributed it to.'

Joel looked doubtful. Sam backed me up with supportive grunt, so I continued.

'Therefore when the blood chandelier episode happened and you all saw the words on the wall, you also assumed that they were connected, right? And connected to what Mary had seen. Therefore supernatural or further evidence of haunting.'

'But they weren't there before,' Joel whined. 'Not before the lights went off.'

I didn't want to get drawn into particulars right now. 'I agree that it's odd that they were there at all, but there will be a reason for that. The chandelier episode was probably random. I mean, what evidence did Mary have that the place was haunted anyway?'

'She seen things. That woman round the place.'

'Lots of explanations for that.'

Sam raised his eyebrows. 'Such as?'

'Well, there's pareidolia,' I said, and smiled at Sam. 'Have you heard of that, Joel?'

He dropped an inch into the seat and shrugged.

'Shall I or will you?' I asked Sam, aware I was playing a dangerous game: everything I knew about the condition I'd learnt from him. I wasn't in a position to show off yet, not really.

He opened his hand. 'Be my guest.'

'Well.' I turned to Joel and tried to make my voice sound kind and motherly. 'This is a very natural condition when you perceive angles and curves that your mind translates into human features or patterns. Sometimes we see what we want to, other times we see what we don't want to.'

Joel's jaw hung low, his mouth gaped open. I wasn't sure if he was really getting it.

'It's called pareidolia,' Sam added then switched his eyes to me. 'Very good, Rosie. And?'

My smile began to falter. 'And what?'

'You were telling Joel there were lots of explanations.'

'She did,' said Joel, and nodded in slow pointless male solidarity.

I squared my shoulders at them both. 'Well, then there's the most obvious explanation. The one everyone skirts around.'

'Yeah?' Joel's eyebrows perked up.

'Being mental,' I said clear and loud. 'It accounts for a lot of reported phenomena.'

Joel flushed. Sam grimaced. 'I think what my colleague—'

'Cheeky,' I cut in. 'Employer.'

He rolled his eyes and continued. 'What the owner of our splendid witch museum means is there may well be a biological, anatomical or neurological reason for Mary Boundersby's convictions. And, by the way, Rosie, not everyone who sees a ghost is mentally ill.'

'I know,' I said. 'And not everyone who is mentally ill is mad.'

'That's an interesting statement for you to make. I never thought you were big on nuance.'

'It's my middle name,' I said, making a note to look it up later. I had a vague understanding of it though the word itself put me in mind of clouds for some reason.

Joel was tucking himself up, retreating once more into the folds of cloth. 'But we *all* saw the chandelier and the words on the wall,' he sulked.

'Yes,' Sam interjected. 'And that would lead me to believe that it was a human hand that had written the slogan, possibly for that very reason. For everyone to see.'

'But that's going to make the customers cancel. They so flighty. It could ruin—' Joel stopped as an invisible light bulb went on over his head. 'But Mary heard groans. And,' he sat up and wagged an accusatory finger at me, 'she seen her close up. A few times.'

'That could be pareidolia, though,' I said in a kind of 'wise' voice as Joel's phone went off.

The kitchen boy uncurled and smiled at the screen. Licking his lips he scrambled to his feet. 'Gotta take this,' he said, than legged it from the table greyhound-quick.

A cheer went up around the TV screen. I looked over and saw six footballers on the telly hugging and slobbering over each other in a demonstration of heterosexual respect and camaraderie. Yeah, right.

When I looked back Sam was leaning over the table, arms folded, staring at his notebook.

So?' I said.

'Working in reverse,' he said, not moving his eyes. 'It seems we've got a murder.' He picked up his pencil and tapped a couple of sentences at the top of the page. He'd underlined them both.

'Yeah,' I said. 'Nasty. Cut throat.' The words made me shudder again.

'Some threatening and gruesome writing on the wall. Then ghost sightings.' He laid the pencil neatly at the bottom of the page. 'Hard to imagine these things aren't connected.'

I agreed. 'Someone's trying to mess with their heads?' It seemed the obvious solution.

'Or slice them off altogether,' said Sam. 'Which means, dear Rosie Nuance Strange, we should take much care to keep hold of ours.'

CHAPTER FIVE

After fifteen minutes Sam went outside to look for Joel. When he came back shaking his head I realised the kitchen boy had scarpered.

We finished up our drinks and then decided we should call Ray Boundersby. He was our client after all, and it sounded like he could use us.

I went straight through to voicemail so left a message.

But when we were on our way back to the car my phone rang. And it was him.

'Listen,' he said. He had a brownish voice streaked with the East End. 'Sounds like you know the score. I'm with Mary at the station. Now, they're barking up the wrong tree here but they're barking hard. We don't reckon they'll be charging her anytime soon, so they'll have to let us go at some point. I want you round her flat by nine o'clock tomorrow morning.'

'I'm sorry, Mr Boundersby,' I told him. 'I've got to work tomorrow. I think Sam will be able to make it though—'

'Don't talk nonsense, girl,' he growled. 'For starters, I'll double your fee.' It was already quite healthy enough, to be honest. 'And for dessert, I'll serve you this – it's not that I don't take no for an answer. It's just that nobody's ever said it since the 1987 job with Frankie the Flyover. Not that any connection could ever be proved. In court. So see you tomorrow.' And he hung up.

Sam was waiting. 'Well?'

I was fond of my kneecaps. I wanted to keep them. Intact, preferably.

'I think I'm going to take my first sickie,' I said.

Then I told him why.

When my phone buzzed again I jumped so high I nearly punched myself a sunroof.

It was a text from Ray with Mary's address.

'That's north London,' Sam commented. 'I won't be able to make it up in time. The connections from Adder's Fork are notorious.'

I stared at him blankly.

'Any room at the inn?' he said, trying to send me what I think he thought was a cheeky grin.

'There's a small spare room but it's filled with junk,' I told him.

'Sounds like a home from home,' he smiled.

Inside my stomach a butterfly began fluttering hopefully.

It took us the best part of an hour to get back to Leytonstone.

My flat was in a purpose-built block on a road that led down to the high street. On the far corner there was a bar that attracted a crowd of youngish people and locals during the week. Though at the weekends when it played thumping house music late into the night it was mostly populated by flashy coke-heads.

So I was surprised when we parked up and Sam suggested we have a drink there later.

'It's open mic tonight,' I said ominously.

'Great.' He clapped his hands together with something approaching enthusiasm. 'Spoken word?'

I stopped myself from laughing out loud. 'More like *X Factor* rejects and wannabe stars of the West End. That sort of stuff. They seem to always end it by murdering the Kings of Leon. It's terrible.'

'Is that legal?' asked Sam and I laughed, then realised he didn't know who the Kings of Leon were.

'Well, let's see how it goes. We've got the evening to ourselves,' he said, almost affable. 'We don't have to decide now.'

My flat was a wide, clean rectangle, mostly glass on the outside wall and white paint on the inside. It was made up of one long room on the side that looked towards the bar. This was an open-plan space comprised of kitchen, dining room and living area. Behind this was a small bathroom. On the opposite side was the master bedroom with small en suite, and two box rooms, one of which I had annexed as a walk-in dressing room. The other doubled as a laundry/junk room and occasional guest accommodation. I had an Ikea chair that turned into a bed. It was already in its bed form, from when my friend Cerise had last crashed, so I changed the sheets, shifted the laundry basket and squirted some air freshener about the place.

I was on the fourth floor, which was irritating when the optimistic, or possibly arbitrary, five-person-capacity lift/coffin was out of order, but a bonus on evenings like this, when the sun had finally broken through the cloud and I could sit out on the balcony and bask in the last of its rays. Being to the east we got a good view of the City with its nest of skyscrapers and, though Leytonstone was seven miles from central London, I always felt that wasn't too far from the glitz if I ever fancied popping over.

'Nice,' said Sam, once he'd given the place a once-over and stowed away his equipment and spare pants.

I got out a bottle of wine. To my great surprise he expressed a desire to have a glass. In my experience Sam didn't drink much at all. Well, not like a normal person. But here he was looking quite relaxed, which was odd considering we'd just been to the scene of a crime. A murder in fact. Though, on later reflection, I thought that considering his field of study it might have made him feel like he was on familiar turf – the macabre was his bread and butter after all.

I suggested we enjoy the view on the balcony and he followed me out.

There wasn't a great deal of depth out there but it had a good length running from the kitchen down to the living area which was at least twenty-four feet. My neighbours, Peter and Sue, who did something unknown in the City had put up some wicker fencing where our balconies met, presumably to stop me looking over if we were out at the same time. Not that I wanted to: I'd suggested to her a few months back that she probably shouldn't go near Lycra, but evidently Sue ignored good advice. Peter was also a big man, swaddled in layers of fat, in possession of a neat trim face with a little light-brown goatee. However, beneath that his chin sloped into his chest, which in turn barrelled out to his stomach. In profile, he put me in mind of a small human ski slope. He liked to relax outside with his top off. When they got pissed, they got frisky and chased each other round the flat. It was like having a ringside seat at London Zoo when the seals were in season. Even before they'd stuck up the wicker I'd erected my own grow-bag in the hope that bulbous green tomatoes might put them off a bit or make them think of food or at the very least block the view. Apart from that, they were fine neighbours. Sue had a key and watered my plants whenever I was away. When they went to their flat in Alicante, I repaid the favour.

'A lot of greenery,' Sam said, settling down on one of the two cane recliners. There was just enough room to leave a foot-long gap between the footstool part, as long as you didn't fully extend it, and the balcony wall. A mosaic table stood between the seats just big enough to hold a wine cooler and two glasses, which was pretty much all it ever needed to hold. Usually one. Outside the kitchen I'd positioned a patio table and two chairs if I ever wanted to dine al fresco.

I poured the wine out and we clinked glasses.

'Not what I expected,' said Sam and positioned a cushion behind his neck. 'Didn't know you had green fingers.'

To me, the balcony looked like your slightly more crowded but average Londoner's open space. Working-class people who lived cities could rarely afford much so you had to make do with what you got. I had nothing flashy or exotic going on, just standard English classics: down from the tomatoes stood a tub of sweet peas that I was trying to cultivate. Dad had brought the young plants over from his allotment. We both loved their intense fragrance. I placed them just under the living-room window so when they bloomed, hopefully in a few months, I might be able to sit on the sofa watch *CSI* and breathe in their heavenly scent. Bliss.

By the kitchen window I had a few planters designed for a similar purpose – honeysuckle, lavender, jasmine – and a titchy greenhouse with some practical pots: chillies, which I was keeping a close eye on in case it was still too cold for them yet, basil, rosemary, thyme, coriander. All bought from the local Tesco Express and replanted. Splashes of colour were provided by this year's crop of narcissi, daffs, tulips and a bunch of Dad's hardy geraniums in cotton pinks and bright fiery reds that for some unknown reason always made me think of the 1950s. I'd popped them into hanging baskets along with some trailing lobelia that the packet had optimis-tically described as sky blue. Of course, I was named after a certain flower, so I had to have some of them about the place too but they weren't going to bloom for a few more months. There was nothing extraordinary about any of it.

'It's pretty out here,' Sam continued, bending over to pointlessly sniff a tulip. 'Ethel-Rose's parents ran a nursery. Did you know that?'

I admitted I didn't and asked him, 'Why, isn't it what you expected?' Had he anticipated a bedsit? Or maybe a three-storey house?

'I can't imagine you out here getting your manicure dirty. Though I suppose it's in the genes.'

I shrugged. 'Good nails and gardening aren't incompatible if you wear gloves. In fact, they can come in very handy if you want to dig out small pits for seeds,' I said. 'Nails and gardens are more or less the same thing except one's on your house and the others are on your body,' I held a hand up, palm out, and admired Fang Li's latest artwork. 'I love looking at my nails when they've just been done. I love looking at my flowers in bloom. In fact, the latter's better because I've helped them along myself. Well, with Dad's help occasionally,' I finished.

'Avid gardener, is he?' Sam pushed his fringe back over his forehead and took a sip of wine.

'Allotments take up a lot of time. They're very trendy these days: the local council waiting list has got names on it like Mungo and Josh. So if you fail to keep them well-maintained, they'll have them off you. Dad puts in a good few hours a day now he's retired. Actually, I think you'll be able to meet him. He's on his way over now.' I raised my head and peered over the balcony wall. Cars were parked solidly up both sides of the road. That would annoy him.

'How do you know?' Sam straightened up decorously in expectation of elders appearing.

'I think I heard him cough on the street.' I hadn't but yesterday he'd mentioned it on the phone and sometimes I could tell when he was on his way. Like close family do.

A cloud passed over Sam's face. He swung his feet to the floor. 'Does he, er, know about me?'

Now, that was a question. In a split second I was wondering what exactly the 'about' bit was. A reference to the early blossoming of romance? A relationship of sorts? Or maybe it was just about my acquisition of him, the curator, along with museum?

While all this was running through my head, I think my expression must have been either blank or confused because Sam waved his hand in the space between us like he was muddying water. He darted a fearful glance through the window at the front door. 'I mean, does he even know I'm here?'

I let out a snigger. 'Sam, I am a grown-up gal. I'm allowed to have gentlemen callers in my own place, you know. Just as long as they declare their intentions to my father as soon as they meet.'

He frowned.

'Oh god, I'm joking,' I said. 'Dad's fine. Very mild-mannered.'

This seemed to ease him. 'Yes, yes, quite right.' He smiled but threw a good two fingers of wine down his throat.

He was confusing sometimes. Well, a lot of the time, if I'm honest. There had been a recent episode when I'd seen him chatting up a barmaid. He'd shown a surprising amount of confidence: he knew he was attractive to women and he handled that well, using it when he wanted to. Then at other times he came across as old-fashioned and awkward. Nervy even. It was a paradox.

The doorbell rang.

'Talk of the devil,' I said, and my companion's frown duly deepened.

I sprang up, jumping over Sam's recliner, and slipped into the apartment.

'Shall I …?' He got up unsteadily but I waved him down. 'Just relax.'

I was across the room, reaching for the Chubb lock, when the door opened and Dad blustered in carrying a large marrow and a bulging Co-op bag.

'Got my own key remember?' he said, closing the door.

'Yes, for when I'm away and *emergencies*,' I reminded him pointedly. 'Oh, come on in then. Would you like a glass of wine?'

I was about to explain that I had a guest but Dad was off already. 'You want to be careful of your liver, Rosie. I know what young people are like. Government recommends two alcohol-free days a week. You doing that? Me and your mum have Mondays. She's thinking about Thursdays but I've got bridge then and, God help me, there's no way I can get through an afternoon with Jean Taylor-Brown in my earhole without at least three units to take the edge off.'

'I'll think about it. Listen, Dad, I've got a g—'

'No, I'm sorry. You can try to persuade me as hard as you like but I can't stop, love. I'm on the double yellows.' He marched straight in and headed for the kitchen, not stopping to draw breath or look around, which might have prepared him.

Sam had inched himself inside the door and was presenting with a fixed grin stapled to his face.

But Dad had trooped into the kitchen and begun removing purple-sprouting broccoli from the Co-op bag.

'Don't know why you choose to live round here, really I don't. Parking is dreadful. Trendy though, isn't it? Price you pay, I suppose. Price I pay, more like.' He emptied the remaining tips and groped around the bottom of the plastic back. 'Fish stew in here from yer mother. She said make sure it's heated through, as she left it on the side for half an hour.' He plonked a rectangular Tupperware box on the counter next to the broccoli mountain and raised his head in my direction. 'Mind you, I stuck in a couple of Scotch bonnets so the chances of anything living in it are about the same as finding Elvis tending bar down the Conservative Club.'

Then he stopped speaking. His mouth remained open for just a fraction of a second longer as his brain tried to compute the man standing next to me.

'Dad, this is Sam,' I said watching him politely convert his astonishment into a smile.

Dad was about the same height as Sam, though used to be taller, and I could see him stretching himself now. He took off the cap that he had on, revealing his bald patch, and lifted his pale grey eyebrows to survey the other male.

Sam took advantage of the pause in Dad's monologue to introduce himself with proffered hand. 'Good to meet you, Mr Strange.'

My dad stared at him a moment then put down his cap. Wiping his vegetable-stained digits against the pockets of his cardigan, he grasped Sam's hand and shook it over the counter.

It looked friendly.

'Very pleased to meet you,' said Dad.

Sam countered, 'You too, Mr Strange. Septimus told me a lot about you.'

If I could have foreseen the effect of the curator's words then I would have stashed him in the broom cupboard and told him to shush up, for within seconds Dad's face changed entirely.

First it went blank, then less than a second later his lips opened and he blew out noisily and for a very long time, eventually sucking the air back in so hard it made a whistling sound. Three times he blinked. I could see the colour was draining out of him though he was attempting to rouse himself. This, however, took some visible effort.

He managed to squeak, 'Well then,' before his frame began to crumple.

Tearing his hand out of Sam's he reached for his chest and then, scarily, pitched down on to the counter.

Both Sam and I made for him.

In an unlikely display of heroic agility, my colleague vaulted over the worktop while I swung round it and caught Dad under the armpits.

'It's all right,' Dad was saying between choking sounds.

We manoeuvred him over to a dining chair, still conscious, thank god. 'Indigestion,' he murmured.

'Shall I call a doctor?' Sam asked, mobile in hand and clearly worried.

'No,' Dad said. 'No fuss.' His lips had gone a sort of bluish colour, his eyes red-rimmed and sunken in the shadows of his sockets. 'Water.'

Sam got him a glass at once.

I bent down and whispered, 'Are you all right, Dad?' It was a stupid question but I hadn't seen him like this before and was shocked and worried and clueless.

'Pills. One. Top pocket.' He began to point to it but found the effort too much and gave up, sinking against the chair back. His face was so pale now he was starting to look vampiric.

I reached in and found a blister pack of tablets and popped one into his hand, which was shaking. He knocked it back with a swig of water.

Sam stood behind him helpless.

After another minute, Dad's breathing began to ease though his forehead remained dotted with tiny beads of sweat. After a few minutes more his skin colour returned to something approaching normal.

'What were those pills?' I asked.

'Rennies,' he lied. In other circumstances, I wouldn't have let that go so easily.

I just said, 'Oh, I see. On prescription?'

'That's right,' he said.

I scowled. Dad's pills plainly weren't for dyspepsia.

A couple of months back I'd seen a client/suspect with similar packaging displayed all around him. He had angina, which was worrying but not fatal, though potentially an acceptable condition to lodge a claim.

'Well,' Dad wheezed and knelt forwards, knuckles on knees. 'I best be off.'

It was Sam who answered before I could. 'Perhaps I could drive you, Mr Strange?'

'That's quite all right, son,' he said. 'I'm perfectly capable of getting home by myself.'

'You can forget that,' I said, and began to look for my phone. 'I'm calling Mum.'

'Gawd help us,' Dad muttered. When he saw I was serious and made a surrendering gesture. 'Let the games commence.'

It was late when Sam and I finally sat on the sofa to tackle the fish stew. I hadn't wanted any but Sam insisted I needed to keep my strength up.

As Dad had predicted Mum arrived and got hysterical, threatening to drive them both straight to A & E. But my father prevailed and the situation was quietened when he promised to go to the doctor first thing. Then I discreetly asked Mum how long he'd been taking the tablets but she didn't know anything about them. This in turn prompted indiscreet hysterics and then several arguments which were only defused when Sam pointed out that all this drama wasn't helping anyone especially not 'Mr Strange' who, at this point, was looking very tired and almost green.

Eventually, Mum conceded, but declared they needed to go home at once.

As they took their leave, she held back and whispered, 'He just worries about you, love, that's all.' Which I told her wasn't relevant. There followed much slamming of front doors, car doors and shouting about early nights and doctors, and then they were off.

But Mum's words echoed in my ears all the way back to my living room. What did Dad's attack have to do with me?

Nothing, I suspected. It was most likely one of those random things parents say when they can't think of anything else. But still, it had snagged on something in my brain.

I was still thinking it over when Sam produced two steaming bowls of stew.

'It was when he saw you,' I said, and took a bowl off him. 'That it all happened. Wasn't it?'

He was sitting next to me on the sofa fanning his mouth with his hand. Dad's Scotch bonnets were taking no hostages.

'*Whah whah whah*,' he mouthed turning a complementary chilli-red.

'Actually, no. It was when you said that you were from the museum,' I went on and sipped the stew. It wasn't that spicy. Sam must be a hot-food wuss. 'Why would that give him such a turn? I mean, he knows that I've been down there to Adder's Fork. He thinks I'm going to sell it. Of course, I haven't filled him in on all the developments, as I haven't had time. Plus, I thought that Auntie Babs might have told Mum that I was seeing Ray Boundersby today. With you.' I chewed a caper. 'Maybe Mum didn't tell him.'

Sam had his back pressed right into the sofa and one hand on his knee as if he were bracing himself. He undid the top button on his shirt and breathed out. I saw a couple of dark chest hairs peep over the top.

'It was,' he said blowing out for a long time, 'at the mention' – pause to breathe in and fan mouth – 'of Septimus.' There was a noisy swallow and a grimace. 'Unless,' he put the spoon down on his tray and took a glass of water, 'that was a timely coincidence.'

'But why would he be so upset? I mean, I know he fell out with him when I was eight but that was over twenty-five years ago. He doesn't like the museum. Doesn't believe in any of that stuff. Doesn't want me to hang on to it. All of this, I know. But I didn't think he was that *passionate* about it. He's not a passionate man.' I tried to stifle a yawn.

Sam shaped his lips into a perfect circle and steadily breathed in and out. He was sweating. A lot. 'I doubt he approves.'

'Well, you're right there. But why so strong? Do you know?'

He gave up on the stew and placed the bowl on a nest of white side tables. Some of the liquid splashed on to the top. I tutted. He took another long draught of water. 'I suspect it goes back to your grandmother,' he said, and sat back.

I couldn't stomach any more either so gestured for him to put my bowl next to his. I'd clear them up in the morning. 'Ethel-Rose? Why would it go back to her?'

Stretching out on the sofa, I nestled my head against a cushion. The day's stresses were finally receding, leaving me more than a little heavy-lidded and drowsy.

'Because, in many ways, it's a monument to her,' Sam's voice had become soft. Lulling even. 'And Celeste too. That's your father's mother and sister. Both gone. The memories are bound to be troubling.'

I pictured a family snap that I'd seen at the Witch Museum – Septimus, Ethel-Rose, Dad and baby Celeste. They were at some party, maybe someone else's wedding reception. Their clothes were splendid – neat, boxy and formal. Ethel-Rose was especially sumptuous in a full-skirted dress, complete with stiffened petticoat. She had scarlet lipstick on and looked particularly vivacious.

'Gone?' I said, trying to hang on to Sam's words. In all the photos Ethel-Rose seemed so ... present. 'Where did they go?'

In my head, I roamed over the baby form of Celeste in Septimus's proud arms – all lacy bonnet and mittens. She was sound asleep. Just like I would be soon. But possibly not so happily.

'We don't know,' said Sam, sounding very far away. 'Not your grandmother, it's true. That's another Witch Museum mystery.'

Yet I too was retreating from the world, travelling into a cosy blackness that I could no longer fight. Though later on, these words would have me reeling.

CHAPTER SIX

Prostrate on the sofa, a couple of tasselled throws twisted across my body and half over my face. I pushed them back and felt an annoying crick in my neck where my head had lain awkwardly on the sofa arm.

For a moment confusion netted me: why wasn't I in my comfortable bed with its soft Egyptian cotton sheets? Then I remembered Sam had been here last night. My god – had he literally bored me to sleep? Surely not. He was too good-looking for that. Maybe I had bored myself to sleep?

No, I reflected, it had been late. I must simply have been tired. And worried, I thought, as I remembered Dad's funny turn.

There was no sunshine in the room. Over in the west the sky was becoming navy. If I had a view to the east I thought the sun might be about to rise over Essex. That put the time between 5.30 and 6 a.m.

I threw off the blankets and stretched, then I peeked into the spare room. The duvet was bumpy with a mess of brown hair sticking out one end. I shut the door and, wrapping one of the throws around me, went into my room and tried to get back to sleep.

It wasn't going to happen.

My brain was awake even if my body fancied forty more winks. I gave up, showered, made some strong coffee, did my face, then just after seven o'clock I got on to my laptop. I had intended to google La Fleur but got distracted by an offer for Russian volume eyelashes in Walthamstow.

Someone behind me grunted.

Sam was leaning against the countertop in one of my dressing gowns. I must have left it in the spare room. Or maybe my friend Cerise had. It was a silk kimono that had been a gift from Auntie Babs and it lent Sam an air of extreme decadence. Especially as his hair was all mussed up, eyes a bit on the dewy side. He actually looked rather wild. And more than a little sexy. The V-neck gaped to reveal a cluster of dark hairs. I swallowed and turned back to the screen.

'Help for male pattern baldness?' he said. 'Is there something you haven't told me?'

'What?' I was trying to watch his reflection on the screen. I couldn't. It was too bright. 'Oh, that's just an ad. There was a beauty offer.'

Sam yawned and scratched his chest. 'Is there any coffee?'

I pointed to the counter and watched him pick up the ends of the kimono and sashay over. He was enjoying the feel of satiny fabric against his skin, you could tell.

'I'll buy you one for Christmas,' I smirked.

'A coffee? How generous.'

'No – a kimono, you plank. Suits you.' I laughed and waited for his comeback.

'I always did have a thing about Bruce Lee,' he said, adding milk to his mug and taking a sip.

'Who'd have thought?'

He sent me a wink.

Well, that was interesting. Sam was being very playful indeed this morning. I wondered why briefly, came up with nothing so left off thinking and asked him to refill my mug.

'No need to ask if you slept well last night,' he said, once he'd handed over my drink and settled on the chair beside me. 'The snoring was a bit of a giveaway.'

I looked at him uncertainly. No one else had mentioned snoring before. Well, apart from one dick called Jacob who I had foolishly got involved with after a work's night out. But Jacob lied about everything.

Sam pursed his lips and pulled the kimono tight across his chest.

My god, he looked dead camp like that.

'How much is that offer anyway?' He leant close in. The silk fell open just enough for me to glimpse a pink nipple in amongst the hair.

'Oh goodness!' He stood up abruptly and pointed at the screen. 'Is that right?'

'What?'

'The time.'

I squinted hard at the bottom right of the laptop. '7.45.'

Then I realised the implication. 'Ray Boundersby! We've

got to be at Mary's flat. Oh god, and I've got to phone in sick. Can you be ready in five?'

But he was gone in a flap of silk and a slam of the bathroom door.

I crept into my bedroom and phoned my boss, Derek.

'Morning?' he said, suspiciously. Derek had a nasal twang that made him sound dull and boring. But he was actually quite sharp. Well, I shouldn't over-egg that – he was of average intelligence. 'To what do I owe this pleasure?'

I did a lot of coughing down the phone. 'I can't come in. I've got, er, sickness.'

'What sort of sickness?' Derek asked. To be fair, he didn't sound sceptical. It was more like surprised. I was rarely off work.

I made my voice noticeably husky. 'Illness. In the head. Throat. Stomach. Groin.' I heard him breathe out loudly. 'Women's problems. All over, really.'

There was a long moment of silence which I resisted breaking. It was a trap to make me say too much, fill up the space with honesty or transparent lies. It made me sweat but I managed to keep my mouth shut.

Derek gave up waiting, sighed and then asked in a bored, resigned tone. 'How long will you be off, then?'

I hadn't thought about that. 'Don't know.' I pretended to sneeze.

More silence. Then, 'Well, as long as you're in for Thursday.'

'What's Thursday?' I asked, forgetting to make my voice croak. 'Oooh, it hurts,' I added for effect and rubbed my throat.

'Team meeting. Important. I need to talk through the case allocations. Might have to get some outside help on the Bassett case.'

'Er, yes, that should be fine.' Cough, cough. 'As long as I can get out of bed.' Wheeze, splutter, gasp, hawk.

'Are you all right?' Sam had stuck his head round the door. I jumped up and mouthed *Shush*, putting a finger on my lips and then jabbed furiously at the phone.

Derek drew breath in. 'Is there someone else there, Rosie?'

'No.' I shook my head and looked at Sam. 'No one else is here, boss. It's the radio.'

'And coming up it's *Thought for the Day*,' said Sam loudly and retreated into the hallway.

'Sorry, Derek,' I wheezed. 'Feel sick. Period pain. Heavy flood. Gotta go.'

'Okay.' His voice had got fainter like he was holding the phone away from him. 'Thursday then and I'll expect to see some self-certification—' he said as I hung up.

Men, honestly. Absolutely no subtlety.

We reached the address Ray Boundersby had given us at nine o'clock on the dot, thanks to some very London driving. By me, of course. I wasn't going to let Sam get his key in my ignition again. And that wasn't a euphemism.

Mary Boundersby lived near Old Street, at the top of block of apartments that had once been commercial buildings. A section of the ground floor remained a bank, which was just opening up its doors, welcoming no one in. We followed the perimeter round to a flash Scandi-type wooden door where we declared ourselves through the intercom and got buzzed in.

There was no one in the hallway and the only way was up so we climbed the stairs. Sam moaned about the lack of lift, which I thought was fairly rich coming from someone who lived in Dark Ages Britain.

The communal landing at the top had two doors. We caught our breath and waited for one of them to open. Promptly the left unlocked and out came a skinny man with startling light blue eyes and curly black hair that was on its way to transforming into dreadlocks. He wiped his hand on a grubby khaki T-shirt introduced himself as Tom Limbert, 'Mary's boyfriend', then led us into a narrow hallway, shuftying secret glances as we passed.

The flat smelt of synthetically enhanced domesticity – shop-bought 'fresh linen' room fragrance. It had just been sprayed. Probably to cover something up. Stagnant air, smoke, sweat? Maybe all three. I imagined this was probably quite a stressful time for the residents.

To the left there was a bathroom and bedroom, to the right a long open-plan kitchen-diner and lounge that led on to a short square balcony. I could see the unmistakable stocky outline of Ray Boundersby silhouetted there, a solid slab of flesh. Auntie Babs had sent me a photo of him and helpfully added that he'd killed someone during his criminal career. Truth to be told, though my aunt wasn't a stranger to hyperbole, I could tell, even from this distance, that this was a man you did not want to mess around.

As we turned into the living area I clocked a woman

perched on the sofa. She was all wrapped in a pastel-pink blanket. This had to be Mary Boundersby for the poor gal had inherited her father's bulky frame. There was a similar genetic roundedness to Mary's build which fell short of stout. Though she wasn't pudgy either. In fact her feminine curves lent her a nuzzly kind of softness that my mum would have called 'homely'. Her face, however, was very pleasant and softened by two huge luminous hazel eyes, definitely not Daddy's, probably Mum's. But they were currently watery and red and magnified by large tortoiseshell geek-style glasses. Her hair also matched her frames, or maybe it was the other way round. Anyway, it was a nice do, a salon job. You couldn't get a home kit that brought out all those amber, caramel and bronze hues. But it was limp and long with a centre parting that gave her a hippie kind of look. She was very pale, possibly anaemic and didn't look up when we entered into the room.

'Rose Strange?' Ray Boundersby walked straight to me, hand held out like a huge paddle.

I took it and let him crush it, while with the other massive bat/hand he patted me heftily on the back disrupting my outward flow of breath so that I ended up telling him it was 'Nice to finally meet you-oo-oo-oo.'

Ray Boundersby's handshake was robust and firm and borderline frightening. Pretty much like himself. He could only have been a couple of inches taller than me so scratching five foot eight and a bit, but despite the lack of height – he certainly made an impression. Bulldog fit and visibly very strong, waves of knotty unease were fidgeting off him. His jaw was clenched all the way up, beyond his ear. It didn't slacken when he smiled.

When he stopped yanking my hand about he swung over to Sam. His legs were sturdy and thick but short and that lent him a bit of a waddle. I watched him compress Sam's hand. He did his best not to wince as Ray's shoulders went up and down: two round sinewy boulders covered by a slick navy suit.

'Get them a drink,' Ray barked to Tom, who scurried off into the dark of the kitchen. There was no natural light in there but I think he might have been glad for the shelter of the shadows.

With a nod of his head Mr Boundersby indicated we should sit on the L-shaped sofa. His daughter was occupying the nexus so Sam and I took an end each and looked at her.

She didn't acknowledge us, just kept glaring at the floor with a puzzled expression, saying nothing though her lips were moving silently.

Ray pulled a chair over from the dining table, spun it round and sat on it, Christine Keeler style. There was another large boulder at the top of his legs, visible between the rungs of the chair back. I tried hard not to look at it. His posture was shouting out that he was all man. I doubted there would was anyone who'd disagree.

'She's taken it bad, you can see.' He'd reduced his volume now to what I imagined he thought was relatively low. In reality it was just beneath 'shouty man'. This was what my friend Cerise termed the level at which the hard of hearing, the mental, members of debating societies and those perpetually used to going unchallenged often spoke at. Ray was the latter. He sniffed, rested his chin on the top of the chair back and stared at Mary. There was a lot of love in that sad gaze.

His daughter's fuzzy unfocused eyes ranged over him, then turned round and regarded me and Sam with indifference. I wondered if she was all there.

'Hi,' I said, and tried to smile my absolutely bestest warm smile. 'How are you feeling?'

Mary's eyes focused but she didn't speak. There was either such a lot of stuff going on behind them that she couldn't work out where to start, or not much at all.

I waited. She gulped down a large breath, looked down at the floor and opened her mouth. Her shoulders were hunched and she was sitting right on the edge of the sofa looking like she might at any minute either fall flat on her face or take off and run shrieking out the door.

'She's shocked, isn't she?' Boundersby said after a couple of long minutes of silence.

'I can see that,' Sam piped up from the other end of the sofa. His voice loosened. 'Hello, Mary,' he said, 'do you think you might be able to tell us what happened?'

She reacted to her name: the eyebrows twitched. Her face lifted and rotated to Sam. He gave her a tender smile, all crow's feet and cheekbones, and edged along the sofa minutely, not wanting to startle the girl nor crowd her out. 'I'm sure you've been through this with the police already but we have certain specialisms that may help with this kind of thing.'

When he spoke like this, I was reminded of his other side, the darker one that took on ex-Serbian mafia types in hand-to-hand combat, the man that was on first-name terms with government agents in the Civil Service X-Files or whatever they were. One day I really needed to sit down with him and have a good long chat about all of that. I wanted to know how much he and my grandfather were involved. What they had done and why they had done it. Over the past couple of weeks there had been no time to discuss much of anything. Other things always seemed to be more pressing. *Plus ça change.*

I watched Mary consider his words. 'Well, it's so difficult and upsetting,' she said, and then paused. Her voice was deep, a bit like her dad's, though she enunciated her consonants. Definitely a different accent going on there. I reckon she'd been sent to some posh boarding school once the family had relocated to Essex and gone legit.

Now her eyes were back on the floor but they were dancing around. She twisted the blanket between her fingers.

I looked at Sam, who shrugged so lightly I knew no one else could see it and mouthed, *Patience.*

I got the message and sat back into the sofa. If Mary was going to continue in zombie mode, I'd take the opportunity to find out what the room might tell me instead.

Not much, it appeared. The sofa was white, modern, comfy. Not expensive. Not cheap. On the wall facing it was a huge plasma television. Expensive. Not cheap. A wicker chest which doubled as a coffee table, dining table and chairs all looked pristine like they had been purchased recently. Not expensive. Not cheap.

On the dining table was a bottle of brandy, three unwashed glasses, a couple of dirty white mugs with brown drips down the sides and a bowl of slatted wooden fruit. I always wondered why people bought that stuff. Why not real fruit? It was so much more colourful and attractive. Did they not like colour or taste? Mary worked in the restaurant so I knew she probably did like food. And she obviously ate a fair bit of it. Maybe she didn't like interior design and accessorising.

There were a couple of photos of Mary with Ray and a tall elegant blonde woman, who I presumed was her mother. My aunt had told me she was a 'lady', whatever that meant, and always had 'beautifully ironed clothes'. It was beyond me how you measured such a niche skill but Mrs Boundersby evidently was an expert and, as such, the envy of women of a certain age in our shrinking home county. I sighted a couple of photos of Mary with some friends on top of a mountain in ski season, but none of her and Tom. Which probably meant the relationship was fairly new. I was betting if I checked, there would be just one lonely toothbrush in Mary's bathroom.

The place wasn't cluttered. In fact, things looked a bit semi-permanent. One level up from student accommodation. She hadn't lived here long, I thought. Possibly it was her first flat. Late-twenties used to be late for first-time buyers, but not any more. Inner-city house prices and astronomical rents priced most young people out of London. Into the suburbs if they were lucky. Into the Home Counties if they weren't. Or if they really wanted to stay within the glare of the bright lights then into houses of multiple occupancy. Unless they were in banking or something corporate, inherited a chunk of wealth, lived on estates or had concerned parents with disposable incomes. I reckoned Mary's dad had helped her.

The only piece of decorative art that I could find was a framed Escher print, *Relativity*, with its confounding staircases and bulb-headed occupants calmly defying gravity.

'It was the ghost,' Mary suddenly piped up. Her voice was low and scratchy, like she'd strained it. At least she was looking up now, engaging, making eye contact with Sam. 'She's been plaguing me for months. It was her. She killed Seth.' Then she hiccupped out a sob.

I realised I had been wrong: there was a hell of a lot going on inside her. Warring emotions, fracturing recall, impossibilities boiling with discomforting conclusions. Mary had been having a hard time articulating her experience. Sometimes words weren't enough. Plus, she'd probably been up all night and been questioned down the nick all day yesterday. I suspected she was quite weak.

Ray breathed out a long breath. I think he was relieved his daughter had broken her silence.

Sam nodded and clasped his hands together roughly. 'To build a picture of what happened, we need you to tell us as much as you can. Will you start right back at the beginning?'

Mary squinted. 'Back in December?'

That muddled me – I thought the chef had been killed Saturday night. But Sam was right on it.

'Is that when you first saw it?' he said, not missing a beat. 'This ghost?'

Mary nodded slowly. She was watching his face. Probably, I suspected, for hints of exasperation, anger or incredulity. As alibis went, those of a phantom nature weren't well received by police.

'See,' Ray butted in, glowering at me. 'This is what I wanted you to sort out.' He stabbed a finger in my direction. His jaw was clenched solid when he wasn't speaking. It made me feel a little panicky. 'When I contacted your auntie Barbara I was hoping for an immediate response. I didn't want it to get this far.'

I looked at Sam. So did Ray. 'You should have come up to see me …' There was more than a portion of blame in his voice but Sam chose to ignore it and turned his body away from the father so that he was fully facing Mary, one knee up now and lounging over the sofa. He was opening himself to her, taking any suggestion of confrontation out of his body language. 'Tell us about it now, Mary. We won't laugh, I promise.'

Speak for yourself, I thought but didn't say. Then cancelled that entirely. We were talking about murder after all.

'Okay,' said Mary at last.

'December you said,' Sam led her on.

'Yes,' she said. 'That's right. The first time, it was the night before New Year's Eve.'

CHAPTER SEVEN

Mary's voice was faltering. She was strung out but, all things considered, she did a good job of communicating the facts.

'We weren't going to open for New Year's Eve,' she explained. 'So the next restaurant day was going to be the third. I was doing a final double-check on everything. Making sure that fridges were closed. Securing the site. '

Ray stood up. With one flick of his wrist, he spun the chair round and settled on it legs crossed. 'No one up town, then. Everyone's at home, in the commuter belt, with their feet up, patting their turkey bellies, or if they're out, they're keeping it local. That in-between week's always dry as a nun's—'

'Dry as a bone, he means.' Mary hurried on. 'We'd closed earlier than usual. It'd been that quiet. I let half the staff go about nine. The rest cleared off a bit later. I'd locked the front doors. Always do when I'm finishing up on my own. Then I made sure the gate on the yard was secure.' She looked at Sam and sniffed. 'We'd had some kids yanking it about, vandalising stuff. So I was to lock up the kitchen when I heard something in the cellar.'

Ray added, 'It's not unusual to hear things in that place. That's why she didn't call anyone, see.'

Ah, I thought. The police must have asked about that earlier. I presumed the fact she didn't call anyone meant there was no one there to corroborate her account.

Ray carried on. 'The cellars, floorboards, walls, beams. They're old. The City is ancient. The foundations of La Fleur go way back. Things creak, things groan. Sometimes they squeak. And yes,' he curled his lip, 'we've had rats as you're probably aware.' His massive shoulders shrugged up and down. 'But you know what they say – you're never more than six feet away from one in London. It's a fact of life.'

Gawd, he was a gasbag! How much did I want to tell him to shut up? About as much as I liked my kneecaps. I sucked in a breath to calm myself. Ray clocked my expression but interpreted it as squeamishness and let out a short grunty laugh. 'Don't worry, Rosie. There's no bubonic plague any more. Rats can't be helped. Not when food's about.'

'Ray.' Sam put a hand out to him. 'Let's just hear it from Mary. We need to listen to her version really carefully.'

Inwardly I gasped and huddled protectively over my knees, but Boundersby apologised and put a finger on his lips, play-acting like he was a little boy chastised. And he didn't interrupt again.

'Notebook, Rosie,' Sam said to me and rotated an index finger in the air. It so irritated me when he started getting bossy like that. I was his guv'nor, after all. And I had a strong streak of healthy defiance that resurrected whenever men started telling women what to do.

Having said all of that, however, I was used to it: whenever we did 'living together' checks at work, there would always be one lead, one note-taker. It was a useful methodology and I understood what Sam was doing right then, so shut up, ground my teeth and fetched my notebook out. See, Mary was responding to him. Sometimes it happened like that. Sometimes they responded to a woman, sometimes a guy. Depended on the personality. Mary responded to men. Or, at least, she was responding to Sam. So he was right – I should be note-taker and jot down anything he deemed of interest. When it came to ghosts – that seemed to be everything.

'Go on, Mary,' Sam urged. 'You heard a noise in the cellar. Can you describe what it was like?'

Mary screwed her face up and looked over Sam's shoulder into the past. 'I knew straight away that it wasn't a rat. It was too slow.'

I wrote down, *30th of December. Not a rat. Too slow.*

'Why?' said Sam. 'How was the noise slow?'

She thought hard for a minute then said, 'It scraped on the floor. Like metal being dragged across the cellar. But not something really heavy. Not machinery. It clinked, that time. And rattled.'

Sam's eyebrows rose. His mouth tightened. I'd seen that look before. Irritation. I wasn't sure why. 'Like what?'

'I thought it might be a bag of bottle tops falling open, at first.' She turned to me. 'I try to recycle them, you see. I'd put a bag down there earlier. It was only plastic, lightweight, so I thought that might be it – that the bag might have ripped or fallen over and the tops were spilling over the floor. But anyway, it went quiet again and I was tired so I thought I'd sort it out when I was back in. It was just as I was leaving through the double doors that I heard it again. It wasn't as light as bottle tops, the noise. It was heavier. Like a chain.'

Oh, that sounded a bit murky. 'Was there a chain in the cellar?' I asked.

'No,' Mary said. 'Why would there be?'

I didn't know what people kept in their cellars and I kind of wanted it to stay that way. 'Did you go down?'

She nodded wordlessly. We all waited.

'The light switch,' said Mary, 'is near the lower rungs on the steps down, so it was very dim. But I couldn't hear anything. I listened to see if there was the sound of breathing, if someone was down there. But there was nothing. Only this strange smell – fumy. Like flaming coals. Gases. Though I couldn't see anything there – no burning. I was about to flip the switch. Then I heard her whisper.'

Sam sat up straight. 'Actual words,' he murmured to himself.

'They were indistinct,' she said. 'Like she couldn't talk properly. Like there was something wrong with her mouth or tongue. Like groans …'

Of course they were, I thought but didn't say. No self-respecting ghost talks clearly or properly, do they? Have to have a bit of blathering and moaning going on. Can't have a straight-up, clear conversation with the dearly departed, can we?

'It,' said Mary, becoming more animate, 'sounded female. Or maybe like a child.'

She cleared her throat then in a creaky low voice stated, 'She said, "Vover vere."'

I waited for someone to respond.

No one did.

'That's what I heard,' Mary explained. 'I just stood there, frozen. Then after, I don't know how long, I plucked up the courage to turn on the light. And it was so odd.' She cocked her head to one side and squinted. 'It was like all the darkness in the room was suddenly sucked into the middle.'

Ray shouldered forwards. 'It wasn't a fire?'

'Not a fire, no,' said Mary. 'It was hard to describe. It happened so quickly, I only caught a glimpse of it.'

I was aware of Tom inching out of the shadows of the kitchen, head down listening.

'And what did you see?' Ray went on. He and Sam were both leaning in towards Mary as if straining to hear her. I wished again silently that he'd shut up. I wanted his daughter to speak for herself.

'It was like a funnel of darkness. But I had the sense it was shrinking, that it had been bigger before and was now contracting and disappearing.' She paused and rubbed her left eye. It was sore and red-rimmed. I thought I saw a tear spill out of it, but she smoothed it away. 'Crazy, crazy, I know,' she said, and shook her head. 'I can hear myself telling you this, and I'm listening to myself and thinking, *You sound as mad as a hatter, Mary Boundersby*.' She smiled, then let out a high-pitched peal of laughter. When she finished, she went on, her mouth set in a serious line as if she hadn't just chuckled at all. 'And, you know, I did think at the time that

I was totally losing it but that's what it was like. I'm telling you straight.'

'See,' Ray butted in. Again. 'She didn't tell anyone because she thought she sounded loop the loop, radio rental. I mean you would, wouldn't you? You can see that, why she'd do that, can't you?'

'It's very common,' Sam concurred. 'The first thing that people do when presented with challenging or irregular experiences is doubt themselves, the validity of their experience. That they've seen what they have.' He smiled gently at Mary. 'You should know that it suggests that you aren't mad, actually, because you realise it's abnormal.'

'That's good to hear,' Mary said, and laughed. But this time it wasn't overly manic.

'Anything else? Anything at all? It might seem trivial to you,' Sam asked, and made a scribbling gesture at me.

I thought about what she'd described and duly noted down *funnel* and *crazy*.

Mary's fingers entwined. Her hazy eyes began wandering again. 'I didn't see this but I had the mental impression of dark matted hair.' She gulped. 'And thinness. And blood.'

She winced, then collected herself. 'I can't remember any more. The whole thing was over in a matter of seconds, like I said.'

'And there was nothing else there?' I asked just to be clear. 'Nobody? No rats. No chain?'

'I checked. Nothing. No one.'

'And then you went home?' Sam asked.

Mary nodded.

'So, earlier, you said "that time". When was the next event?'

'About a week later, at work. I was just staring out the office window into the yard, I can't remember why. You know, you do that sometimes, don't you? When you're busy. You forget what you're meant to be doing. And I was just dawdling for a moment, in the office, and I saw this woman come across the yard. Just like that. She walked across it. So I knew I wasn't imagining it – I mean it wasn't a mere glimpse this time. I saw her go all the way across the yard.'

'You sure it wasn't a real woman?' I asked. 'You must have people constantly walking about your yard. And you can't be the only female member of staff? Presumably there are also trade suppliers and deliveries.'

Mary shook her head. 'Somehow I knew that she wasn't living. But it was different to the other time because I could see her clothes really clearly. I saw them Saturday night too. With Seth ...' She flinched at the memory.

I waited to see if she'd tell us what they were like. I was genuinely interested in what was currently on trend in Spooksville.

Mary squinted again and this time I did see a tear pop out of one eye. Quickly, she wiped it away. 'Made me think I was mental. But I could see this very wide-brimmed hat. I've seen her wear it twice now.'

I started writing it down but snuck a sideways glance to see what Sam was making of it all.

'And she had a shawl over a laced bodice and full skirt. You know the kind of thing. Georgian. The dress was detailed, I remember. Pale blue.'

'Was there sound?' asked Sam. He was leaning right in to her, all ears, as it were.

Mary thought about the question. 'No,' she said after a long pause. 'I don't think so. Not then. I can't recall any. I just remember suddenly feeling very bad – there was this huge feeling of dread that came over everything. Then she crossed the yard and just disappeared,' she finished.

There was silence in the room again. The wind rustled the curtains. The grey voile billowed towards us. Somewhere outside in the road a bus honked its horn. A woman shouted. Traffic hummed and screeched. A solitary bird somewhere up above chirped happily. Life was continuing as usual.

There were things that people did when they lied. Often they didn't have a clue they were doing it. Erratic vocal undulations were one. Fidgeting was another. Turning their face away, pausing so they could make up an answer and avoiding pronouns in their speech. These were all telltale signs. Mary was doing none of them. Maybe fidgeting a little. Right now, she was rubbing the back of her neck. She had done that before and kept hunching her shoulders. It was either a habit, an injury or bad posture taking its toll. That kind of thing rose to the surface when you were stressed.

'You okay?' I asked, realising as it came out that it was a really stupid question. I glanced at Ray to see if he was going to tell me just that but he didn't. He was biting his lip. Probably his tongue too.

Mary dipped her elbow and stopped massaging. 'Uh-huh,' she said. 'Whiplash injury. I had a car accident a few months ago. Nothing serious.'

That would explain it. That and the huge anxiety she was undergoing through the retelling of her traumatic discovery.

Unable to sit still any longer Ray got up from his chair, shook out his hands and went and leant against the wall, next to the telly. He smoothed down his trousers and said, 'She told people this time though. Didn't you, Mary? You told the staff.'

'Yes, the kitchen staff were in. There are windows around the door so you can see into the yard. I asked them if they'd seen her too.'

'Had they?' Sam asked.

'No,' she said. 'Not then. But a few days later MT said she'd seen something.'

'That's right, she did,' Ray added. His hands were behind his back now and he was leaning on them, perhaps to stop himself twiddling his fingers and giving away his anxiety levels. 'I was there that night. She came rushing out of the ladies and said she'd seen a ghost in there. Just staring at her.'

I wrote down *staring*.

'Marta Thompson,' Ray explained, 'is our hostess, or butler. *Maître d'hotel*.'

Mary nodded. 'She heard someone in the toilets.'

'And it wasn't a customer?' I asked.

'They were groaning apparently,' Tom said.

'Food poisoning?' I asked.

Sam tutted.

Ray shot me a very nasty look. 'That came later,' he said, and managed to make the statement sound like a threat.

Mary looked over to her father. 'I think it was some kind of warning because the next day was Friday the fifth of February and then *everyone* heard it.'

I noted the date.

Ray sighed. 'Yes, the night we had the rat incident. Two or three of the buggers actually ran across the dining floor in clear view of everyone. Very bold. One ran right upto a journalist too. You bet your life there was a lot of moaning that night. All across social media. Not ideal.'

'Yes, but *everyone* heard her,' Mary repeated, and I understood what she was getting at. There were lots of witnesses this time: not just this MT person, but the diners and all the restaurant staff. It wasn't singular insanity.

Tom appeared behind the sofa with a tray of mugs. 'They did.' He put it down on the wicker chest for us. 'Every single diner in La Fleur heard it.'

I noticed as he leant over to hand me the drink there were huge dark green sweat patches under his arms. Greasy fingerprints remained on the mug. 'I was there that night,' he said. 'Up at the bar, waiting for Mary. It was real loud. Just before the rats.'

'Were there words?' Sam asked.

Tom shook his head. 'Not that I could make out.'

'What did they do?' Sam looked at him. 'The staff?'

'Nothing,' said Tom. 'There wasn't really time to talk about it because suddenly the rats happened and then everyone sort of forgot about the moaning.'

I nodded. 'Priorities, I suppose.'

In a restaurant, yes,' Ray agreed. 'They demanded immediate action, I'm sure you can see that.'

I nodded. 'A lot of people were witness to both incidents then?'

'Yeah,' said Mary. 'But people, the staff, knew it was her – the ghost.'

'Knew she'd brought the rats?' I asked.

Mary shook her head, 'No, I didn't mean that. But probably. What I meant was we all knew it was the ghost wailing.'

'How?' Sam came in quickly. 'He had been paying close attention.'

'It was obvious. To me anyway. I told them.'

But Sam clearly didn't think so. 'How did you know the noise had come from the apparition you'd seen?'

All of us looked at Mary, who frowned. 'I just did. What else could it be?'

There were a lot of explanations for a sound like a wail: metal screeching on metal, dodgy pipes, bad plumbing, wind in the eaves. But I didn't say anything. I just sat still and waited for her to continue. When none of us moved, Mary grimaced and said, 'It was high-pitched again and female. You can tell, can't you?'

Tom bobbed his curly bonce up and down quickly, animating the thickened curls.

'The *same* female?' Sam continued.

Everyone looked at Mary again.

'Oh.' She fiddled with the blanket. 'I don't know now.' Her forehead was full of lines. It made her look knackered and much, much older. One hand let go of the blanket and crawled up over her face. She wiped her eyes, then felt round the back of her neck again. 'I can't remember. But it had to be, didn't it? Had to. Because after that everything seemed to unravel. Everyone was talking about her. Femi, the sous chef, was muttering that Fleur de Lis Court was cursed. He didn't want to say before, but it came out that all businesses on the street had had a run of bad luck.'

Sam was making notes now too. 'Because of the curse? Was it anything specific?'

'What?' Mary's pale face turned to him.

'The curse?' Sam spoke up. 'Were there any specific aspects to it or was it general bad luck?'

Or bad investing and the financial crisis, I thought. Or maybe simply bullshit? People loved stirring things up, having a bit of a gossip, creating some drama. They didn't realise what it could lead to.

Mary shook her head. There were dots of sweat across it. 'At that point I didn't think it was the restaurant that was cursed.'

'Really?' That surprised me.

'No,' Mary sighed. 'I thought it was me.'

'You?' I said. 'Why?'

'Because I saw her again.'

'In the cellar?' It was a good a guess as any.

'No.' Mary rubbed her neck. 'Here.'

'Here?' I wondered for a moment if she was referring to her back. 'Where here?'

'She walked across that window.' She thumbed the wall

behind her. We all looked through the voile curtains to the narrow street and buildings across the road. The casement was wide and propped open with an aluminium rod.

'Is there a balcony out there?' I asked.

'No,' Mary said, and hid her face. 'Only at the front. There's a sheer drop behind the window. That's when I knew she was haunting me. And that it was a real ghost.'

'Do you keep it open all the time?' I asked.

'I'm on the third floor.' She cast a guilty glance at her father. 'It's not a security risk.' They'd had this argument before.

'But you say someone walked past it,' said Ray, sounding exhausted. And I realised he was on the same page as me. He loved his daughter but he wasn't buying the ghost theory.

'It was a ghost, a spectre, an *apparition*,' Mary repeated with emphasis. 'Obviously they don't observe the same rules.'

Ray shook his head. 'Something strange is afoot for sure,' and he turned away from his daughter and glared at us.

'I saw her, Dad.' A plaintive note had crept into Mary's voice. 'Like the one in the yard. 'Cept she had her bonnet on again then. It was a ghost.'

But Ray put his head in his hands and groaned. Then he brushed those short, stubby and very strong fingers through his well-oiled hair.

'She tells the truth, Mary does. You know that, Ray.' It was Tom. This was the most forceful and emotive thing I'd heard him say since we arrived. He stepped over to the couch and sat down next to Mary, reaching for her hand.

She took it and held it tightly, then gave him a weak smile. They looked like a sweet couple.

I heard a splutter from the chair. Ray was wiping his nose. His eyes were bright and vivid. He had the look of a powerful man who had faced fear before but was fighting down his worst terror. 'You've got to get to the bottom of all this. She's all I got, Mary is. She took it bad after her mum died but she's just getting back on her feet and – and I bought that place for her – to set her up with a business. A trade, you know. So she could be purposeful. It always pays to have a purpose. A meaning. A reason to get up. And now, oh god, I can't believe what's happening. You've got to find out.'

I didn't know whether to go over and pat Boundersby's back or pretend I hadn't seen anything. I looked down at my knees and decided to address Tom. 'So were you here? When Mary saw the thing? The apparition?'

He shook his head roughly. 'I came over and looked around obviously. But nothing. I thought maybe Mary was working too hard.' He raised her hand to his lips and kissed it. 'She does that.'

The whole of his girlfriend's face brightened briefly.

'At least someone does,' Ray muttered, eyes fixed back on the floor. He hadn't thought anyone had heard it. Interesting. I made a note to ask Tom what he did or didn't do for a living. There was obviously tension there.

Ray's face was tense. 'And at La Fleur things got worse and worse: a customer found a cockroach in his food. Subsequent to that a swarm of them showed up round the bar, hogged the limelight then scarpered, but not before every fucker had tweeted pictures.'

'The toilets backed up,' Tom added, blinking. His eyes

were the same colour as forget-me-nots. Quite attractive, though his front teeth were a little overlong. 'Then there was that awful writing on the wall.'

'Oh, yes,' I said. 'We heard about that. Sounds well nasty.'

'Who from?' snapped Ray, his face pinched and red.

'Bumped into one of your staff,' I said. 'Yesterday. Joel Rogers. Nice boy.'

I didn't mean it.

Ray looked relieved. 'Oh, Joel, yes. Well good. We tried very hard to shut that one down. Everyone who was in that night got a free meal on the house. Cost a bloody fortune. I had to pull in a lot of favours to keep it out of the press, but we managed to neutralise the damage, thank Christ.'

Sam clicked his tongue. 'And I understand it read,' he flicked back a few pages of this notebook. '*Till the blood gushed from her eyes*. Why did it say that? Anyone know?'

'No, no one.' Ray shrugged. 'Not a Scooby.'

I chipped in my own penny's worth. 'It's fairly specific. Were there any incidents it could have referred to? Accidents in the kitchen, perhaps?'

'People cut and burn themselves all the time in kitchens,' said Ray. 'But nothing's happened with eyes. That I'm aware.'

Mary joined her father with a shrug. Tom shook his head.

'And then Seth was murdered?' Sam went on.

'No,' said Mary. 'I saw her again. In the yard. No bonnet. Thin and red and wretched.'

Sam nodded her on. 'Go on.'

'It was kind of weird. The motion sensor lights were off but I saw the moonlight on her arms. They were thin, like bones.

There was that burning smell again. Charcoal. And she was pointing across the yard. But it was only for a moment. I went to the door to see if she needed help but when I opened it she was gone again. That time I felt so bad. Really bad. Worried. Like something terrible was about to happen. Like she was trying to warn me. That was last week.'

'Then we had the food poisoning,' said Ray. 'Friday.'

'I thought that was what she might have been warning us about,' Mary said. 'But it wasn't, was it?' She looked down at the floor.

Tom put his arm across her shoulders and said, 'Shh.'

We were coming to the climax.

'I'm sorry to mention it but we do need to know what happened the night you found the body,' Sam said as gently as he could.

Mary balked at the prospect of recounting it again, but managed to rally her courage and tutted. 'I don't know why she did it. Gutted him like a fish. I didn't think she had the strength.'

That was an interesting comment to make.

'Why not?' Sam asked. I guessed he was thinking the same as me.

'Because of the blood and the lacerations all over her. She looked so weak.'

'The lacerations?'

'She doesn't have them all the time. Sometimes she is dressed well. With the bonnet. Other times she looks very different. Terrible. Abused.'

Sam scrawled in his notebook. 'So what happened? In your own time.'

And Mary detailed the whole event. How she had forgotten Tom's present and returned to work with an absence of maybe twenty-five minutes. She told us she had located the package and was about to leave when she heard sounds. Then how she witnessed the spirit pass over the floor, bloodied and ethereal. She described descending into the hell of the cellar, the scene – the body of Seth hung up high on a hook, gashes and wounds to his body, throat slit and guts spilling.

It was a hideous tale. At the end of her story, I felt sick and appalled. That someone could do that to another human being was beyond me.

Ray turned his face away from us. Tom paled so dramatically I thought he might faint. Only Mary kept herself together through it all. Trying hard to remember whatever she could, desperate to please, to help us.

Eventually, afterwards, when we had collected ourselves, Sam spoke. 'I need some extra detail, if you don't mind trying?' I thought Ray was going to intervene and stop the interview – Mary was clearly distressed – but he didn't. He nodded to his daughter and said, 'Go on, love. Try.'

Sam sent her a pleasant smile. 'So how did she get out? Of the restaurant?'

Her eyebrows lowered. 'I don't know. She must have walked through the door. She can walk across windows three floors up, can't she?' And then she pulled her arms in and crossed them over her. I had a sense she was shutting down.

Again the room lapsed into a fraught silence until Ray shook his head and spoke up. 'You know Mary cut him down? She's got his DNA all over her and vice versa.'

Oh dear, I thought but didn't say.

Sam was obviously pressing Mary for something. 'And no one else came in or out afterwards?'

'No, not until the police showed up.'

Her voice began to tremble. 'Which means it had to be the ghost. Because if it's not the ghost, then it was me, wasn't it? I did it and I've gone mad.' She pulled up the blanket around her shoulders and started rocking. 'I don't want to be insane. I don't want to have killed Seth. Why would I do that? Just because his hygiene wasn't good. It wasn't a massive deal, was it, Dad? Not in the bigger scheme of things.' Her breathing had started to accelerate. 'Oh god. I don't want to go to prison. Or a nuthouse. I don't want to. How can this be happening?' She let go of the blanket. It slid off her shoulders. Then she hit her chest. Hard. 'What's wrong with me?'

'Shh,' said Tom and put his arm round her and pulled up the blanket again. 'It's going to be okay. I won't let anything else happen to you.'

'You are not going down,' said Ray, his voice firm and measured. 'These people,' he gestured between Sam and I, 'they're going to find the ghost.' He was speaking at a pinched, measured pace. 'Aren't you?' Then he smiled.

But it wasn't a nice smile. More like the kind that would spread across Dracula's face if he happened upon an unsupervised play-school.

Before either of us could respond, he turned back to Mary. 'And if they don't, I'll shoot them.'

CHAPTER EIGHT

Once my pulse had slowed down enough for me to detect any sound other than my banging heart, I was relieved to hear Sam laughing, though it was extremely high-pitched and squeaky. Once he stopped, he told Ray that we'd absolutely need to look around the place. At length.

'Not today.' Ray's voice returned to his regular 'convivially menacing' mode. 'The whole place is out of bounds. Crime scene, innit.'

I looked at Sam, who shrugged. He appeared to be taking the whole 'threat to life' thing quite well.

Snapping his notebook shut, he asked, 'Well, we'll get on with interviewing the rest of the staff. Do you have their addresses to hand?'

Ray shook his head. 'Not on me.'

'I can get into our system remotely,' said Mary. 'But my laptop's with the police.' She paused and looked hurt.

'Use mine,' said Tom. 'I'll nip home and get it.' Then he put his hand on her knee and gave it a rub. She didn't smile but leant her head on his shoulder.

'You know MT's anyway, don't you, Tom?' Ray scowled.

'Give it to Rosie and Sam. They can start with her.' He pulled his jacket together and smoothed down the front, then walked over to us. 'I'll let her know you're on your way over. Mary will email you the staff list. As soon as I hear about La Fleur, I'll contact you about access.'

Then he dismissed us with a nod of his head and went to his daughter. Picking up Mary's hand he pulled her to her feet. 'But right now, I want you, young lady, to eat something.' Then he sat her down at the dining table.

Left alone on the sofa Tom sighed, then he got up and ushered us out. In the hallway, with the volume of his voice just above a whisper, he relayed MT's address.

'Why do you have it? Are you friends?' asked Sam.

'Yes,' Tom nodded. 'We were at uni together. It's through MT that I met Mary.'

'Oh,' I said. 'You're obviously very fond of each other. When did you meet?'

'Christmas party,' he said, and leant across me to open the door. I got a waft of his body odour again. It was animally with base notes of brine. Pungent. It wasn't hot in there. But I suppose he'd had quite a night of it and one had to take Ray into account. The bloke was enough to make anyone break into a heavy sweat. Especially if you were shagging his daughter.

'Thanks for doing this,' he said, as we went on to the landing. 'Mary is innocent. You get that, don't you?'

I pressed his moist palm and nodded. 'Seems so.' I didn't want to commit. 'Do you work at the restaurant too, Tom?'

'Oh no,' he said. 'I'm a historian. Well, that is I'm looking for something in that field, you know.'

I said that I did know, though I didn't, and was going to commiserate (there can't be too many jobs around for historians) but Sam leant across me, thanked him for the coffee and shook hands. I wiped mine off against my jeans, and assured Tom we'd do our best to get the bottom of everything.

He grinned, then looked guilty for grinning, frowned hard, sighed then quickly turned round and closed the door.

'Why are we doing this?' I asked Sam as we pulled up in a space on a street near to the address we'd been given. Not as salubrious or as central as Mary's, I noted. It was a postcode that had yet to become gentrified. The type of place people stayed in because of income or because they were born there.

'You heard Mr Boundersby,' he said, stretching. He'd been bent over his phone all the way over here. 'Because it's up to us to work out what the hell is going on.'

'But shouldn't we be leaving it to the police?'

'I doubt they're going to stretch their resources searching for a spectre in period dress, don't you? They'll probably just get a psych test done and leave it at that. The evidence seems to point to her and, like Joel said, they do tend to take a hard look at the first person on the scene. Poor Mary's got the victim's DNA on her. I imagine her fingerprints are going to be down in the cellar too. She didn't mention the murder weapon though. I don't know what that was. Presumably a knife of some sort?'

I shook my head and peered out the windscreen. Looked like rain. 'Dunno. I expect there'd be plenty around in a kitchen. Unless it was a phantom knife.'

Sam pulled his bag across his legs, undid his seatbelt and turned in my direction, looking beyond me as he thought. 'The only thing that doesn't scream suspect number one, is her lack of motive. Though they could say she lost her temper after the food poisoning. Seth was ruining the reputation of the restaurant. Running it down.'

'Yeah, but whipping, gutting the chef because of a few bad prawns ... Bit extreme, isn't it? She didn't strike me as the extreme type.'

'I know what you mean. But the ghost theory?'

'Yeah. That's even dodgier.'

Sam sighed. 'Extremely unoriginal – clanking chains and moaning.'

'It's not a dungeon, though,' I commented out loud.

'Eh?' Sam asked. 'What's that got to do with anything?'

'Chains and moaning. Makes me think of dungeons. Like Septimus's Inquisition waxworks at the museum. Prisoners, torture. That kind of stuff. But it's a *restaurant*,' I emphasised the last word. 'So in terms of location it's far less clichéd. It didn't feel like she was churning out the usual ghostly guff.'

'You might be on to something there,' Sam nodded. A shard of late morning sun cut through a brief hole in the clouds and danced over the golden threads in his hair. When he looked at me the light hit his eyes and turned them a beautiful honey brown. 'But similarly,' he went on, unaware of the sudden desire in my gaze, 'she didn't deviate from her tale one iota.'

I was being far too indulgent here, so turned away.

Out of the corner of my eye I saw Sam look down the

street. 'Even when she was broken, crying, she kept to her story. I believed her.'

'Me too.' I said. Now he was looking in the other direction, I grabbed the chance to admire the firmness around his chin, that strong chiselled jaw. *Oh, Sam*, I thought, *you are so wasted, hidden away in that dingy old museum.*

'I think that Mary certainly believed what she'd seen.'

'What?' I had been slightly distracted.

'I believe that she believed what she was telling us.'

'Yes, I know,' I said, dragging my eyes away from his face and making an effort to concentrate. 'It's weird.'

'It is indeed.' He stopped looking at a woman sweeping her small front yard and undid his seatbelt. 'Although I'm sure her father has probably lied in the past.'

I nodded. 'Without a doubt.'

'She could have learnt tricks from him. About how to lie convincingly.'

'Could've done.' I conceded. 'It just didn't feel like it.'

'Yes,' he said. 'And there we go, agreeing again, Strange.' He looked back and smiled. 'If we're not careful, we'll be married with children quicker than you can say, "Hell will freeze over."'

I jumped in my seat, looked at him grinning at me, then quickly glanced away again. A blush was on its way. Why had he said that? Did he want to marry me? Or was that the kind of thing you said to someone who you had absolutely no interest in marrying? It bothered me that he could make me blush when no one else ever could. I just couldn't help it.

Covering up my discomfort, I laughed a little too loudly, patted my hair and slid out the door so I didn't have to face him.

Over the other side of the car Sam got out and stretched. I refused to look at his body, despite a pressing feeling in my stomach.

'Interesting though,' he went on, oblivious. 'That there have been instances when everyone has seen the phenomena. That there have been scores, sometimes, of witnesses.'

'Oh yes,' I said, avoiding eye contact and ambling on to the pavement. 'The writing? The blood? Very public.'

'Yes, now both of those facets are interesting. Over the years there have been some well-publicised incidences of spectral writing.' He caught up with me. 'One of the most famous cases was at Borley Rectory.' He added as an aside, 'In Essex. Just.' I could feel his breath touch my cheek. It was tickly. I wanted to touch it but kept my eyes on the turn to Marta Thompson's house.

'Allegedly it was the most haunted house in Britain. As declared by Harry Price, psychic investigator.' Sam struck out hefty strides down the road, his frame upright and animated by mental energy. 'Now, if I remember rightly there were several witnesses at Borley who attested to pencils rising up into the air, scrawling messages on the wall. Pleas for help, for light and for Mass.'

Despite my scepticism in such matters I felt a chill run through me. It's normal to be scared of the unknown so I didn't give myself a hard time about it. Like we told Joel, that sort of thing usually had a mundane explanation. Usually.

'However, most experts think they were written by the occupants of the house,' Sam concluded. 'And not a spirit at all.'

See, I was right. 'Why? What for? Attention?'

'People do things for all sorts of reasons. Human nature is one of the most confounding phenomena I've ever encountered.'

'I don't think that's what's happened here though. At least I don't think Ray and Mary are happy with the quality of attention these incidents have inspired.' I was picturing La Fleur full of diners, horrified and disgusted by what they were seeing. Didn't bode well for a fledgling business. 'The writing's on the wall,' I murmured out loud, thinking the words through as I articulated each one.

'A doom-laden portent? Is that what you're suggesting?' Sam ducked to my side to let a tall man in a grey fleece pass us. His dog stopped to sniff the ground, then growled at me. Maybe he could smell Hecate.

I returned to Sam's question. 'For the restaurant certainly. No one wants to read about bloody eyes turning up while they chow down on their meatballs, do they?'

Sam stopped, then began nodding. 'Of course, there's the food connection.'

'What connection?'

'The phrase. I do believe people are subconsciously drawn to certain things. So you're right to mention "The writing's on the wall".'

'Uh-uh,' I said. 'So where does it come from?'

He grinned. 'You really were brought up secularly, weren't you?'

'Yes. Faith is illogical. Dad didn't want us influenced by things that couldn't be proved.'

Sam nodded at me. 'So I see.'

'Where did "the writing on the wall" come from then? Is it relevant?'

'I'm not sure but certainly the story is set in a place with food and excess and riches – Belshazzar's feast. In the Book of Daniel. Belshazzar is having a great old time feasting and dancing and quaffing from golden cups stolen by his father. From a temple too, the naughty boy. Suddenly, out of nowhere, a hand appears and writes on the wall. But it's illegible. Even his wise men can't work it out. Then Daniel arrives and suggests it means that when Belshazzar's father was proud and arrogant he was deposed by God. So Daniel warns Belshazzar that things might go that way for him too. That very same night Belshazzar is killed.'

'So it was a warning.' I murmured.

'Or maybe a prophecy. Because death followed.' We turned the corner. '*Blood gushed from her eyes*,' he crooned. 'A prophecy? For whom?'

'The blood ended up gushing from Seth's neck and stomach though, didn't it? There was nothing coming out of his eyes.' I saw up ahead house number 44, where this MT lived. It was a bland little terrace clad in rectangular grey-and-pink paving tiles. Ugly. 'And Seth was a bloke,' I blurted with amazing insight and perception.

'I understand that to be true,' said Sam. 'Though shortly after the words appeared, allegedly without a disembodied hand writing them, didn't blood gush from the chandelier?'

'No, that happened before the words on the wall,' I corrected. 'Joel showed us that snippet of footage. It was really awful. Reminded me of that scene in *Carrie*,' I mused. 'That's a film.' I didn't think Sam's grasp of popular culture was particularly wide.

'Thank you for that,' he continued. 'But I wonder if that's what precisely what it was meant to do.'

'Remind us of *Carrie*?' I couldn't buy that. 'Naaah.'

'Not specifically perhaps. But that's iconic horror-film imagery, isn't it? Blood dripping from ceilings or walls or out of taps or through lights? It's a recurring motif that connotes haunted houses, madness, possession, brutality, demonic forces, the supernatural. All of that.'

We paused outside the stubby garden with its iron gate half off its hinges. Weeds were growing out of the cracks in the paved path that led up to the front steps.

I considered Sam's assertion. I'd seen a fair few horror films in my time. He wasn't wrong.

Taking my silence as consent, he went on, 'The colours, the terror, the sheer unexpectedness of it, the drama. It's so visceral it evokes strong human responses. In fact, I would suggest that it is well-used, a recurring scene or effect within the horror genre, precisely because it is so extraordinarily spectacular.'

I pulled the gate open and let him pass, turning the proposition over and coming to the conclusion it was a well-made point. 'So are you suggesting it was stage-managed?'

He waited for me halfway up the stubby garden path. His voice was lower as he spoke. 'Ray Boundersby has not long bought the place, you said.'

I had zero recollection of that. 'Did I?'

He paused and put a finger to his lips, 'Well, maybe it was your auntie Barbara who did.'

An unpleasant thought struck me. 'Are you getting me confused with Auntie Barbara?' I loved my family, truly I did, but my aunt had lived in Spain for a fair few years and was no stranger to the sunbed. Her furrowed, mahogany exterior was distinctive and very memorable and, as such, she did not, to my mind, present a particularly flattering doppelgänger.

He raised his eyebrows and tutted, reluctant to be drawn into a potential argument. 'I confirmed it online, during the drive over here. He's only had it for nine months.'

'Mmm.' I got on to the doorstep, so I could check my reflection in the glass of the front door. But the sun had chosen that moment to put in a rare appearance and threw my face into shadow. 'I go for a spray tan over sunbeds anytime.'

Sam's forehead wrinkled. 'What? What's that got to do with the price of bread?'

'My skin.' I turned my face to his and pointed. 'I like to keep it protected and well-nourished. It's an investment in the future, you might say.'

His eyebrows had pulled together hard making one big fat wrinkle on his forehead. He should really start considering Botox.

'Unlike Auntie Babs,' I prompted him. 'Who has lived a full and fun life exposed to UV rays.' There was no response. 'The consequences of which show on her skin.'

An eyebrow fluttered up, then my concern dawned on him. 'Oh, for god's sake, Rosie, you look nothing like your aunt. I can't see a family resemblance at all.'

'You can't?' Now I wasn't sure whether or not to be offended. After all, she might share certain aspects with the queens of the dried fruit scene but Auntie Babs remained a comely specimen of femininity: slender, agile with big shiny hair and, I was told on good authority, still sexy to those that liked that sort of thing, like some of my dad's friends from the allotment. And Del, her husband, obviously. And maybe Ray Boundersby.

Sam shook his head. 'You take after the other side of the family, the Strange side – Ethel-Rose, Celeste. Everyone comments on that, don't they?'

I pouted for no particular reason. 'Yes. Suppose.'

He stepped up on to the doorstep and reduced his voice to a whisper. 'I only mentioned Barbara because we were at her place at the time. In her salon. When she was telling us about Ray and his business. She implied he'd only had it for a little while.' He swung his bag over his shoulder, straightened his jacket and said quietly, 'I imagine that a man like Ray Boundersby might have made some enemies before he went legit, don't you?'

I narrowed my lips like a proper detective and nodded slowly. 'Mmm. That is a possibility. Or even a probability. But there's got to be other, less complicated ways of exacting revenge. Why kill his chef?'

'Framing his daughter would certainly hurt.'

'Oh, come on.' I wiped my lovely gold leather boots on

the doormat. 'How could anyone have guessed Mary was going to return when she did? No one knew she'd forgotten the present for Tom. Not even Tom. It was a surprise. She stumbled over the scene by accident. It was chance. The girl was only fouled by the fickle finger of fate.'

Sam frowned. 'And so we return to the ghost.'

'Who no one else saw. There was, after all, no one else there to see it.'

'Although there is someone else who has witnessed the apparition in the restaurant. Come on,' he said. 'Let's find out exactly what the butler saw.'

CHAPTER NINE

As Sam raised his hand to knock, the door opened of its own accord. A fitting entrance, I thought. There was even a slight creak to its hinges. All that was missing was a cackle of lunatic laughter. Which I could quite happily supply, if requested.

'Hello?' Sam halted his hand mid-air and craned his neck to the darkness.

A short thin blonde poked her head round the door, blinking at the sunlight. When her eyes began to adjust she squinted and looked us up and down. Settling back on our faces, she clicked her tongue and shook her head a bit, as if she was lamenting our appearance with an unseen friend.

'Hello?' I said brightly

The woman's slim tanned hand twitched on the door. For a second I wondered if she was going to have second thoughts and shut us out. At which point my own personal workplace habits kicked in – I took a step towards her and stuffed my foot on the carpet, just inside the perimeter of the house. There was no way that door was closing on me. It got my goat when that happened on the job, which was fairly common. But on this occasion not only were we fully authorised, we were on a mercy mission. We had a God-given, or at least Boundersby-endorsed, right to be here.

'Marta Thompson?' I asked, suddenly unsure if we'd got the right house.

Hard sapphire eyes re-appraised me. The manicured hand came off the door and slapped on to a scrawny hip. Both elbows were now stuck out, creating little triangular barriers across the threshold. 'And you are?'

'Here to see you,' I continued unfazed. A camel coat was draped loosely over her shoulders. 'On your way out, were you?'

'Yes,' she said, holding my gaze. I could smell extra-hold hairspray on her honey-blonde locks. In the brief sunshine, the curls, which were voluminous and full, shone like burnished gold. A very professional job. 'I'm late for lunch,' she said, and jutted out her chin.

Sam shuffled up behind. 'Nice to meet you, Ms Late for Lunch. I'm Sam Stone.' My colleague stuck out his hand in greeting, an enormous grin plastered over his face.

Cheesetastic, I thought, then realised, good god, he's trying to flirt.

Rather surprisingly, this approach seemed to defrost Marta Thompson for she responded with a thin smile and took his proffered hand. Dainty French polished nails crept over his fingers. 'It's a pleasure,' she said. From under the long curled fringe her eyelash extensions fluttered sweetly. They were way more obvious than mine.

'I'm so sorry to disturb you like this, Ms Thompson,' my

colleague cooed, breathily, 'but we're here at the request of your employer, Ray Boundersby,'

Marta Thompson regarded Sam a moment then made some internal decision which prompted her to let go of a big hefty sigh. No sooner was it out then the unbecoming scowl disappeared and her face transformed into a merry smile which revealed an ultra-pearly set of small teeth. Probably bleached. Home kit maybe. 'Call me MT,' she purred. 'Everyone does.' Though the way she said it sounded like an order.

'Thank you,' Sam said still beaming.

Her eyes lingered on him a moment, then she leant coyly into the door, lengthening her spine along the edge of it, pushing her chest out in a none-too-subtle fashion. 'I suppose you're these ghostbusters I've been hearing about?'

I wasn't going to be pressured into discussing sensitive matters on her doorstep. 'My name is Rosie Strange,' I said in such a mannered way Michael Caine would have been proud. 'Can we come in?' I left off the 'please' as the blocking business was really starting to get on my nerves.

'I'm on my way out to lunch,' MT whinged again, but a twangy note in her delivery suggested she was on to a loser with this one and she knew it. 'Can't this wait until tomorrow?' She made a last-ditch attempt to persuade Sam and widened her eyes.

I'm glad to say my colleague shook his head. 'I'm afraid not.' Then he shifted his weight to his rear foot and leant away from her leaving a respectful distance between the pair of them. Him and her, that is. 'I take it you've heard the news about Seth?'

There was a moment's pause then MT cast her eyes at the floor. A flash of uncertainty passed across her pretty bronzed face. 'Awful, awful business. I hope they get the bastard. Really I do. It's gutting.'

A choice selection of words, I thought and watched her poke a stray leaf out of the hallway with her shoe, a high-heeled patent number in nude. The beigey colour matched her lipstick. She was well accessorised, for sure, but I had to say I never really understood why some people went for neutral shades when everything else about them was so obviously enhanced. Cosmetics, I thought, were all about providing contrast. Making things stand out. That said, I could see a dusting of shimmer bringing out her cheekbones and there was a good lot of liner defining those hard blue eyes but the natural lips were a bit pointless, if you asked me. Made them fade into her chin when a nice bright red would have said, 'I'm here. Look at me.' No, I wasn't a fan of subtlety. Not that you'd notice.

The leaf popped over on to the step and was picked up by a breeze. MT took in a deep breath and breathed it out with a new briskness, lifting her head and meeting my eyes boldly. 'But, you know, life goes on. I didn't know Seth that well and I've got a lot on my plate at the moment. Can't you—'

'Yes, of course. We'll be very quick, thank you,' I said, and propelled the bulk of my body past Sam, setting myself right on course for a boob-to-boob collision with MT. An uncomfortable collision that could be easily averted if she backed down and retreated into the hallway. Which she did, pretty instantly.

Except it turned out not to be a hallway. The front door opened straight on to a modestly furnished living room.

'I don't know what help I can be,' MT said, almost by way of protest, as I marched past and in, casting around for somewhere to park myself.

It was a traditional working-class terraced house with a living-room-cum-diner that led into a small galley kitchen and yard at the back. I reckon if I'd met her outside of it, like a *long* way outside of it, not just on the doorstep, I might have expected her living accommodation to be a little more high end. This place felt like it was mismatched with the owner of those immaculate shining locks and camel coat.

At the same time I was aware that although the world of London restaurants might sound like a glamorous vocation, a lot of workers, especially the ones that had families to support, would often have to claim extra income support and credits just to get by. Catering and hospitality wasn't an industry known for its astronomic pay. Unless you got right to the top. Yes, chef.

There were some obvious signs that MT was sharing her living accommodation with others: over the back of one of the sofas were heaped jumpers and cardigans, (different sizes, I noted), a football trophy stood proudly on the mantelpiece and a woman in a tracksuit was lounging lengthways on the sofa watching TV. Ain't no flies on me.

It was only when I stood in front of her, coughed and said 'hello' that the lounger heaved her eyes away from the screen and smiled wanly. I wondered if she was massively stoned.

'This is Hannah, one of my flatmates,' said MT. With reluctance she shut the door thus abandoning all hopes of immediate escape. 'She's trying to enjoy her last day of freedom,' she said, insinuating we were spoiling it, and hung her coat over a stand. 'School starts again tomorrow.'

'Hi there,' said Hannah without interest and returned her eyes to the screen. 'Sorry to hear about Seth.' She picked up the remote and turned the volume down, but only a bit. There was an old rerun of something with Angela Lansbury on.

'You look slightly too cool for school,' said Sam, trying a polite smile. He was hovering near the sofa weighing up whether it was clean enough for his chinos. There were indeed a lot of stains on it: circular rings from the bottoms of cups, and unidentifiable bits of organic matter that might once have been dinners. A smattering of popcorn crumbs seemed permanently wedged or maybe glued in between the seat cushions.

'Sorry,' said Sam, backing away from it. 'I didn't mean that impolitely.'

Oblivious to his scrutiny the woman, Hannah, picked up a tumbler of dark brown liquid that was sitting on the carpet and sipped it. 'I'm a teaching assistant,' she said.

Well, that explained the strung-out appearance. My friend Cerise had worked in a school once. She didn't last more than two weeks and spent a fair few days afterwards twitching in her living room, occasionally shouting, 'Settle down', to no one in particular. We called it post-traumatic teaching Tourette's. So I got where this Hannah was coming from and said, 'Ah right. You have my sympathies,' then went and sat on the arm of the least grubby piece of furniture in the room before Sam nabbed it. I tried the seat but the stuffing was coming out and I could feel the springs beneath the fabric on my bum, so I nipped up on to the arm. That at least appeared relatively clean.

Sam, however, was bravely going for the sofa. He screwed his face up and looked pointedly at Hannah's sprawling legs. She smiled but didn't move so he came and sat by me on the other arm of the chair. He looked a bit wounded. In my job I was used to rudeness. Occupational hazard. Sam, however, was, on occasion, surprisingly sensitive.

MT clapped her hands. 'Okay, then let's get to it,' she said, and went and stood in the middle of the room. 'What are you after?'

It was kind of weird, her standing there while the rest of us had chosen a seat but, as homeowner, it was her prerogative. Maybe she preferred lording it over everyone. Or maybe she was just used to it. After all, as a hostess-cum-receptionist she must spend most of her working hours on her feet.

I sent Sam a go-ahead nod.

'Well,' he said. 'We'd really like to hear more about when you saw the La Fleur ghost, please?'

Hannah jerked to attention.

MT began moving backwards slowly until she reached the wall. Then she leant on it. 'Is that relevant? To Seth's murder?' She clutched her throat. The question seemed to have upset her.

Sam nodded. At the same time I said, 'We don't know. Just answer the question please.'

A moment passed while MT thought about it. 'Okay, well I only saw it once.'

Hannah muted the television. 'Am I hearing this right?' she said, incredulous. 'You've seen a ghost?'

MT shook her head. Blonde locks tumbled forwards and spilt over her shoulders like a glossy hair waterfall. 'I wasn't sure. It was too weird.' Then she turned back to Sam. 'I mean it's not what you expect to see, is it?'

'Poor you,' he said. 'Must have been quite a shock.'

His words were dripping with sympathy. He sure hadn't been like this with Mary. But then Mary wasn't a blonde-haired and blue-eyed rake, was she?

'It was,' MT admitted. 'Ghosts in your workplace! It just never happens, does it?'

Sam smiled his crooked smile. 'Oh, more than you might imagine.'

She responded with some simpering and flashed her teeth. 'Of course. Your occupation. So silly of me.'

'Not at all,' said Sam, with a little manly shake of his shoulders.

It was like I wasn't in the room at all.

Hannah wasn't liking it either. She pouted and pointed an accusatory finger at her flatmate. 'You didn't tell me! I can't believe you didn't tell me. You know I love stuff like that.' She looked at me and shook her head. 'She knows I love stuff like that. I've got bookshelves on ghosts and UFOs. I love all that.'

MT clicked her tongue. 'I'm telling you now, aren't I?' Then she rolled her eyes at Sam in a 'save me' way.

I leant forwards. 'But you did mention it to your work colleagues, didn't you?' I flicked open my notebook. 'This was at the beginning of February?'

'That's right,' she said, and shifted her eyes away out the window. 'After it had just happened. I was confused. Upset. Flustered. I needed to talk.'

'As you would,' Sam warbled, beside me.

She caught his gaze and sent him another thin grateful smile.

For god's sake. I cleared my throat and checked my notes. Time to get some speed on this interview. 'And the sighting took place in the ladies, didn't it?'

'Yes.' MT nodded. 'It was after a shift.'

'A what?' I said, and raised my eyebrows, sensing mischief.

MT narrowed her eyes. 'A shift.'

'Oh, a shi*ft*,' I emphasised the 'F' and tried to look innocent. 'Sorry, I misheard.'

Hannah giggled. Sam's face tightened. He crossed his legs then uncrossed them again.

'And what happened?' I went on, keeping my mouth a flat neutral line.

'I was coming out of the toilets—'

'After your shi*Fffft*?'

MT pushed her butt off the wall and straightened her narrow shoulders in defiance. 'After work,' she said stiffly. 'I was in the doorway.'

I tapped my notebook with a pen. 'Of the toilet?'

'Of the cubicle,' she said with precision.

'And what?' I asked. In my notebook I wrote, *toilet cubicle*.

'And this thing brushed past me.'

'Can you describe it?' Sam leant forward on his knee. 'How did it move?'

'It's hard to remember.' MT's eyes were fixing on him. As she spoke she began twisting a curl. 'Sort of drifted.'

'Above the floor?' Sam asked.

'Yes,' she nodded. 'Above it.'

'So, MT,' I said deadpan. 'Let me get this right. You're saying that after your shift you encountered a floater?'

There was a moment of impasse, then on the sofa Hannah burst out laughing. Sam sprang off the armchair and caught my arm. 'Can I have a word with you, Rosie? Now!' And then he frogmarched me to the front door.

'What's got into you?' We were wedged into the furthest corner of the room.

'Oh, come on,' I said. 'It's a joke. Literally. You can't be buying this.'

'Buying what? She hasn't got started yet.' He bent closer to me so I could smell the slight tangy whiff of grapefruit. He must have used my shower gel this morning. I liked that notion. 'Rosie!' he snapped. 'Concentrate! Mary said she saw something there too and you didn't give her the third degree.'

'And you didn't slobber over Mary the way that you're—' I stopped myself from finishing that sentence, instantly regretting what I'd given away. It wasn't like me to be so unguarded.

'What? What are you talking about? I'm not slobbering. I'm allowing her to talk. In fact, it would be nice if she could get a bloody word in without you making some acerbic comment. You're the one,' he said, pointing his finger at my chest, 'who suggested we should allow subjects to talk without interruption. "Don't make too many requests for clarification," you said. "It's an important technique," you said.'

It was all true. Clearly some random emotion had queered my pitch. I needed to check it, rein it in and apologise. Which I did promptly.

'Accepted,' he said. 'Now we need to go in and rebuild rapport.'

'Okay,' I told him. 'You continue, then.'

'You apologise.'

Oh god. I didn't want to. I might have reacted irrationally against MT's mild flirtation but there was no need to prostrate myself on the floor. 'Must I?'

'You must.'

'I was only saying—'

'Apologise.'

Back in the living room MT and Hannah were waiting for us with eager eyes.

'Sorry,' I said. 'Nerves. We're not used to murders. Well, not recent ones.' I shrugged and tried to laugh.

MT didn't. Just rotated those crazy ice-blue orbs and bolted them on to my face. For a moment I felt like I was being pulled into an icy lake. Then she cracked a smile and said, 'It's okay.' Which, credit where it's due, was actually rather gracious. She could have frosted me out. But she didn't. That was decent.

With her next sentence MT went even further and threw me a conversational olive branch. 'So, Rosie, how long have you been doing this?' Again, very nice of her. Considering.

However, the most accurate answer to this question was just over a week. There was no way I was going to let on about that. Any moral high ground would be utterly lost, if there was any left to fight about.

I expertly batted the question over to my partner. 'It's been a while now for you, Sam, hasn't it?'

Back on top of the armchair, Sam nodded like a happy dog. 'Yes. I've been in this area of study pretty much since I was twelve.' Which surprised all of us.

MT asked him how that had come to be but he shook his head and told us it was a very long and boring story and went back to asking MT about the incident again.

'Yes,' she said. She was sitting on the sofa now, next to Hannah, who had turned the telly off and was leaning forwards, hugging her knees, enthralled by the whole thing.

'It was eerie, you know. One minute she wasn't there, the next minute she just walked straight past me. All dusty and white, just moving across the space between the sinks and the cubicles, not looking at anything but staring straight ahead. Then she just disappeared into the wall. It was horrible. The strangest thing I've ever seen.'

Sam was scratching down some notes. 'And you say she *drifted* across the floor?'

'That's right.' MT sent me a wary glance.

I looked out the window and kept my mouth firmly shut.

'And you were coming out of the doorway, were you?' Sam went on.

MT nodded.

'So did you see her when she was approaching? On your right? Or was she in front of you? Did you see her profile? Or her back? What angle was it?'

Briefly the MT's eyes widened. Then they relaxed as she went into recall. 'She was in front of me.'

'Did you see her profile?'

'No, I don't think so.' Then she stopped and said, 'Actually thinking about it now, I think she had a long, sharp, bony nose.'

'Oh,' said Sam. 'That's good. Helpful.'

While he was noting that down, I asked, 'What was she wearing? Do you remember?'

'Yes.' MT nodded, hair rustling all about. 'An old-fashioned dress with a big full skirt. And a bonnet.'

Sam looked at me. Same as Mary. 'And this definitely wasn't a real person dressed up?' I went on.

MT shook her head. Hannah smiled. 'This is so cool.'

Sam scribbled something else in his notebook. 'What made you think it was a ghost?'

MT pushed a hand through her hair and sat back into the sofa. 'I knew the place was haunted,' she said.

Hannah looked pissed off. 'You so should have told me.'

'How did you know that?' I asked. 'From Mary?'

MT stared at me a long hard minute, then said, 'Actually, I heard it from other people.'

'Who?' I asked and picked up my pen.

'Some customers.'

'Really? Can you remember their names?'

She shook her hair out and ran a hand through it on one side. 'Henry Warren, one of the regulars, may have mentioned it,' she said slowly, as if she were delving deep into her memory. I wrote it down.

'And the staff, obviously,' she went on and then paused. 'Hang on, it actually might have been Seth, who told me that Henry had told him?' She chucked her chin. 'Or maybe Henry told me that Seth had spoken to him about it. Yes, I think that was the right way round.'

'Anyone else?'

'Not to my knowledge.'

'Thank you,' said Sam again. 'And I wanted to ask about the night of the writing on the wall.'

'Oh, yes.' MT straightened her pencil skirt.

'Can you tell me what happened? In your own words.'

'Actually, I can't,' she said. 'I wasn't in that night. Off sick with flu.'

A mobile somewhere in the room began to buzz. MT fished around in her handbag and muted the ring. I guessed it was her lunch date wondering where she was. 'That's all I know, really,' she said, and put the phone on the arm of the sofa, face down.

Her fingers inched to her knee and tapped it three times. 'Well, if you've got no more questions?'

Sam flipped his notebook shut and put it in his bag. 'You've been very helpful. Thank you for seeing us, MT. We may need to talk to you again sometime.'

I doubted we'd need to do that – she been helpful enough but not earth-shattering quite frankly.

'Of course,' she said, and stood up. 'Okay, then. Well, I've got to dash. Hannah can see you out, can't you, H?'

Hannah mumbled something while MT grabbed her coat. In a blink of an eye, the door slammed, the letterbox rattled and MT was gone.

'She's always like that,' said Hannah. 'Rushing off from one thing to another. Don't take it personally.'

I grunted. Sam said, 'Of course not. Busy woman.'

'Now,' Hannah clapped her hands together and smiled. There was a worrying glint in her eye. 'How 'bout you tell me all about your job. Sounds fascinating.'

We emerged quite a while later, after Sam had amused Hannah with a couple of nuggets of information about our last case, then done his very best to deflect the rest of her questions, banging on at length about the intricacies and details of his PhD. This eventually had the desired effect of glazing Hannah's eyes. She was, she began to insist, more of a UFO kind of girl. Nevertheless she did promise to come and visit the museum one day, which we both made delighted sounds about. We weren't proud. You took customers where you could.

'Not sure what we got there,' I said as we walked back to the car. 'With MT. I mean she gave a suitably vague description of the apparition. Period dress, as Mary described.

It's consistent, but that could mean they conferred. Or Mary told the staff and they told MT.'

'Or maybe MT saw what she was expecting to see because she was spooked and because of the stories in circulation.'

I considered it. 'I expect to win the lottery if I buy a ticket. It ain't happened yet.'

'That's different. I'm saying that if people expect to see ghosts, then they will,' said Sam. 'Sometimes it's even involuntary.'

I made a *pfft* sound with my lips.

'Honestly, Rosie,' he said. 'The human brain is a wild and untamed thing. We're only just beginning to understand its complexities.'

He would have no disagreement from me. I had to read government policy documents. There was no greater illustration of bizarre and twisted minds.

'And,' he said. 'Did you know that belief in ghosts is actually on the rise? A recent survey found that fifty-two per cent of respondents said they believed in them.'

It never ceased to bewilder me how so many people could express belief in something they couldn't prove. Like Santa. Or the tooth fairy. Or God. 'That's amazing,' I said, and added a low whistle.

'I tell you what's also amazing, young lady,' Sam went on.

I took a moment to enjoy his use of 'young'.

'That that glorious woman didn't kick us out of her house earlier. Behave yourself, Ms Strange.'

Eh? I thought. 'What glorious woman?' I said.

'You must have notice how stunning she was,' he said with a smile.

'Who?' He had me there.

'MT.'

'No, Sam,' I sighed. 'I didn't actually.'

'She was immaculately turned out.'

'That's what women do when they have a hot lunch date. They get dressed up.'

'Oh,' he said, deflating around the shoulders. 'Do you think she was seeing a man?'

I looked at him and considered the possibility he might be intentionally winding me up. 'Well,' I said to him. 'Yes, if she's straight, which I think she probably is. I didn't have my gaydar going off, did you?'

'Not my gaydar, no.' He grinned idiotically. The moron.

I was starting to feel uncomfortable but decided to ignore the feeling and just get in the car so we could hop on our way. 'But that's a point actually,' I said, as I opened the door. 'She *was* going out. Ray said he was going to phone to say we were coming, didn't he? So why was she buggering off to lunch *before* we arrived?'

He shrugged. 'Hot date, like you said. I expect she has a lot of those.'

Was that 'wistful' I was hearing in his voice? Surely not.

'Not a particularly difficult choice for her to make,' I sniffed. 'Hot date versus ghostbusters.'

'Oh, Rosie,' Sam moaned. 'Don't you start. It's bad enough from Joel and MT.'

I giggled, glad he'd said something negative about her,

and turned on the engine. 'Home, James? To mull over what we've found out and sort out a plan?'

'Good idea.'

But before we'd reached the bottom of her road, he was back on it again. 'So what makes you think she was going off to see a man?'

'Obvious.' I said. 'Roots not long done. Gone to town on the make-up. Nice mani. French polish. Bet she's had a recent pedi too.' And, I refrained from adding, her low-cut top was a dead giveaway – we'd all copped a glimpse of those cosmetically enhanced mammaries.

Sam leant his head against the window and sighed. 'She's obviously a woman who likes to look good. And surely she does indeed.'

I raised my eyebrows but carried on driving. I hadn't seen him so taken by a woman before. Not so dramatically anyway. It was quite un-Sam, really. He veered more towards repressed British male specimen than bold metrosexual. And yet over the past week or so I had also started to entertain the idea that something hot and dark lurked beneath that surface. I'd glimpsed it once or twice. Even so all this fawning was really quite atypical. And a bit sick-making.

We drove on for a couple of minutes then softly, he muttered, 'She's incredible.'

'Incredible? Really?' It popped out before I could stop it. But I couldn't see what was so astounding about the girl. Sure, she'd made the most of what she'd got but no more than the majority of my friends did. MT weren't no Angelina Jolie, it had to be said.

'You've got eyes, haven't you?' Sam nudged me.

'Careful. Not while I'm driving.' He was usually anal about that sort of thing.

'She was gorgeous,' he went on. 'That hair, it's magnificent—'

It was pretty good, I had to concede, but not entirely a gift from God. 'Ah, yes. Extensions,' I told him. 'My friend Cerise quite often sticks them in. They're easy to spot if you know what you're looking for – all those clips, hairnets, stray synthetic mono-fibres.'

'Really?' He sounded shocked. 'Well, they're, er, still magnificent. And those eyes, absolutely startling.'

'Coloured lenses, I expect.' I was thinking back to their sapphire luminescence. 'I've got some that make my eyes look amazing too, you know.' I made them big and flashed them at him.

He was bloody well looking out the window. Like a lovesick fop. 'But, I mean,' he continued to moon. 'Hers are huge too, aren't they? It's not just down to the lenses. If indeed that's where that brilliance originates.'

Jesus. 'Well, I expect it does come from contact lenses and the "hugeness" as you describe it, can be very easily achieved with the right skills. Make-up is an art. Like any craft you have to put in the hours and practice to get it right. She's good, I'll give her that. Reckon she's gone for an eyelash perm to get the kink going on there, then layered on the mascara. Overdone it a bit if you ask me. I hate it when it goes clumpy like that. All those flakes. They get in your eyes and then you end up with those nasty black bits in the corners. My friend

Cerise calls them eye bogeys. That's what MT's got coming her way,' I said. 'Eye bogeys. Poor girl.'

It had no effect. His adulation was ridiculously undiminished. 'Fantastic skin,' he mused out loud, pretending to talk to himself. Jeez he was getting irritating. 'Glowing and sun-kissed. Very "Girl from Ipanema".'

'The "Girl from Ipanema" was dark-haired.' I stopped myself from adding, *like me*. 'And Brazilian. A bit more tasteful. MT is more your brassy "Blonde Ambition" kind of chick, don't you think? You know, a bit "Material Girl". A bit "Desperately Seeking …"' Still no response in the passenger seat. 'And tan-wise you can do wonders with a dab of bronzer on the cheekbones. And I saw dark wrinkles round the wrists. A dead giveaway. Her "Ipanema" look comes straight out of a bottle. Home job too. I prefer salons, personally. Less imperfections.'

My colleague, however, was in for the fight. 'Oh, come on, Rosie, even you have to concede she's got a breath taking figure for someone so petite.'

'Short,' I corrected. 'And those tits aren't real, Sam.'

A tremor passed through the front seats.

'The waist certainly is,' Sam bleated.

I remembered the way she came in from the hips. 'You can thank Gok Wan and his high-tech shapewear. He's a blessing to girls without a good outline.'

'Shapewear?'

'Modern speak for corsetry.'

'She's not big though, is she? She's slender. Lithe.'

She was. I sniffed with distaste. 'People that thin don't like food.'

'Ah-ha,' he said with glee. 'But we caught her going out to lunch.'

'She was going to meet a man.'

Sam made a 'pooh' noise with his cheeks then turned to face me in the seat. 'What's the matter with you?'

I kept my eyes on the road but thought his voice sounded like he was smiling. 'What's the matter with *you*?'

He turned his face away and looked out the window again. I thought there was a slight shake to his shoulders but I wasn't going to dignify him with a glance. I think that was exactly what he wanted me to do. Instead I drove on.

Within a minute he'd started humming a tune. 'Don't Cha.' Pussycat Dolls. I recognised it straight away.

Pathetic.

I screwed up my face and made a huffy noise.

What was I doing? I wondered, as we stopped at the roundabout. Sam was perfectly entitled to be attracted to other women. I was attracted to other men, and anyway we didn't even know if we were attracted to each other. Or at least I didn't know if he was attracted to me. And anyway, I was his boss and all that.

I repressed a sigh. It was complicated, I shouldn't be making it worse by acting like an idiot. I ought to be more generous, have a little more grace. 'She was quite stylish, I suppose,' I said, with gargantuan generosity. 'Though it takes one to know one in that regard.' A point well made, I thought.

His gaze brushed my cheek and neck but I still wasn't going to look at him like he wanted me to. I heard him sigh and wondered if he was summoning MT up mentally, going over those inches that looked about as curvy as a little boy. A little boy with big false knockers.

'You're right,' he said dreamily. 'Stylish. Alluring. Glamorous.'

'Glamorous is easy if you know how,' I said, and pushed my foot down hard on the accelerator. As I did, I caught sight of my lovely boots. Black and gold. Black-and-gold leather. Amazing. Now that was glamour.

'Now that's glamour,' I said to Sam, trying at the same time to nod at my feet.

'What?' his attention drifted back into the car.

'Glamour,' I repeated. 'Now that's glamour.'

'Glamour,' Sam said, chewing the word over carefully. Then he paused and sat up straight. 'Oh, Rosie, you've just said something incredibly interesting.'

'And you're sounding surprised because?'

He shook his head. 'How funny.' Then he rummaged in his bag and pulled out his notebook. Flipping the pages over, he started chuckling quietly and making notes.

I waited a couple of minutes for him to explain. When he didn't I said, 'Are you going to let me in on this or do I purely serve as the butt of your jokes these days?'

'A very nice butt it is too,' he said.

This time I did dart a look at him. But his face was angled down, the expression hidden in shadow. Though a slight repetitive heave to his shoulders suggested he might be chuckling again.

'Come on,' I said. 'What are you talking about?'

'Oh, it's a witch thing,' he said smothering – yes, it was there – a definite laugh.

'Go on then.'

He sucked down a long breath and tried to make his voice steady. 'The glamour. Have you not heard of it? I've never thought about it before but it really adds credibility to my theory about Essex Girls and Essex witches. You know how I think that recent stereotype may well have grown out of the former.'

'Uh-huh. You're not going to tell me the Essex witches were glamorous, are you?'

'Not quite. But glamour originally was the ability to make people see something or someone in a more positive light or more attractive way than it or they really were.'

I considered this a moment. 'Yep, that sounds about right.'

'No,' said Sam. 'It wasn't cosmetic but a spell. A bewitchment. Something illusory that could be used by witches to seduce men.'

'Oh, typical,' I said. 'Poor men. That seems like a "she made me do it, your honour". Always the woman's fault.'

'I'm not defending it. But that's what it was. It had a demonological context.'

I was getting his drift. 'Are you suggesting this aspect, this glamour, the witch thing has descended from the witches to the Essex Girl?'

'It's something to consider: Essex Girls *are* glamorous. An aura hangs around the stereotype that points to this enhancement and illusion. Oh yes, all those unsubtle bewitchments wreak havoc over men, don't they? The glamour tests, pulls and sometimes breaks the male will. The Essex Girl threatens because she is attractive. That's why she's put into a box, a stereotype, in the first place. So she can be controlled. And disempowered.'

'Like women accused of witchcraft.'

'Also controlled. Also disempowered by their label.' Sam paused. '*The Hammer of Witches* by Kramer and Sprenger.'

'The what?'

'Also known as the *Malleus Maleficarum*. It was a medieval best-selling guide to witch-hunting. Written by two Catholic clergymen in Germany. Had a how to spot a witch section, how to hold a trial, how to prosecute, interrogate and torture. And there was a whole section in which they debated how witches "by some glamour" turned men into beasts.'

I could have laughed at what he'd said if the rest hadn't been so damn hideous. I'd seen pictures of equipment that witch-hunters used to extract 'confessions'. We had a whole wall of them in the Witch Museum. Though they were unlabelled. I'd decided to start researching so we could explain what they were used for. I'd got as far as the heretics fork and found myself too traumatised to continue.

The image of the torture device made me cringe in the driving seat. 'I suppose they weren't talking metaphorically?'

'Doubtful,' said Sam. 'Everything was taken rather literally back then.'

'God,' I sighed. 'Were these women really so threatening?'

'Indeed.' He buried his face in his bag and rummaged. 'And sometimes also threatening to other women. If you can believe that?'

I detected a note of light sarcasm in his voice and shot him a glance but he was still hunched over his bag.

'Ah-ha, here we are,' he said, and brought out a slim, printed black volume. He turned to a page then read out, '*Glamour, when it was defined during the witch craze, was the demonic ability to confuse reality and distort the senses. To create an illusion.* Though, generally, it was a power that wasn't used by the witch but attributed to her by her persecutors.'

'What do you mean? That it didn't really exist? People just said it did to get the witches, or—' I remembered he'd been quite a stickler on that point, 'Sorry, I mean, women accused of witchcraft – to get them into trouble. Convicted.'

'Yes, it also functioned as an excellent excuse,' he said. 'If a man slept with a woman deemed unsuitable, usually because she was of a lower class, then he could cry "glamour"! The scheming seductress had used a spell to make her appearance seem more attractive him so she could charm him into bed.'

'I suppose it was also a good excuse for rape.' I tutted loudly.

'Could well be,' he said. 'Box junction.' Then he waved his hands at the windscreen.

'I can see it thank you very much,' I told him.

'Then why are you sitting in it?' he asked.

'Because that car didn't move like it should have done.'

He sighed and twitched his hands. Someone behind me blared their horn.

'But anyway, I was saying that there were men, probably still are, who were frightened of women and this glamour.'

'Yes, they're called misogynists.'

Sam said nothing.

I moved out of the box junction and felt him relax next to me. 'Probably the biggest glamour,' he said, 'the biggest illusion of all was the myth of demonic witchcraft. That it existed like they thought it did.'

I made an agreeing noise.

'But dear gal, thank you.'

'For what?' I said.

'For mentioning it. Glamour has been a timely reminder: we should certainly take heed.'

'What do you mean?' I said.

He smiled and tapped his nose. 'That which the wise among us are loath to forget – things are never really what they seem.'

CHAPTER TEN

I rotated my glass. The action made the ice tinkle inside. I liked that sound a lot. And it was important to relax and unwind after an intense day like the one we'd just had. That's why I'd gone for spirits. Medicinal. Sam returned to type and ordered a Coke. Personally I would have preferred to go a bit further field to somewhere that wasn't full of neon and white leather. However the location of the Buzz Bar, opposite my flat, meant that it was staggering distance. Not just for me, unfortunately, but also the hordes of marauding drunks who took up residence from Friday to Sunday, fagging, screaming, shouting, fighting and regularly sauntering over to urinate in our communal entrance. Or sometimes copulate. Or from time to time, I'd also been told, to snort a ton of class A's.

It was Sam's idea to come here. I was so flabbergasted that he'd suggested a drink that he could have led me anywhere. He didn't usually. I, personally, was always quite up for one. But right now I was most definitely in need of a little snifter to settle my nerves: Mum had phoned in the afternoon to say the doctor was sending Dad for further tests. I had a very dry mouth and clammy hands as I told her not to worry, that it was perfectly normal and encouraging that the surgery was investigating everything, taking it seriously. Sam could see how it rocked me. So he brought me here.

'I'll get them in, you go and find a table. What you having?' he asked as we leant on the bar.

'A Buttery Nipple please.'

He stopped and took a breath, reddened slightly on his cheeks then said, 'I don't quite know how to respond to that.'

'It's a cocktail,' I told him, unable to stop myself grinning at his expression. It lightened the atmosphere a bit, which was good. Buttery Nipples had a tendency to do that.

'I'm not asking for a Buttery Nipple,' Sam returned with priggish dismay.

I tutted and went off to get a window table, 'Just ask Jamaal for Rosie's favourite. He'll do the rest.'

'Thought you didn't come here often?' Sam called after me.

'Oh, you know – birthdays, bar mitzvahs, divorces …'

There were some free stools at a tall table by the exit that looked out on the flats. It wasn't inspiring but if you leant forwards and craned your neck, you could just about see the green foliage peeking off my balcony. Felt comforting to know my plants were there. I checked my phone. One message from Mum saying Dad seemed fine and that they were going to have halibut and an early night. I put the mobile on the table and stared at it. Was I partly responsible for Dad's attack? Had I unwittingly brought it on? Was my lingering at the museum, my dwindling resolve to sell it straight away, was that making my poor father ill?

The thought troubled me more than I expected. Of course my first impulse was then to stop mucking around and go back and put it on the market. But my second reaction, which was rooted in a tumult of emotion, was to be sad. And somewhere else, in a place without thought or emotion, I experienced another feeling or notion or, I don't know what you'd call it – a conviction that stopping this, severing these new-found connections with the past, that all of that would be wrong.

But if Dad's health was at stake …

I took a deep breath in and smelt the stale stench of week-old Sauvignon Blanc, rancid orange juice and beer. If it had to be done, then it had to be done. If we could find some time after we'd sorted out this business at La Fleur, then we should go back and start an inventory. I'd tell Sam that was his new priority and to forget about fixing the place. If I had to get rid of it, then at least an inventory might bring to light some valuables and maybe there would be some items I could salvage for myself as a memento of sorts. There was such a lot there.

Sam set our drinks on the table. 'Nice chap, that Jamaal,' he said. 'Knows all about your nipples.'

I was going to make a joke about him and half the neighbourhood but I thought it might give the wrong impression, so instead asked, 'What killed Septimus?'

The question had been at the back of my mind since I saw Dad pitch forwards and clutch his chest. Well, it would, wouldn't it? I couldn't think of a way of introducing the subject in a more subtle manner so there was nothing for it but to come straight out and call it.

I don't think Sam minded. He kind of squinted at me, and said, 'Heart.' Then he took a long swig of his Coke.

'He was fit up until the day he died, though,' Sam added, suddenly and quickly. 'Your dad has got good genes. Try not to worry too much.'

'Difficult,' I began, but my phone which was on the table between us, beeped very loudly and insistently. Two messages arrived, one after another.

'Who is that?' Sam turned the phone round towards him and read the sender's ID on the screen. 'Ray.'

'Let me see,' I said, and grabbed it back. I didn't like other people reading my stuff. The messages were both the same. Mr Boundersby had either accidentally pressed send twice or he wasn't taking any prisoners and wanted to get his message across. 'He says the crime scene's going to be released soon.' I told Sam. 'He wants us at La Fleur at 10 a.m. prompt.'

'Does he say prompt?' Sam asked.

'No. He says,' I pretended to read off my phone, '*or else I'll shoot you.*'

Sam jumped to his feet wobbling the table in his haste. 'Good god.'

'Just joshing,' I told him and nudged a beer mat into the spilt Coke. 'The words he's used are *on the dot.*'

Sam sat back on top of the high stool. 'And what Ray Boundersby wants, Ray Boundersby gets.' Then he took down a very long slug of his drink. 'I'll phone the museum and let Bronson know we'll be up here for a bit.'

He pulled his bag on to his lap and began fumbling for his mobile. There wasn't a problem with him staying over at my place, though I did have an issue with him wearing the same pants for the foreseeable. We definitely weren't yet at the stage where we'd be comfortable washing each other's smalls. Thank god.

'Sam,' I said. 'You'll need to pop over to Matalan and buy some clothes, won't you?'

He brightened visibly. 'You don't mind me staying?'

'No? Do you?'

'Cards on the table,' he said. 'I'd love to.' He found his phone, which immediately began ringing. 'Oh,' he said. 'Talk of the devil … it's Bronson!'

I could tell from the fall of Sam's face as Bronson spoke that it was serious.

He punched the speaker button and said, 'Rosie's here too. I'm putting you on speaker.' Then he looked up. 'Someone's broken into the museum.'

'No!' I said, then shouted at the phone, 'Bronson, you okay? Are you hurt? What happened?'

The caretaker's voice crackled over the line. 'I'm fine thank you, Rosie dear. I wasn't there. One of the neighbours called in to say they saw a suspicious light in the front yard so I've dropped by to check. Window's smashed at the side.'

I thought of the beautiful circular stained glass in the office and asked if it was that one.

'No,' he said. 'Thank goodness. Not the rose window. Further back, in the kitchen.'

Ah, that wasn't too bad then. That was an ordinary PVC job that looked to the side and rear of the museum.

Sam's face was all pinched. 'So what have they taken, Bronson?'

There was a pause on the line, then the caretaker said very slowly, 'Well, that's the thing, Sam lad. They've not taken anything.'

I frowned at Sam who responded similarly.

'No,' Bronson went on. 'Whoever has broke in has, er, *left* a few things in here.'

'What?' I asked.

There was another lengthy pause then he said, 'I think you'd better see for yourselves.'

CHAPTER ELEVEN

Bronson was waiting for us outside the Essex Witch Museum. In the pale moonlight, it looked more like a skull than ever. The whitewashed walls gleamed like bare bone. The glass of the 'eye windows', though dark and hollow empty sockets, caught the light and glinted with animation. The museum was disturbed. Someone had violated it.

As we crunched over the gravel of the drive to the caretaker the breeze stirred the line of pine trees that formed the property's border. 'Shhhh,' they whispered, urging us to caution.

Except of course they weren't, because trees can't talk.

'Thank you for coming down so quickly,' Bronson said when we reached him. He had on his usual garb, a yellow sou'wester and matching jacket that gave him the look of a fisherman in search of his boat.

I popped a kiss on his cheek, brushing the thick grey moustache, and thanked him for waiting. We'd left as soon as we got the news but because of my Nipple (buttery variety) I was over the limit so Sam had to drive and kept very firmly to the speed recommendations, doubling the normal length of my journey to Adder's Fork.

Sam shook his hand, then wiped it on his jeans. The caretaker's hands were perpetually damp.

'Come on then,' said Bronson and picked up a bucket.

'Yep,' I said. 'Show us the damage.'

'Oh.' He slowed as we crossed the lobby to the 'Abandon Hope' door. 'There ain't no damage. Quite the opposite.' He beckoned us in. 'Apart from kitchen window, that's all.'

'See,' he pointed to the floor of the corridor that led into the main body of the museum. 'It starts there.'

Sam and I followed his finger to a series of tiny round objects scattered across the lino.

'What is it?' I asked and went and squatted over them.

'Rose petals,' Bronson said quietly. 'There's a whole trail of the buggers. Will take me a good hour at least to clear up.'

They were mostly yellow in colour but had fine tips tinged with both a reddy-pink and lavender. And they were fresh too. 'A trail?'

'Yes, come see.' He disappeared round the corner into the artefacts display area, the one that Sam had worked on with Septimus. It was the lightest, airiest space in the museum because of its high ceilings and skylights. The spotlights fixed to the old wooden beams illuminated elegant cabinets full of neatly labelled historical artefacts and folklore paraphernalia.

Bronson was right – a narrow path of petals led us past the cases and several witchcraft exhibits, tableaus which I called 'witch scenes', and through to a space referred to as the 'Talks Area'. It was usually set out with benches that faced a small platform from which Sam did his lectures and 'community-facing engagement', whatever that was. But tonight these had been pushed aside. In the centre of the clearing was the strangest of sights.

'Wow,' said Sam and put his hands on his hips.

'Indeed,' Bronson nodded.

'It's kind of beautiful,' I said. 'Flowers.' For there were hundreds of them, in vases, sprouting from buckets, bunched into plastic plant pots, dotted all over the space. In the centre of them all, on a podium, was a huge stunning bouquet like an exploding firework of colour – yellows, purples, whites, blues. It looked gorgeous.

'Bronson,' I laughed. 'It looks like you've got an admirer.'

But he didn't laugh back. 'This one here,' he made his way towards the central bouquet and pointed at a cluster of beautiful roses. 'Do you know what it is, Rosie?'

Sam had sidled up behind us. 'Bronson,' he said. His voice sounded strained again. 'Do you think you should …?'

But the caretaker sent a gesture back with the minutest shake of his head. 'Look around you, lad.' Then his twinkly blue eyes fixed on me. 'This,' he gestured again to the roses. 'It's the Ethel-Rose rose.'

'Oh,' I said. 'The same name as my grandmother.'

'That's right,' he nodded. 'It was created and named for her. By your great-grandfather on the occasion of her first birthday. Lovely isn't it. Your great-grandfather chose the colours himself – yellow for joy, pinky tips for love and gentleness, and mauve for splendour.'

I was frowning, trying to work out what he was going on about and reached out to pluck the rose from the bouquet. In the quickest movement I'd ever seen, Bronson knocked my arm back and caught my hand in his. 'Sorry,' he said. 'Don't touch it, Rosie love. There's belladonna in among the stems.'

'Bella Who?'

It was Sam who answered. 'Deadly nightshade. The queen of poison plants. Now you mention it I can see it too. There's quite a lot.'

'Why is it there?' I bleated. Surprisingly it was pretty with a purple hooded flower, yellow stamens and blue cherry-like berries. 'That's not very nice.'

Bronson released my hand and pointed in among the stems. 'There's nettles in among them too. See.'

I looked past the deadly nightshade to a straggled hairy stem which I recognised, from lots of experience on my dad's allotment as a stinging nettle. 'Strange for a bouquet.'

'There's wolfsbane there,' said Sam, edging towards the bouquet. 'Also known as devil's helmet. You know, in mythology, the goddess Hecate was meant to have invented it. Talking of which, she's not around, is she?'

Bronson shook his head. 'That cat's got a six or seven senses, for sure. Not seen her tonight. Reckon she scarpered when it happened.'

'Look,' said Sam. 'The wolfsbane is almost hidden behind those orange lilies but you can see white flowers there. They look a little like snowdrops. Just a sniff of them can make you feel unwell.'

'Oh,' I said. 'Do you think that's what they wanted? To make us sick? Maybe it was someone from La Fleur?' I thought about the restaurant's name. 'Perhaps we're getting closer than someone likes?'

'But who would put them here? Like this?' Sam bit his lip in thought. 'It would be more effective to send a bouquet to your flat, wouldn't it? Then you would physically have to handle the blooms and stems – unwrap them, put them into a vase, arrange them etc. But these, they're set up already. Arranged. Almost as if whoever did this didn't want you to touch them. Just to look.'

'I suppose so,' I conceded and stood back to take in the huge display. 'But who would go to such effort?'

'Who, yes. Well, that I don't rightly know,' said Bronson and carefully flattened his moustache.

'And why?' Sam wondered out loud. 'That's the more troubling question.'

'Oh, I reckons I know why,' ventured Bronson.

Sam and I both turned towards him.

'It's a message,' he said. 'I been here since half seven and not doing much but looking at it. It's a message.'

'How d'you work that one out?' I said.

There was a chair at the back of the area, which Bronson went and got. He offered it to me, then when I declined, sat in it and leant forwards, hands on knees. Sam sat down on the floor next to him.

'Now, if you look at it from here, you can see that these red flowers in the buckets,' he motioned to what, from this angle, now looked like an outer ring of flowers. 'They're all begonias. Old Mrs Bronson used to go in for flower arranging back in the day. She was very big on the meanings of flowers. Said it gave her arrangements an added layer of enigma. See, the Victorians went wild for that sort of thing. Had a whole language of flowers. Begonias, I remember Grace saying, were such bright and charming blossoms. Didn't seem right that their meaning was so different. You see, the begonia is meant to stand for fear. If you give it to someone else, then it means "beware".'

I crossed my arms and squinted at the display. The vases and buckets and pots had been formed into several decreasing circles around the main bouquet. Bronson was right about the ruby red ones, the begonias, for they did form the outside perimeter of the piece or arrangement.

I carefully picked my way through the scarlet flowers to the second ring.

'I know what these are.' I bent over a pot of bright yellow-and-orange blossoms. 'Marigolds.' I had grown them on my balcony last year and tried to use them in salads. 'They're not poisonous. They're edible. What do they mean?'

Bronson shrugged, trying to remember.

But Sam was already jabbing at his phone. 'Oh! Pain and grief!'

I raised my eyebrows. Bronson nodded slowly. 'That's right,' he said. 'Now you mention it.'

'And these,' I moved in towards the centre and hovered over a couple of jam jars that had been planted with sweet-smelling pink-and-blue flowering plants. I loved them. 'These are hyacinths,' I announced.

Sam swiped his phone then looked up. 'I am sorry. Please forgive me.'

'For what?'

'That's what they mean,' he said, and frowned.

'Told you,' Bronson's full baritone resonated across the space. 'Mark my words – it's a message.'

On the interior ring there were three buckets and one watering can, each filled with a different plant. Little shoots of lobelia poked from the spout of the can. They looked exactly like they did on the packet that I had stuck in the soil of my hanging baskets. I fingered their delicate blue petals and named them. They were so pleasant-looking they had to have a positive meaning, I was sure.

Sam shook his head. 'Malevolence.'

'Christ!' I said, and stepped back, almost knocking over a bucket behind me. I righted it and looked in to find there was actually no water in there. There was a small branch poking out. 'Chestnut,' I declared.

It took Sam a couple of seconds to find the meaning. 'Do me justice,' he said very slowly as if he were just as surprised by the meaning as me.

I was becoming more and more unsettled. It was beginning to look like Bronson was right.

A small bunch of flowers inside the can were withered. 'I don't know what this one is.'

'Can you describe it?' Sam asked. His voice had got its edge back again.

'Lots of foliage, dark green. The flowers look like daisies, but they're large and yellowy-orange with brown centres.'

Sam got up and came over and took a picture on his phone. After a few seconds he said, '*Rudbeckia*, or the coneflower, or goldsturm. Or black-eyed Susan.'

'And?' I said.

He nodded at the caretaker. 'Justice again.'

'Okay,' I said, and pointed to the final bucket. 'Well, we all know what these are.' I indicated the slender-stemmed flowers with their floppy red heads. 'Poppies.'

'The fallen,' Bronson murmured.

'So that means this central bouquet is full of orange lilies ...'

'Hatred, jealousy,' said Sam.

'That frothy foliage has come from asparagus. Dad's got some on his allotment.'

'Fascination?' Sam added, as if it was the uncertain answer to a question he didn't understand.

'There's a wreath of ivy wrapped around the base like a garland. Some small leaves turning into bigger ones. Quite fresh and shiny and full ...'

Sam shook his head and looked at his phone. 'Marital fidelity.'

'Oh,' I said. What did it all add up to? 'Then there's all these others, the bad ones, the poison brigade.'

'Which are pretty evident in their meanings,' Sam continued. 'All clustered around the Ethel-Rose.'

I folded my arms and stepped back to regard the display. 'So – beware, pain, grief, malevolence, justice, the fallen, fascination, marital fidelity, poison and roses. What does it mean?'

'I was wrong,' Bronson said finally. 'It's not a message – it's a warning.'

I remained quiet for a moment then asked Sam and Bronson. 'Do you know how Ethel-Rose died?'

Bronson looked at his feet. But Sam met my gaze and said, 'No idea.' Then he sighed and added. 'No one does. I wasn't sure how much you knew.'

'So what are you saying here, Sam?'

'Let's go upstairs and light a fire,' he suggested.

'I'll get on to that right away,' said Bronson and darted out through a side door.

'Come on, what's the big deal?' I was starting to feel annoyed.

Sam folded his phone away. 'Okay, well it was a very strange affair.'

'Had to be, didn't it?' I said with a sigh. 'Go on then.'

CHAPTER TWELVE

Ethel-Rose was a vivacious young woman. Bright, with a personality that switched between infectious cheer and reflective solemnity. This I knew from my dad. His mum, he had told me, was beautiful too with an evident glamour that lent her the charisma of a ballet dancer or a movie star. This I also discovered for myself, after viewing the Strange family portrait that hung over the fireplace in the museum lounge that Sam and I sprawled in while Bronson boosted the fire.

I also thought, though no one had mentioned it, that she was quite sexy.

In the picture she'd chosen a sumptuous pink evening gown, taffeta or silk or a fabric similarly shiny, which revealed just enough décolletage to titillate decorously. The painter had certainly appreciated the view, you could tell. He'd worked hard on the cleavage and her eyes – which turned out wide and lashy and kitten-green. Certainly I thought he'd captured a spark, a moment of impish mischievousness in them. Or maybe that was just me.

More recently I had learnt from Sam that Ethel-Rose possessed another interesting quality: she was allegedly clairvoyant. That is, my grandfather, who seemed to have once been the expert on such matters, thought her so. In fact it was this rather unconventional aspect of her character that had brought her to his notice. He had been assigned to investigate her case which he approached with every intention of catching her out. But he couldn't and ended up marrying her. I wasn't sure how I felt about this. I wasn't sure about any of that malarkey. Though I had taken my foot off my own brakes of late, having learnt from Sam that absolute scepticism could be just as blinding as absolute faith. And despite loud protests to the contrary, it did resonate somewhere within.

Sitting back into his armchair Bronson took a sip of the brandy he'd found in the cellar, and said, 'She was a beauty, your grandmother. I was only five years old when she disappeared but my father—'

Eh? I sat up straight. 'She disappeared?' I thought she died. 'What do you mean "disappeared"?' Dad hadn't mentioned that.

For a moment he seemed doubtful, then Sam came in and said, 'I told you. The other night. When we were at your flat. It's another Strange family mystery.'

'Did you?' I said, not really able to remember. But anyway, that wasn't the point. 'Sorry.' I nodded at Bronson, eager not to put him off. 'Please. You were saying your father …?' Though internally I was almost quaking.

'Yes,' he said sending his mind back to his childhood, I supposed. 'My father remembered her very fondly. He used to work with her father, your great-grandfather, Frederick, at his nursery. He was a lovely man, Fred. The wife though, she had, what you'd call "airs and graces". Reckoned herself as a bit of a madam. Not that she had any cause to set herself above the rest of the village from what I heard. Pair of them arrived in Adder's Fork during the First World War. Fred's lungs were weak and they'd been living in the East End. His family ran a cigar factory.'

'They were called Romanov, weren't they?' I remembered this from one rare occasion that Dad had reminisced about the family.

'That's right,' Bronson concurred. 'There were rumours they were distant relations of the imperial Romanovs. But I think the wife, Anne, put that around. My dad told me he'd heard her telling her husband it didn't do no harm and opened doors that might have been closed to common tradespeople with peculiar surnames.'

Not a bad idea, I thought, given the amount of xenophobia that must have been around at the time.

'She, Anne, had come from the East End too. Father had been an Irish navvy, mother apparently from a gentle family that had lost its fortune. They'd come down after the first Zeppelin raid so Fred could have some country air. Lived in that nice cottage on Hollypot Lane in the village. Beautiful, covered in honeysuckle, flowers everywhere. But the grandma, on her side, she came down to see them once and never went away again. Her name was Roisin. She was Irish and I believe it was her who first taught Ethel-Rose to read the tea leaves and the palms. Filled her head with all sorts of nonsense about fairy folk too. And I think when she died, Anne hoped that would be an end to it. But along comes Fred's sister, Rozalie – see Ethel-Rose was named after the pair of them – the grandmother and the aunt, and by god, they both left an impression on the child.'

He shook his head at the fire, then looked at the portrait above it and smiled at some memory. 'Anyway Rozalie was just as bad as Anne's mother. With her, it was all tarot and spiritualism. See after the war, with so many lost, there was a lot wanted to get in touch with the dead. It wasn't uncommon.'

'What?' I said, surprised to be hearing this. 'So did Ethel-Rose do séances then?'

Sam cleared his throat. 'Not séances as such, I believe she called them "public meetings". Rozalie encouraged her. And, as I told you, this is how Ethel-Rose and Septimus met.'

I turned and lent him the full force of my gaze. 'Go on.'

'Okay,' he said, though he seemed to me a little reluctant. 'This is what I know from Septimus.' He was distancing himself. 'She'd done a few in the village hall but they'd been attracting more and more people. Rozalie hired the ballroom at the old town hall in Litchenfield to accommodate everyone. The place was packed to the rafters. Word had got around. It was 1943 and the country was at war again. As Bronson quite rightly points out there were a lot of grieving people then who were desperate for hope and/or answers.

'Your grandmother started off with the usual requests,' Sam went on. 'Finding mislaid lockets, wills, imparting messages of love from those who had passed on. However, towards the end one lady in black stood up and asked for her son. Ethel-Rose was in two minds as to whether to help, ironically.

For she was very tired and well over her time but the sight of the woman apparently moved her. According to Septimus, she used to say that when she reached out it was like tuning into the "frequency of the dead". Whatever, she swore that, that night, when she sent her mind into the blackness she heard the woman's son speak. In a later interview, she testified that the boy was confused, lost in a wild vortex he supposed might be the roiling sea. But hearing her summons, he duly reported for duty giving his name and squadron. There were others with him too, pleading for help, whispering in low voices. "We," they allegedly insisted, "are on *Burnstow*." When Ethel-Rose repeated this a murmur rippled through the crowd. The mother of the boy, the woman in black, she immediately cried out and then fainted. Within seconds two men in brown suits, who had been sitting at the front, got up from their chairs, ascended to the stage and there, in front of the gathered audience, they arrested Ethel-Rose. There were also, unfortunately, press in among the rows.'

'Why?' I said. 'Why did they do that? Arrest her? She wasn't breaking any rules, was she?'

Sam shrugged. 'Depends what you believe. She was arrested under Section 4 of the 1735 Witchcraft Act. You see, the ship that Ethel-Rose reported the spirit sailors were aboard, the HMS *Burnstow*, had been sunk but one week previously, torpedoed by a German U-boat with a loss of 547 lives. To maintain the country's morale this news, however, had not yet been released.'

'Oh,' I said, sucking down a deep breath. 'So how did she know? That it had been sunk?'

Sam took a swig of his tea. 'How did she know indeed?' Then he fastened his eyes on me and blinked. His voice was conspicuously steady, his face rigidly calm. 'Ethel-Rose Romanov became a cause célèbre. There were clamours and protests about her arrest. It caused a bit of a public uproar. So,' he went on. 'To demonstrate that something was being done the Home Office deployed a young freelance operative with some experience of the MI6 Occult Bureau. Enter Septimus Strange.'

'Ah-ha!' I said. The picture was becoming whole. 'But did everyone think she was a witch or something?'

Bronson, this time, took a breath and shook his head. 'No. Not here. Everyone thought it was a bit of a joke.'

'Yes,' agreed Sam. 'Ethel-Rose was arrested under the Witchcraft Act but that was an excellent act of dissembling. It was the easiest thing to slap on her and the perfect distraction. The serious question that they really wanted to interrogate her about was where the leak in the department was. Or had she somehow heard the news from abroad?'

'Oh,' I said. 'Spying?'

'Sort of,' he replied. 'The Witchcraft Act was helpful because it lent cover and, like I said, people were desperate to believe in something more.'

I frowned. 'So was she a clairvoyant or not?'

Sam shrugged. 'Why are you asking me?'

'Because you had my grandfather's ear.'

'Well,' he said, 'you know that I believe that some things can't be explained.'

I nodded vigorously. 'And some things can. So Ethel-Rose …?'

'I don't know. There could have been some form of telepathy going on. Ethel-Rose was allegedly clairaudient – she heard voices. But Frederick's family were from Prague. He listened regularly to international radio broadcasts. Ethel-Rose herself was a telephonist; maybe she had heard something about the HMS *Burnstow* without realising what it was. I don't know. Septimus, though, approached her with an open mind at first. He put her through quite a lot of tests and examinations and she proved unusual. Her results were extremely positive. She seemed to demonstrate certain gifts, keen perceptions, and in uncovering them, his admiration for her grew.'

'I bet it did,' I said, and laughed at my own joke.

'Rosie,' said Sam. 'Really! This is your grandparents' love story.'

'Yes, you're right,' I said, suitably chastened. 'Go on.'

'Eventually he was able to use his ministerial contacts to pull a fair many strings and negotiated a release. Two months later he returned triumphantly to Adder's Fork with Miss Romanov.'

'That's quite a long time to be held in custody, isn't it?'

'Like I said, there were those that thought she may have been a spy. Could have been worse. But it was the war. Things didn't run smoothly and fairly. On the positive side when they returned to village, the pair were in love.'

'Ah, how sweet.' I avoided his eyes.

'When Septimus proposed on VE day, Ethel-Rose readily accepted. They married on 2 October in 1945, an autumn wedding shortly after the war ended. Soon they moved into the cottage with Rozalie. Fred and Anne had upgraded to a bigger house a few years before. Ethel-Rose's aunt, however, continued to urge her niece to use her gifts. She believed they were a gift from God. That it was evil *not* to use them. Septimus insisted that even though the war was over there were those who would be watching Ethel-Rose and not with her best interests in mind. He was evasive about who these people were,' Sam said. 'I never did find out who he was referring to. Wouldn't be drawn.'

'Why would that be?' I wondered out loud.

Bronson piped up. 'My father always said Septimus was afraid for her. For Ethel-Rose.'

I took a moment to think about this. Who would be watching out for my grandmother? 'Someone connected to the Occult Bureau?'

'I honestly don't know.' Sam shook his head again. 'But he thought it very important for her to lie low. He didn't want her gifts to come to public notice again. Maybe it was the scandal that they'd caused. The drama. I think he'd indebted himself to certain government agents when he got her out of detention. Maybe he didn't want to go through all of that again. I don't know. But anyway, for a while, it worked. An uneasy truce existed between Septimus and Rozalie. The next few years were fine. Edward George Strange was brought into the world.'

'Dad,' I said, and nodded and smiled.

'Indeed,' said Sam. 'And then in the summer of 1952, Celeste was born.'

We shifted our collective gaze to the portrait hanging above the crackling fire.

Septimus looked noble, tall and straight, Ethel-Rose all rosebud-pink and slinky. They cut an attractive pair. Dad scowled in his sailor suit and Celeste struggled in her christening robes, lobster-red and squealing. Such a traditional, conservative painting. And yet how unconventional they all must have been. Who'd know to look at them?

'There was a brief period of joy and then rather suddenly Fred died. He was seventy-five, which was a good age considering his lung problems. However, it was sudden and had rather a dramatic effect on both his wife and daughter. Anne locked herself away and wouldn't be persuaded to come out. Ethel-Rose fell into a bout of depression. She had had quite a difficult childbirth with Celeste and still had Ted running rings about her and Rozalie at the cottage. I think she may have been relying on her mother to help her out, but Anne insisted on staying in the dark. I know there were rows. Between mother and daughter, and husband and wife. Not too many, your grandfather said, but enough to make the police look at him with suspicion after she disappeared.'

'Yes,' I said. 'So here's the rub. How?'

'As I said, Anne was morose. Rozalie, of course, thought the best way to ease her pain and help her to move on was to put her in touch with her husband, Fred. Though they had rarely seen eye to eye on this before, it seemed that the grief-stricken Anne very soon came round to Rozalie's thinking.'

I shrugged. 'Bereavement does weird things to people. Especially in that regard. Makes them vulnerable.'

'Problem was Rozalie,' said Bronson and crossed his legs. The alcohol had made his skin flush scarlet. 'She had a big mouth. I think Septimus never really forgave her for that. She thought if Ethel-Rose was going to do this one last time, then she should help as many people as possible.'

'I see,' I nodded. 'Go out in a blaze of glory?'

Sam gave a sad smile. 'She should have been in PR. She really was ahead of her time – hired the village hall.'

'So Ethel-Rose agreed to it?'

'No, not initially.'

Bronson came in again. 'That Rozalie, she just disregarded that. She told her friends. One of these had a relative in Canvey Island and there had been terrible floods there. Lots of people drowned. The woman from Canvey told her friend from Jaywick, where there'd also been fatal flooding. A whole load of them came down.'

'Septimus of course was livid,' Sam went on. 'He forbade her to get involved in such a thing.'

'Is that what he actually said? I asked, ears prickling at certain archaic words. 'Forbid?'

'I'm paraphrasing. As you well know sexual politics was rather different back then. However, there was a period when the whole thing was called off. But then your grandfather was called away, at the last minute, on a job.'

A thought crossed my mind. 'Did Rozalie have anything to do with that?' She sounded quite conniving.

'I don't know,' he said, as if it had never occurred to him before. 'But unguarded, as such, Ethel-Rose was persuaded to perform.'

'Oh dear,' I said in an exaggerated manner. 'What could possibly go wrong?'

'Quite,' said Sam. 'Well, it was spring and by all reports a warm night. Anne and Ethel-Rose walked to the hall chatting casually. It was one of the first times that Anne had been out since the funeral and it emboldened Ethel-Rose. However, when the pair of them arrived at the village hall, they had quite a shock. A dozen of the villagers were protesting outside. There had been a change of hands at the vicarage and the new incumbent was of the fire-and-brimstone school of preaching. While Albert, the previous vicar, had looked upon Ethel-Rose's divinations as a bit of fairground fun, the new regime, under the Reverend Roger Winsome, was not so tolerant. He had met with other villagers concerned that Adder's Fork was attracting unwanted types, low of class and clearly low of standards, and becoming, they believed in the eyes of the outside world, a village associated with dark arts and black magic. Forming an alliance with the disgruntled villagers the new vicar used Ethel-Rose's meeting to proudly proclaim his zero-tolerance moral crusade, and no doubt publicise his new-style leadership. The meeting was, the group shouted loudly, "Unwholesome, unholy and unwanted." But, this time, her mother pushed her on. Mrs Romanov was hell-bent on communing with her dead husband. Even if it was to be at the expense of her living daughter.'

'That was a bit of a turnaround,' I said, reflecting that this Anne woman was, in fact, my great-grandmother.

'It was.' Sam paused and set his drink down. 'Sometimes it can happen like that, can't it?' He glanced at me. 'That which initially repels turns in on itself and becomes absurdly unstoppable in its attraction. Sometimes,' he said, and coughed and went on more quickly, 'Anyway, inside it was just as turbulent. Not only was there a police presence, but Ethel-Rose also sighted men who looked like the types in brown suits who had arrested her before. It didn't help her nerves. Then, of course, there were the bereaved in various states of hopefulness and distress.

'After a short introduction by the elderly Rozalie, Ethel-Rose began. Her priority was to reach out to her father, Fred, but others had requests too so she tuned in to the frequency of the dead once more and let the voices draw near. There was a whole gaggle of them desperate to speak and as they broke forth, Ethel-Rose repeated their messages.'

That was quite a lot of detail for Sam to reel off, I thought. Maybe Septimus had written up a report. He was an investigator after all. I wondered if Sam had access to it.

'At some point,' he was saying, 'a protest group burst into the room. On the stage, Ethel-Rose faltered. Someone in the crowd shouted out that she'd lost her wits and others began to jeer. But according to Anne, in among the clamour of voices, Ethel-Rose heard her father speak. We don't know to this day what he was meant to have said, but we do know that Ethel-Rose suddenly became frightened and clutched her throat. She began to scan the faces in the crowd. Someone cried, "Charlatan." Then Ethel-Rose screamed and flew from the stage. Her actions caused even more uproar and people began to rise to their feet. A fight broke out – half the protest group were pounced upon. The police waded in; the brown suits were co-opted to help contain the situation. On the stage Anne and Rozalie appealed for calm. But somehow in the middle of this commotion Ethel-Rose Strange simply disappeared.' He paused and looked at me.

I hadn't been expecting this ending. That it would end so abruptly and simply. 'Are you saying that was it? That she was never seen again?'

'Yep,' he said.

'What about the rest of the protest group outside? They must have seen something.'

'According to Septimus, they were trying to get in. But it was chaos. The place only had a small entrance. People were trying to leave in swarms, getting out of harm's way, avoiding arrest or a clip round the head. Others were trying to get in. At one point someone shouted that a fire had started. A couple of windows were smashed.'

'Shit,' I said. 'Was there a fire? Was anyone hurt?'

'No. False alarm. Maybe mischief. Obviously the parish weren't best pleased. But they had bigger things to worry about. A lot of them were interviewed by the police.'

'And no one saw her leave? Or where she went? She couldn't have just vanished into thin air. We both know that's not possible.' I narrowed my eyes. 'Or is it? Is this something else I don't know about?'

'No. Not that I'm aware.' Sam smiled briefly then shook his head. 'I agree it's odd. Believe me, I asked the same questions. As did your grandfather did before you. And, no doubt, your father.'

'She just disappeared,' said Bronson and looked into the fire. 'No one ever saw her again.'

'But how could that happen?' I said. 'How could a woman walk off the stage and never be seen again? Wouldn't happen now. Not with CCTV, but I suppose back then ...'

'The worst of it was,' said Bronson, and reached for the brandy, 'there was rumours that Septimus had killed her.'

'What?' I said, momentarily outraged for the grandfather I had barely known. 'That's ridiculous. He wouldn't do that, would he?'

Sam's eyebrows rose briefly, but quickly and forcefully settled down again.

'I mean,' I added, 'from what I can remember and what you've both told me of him, you know, he sounds decent.' Another thought dawned on me. 'But didn't you say that he'd been called away. On a case?'

'That's right,' Sam agreed. 'Forgive me for telling you with such indelicacy but I thought you should know that he was, for a very short period of time as Bronson has affirmed, under investigation. I wouldn't want you to think that I was keeping that information from you. But you are correct: Septimus had a bulletproof alibi. And that's what the police discovered too.'

'But mud sticks,' said Bronson and shook his snowy white head.

I watched him refill his glass and asked, 'So what else were people saying?'

'Some thought that she had been arrested by the government again. A few believed the men in brown suits had found her and taken her away. Thrown her into prison or an experimental centre.'

'Really? That's kind of weird.'

'I know. And unlikely. The idea that had most currency was that she had simply run off. That she was having an affair and went away with her lover.'

I contemplated the likelihood. 'An affair,' I said. 'Is that possible?'

Sam shrugged. 'It wasn't impossible. She knew a lot of people in the village. She was still attractive.'

'But that meant she would have willingly left behind Ted and Celeste too.'

Bronson snorted. 'And all her clothes and all her money. Doesn't happen, does it?'

'And,' I added, 'without so much as a goodbye to her mother and aunt. And what a way to leave.'

'That's what Anne and Rozalie thought too,' said Sam. 'They favoured the brown-suit option. Though this time Ethel-Rose never returned to the village. They couldn't work that one out. She should have been released at some point. Why not come home?'

'So what did Septimus think had happened to her? Seriously?'

Bronson coughed and started to construct a roll-up. 'I think he suspected foul play. But by whom he could never work out. There were a fair few suspects.'

'You mean the Christians and moral outrage brigade?'

'Did think that for a while,' he said, and poked some errant strands of tobacco into the cigarette. 'That one of them might have got carried away and had a good shout, maybe a shove, but murder? I don't reckon so. They was Christians.'

'But Christians were happy to kill witches,' I ventured.

'Nah,' said Bronson. 'Not this lot. They were all propriety and moral high ground. I don't think Septimus believed they had anything to do with it – he was always so tolerant of Audrey Winsome.'

'Audrey? The protester outside the museum?' I recalled the wild and ragged form of the old woman by the sign. 'So she was the vicar's daughter?'

Bronson nodded and took out a lighter. I didn't object. 'That's right, Rosie love. She was there that night. Only thirteen. Gave a statement to the police. Said she saw something out back in the trees. Though she said the Devil was there too,' he said. 'So you know.' He shrugged and tapped his head.

I made a mental note to invite Audrey in under the pretence of discussing selling the museum.

'She's apparently always been a little on the hysterical side. Eccentric,' said Sam. 'Not entirely surprising as her father was rather much an acquired taste.'

I recalled Sam's description. 'Fire and brimstone.'

'That's right. Though there were others Septimus mentioned when we talked about it. These unknowns, whomever he had wanted to shield Ethel-Rose from. He never told me much, but I remember him saying something about a family, foreign, who was on the radar of the Occult Bureau.'

'Really?'

'I think. I can't remember too well either. It was a while ago that we last spoke of it. But I'm sure we could find out. Septimus kept reams of notes and files. Plus, Monty would have access to records about those sorts.' He smiled. 'As we are well aware.' Then unconsciously he rubbed his arm. He was still healing from a couple of cigarette burns inflicted by some vile Serbian cheat, who could have done a lot worse had not our friend Monty intervened.

'Oh yes, Monty,' I said, and sort of changed the subject. Mr Monty Walker was indeed an excellent bloke to be acquainted with. Charming, elegant and well connected, he worked for the government in the weird X-Files department or whatever it was called. I owed him dinner, so made another note to talk about it then.

'Anyway, in the absence of a body,' Sam went on, 'the police concluded that Ethel-Rose had simply had enough of everything – notoriety, scandal, her mother's grief, her husband's control, family squabbles, bawling children – and had upped sticks and buggered off somewhere else to find a new life and a new husband.'

'Hmm. Septimus must have been devastated.'

'He was. Indeed he was. Rozalie too. She died, shortly after, and bequeathed the cottage to him. He thought she had done it out of guilt. But he couldn't bear to live in it any more so sold up and bought the building that was to become the Great Essex Witch Museum. Partly I think it was about sticking two fingers up at the Christians and partly about trying to convert the rest of the pitchfork brigade. He was all about challenging prejudice back then and, as such, he would brook no clairvoyance or chiromancy or anything like that. I think it left a bitter taste in his mouth. Wouldn't have any of Ethel-Rose's things in the museum either. For he thought, as I think your dad does now, no good ever came of it.'

A small parcel of guilt landed in my stomach and began to unwrap itself.

Unaware of my conflict, Sam continued. 'Septimus became quite puritanical about it actually. Until Celeste came of age and started nagging him. She had a different approach. Despite her mother's absence, or maybe because of it, she meandered towards the same hobbies Ethel-Rose had toyed with before. And it seemed she had some flair for it too. Tarot was her favourite medium. But Septimus was absolutely terrified he might lose his daughter as he had his wife. As irrational as that might seem. He didn't want anything to happen to her and so was very protective. Possibly quite authoritarian about it. Anyway, over time he softened. Celeste used the opportunity to bring in new exhibits that she believed had an effect on people, whether that be psychological or magical, as it were. She said they were both the same anyway. Celeste was a child of the sixties, you see. The world was in revolution and thus the museum changed tonally.'

I was about to tell Sam that I had noticed that – the difference in some areas – but it didn't seem appropriate now.

The three of us lapsed into our thoughts.

Bronson lit his fag. 'But that was the end of Ethel-Rose,' he said between puffs.

'Until tonight,' I added, and held his gaze.

'What do you mean?' Sam leant forward to me.

'Well, Bronson's right about one thing. Those flowers.

Someone knows more than we do. Those flowers are a message.'

'Or a warning,' said Sam.

'After all this time.' Bronson breathed out a smoky sigh.

'After all this time,' I agreed.

CHAPTER THIRTEEN

I could feel the sunshine on my cheeks, the scent of honey-suckle on the old cottage wall and then an incredible doom-laden claustrophobia descended.

When I opened my eyes I realised I was back in Septimus's four-poster bed. Something furry rubbed against my shoulder. Hecate had come to wake me up.

'Hello, gorgeous,' I said, and gave her a stroke along the spine. 'Had a funny night last night.'

When she meowed, it sounded absurdly like 'I know'.

I sat up and for a moment was touched by a wild fleeting fancy. 'Did you see who left the flowers too?'

But she just stared at me, then slipped off the bed. I watched her paw the door to and disappear round it with the twitch of her tail. *I'm going mad*, I thought.

There was a photo on the wall opposite the bed. I got out and inspected it again. Ethel-Rose had been captured in a moment, giving in to a full-throated laugh, flinging one hand out at the camera. In the other she held a boy on her hip. Dad, a mere toddler, he grinned at the photographer. He was much younger in this picture than he was in the family portrait. A plastic spade in his hand, he looked very happy. Of course, I thought, they were on the beach. Ethel-Rose was up to her ankles in surf. What a shame it had ended so tragically for her.

For them.

I'll sort that, I thought, as someone knocked on the door. If I could, I'd find out what happened to her. It wouldn't help Septimus but it might find some resolution for poor Dad. How tough for him. Talk about abandonment issues.

'Coffee?' Sam began, walking into the room. He had a mug in each hand, and one stretched out to me, but stopped abruptly when he took me in.

I hadn't brought any clothes with me but had eventually found a pink nylon nightie in one of the drawers in the bedroom that must have once belonged to my grandmother. It had fabric flowers on the neckline and was old and fairly see-through.

Sam dropped his gaze to the floor. 'Oh, I …' he stuttered.

'Come on, Sam,' I said, and giggled. 'You must have seen someone in a fifties' baby doll before.'

'Well, er, no actually.'

'You haven't lived,' I said, and took up Granddad's old dressing gown. 'Okay, you can look now. I'm frumpy.'

'Oh yes,' he said, a slight blush to his cheeks. 'Here's your coffee.'

I thanked him back and sat on the edge of the bed. 'You know, Sam, I was thinking: all we need to do is track down whoever is growing the Ethel-Rose, then we'll find the owner of the flowers left last night. Can't be many of them about.'

He leant against the wall and sipped from his own mug. 'Not as easy as you might think, I'm afraid. You know your great-granddad had a nursery. During the war, he had to turn over all the flowerbeds for vegetables. Dig for England, etc. He saved all the roses by handing them out to anyone in the village who cared to have one. There are loads of them now, all over Adder's Fork.'

'Oh,' I said. I couldn't think of anything else. 'I don't suppose we'll bother telling the police?'

'That we had a break-in where nothing was taken but a floral offering left behind?'

'Yes, I see what you mean. But,' I added, 'it does suggest someone knows something else. Maybe there's new information? We should do something. Perhaps ask around the village? I mean, someone has just flower-bombed Ethel-Rose's mystery into our lives.'

'I agree it's worth investigating, but not until we've sorted our present case.'

'But whoever did the flower bomb wants us to look at it now.'

'Life goes on. We've got other priorities.'

'I know,' I said stiffly. I think I was aggrieved for my grandmother. 'But they don't know that.'

'Which means,' said Sam with a glint in his eye, 'if we don't do anything, then they might "flower-bomb" us again.'

'Okay,' I softened. 'So we keep an eye out? Yes, that's a good idea. But I propose that we start thinking about this mystery in the future. Well, I'm going to anyway,' I finished off in a slightly over-pouty manner.

'Yes, we'll see what happens. But right now you need to get dressed.' Sam pointed at his watch. 'You know what Boundersby's like. We must get a move on – there's a murder scene to survey.'

CHAPTER FOURTEEN

It was horrible. It was odd. It was a mess.

Not having experienced anything like it before I assumed that after a murder there would be people who cleaned up the crime scene and put everything back. Made the place look normal, rid it of its terrible connotations.

That assumption was, at present, incorrect.

The cellar looked like a slaughterhouse in a snow globe.

A brown puddle of dried muck, which I was trying very hard not to look at, dominated the floor. My guess was it had once circulated through the veins of Seth Johnson. Above this dark reckoning, a nasty hook hung down from the low ceiling beams.

Some extremely bad stuff had gone down here.

Despite a natural instinct to turn and leg it back up the stairs I made myself move further into the cellar. I had to at least try and look like I'd done this sort of thing before. Which I hadn't.

Blimey O'Riley, the place stank to the highest heaven. It was a million miles away from the sweet-smelling Witch Museum. I put a hand over my nose in an attempt to keep the musty smell of death at bay. It was seriously making my stomach churn.

Over in the recess beyond, I could make out several wooden shelves stacked with foodstuffs and equipment. Some of them had been sectioned off with plastic sheets. Maybe forensics, maybe La Fleur practice. I lifted one and peeked into the shadows. Nothing much to see there – more tins and sacks – though my hands came back grainy: everything appeared to be covered in a thin, white film.

'What is it?' I asked Ray, who was not moving further than the foot of the stairs and holding a purple hanky to his nose. 'This stuff?' I rubbed my thumb and forefingers together and sniffed it.

'Flour. It's all over the place,' he growled through the fabric.

'Why?' I asked. Was that part of the murder or had there been an accident earlier in the night?

'How do I know?' Ray said. He didn't show any obvious symptoms of fear or shock when he spoke but I noticed his lips pursed when he wasn't using them. And he'd been really gobby since we got here.

'Sorry.' Still, I had to be careful not to offend. He was the boss and there were the kneecaps to consider. 'I didn't mean anything – I just wondered if it spilt during the night on Saturday? While the place was open, when they were cooking?'

'Nothing was entered into the log.' The purple hanky moved up and down. 'From what the police said, I think it happened afterwards.'

'Really,' I said, and stopped myself asking 'why'. 'That's odd.'

Ray breathed the hanky into his mouth then spat it out. The flour in the atmosphere was getting into my lungs too. 'Probably,' Boundersby went on, 'they were hoping to contaminate the crime scene. Destroy evidence – finger-prints, DNA.' Then he turned his head up towards the top of the stairs and took down another breath.

'Everyone's fingerprints will be in here, I'd imagine,' Sam said. 'Am I correct in assuming all the staff would be down at one time or another to replenish the stock? Food or napkins. There's tablecloths down here too?' He prodded a finger towards the bottom of a nearby shelving unit. I followed it to a large silver blender in a see-through plastic cover, then saw, beneath it, that blood had seeped into the cracks of the tiled floor.

'Yes, correct,' said Ray.

More smears were evident on the wall behind him. They continued up the stairs like a mad artist's brush strokes.

It was so gross I turned round so I didn't have to see it but it was useless – you just couldn't escape the gore. Smudges were apparent on the light bulb that illuminated the subter-ranean space. The light it cast was dappled in shades that related to the thickness and density of the dried blood.

I couldn't stop myself: I shuddered and swore, then said, 'Why would someone do that to another human being?'

Ray unpursed his lips took another breath from the direction of the less contaminated upstairs and said, 'Looked like he'd suffered some sort of lashing. There were cuts to his torso. Deep

ones actually that went through the skin and fat to the …'
his eyes left mine and settled on Sam, 'organs. Not the heart
though. So it weren't fatal. What I reckons really done him in
was the throat slit. That's a messy matter. Spatters everywhere.'
I didn't want to know how he knew about that particular detail.

Ray nodded at the hook, which had congealed mauve-
russet splashes on it. 'He was strung up on that.'

'But why?' I said again. 'What's that all about?'

The burly restaurateur shrugged. 'That's why you're here.'

Sam, fully prepared, though God knows how, had put on a
face mask. 'Surely that rules Mary out? How heavy was Seth?
She would neither have been able to overpower him nor lift
him up on to the hook presumably.'

Ray shook his head and pointed to the nearest wall.
'Pulley,' he said.

The rope coming out of it was halfway across the floor.
'Mary cut him down when she found him,' he explained.

'Why do you have it there?' asked Sam. 'This hook? Does
it have a purpose?'

'Never got rid of it. Sometimes we've hung cured hams
on it.'

The thought made my stomach convulse again. If I spent
much longer down here, I'd end up contaminating the crime
scene myself.

Sam walked right up to the hook and tapped it. There was
a slight echo to the noise it made. Which was odd as the place
was quite full. The acoustics must be a little screwy. That's not
unusual in basements and other subterranean spaces. 'Looks
old,' he said. 'Has it always been here?'

Ray grunted. 'Since we bought La Fleur.'

La Fleur, I thought. The Flower. The Flour. Does that mean anything? But I didn't say it out loud. I didn't want us down here any longer than was absolutely necessary. Apart from the smell and smears, the place was totally creeping me out: beyond the bloody murder, if that wasn't enough, I could feel another dark discord. It was hard to describe, but I could really imagine Mary hearing chains down here. It seemed to fit. Somehow. I didn't know in which way, exactly, or why. But maybe that would come. And again, I found myself believing Mary's testimony. Of course, on the other hand, my imagination could purely be galloping away as a result of the current multisensory onslaught. I'd have erred that way a couple of weeks ago but now I found my inner voice telling me to keep an open mind.

I was developing nuance.

I'd looked it up last night in bed. It referred to subtle differences. That wasn't going to come easy, so I'd made a commitment to keep my mind alert to it. After all, I'd declared it to be my middle name. Rosie Subtle Difference Strange. Didn't trip off the tongue, I had to admit.

The light, suspended by a short cable, started to jiggle: Sam was tapping the hook again. As a consequence there were shadows dancing to and fro absolutely everywhere. I so wouldn't want to be down here if it went out. The effort it was taking not to puke or run away was making my eyes tear.

It was easy to see why Mary had been spooked. Or seen something down here that she believed was ghostly. 'So this is where Mary also said she saw the ghost? Originally?' I asked Ray.

'It is where Mary *saw* the ghost,' he said with firmness and omitting a few pertinent words.

Sam was smoothing over one of the ceiling beams. 'Interesting,' he said, and put his hand on his chin, tipping up on his toes and craning his head closer to the wood. 'A demon trap.'

'What?'

A circle had been carved into the beam. Within it, the petals of a simplistic flower had been engraved.

'It's an apotropaios,' said Sam and, slipping his phone from his jeans pocket, took a photo.

'What's that when it's at home?' Ray growled over my shoulder and made me jump. I hadn't been expecting him to be that close by.

'This one is a daisy wheel,' Sam went on. 'Look you can see how someone has carved it in.' His finger traced the circle and then the petal pattern within it. 'It's a ritual protection symbol. The idea was that demons and evil spirits were very stupid and that if they saw this they would follow the line to its conclusion. Of course, these lines interlink with each other so the demons would stay in them for ever trying to find the end.'

'Demons?' said Ray and shuddered. 'So that's something that adds to Mary's statement, right? Someone else thought the place was haunted too?'

'A long time ago, I'm sad to say, Ray. Look at how dark and aged these cracks are.'

We bent closer.

Just at that point someone shouted down the stairs, 'They're here, Ray,' and we all started. I hadn't realised how quiet it was in the cellar. The hum of traffic and commotion of millions of people swarming over old London town was completely blocked out. The cellars must be virtually sound-proof. Thick walls probably. Old.

'Right, have you seen enough?' Ray began to back up. 'Because I want to get the cleaners in. I can't …' he began, 'I can't stomach …' Then he gagged, stuffed another hanky in his mouth and began climbing the stairs.

Sam continued to snap away at some more marks further down the beam. His seeming indifference to the blood and guts was unexpected but admirable. 'Where's the flour bag?' he called up the stairs to Ray. 'Did they find it?'

'No one's mentioned it,' the boss shouted over his shoulder. 'Don't mean nothing though.'

'Can we go now, Sam?' I asked. 'There's not much else to see is there?'

'Meet you upstairs,' he said, bending down to the floor. 'I'll be two minutes.'

Ray instructed us to get out of the way while the cleaners made the restaurant safe. They had taken over the yard as well, so we set ourselves up at a more private table close to the spiral staircase. I referred to Ray as the boss – he was employing us too now. He smiled wearily when he heard me and suggested we spend the rest of the day talking to the staff. There were several coming in, he said. Ones who couldn't afford to lose a day's pay. Tragedy might strike but life had to go on. Some of them had families that depended on wages earned at La Fleur. Those who turned up were expected to get involved in some more deep cleaning and polishing to spruce up the restaurant for its reopening tomorrow.

I was laying out the table with notebooks and water and had opened a voice-recording app on my phone, ready to capture the staff interviews. It made me look like I had a clue, even if the reality was rather different. From time to time the doors to the kitchen opened and I caught glimpses of the professional cleaners erecting a tent-like structure in there. Occasionally a whiff of hard-core cleaning fluid would leak out. It was marginally less vomit-inducing than the odour of decaying body matter.

'I didn't like it,' I told Sam, when I'd finished setting the table.

'It's a crime scene,' he replied eventually. He was taking things out of his big brown suitcase and laying them on his side of the table. 'You're not meant to like it. Unless you're a ghoul.'

'That's your job description, isn't it?'

He sent me what he thought passed for a hard stare.

'But doesn't it make your flesh creep? This whole thing?' I shuddered for the third time and said, 'Brrr,' as if I was cold.

'I refer you to my previous answer,' he said without looking up and muttered something else about magnetics that was not meant for me.

'And, I might add,' I said, really feeling I should get a pressing concern off my chest, 'Sam, I'm worried that we're out of our depth here. I mean, how can we solve this murder? We're not detectives. We don't know anything about it …' I struggled. 'I mean, do we look like Sherlock Holmes and Watson? Or, just to balance that, Cagney and Lacey? No, we don't. I haven't got a clue what's going on or what we're meant to do. And this is serious. It's murder. Neither of us know what the police are looking at, what forensics they've found? All that stuff. Stuff that is important and is on *Crimewatch* and usually leads to successful convictions. And do not assume that those guys, the police, are going to share anything with us. Because they won't.' My voice had climbed a fair few octaves as I'd ploughed through the speech. 'Because we're not really credible, are we?'

Sam had put a small electronic device on the table and folded his arms. Despite the gabbling onslaught his eyes were steady.

'You know what I think?' I continued, not waiting for his answer. 'I think we're up a certain creek without a paddle and with a seriously scary man in our canoe. One who is expecting results. And possibly, probably, expecting them bloody soon!'

I sat down and took a breath.

Sam put his hands on the table and leant over. 'Finished?'

'Not sure,' I told him.

'You've finished,' he said. 'We haven't been asked to solve the murder, Rosie. We've been asked to investigate the ghost.'

I crossed my arms over tightly. 'Yeah, I know, but the ghost is meant to have killed Seth. If you believe what Mary said,' I whined. 'And that's another thing. Do we have to believe her? I mean, I do anyway. But what if we didn't? Would he sack us without pay?'

Sam took a deep breath. 'None of this is in our remit either. You need to take a deep breath and calm down, okay?'

I followed his instructions and pointed my face at the front windows.

'Good,' said Sam, watching my chest rise and fall. 'We don't need to work out if the apparition killed Seth. Just to investigate it. I'm not sure that ghosts can kill people.'

'Well,' I whinged, 'how are we going to do that? Investigate the ghost? I've never had to investigate a ghost before. I can't even believe I just said that. My life used to be so straight-forward before you turned up in it.'

He cocked his head to one side and raised his eyebrows.

'Okay,' I corrected. 'Before I turned up in yours. Same difference.'

'Look,' he said. 'It's going to be okay. We're going to do what Ray Boundersby tells us to do and interview the staff. Then, when the cleaners have done their job, we're going to investigate the place, using the equipment we've brought. After that we'll write up a report. That's all. What Boundersby does with it is also not our call.'

'We're going to investigate La Fleur? How are we going to do that?' The thought did not please me. 'When are we going to do that? Not tonight?'

'I don't know. How long does it take to clear up a crime scene? Well, we'll find out.'

'Oh my god. I'm not sure I can go down to that cellar again.'

'I'll take that section then. But there won't be any blood. It will look fresh, sanitised, different. That's why the cleaners are in.'

'But you'll want me here, will you? In La Fleur? Can I keep the lights on?'

'Rosie,' he began, but a deep sonorous voice announced itself across the table.

A tall man with powerful shoulders, a short fuzz of black hair and a very sour face repeated, 'My name is Femi. Ray says I must speak with you.'

Femi Conteh turned out to be the sous, or junior chef, at La Fleur. He had been one of the longest-serving members of staff and was there before it opened to help get the kitchen ready. He was no stranger to hard work and was happy to go for sixteen-hour shifts as he had ambitions to get to the top. All of this we learnt in the first three minutes of our meeting, before he had taken a seat. Femi Conteh did not like to waste his time. Nor did he like wastrels. Not at all.

'Saturday night I went home and to bed. My wife and children confirm. Police have already spoken with them,' he said, when we'd finally persuaded him to sit.

'Uh-huh,' I said, and wrote down *alibi* because it was tough maintaining contact with his intense dark eyes.

'I have no joy that Seth is dead,' he went on. His accent was hard with pronounced consonants, which had the unfortunate effect of making you feel like he was telling you off. 'But I have little sorrow either. No, none. As a chef, he was skilled, yes. As a man, not so.' His eyes burnt as he spoke. Everything around him looked smaller.

'Why?' I asked. 'As a man?'

Femi hunched his massive frame over the table. He was wearing his kitchen whites and took a moment to push the sleeves right up to his shoulders before bending his elbows on to the table. 'I tell you – he drank. Much. He gambled. He blasphemed. He had women.'

I glanced at Sam who was making notes and waited to see if he was going to pick up on this. He raised his notebook and pen and said to Femi, 'So when did you become aware of the ghost?' Which I thought was maybe the wrong direction but then again, Sam was only keeping us focused on the subject we'd been tasked to investigate.

The chef bristled as if he had been insulted. 'I do not like to talk of such things. They are against nature.'

I leant in, to show I wasn't intimidated by his hugeness. 'But you were aware that things had been said about it?'

Femi fixed me with a tight frown. 'I do not like witch-craft,' he said, almost as if he was scolding me, personally. Man, that gaze was blistering. 'I do not countenance the Devil.'

'Me neither,' I went on. The bloke's muscles were coiled tightly beneath his skin. I couldn't help it – I leant back and away from him. Sometimes you had to give in to your instincts. 'Who did you hear it from, Femi? Have you had any experiences with the alleged ghost?'

To my surprise he banged his fist on the table. 'I do not need anyone to tell me evil walks here. You can feel it.' He threw his hand flat on the surface and sucked his teeth.

Sam seemed not to notice this sudden outburst and

flipped back a few pages to put his finger on a line of his notebook. 'Are you referring to the curse? I understand you mentioned it to Mary, after she stated she had witnessed an apparition in the yard outside? Is that out there?' He pointed through to the kitchen and to the courtyard beyond.

Femi eyed the doors fiercely. 'Yes, the yard is there. But the curse, you say? I knew of it before then. Before he told me.'

'Before who told you?'

'Jackson,' he said, and pointed at the wall behind us. 'Before he told of the curse. I—' His hand gave up on the pointing, formed a fist then beat against his heart. 'I knew it. In my soul.'

'And this is Jackson who …?' I made a show of looking efficient and picked up my pen.

'Jackson next door,' said Femi. 'His place is next door. Import-export. He mind the business for his uncle while he back home.'

'Oh okay,' I said, and added Jackson to our list of people to interview. 'What did Mr Jackson say?'

'I knew before Jackson,' Femi repeated. 'This court, this place – evil. This is a wicked part of the city, you know?'

'How wicked?' I asked, not that I disagreed. The feeling I had got in the basement had been potent.

'The demon butcher,' Femi stated plainly.

'Sweeney Todd?' Sam was prodding him on. It didn't surprise me to learn that my colleague knew what the junior chef was on about. Sam was like a macabre Wikipedia. Oh, the things he could tell you about cephalophores. That's headless saints to you and me.

Femi grunted. 'The demon butcher prospered here. In this filth and corruption. These streets have blood beneath them.' I shivered and thought of the tiles with the rusty flakes between their cracks. 'The spirits, they are still here. Still walking.' He finished and darted glances either side to make sure he wasn't being overheard. I remembered Joel doing exactly the same thing. 'Sometimes, at night, you catch a whimpering, you know? Like the creak of a door or moan of floorboard. But it is not such things. It is the evil.'

Uh-huh, I thought, and wrote down *not floorboards or doors – evil.*

'Any particular spirits?' Sam asked.

But Femi shook his head. He'd said enough. 'Evil.'

'And,' I continued, 'this Jackson told you this, did he?'

He nodded. 'But I tell you we all hear – the crying. One day, below,' he jerked his head in the direction of the cellar door, 'I saw salt fall off a shelf and fly across the room. One of the waitresses, she was there; Mary-Jane, she saw it too. And Miss Boundersby, she has seen the evil herself. Out in the yard.'

Yes, we knew that. 'Did *you* see this ghost?' I asked.

'Not me. But it is here,' he said.

Sam wrote something in his book. 'Thank you, that's helpful.'

Femi leant back into his chair and crossed his arms. 'I am a Christian man. God will protect me. He does not protect the unholy.' Then he shot me another weird glance.

I didn't know how to respond, so tried a smile.

It didn't work. Femi grimaced and shot to his feet. 'And now I must clean.'

Then without so much as a goodbye, he turned and left us.

The heating system clanked on and began wheezing.

Sam and I looked at each other. I wasn't sure if he was thinking the same thing as me, so I asked, 'Another suspect?'

He put the pen in his mouth and bit the end. 'He's got an alibi.'

'Yeah, but wife and kids? They'd confirm whatever he said, wouldn't they? Always do on the TV shows.'

'I don't know. Femi was certainly very open about it all. But what's his motive, what does he have to gain?'

'Moral crusader? He didn't approve of Seth's lifestyle. Or, now that the occupant of the top slot has been removed, he could be in line for a promotion? He wants to get to the top of the ladder, after all.'

Sam wasn't convinced. 'If there isn't a restaurant, then there isn't a ladder to climb. He hasn't got enough experience to run it yet surely? And anyway, far too obvious. I would imagine if his alibi wasn't watertight the police would have got him in.'

'Well, we should check out this Jackson then, shouldn't we?' I wrote it down.

A young man slouched into Femi's newly vacated chair.

'Howsitgoing?' he asked, without drawing breath.

It was Joel. Full of gel and wrapped in another extra-large tracksuit. This time it was a dirty blue. 'You found it yet? This ghost?'

'Nice of you to say goodbye the other day,' I said pointedly. 'We went and looked for you.'

Sam tutted. Okay, well, he was the one that had actually gone into the alley but Joel wasn't to know.

'No news, I'm afraid, Joel,' Sam told him. 'But we're collating the information. Might stake the place out soon.' I wondered if he should have told him that.

'How's Mary?' he asked. 'You seen her?'

I replied that we had and that we were also processing the information we'd gleaned from our professional interview with her.

'Good work.' He bowed his head and smiled revealing those triangular teeth. 'Who's next?' And he looked around at the restaurant, which had filled up a bit since we'd been here. Not by much but there were about four more bods in the area, all donning aprons and getting stuck into the mops and brushes.

I looked at the list of several names Ray had given us upon arrival. 'You've got a Mary-Jane and a Jarvino?'

The boy bowed his head again, then stuck two fingers in his mouth and gave a long and very loud whistle. 'MJ,' he yelled to a young woman in a black T-shirt and jeans. 'You're time has come.'

'MJ? Oh, Mary-Jane?' I asked as he flowed into a standing position.

'Indeed,' he said. 'We got three here – Mary Boundersby, MJ and MT.'

'Oh, yes, the lovely Marta Thompson?' said Sam.

'Marta's not Mary, is it?' I frowned.

'I imagine it probably derives from Mary,' Sam replied with a gleam and a grin in my direction.

'That's right,' Joel responded with a little wink at my colleague. 'I take it you met her then?' Then he did something crude with his lips.

'Where does Marta, MT, come from?' I asked to remind them I existed.

Joel sent me a greasy smile. 'Born over here but I think the mother is German. Come over to London for work and met the dad. They both worked on building the NatWest Tower in the eighties. He was an engineer, she worked with the architects or somethink,' he said. 'She always banging on about it, like she built the friggin' thing herself.'

'Three Marys,' Sam murmured.

I was going to ask him if that was relevant but Joel clicked his fingers and started wobbling his neck. 'And here be coming the hottest of the lot.' Then he jumped up and pulled the seat out for her to sit down. Mary-Jane rolled her eyes but smiled. She *was* pretty. She liked him. But not in that way. Not that Joel knew.

'Okay,' she said, and tucked herself into the table. 'Fire away!'

So we did.

MJ was one of the more senior waitresses. She told us she hadn't been here Saturday but had been here on the night of the writing and the bloody chandelier. She had a different perspective, literally. She'd seen the red liquid coming down through the chandelier, then gone upstairs. In the offices that were being renovated she found a new floor was being laid. The old one had been pulled up and someone must have accidentally kicked or knocked what looked like a bucket of rusty water across the dismantled floor. It was a chance happening, she said, and just plain bad luck that it had gone straight through to the chandelier below. Some of it must have got into the wiring and fused the lights. She did her best to mop it up then after she came back downstairs the lights had come back on and people were leaving. She didn't hear about the writing on the wall till later because it had got washed off by the time she returned. All in all Mary-Jane suspected that it was more likely the culprit was someone taking advantage of the blackout to muck around. She darted a micro-glance at Joel. And no, they hadn't had the water tested to see if it was dye or paint. Why would they? The upstairs office was a construction site. Shit happened.

I asked her why nobody had seen the writing go up. She told us that it wasn't busy that night so the mezzanine had been closed. Everyone was focused on the main ground-floor dining area.

You could see the mezzanine floor from our table but not the wall on which the writing was meant to have appeared. In fact, you might only see it from the entrance and a couple of tables. Unless you were standing, you'd have to walk a few yards.

Concluding that it was 'all bullshit' MJ did concede something 'pretty awful' was going on. Though she thought it was all human hands, she did confirm seeing a canister of salt fly off the shelf in the cellar as Femi had attested. However, the waitress pointed out there was a Tube line nearby and that it was more likely that vibrations from the trains had shaken the foundations and thus the shelf.

The line cook, Jarvino, was a Kiwi travelling around Europe. She had been here a month and planned to 'get the fuck out' before too long. Saturday night after work she'd gone straight out to drink at some Australian backpackers' pub, called the Ozzy Dina, and won a wet T-shirt competition. There were photos of her on Facebook which confirmed her presence there. Sam said he was surprised to hear the place was still going. I said I was surprised to hear that wet T-shirt competitions were still going, but she just shrugged and said, 'Free beer.'

She did, however, confirm Mary's sighting of the spook in the yard but hadn't seen it herself. Though she was adamant that whatever Mary had witnessed she absolutely believed. Mary didn't lie or make things up and thus the whole caboodle was really giving her the creeps. Jarvino also mentioned that she'd smelt horrible whiffs about the place but accepted that was entirely likely in a restaurant kitchen and also threw disparaging glances at Joel.

Another prep chef, Tim, reported to us. He had an exceedingly long hipster beard that was mostly orange and which I thought looked rather unhygienic for food preparation. But no one was asking me. The jaw growth was compensated for by lovely green eyes, a chiselled face and well-spoken, pleasant bearing. He'd been visiting his parents in Derby over the weekend. He confirmed MT's version of the floater in the toilet, at least he confirmed after her encounter she was 'in a complete state' to which Sam replied he found that 'very hard to believe'.

I flirted mildly with Tim in revenge and complimented

his beard, which I didn't particularly like, then got the accountant, Kundan, in. She stated for the record that she believed Mary, a growing trend, and that it was all generally weird but hadn't anything else to add and never worked nights or at the weekends. She gave off a really sweet, honest, family-lady vibe. But I told Sam to check her out anyway. We all know looks can be deceiving.

Gabriel, another waiter, was over here from Brisbane. He sat down and took off his whites. Underneath them he was wearing a T-shirt which featured Eeyore. The caption read *Nice ass*. Apart from that he seemed sensible and fairly grounded. He reported hearing the 'odd shriek' which he put down to revellers in the streets about and remarked that there was so much history in London and this area, it wasn't surprising that people's imaginations went wild. He went home after his shift and straight to bed Saturday night. There was no one else around to confirm. I put a question mark by his name.

By the end of the day we worked out that we'd pretty much seen all the workers, apart from the remaining waiting staff, John and Anita, a busboy called Nicky, and Agatha the bartender, all of whom were in tomorrow night.

Most of the La Fleur team, we concluded, were disturbed in varying degrees and said they'd felt uncomfortable in the place but apart from that there were no new incidents to report.

'So,' said Sam, leaning back and steepling his fingers, 'that was rather much a haul.'

'Do you reckon?' I said.

'Well.' He yawned, leant back heavily into his chair and pushed his hands into this pockets. 'They've collectively attested to poltergeist activity, wailing, crying, floating apparitions, bad smells, cold draughts and clanking chains.'

'Line!' I shouted. 'I reckon all you need is a cute child that turns out to be evil and you'd have a full house there.' I smiled at his confusion and added, 'If we were playing supernatural bingo.'

'What?' he said, and mussed his hair up. 'Actually don't answer that. I don't want to know. What I'm saying is we've got a veritable smorgasbord of phenomena. Could be an interesting case study for the museum if we are able to come to any conclusions. Perhaps a paper.' He lapsed into thought for a moment then sat up straight. 'Right, well, we're definitely going to need to do the stake-out. And soon.'

Oh God, I thought. 'Tonight?' I so did not want to sit alone in that blood-darkened cellar. Even if Sam was there too. I mean, who would?

'Depends, doesn't it?' Sam said, and rose. 'Let's go and find Ray.'

Thankfully, according to the boss, the clean-up was going to take longer. He suggested we finish up and come back tomorrow night, adding that he wanted to get his staff together and talk to them. They'd had a shock and needed 'a steer' and a 'pep talk'. I found myself pleasantly surprised by the unexpected soft side of the restaurateur once more.

Sam and I returned and packed up our table. We stowed

away our equipment in a locker that Ray had cleared for us, waved to the rest of the team, then headed for the door.

It was as I stepped over the threshold, coming out of La Fleur, that the weird thing happened: it hit me like a ton of bricks, a feeling that someone had, just then, thrown an invisible shroud over me. And that the shroud was made of an absolutely horrible material. Like, stonkingly, gut-wrenchingly bad.

For a moment it covered me. Entirely. A kind of revolting emotional stew – shards of anger, spikes of fear, a terrible sinking weight around my stomach, dread and doom, helplessness. And pain. Sharp, angled pain. All around my shoulders. It came on so suddenly, wrapping around me and extending to the length of my body, suffocating, shrinking, contracting with me in it, that I howled out loud.

Sam turned round to look at me and gave me a half-laugh.

But I couldn't speak.

An excruciating heat was burning down from the top of my head bringing with it dizziness, acute nausea and a deafening tinnitus in my ears.

With all the strength I could muster, I thrust out my hand to try push the feeling, the shroud, off. Crazy reaction, I know, but I was reacting not thinking things through.

The sudden action, however, overbalanced me.

As I fell back against the glass of the window, the ache in my stomach turned into a bite. I bent double expecting to vomit.

My handbag clattered to the floor. Its contents spilt over the pavement.

The noise, the smashing and rattling, however, seemed to have a weird effect, for it dispelled the nastiness.

In my head I experienced the absurd notion that an invisible hand, a *giant* invisible hand, was flinching, letting go of me, and the horrendous thing, this welter of appalling sensations, simply slipped away.

I sank down and put my hands on my knees, took a breath in and tried to steady myself. My temperature was coming back down but I could still feel a stickiness around the back of my neck. Sweat.

Surely I was too young for a hot flush? I tried to normalise by focusing on the grey cobbles of the street outside.

'Rosie!' Sam's shoes hurried into my circle of vision. 'Are you okay?' He bent over and began to pick up some of my handbag detritus. His face loomed up beneath me, all concerned and wriggly.

'I just, I just …' How could I begin to explain that? It was totally weird. And, jeez, what if it was early-onset menopause?

Screw that.

I made my mind up that I was definitely not going to go into details.

'Rosie!' Sam crawled underneath my face and wiped my hair back. 'You're sweating. Are you all right?'

'I'm fine,' I said, and tried straightening up. For want of something better, or maybe because I wasn't thinking right and wanted to distract his attention away, I said, 'Wind.'

'Okay,' he said, and retreated.

Maybe it was.

Bit excessive though.

I watched Sam pack the bits and pieces back into my bag like a proper gent. I knew I should help but I just needed to catch my breath.

My head rested against the glass frontage. It felt cool there. I was becoming calmer now, breaths slowing.

I had no idea where it came from. Perhaps after last night's Buttery Nipple, the brandies at the Witch Museum had been a bridge too far? Or maybe it had been something I ate? I supposed it could be a delayed reaction to the scene in the cellar. It had been disgusting and gross, after all. Freaky. But I wasn't sure. Nothing like that had happened to me before.

Then again I hadn't visited a crime scene before. Not that I knew of anyway.

'*Tsk tsk*,' Sam was saying, shaking his head and wagging a thin purple rectangle at me. 'Stealing the cutlery, Rosie? Well, really!' He laughed and handed it over. I reached out to grab it but only managed to catch the top section of the linen cloth. The napkin unfolded and a knife and fork rolled out of it and fell to the ground with another couple of clangs.

'I didn't put that there!' I said with sincere indignation, glad to hear my voice was steadier again. 'I didn't take it.' As I brought it up to inspect the linen I saw something dark and squiggly across the width. 'Hang on, there's something written here. Come and shine your phone on this.'

We both gasped as the light revealed a message scrawled there.

Pots Fischman knows, it read. *Tomorrow. Noon. The Traitor's Gate. E17.*

CHAPTER FIFTEEN

The landlord eyed us suspiciously.

He looked exactly like landlords used to in the eighties: white shirt, sleeves rolled up to his elbows, tucked into a pair of grey slacks fastened with a leather belt beneath a big old beer belly. Occupational hazard, I expect. He had a blurred blue anchor tattooed on his forearm and had been polishing a glass pint mug with a handle since we walked in, though I could see a whole fleet of scratched and blurred glasses on the shelves above his head in various shades of limescale residue.

'What do you want with Pots Fischman?' he said. But what he meant was – you don't want to meet Pots Fischman. Though he was curious to know why we did.

'Is he here?' I said again.

The landlord stopped polishing and put the pint glass in front of us on the counter. He rested the tea towel next to it and patted his hair, which was a shiny shark grey and swept back in a DA, the kind of quiff sported by ancient rockers. There was more than a palmful of Brylcreem keeping the structure upright.

'He's not in yet. You police?'

'No,' Sam said. 'Not police. We're independent, er …' he struggled for a word to describe us.

Ghostbusting wasn't going to go down too well here.

'Independent investigators,' I finished.

Though I had never been in the Traitor's Gate before, I had a sense that if I started flashing my Benefit Fraud credentials we would be given an arctic version of the cold shoulder, maybe even booted out on our rears. Believe me – worse things had happened in Leytonstone.

The landlord's expression transformed from scepticism into a leer. 'What's he done then, eh? Does Suzanne know?' Then he straightened up. 'He's not the heir to a fortune, is he? It'd be typical for someone like him to, you know,' he shrugged, 'land on his arse.'

Sam shook his head, 'Nothing like that I'm afraid. We just need to ask him a few questions about someone else.'

He sniffed and nodded. 'All right. Well, he's usually in around now. Sets up out back by the pool table.'

'Thanks,' I said, and was about to follow his directions when he hollered out, 'And so what you having?'

Ah yes, of course, this had the flavour of what my dad would call 'a tinker's pub'. It wasn't just where you went for a drink. It was an unofficial marketplace. You bought, you sold. Everything came into that equation – information included.

'Diet Coke. In a bottle or a can.' I remembered the state of the unpolished glasses above. 'Got a straw?'

'I'll have an orange juice,' Sam suggested.

The landlord looked briefly disgusted, muttered something under his breath and went off to fix them.

Sam leant against the bar and said in a low voice, 'This is a proper East End pub, isn't it?'

'Not really,' I replied, taking in the swirly Aertex ceilings, mock-Tudor beams, and worn-out green carpet. 'No hipsters or property developers.'

'You know what I mean,' he said, and paid the landlord.

We took the drinks out through a narrow hall into the rear bar. There was a large snooker table in the middle. Beyond it a smattering of round tables. I had the impression of dirty redness everywhere – the lino, the painted casements, old photographs of Walthamstow High Street that were dotted about in similarly claret coloured frames.

We had already had a big discussion this morning raking over the possibilities of who might have put the napkin in my bag. Sam agreed with me it wasn't going to be Ray Boundersby; there was no reason why he wouldn't have volunteered this Pots character before. It had to be one of the staff. Sam was edging towards Femi, while I was more inclined to go with Joel. Maybe the charming MJ. Though we had both agreed that it didn't really matter to a certain degree. What mattered is what exactly it was that Pots Fischman knew. If indeed Pots Fischman was a person, which it now seemed he was. Our plan was to show him the napkin and take it from there.

We were playing pool when the elusive Mr Fischman turned up with two cronies and informed us we were sat at his table and playing his pool. It wasn't a great start for it got my hackles up. My fingers twitched towards my ID. I wasn't sure what business this bloke was in but I was pretty convinced it wasn't a hundred per cent legit. There would be consequences to that. Some of which I could use if necessary.

'We just want some information please. That's all.' Sam offered him a chair. He was being extremely polite.

Pots, who we were asked to refer to as Mr Fischman, seemed to be a moneylender of sorts, which I was quite surprised about considering his years. He was swarthy, possibly of Mediterranean or maybe Middle Eastern descent, and, though his face was of that indeterminate range that could have started in the twenties and ended in the thirties, he had a young (immature) way of conducting himself. Exaggeratedly playing with the chunky gold chain around his neck, he sprawled into one of the pews lined up against the rear wall.

'So, who sent you?' he asked predictably. His cronies had already nudged us off our game of pool.

I waited for Sam to answer. There was so much testosterone in the room, I knew if I were to jump in first it might emasculate my colleague. Nuance you see. I was getting there.

'Actually, we don't know,' said Sam and nodded at me. Fischman had become intrigued.

With great theatre I cleared away the glasses, shook out the napkin and spread it carefully across the table. 'This,' I said. 'Was slipped into my bag at a restaurant, last night. Do you know it – La Fleur?'

He stared at the napkin and shook his head silently.

'La Fleur restaurant,' I repeated. 'In Fleur de Lis Court. Off Fetter Lane.'

Pots Fischman sucked his teeth and continued shaking.

'Translation is The Flower,' I added.

'*Je sais ce que cela veut dire*,' he snapped back.

'Sorry,' I said. 'I didn't know you spoke French.'

'What's this all about?' he asked. He had knitted his hands together and lowered his brow.

'You don't have a connection there?' I pressed on.

Sam cleared his throat 'Do you know Seth Johnson?'

'Ah-ha,' he said, and pushed back from the table, smiling. 'He work there? I knew he was a chef. Didn't know where. What's he done?' He pointed his chin at the napkin.

'How do you know him?' I pressed on. 'Professionally?'

'Sure,' he said. 'I spun him out a few bags of sand over the years. He's been a good customer. Enjoys a bit of a flutter on the horses now and then. Well, more now than then. He's always on 'em.' He laughed at the chef's weakness.

'So he's in debt to you?' I asked, beginning to view Pots Fischman with new eyes: he had a couple of heavies, he knew the victim, he didn't have the most noble of businesses. What if Seth hadn't kept up his payments?

Pots was obviously getting my drift too. He sat up a bit. Then he opened his legs wide and put an elbow on the table, so he was occupying a hell of a lot of space. 'No, not any more. Why what's he done?'

'So he doesn't owe you anything now, Mr Fischman? He's got a clean slate?' Sam interjected. He'd got his notebook out and was writing something down. This action seemed to make Pots nervous.

That was something I could work with. 'When exactly did you last see him, please?'

Pots finished watching Sam then answered me. ''Bout two weeks ago. He came and paid off his loan. In full.'

'How much was it?'

He cocked his head and squinted, calculating. 'Then? About 3k.'

That was a fair chunk of cash. 'He was a chef, Mr Fischman,' I said, and tried to make my eyes piercing. 'At La Fleur. Not a stockbroker or a hedge fund manager. That's unusual, isn't it? Suddenly coming in like that to pay it off?'

Pots looked from me to Sam and back again. 'You told Gregory you weren't no police.'

I was guessing Gregory was the landlord then. Funny that. He didn't look like a Gregory. More like a Bill. Or a Buddy or an Elvis. 'We're not,' I added. 'But we're investigators. I take it the police haven't been here yet?'

Now his eyebrows shot up. 'No, they ain't. Whatever he done, I ain't got nothing to do with it.'

Sam also knew weakness when he saw it. 'Did he tell you where he got the money from?'

Pots shook his head quickly. 'Not my business to ask.'

The place was starting to make me feel grubby. I got up as if to leave. 'Well, we'll pass on the information to the police. I'm sure they'll come and find you to confirm.'

'Hang on,' he said, and touched my arm. 'I think he might have said he'd had an unexpected bonus come his way.'

'Those were the words he used? "An unexpected bonus".'

'Uh-huh.' Pots lounged back and crossed his arms again. I couldn't tell whether he was lying or not. I knew body-language experts suggested that when people crossed their arms they were putting up a barrier but sometimes I'd found the complete opposite to be true. It meant they were comfortable or relaxed. Or finished.

'Note it,' I said to Sam who did, then also got to his feet.

'Thanks Mr Fischman, for your information,' he said.

Pots leant forward. 'You gonna tell me what he done?'

Of course – quid pro quo. 'He's dead, Mr Fischman,' I told him.

He looked confused for a moment. 'Shit, no! He ain't the body in the restaurant, is he?' he said. 'I read something 'bout that in the *Metro*. Just said a body bin found in a City food place. What happened to him then?'

'He was strung up like a piece of meat and then gutted,' I said, and turned on my heel. As I did, I was surprised to see one of Fischman's hard men flinch.

It reminded me it was a horrible crime.

And that whoever had done it, ghostly or not, was still out there at liberty, prowling.

'So is that relevant?' Sam asked, as we got outside.

'Difficult to say. Is that what "Pots Fischman knows"?' I shrugged. 'That Seth came into some money? Does it matter how? Or is that precisely what matters? We can't know, can we? I mean he might have got a big win on the horses.'

Sam walked alongside me. '"A bonus", is what he called it. Wouldn't you call a "win" a "win"?'

'Yeah, I would. But a) I'm not a gambler, I don't know the lingo, and b) this has all come out of the mouth of the delightful Pots Fischman. We have only his word it's verbatim. And I don't reckon that's worth the paper it's not written on.'

Sam looked around for the car. 'And it doesn't help us with the paranormal element of it all, does it?'

I had to concede he was right there.

'We should tell the police,' I said. 'It's the right thing to do. But let's do it from La Fleur. We have those other staff to interview.'

'And equipment to set up,' said Sam.

I shuddered. I didn't want to spend the night in La Fleur. Even if it was with Sam. A weird creeping feeling was niggling me.

I couldn't shake the notion we wouldn't be alone.

CHAPTER SIXTEEN

The moon was bright, just off full, arching its way across the metropolitan skyline.

I had come outside to get a bit of fresh air: we had been at La Fleur since early afternoon and because we'd set up as much as we could, equipment-wise, there was little more to do. The restaurant wasn't particularly busy so Sam had nipped up to the mezzanine, ostensibly to check the 'writing' wall, but really to have a little kip: we had a long night ahead.

I agreed to take the kitchen as long as Sam did the cellar. I couldn't sit down there all night, no way. It was spooky at ten o'clock in the morning. At midnight, it would most certainly prompt imaginings in the most grounded of minds. And mine.

The kitchen, however, was not going to be a walk in the park. It had been very noisy during the day: not just with the sounds and yells of cooking, chopping, cursing, boiling and bubbling, but also because there was a lot of clanging and clanking coming from above. The workmen were back in, trying to finish off the offices upstairs. At least, they'd be long gone by the time we began our vigil. I might get a little peace and quiet. Though I doubted it.

The information we'd got from Pots Fischman had been helpful and cast a different light on the victim: we now knew Seth Johnson was a gambler. We'd heard that from the staff. Femi had been rather emphatic about that side of the chef's character. But it had been confirmed by Pots himself, who had first-hand experience of lending to him. Just because Seth had paid Pots off it didn't necessarily suggest that he'd redeemed all his debts. He might have taken out a new one with someone even dodgier. Maybe he'd got himself into trouble with them and they'd made an example of him. It did mean, however, that his death might not have had anything to do with his job. Then again it still might.

I rubbed my chin as I considered this and hoisted myself on to a wide stone bollard that stood at the end of Fleur de Lis Court fronting on to Fetter Lane.

The new information would have to go to the police for sure. I would do that later. But, I thought Sam was probably right – this news didn't help get to the bottom of the ghost thing. I mean Mary had seen a woman in a bonnet leaving the scene. If Seth's murder was tied in with the loan sharks, the idea that someone like Pots Fischman might send in a chick to do his dirty work didn't cut it with me.

Women were generally shorter and, though it bugged me to admit it, not as strong as men. This made them an odd choice of heavy. It was a generalisation of course, but could a woman really have overpowered Seth Johnson? By all accounts he was strong and muscular. Joel had described him as fit. If that was the case, then the only thing I could think of that might have enabled a woman to overcome him was the threat of violence in the form of a gun. But if they had a gun, why didn't they use it? Why go to such elaborate lengths to string him up, lash him and make those sadistic incisions to his neck and body? There was something in that.

I took out my notebook and flicked back over the pages. Our last interviews with the remaining members of staff had been patchy. Nicky, the busboy, who actually turned out to be a busgirl, came over and complained about her pay. Didn't add much else. Another part-time waitress, Anita, encountered *the odd unaccounted moan or two* and reported draughts in the kitchen. Possibly near the back door. I had worked hard on keeping my face neutral.

The waiter, John, had been mentioned in our first encounter with Joel. John confirmed Joel's account of the bleeding chandelier but added that he believed he'd glimpsed a dark shadow on the mezzanine just before the writing appeared. Thus Sam's excuse for a nap. Only Agatha the bartender had a little bit more to add. She was a plump girl with dark black hair and was, I think, Polish. She told us she hadn't known Seth very well, as she was engaged and poor so of no interest to him.

It was a throwaway comment that was muttered under her breath. But obviously it spoke volumes: in addition to his long list of faults, Seth was also, according to at least two people, a womaniser. Definitely a flirt. Perhaps there was an element of jealousy in the killing?

Thing was, I didn't figure it as a crime of passion, as such. True though, there were eccentric passionate elements to the murder. Like I said, the staged, almost ritualistic quality of the way the body had been left, the stringing up, the posing, to my mind indicated something weird and sexual was involved. It was certainly a little bit S&M. Same with the wounds he suffered: whippings. If not so vicious, nasty and fatal, the scenario might have appeared a little nudge-nudge wink-wink.

It would be really helpful to know what a pathologist made of it. Whether those marks we'd been told about were inflicted pre-, post- or mid-mortem. I'd seen the TV shows, I knew they could work that stuff out. Maybe I could do an exchange of information with DS Edwards?

At the end of the day though, however intriguing it was to speculate on this, none of it particularly shed light on the ghostly happenings and sightings at the restaurant. Or did it? Did it mean we were dealing with a sadistic ghost? If ghosts actually existed. Which they didn't.

Or did they? I asked myself to develop nuance.

Who knew?

I sighed out loud and saw my breath make a cloud in the air.

Interestingly Agatha had declared that she knew the place was haunted way before Mary came out about what she'd seen. Said MT told her.

I flicked back through my notes to check that. MT had said it was a Henry Warren but then altered her statement to indicate Seth as the original source. Seth, we couldn't ask.

Femi had reported that the bloke next door had told him first before anyone. Some guy called Jackson. I'd have to talk to them both – Jackson and Warren. When I went back into the restaurant, I'd ask Agatha to get me Mr Warren's contact details from the bookings system. I'd pop next door and see Jackson. Maybe tomorrow.

I flipped my notebook shut and took a final breath of fresh air.

A thin mist was curling through the tall leafy trees across the road. Somewhere down by the crossroads a motorbike backfired. A bunch of birds, black ones, took off from their branches but instead of flying away, circled thirty feet above my head, squawking with fright.

Not an omen. Or a portent, I carefully told myself.

None of that actually existed.

As I walked back up Fleur de Lis Court, one of the birds above let out a shrill caw. The street lights flickered on and off. Shadows danced wildly in the alley.

I stopped and waited for them to straighten out.

The street lamp beside me came on then popped and spluttered.

Electrical interference probably. Maybe a faulty cable.

I wondered if that might affect the EMF monitor.

Oh god, I thought, *this is stupid and ridiculous.*

I was becoming a blimmin' ghostbuster.

CHAPTER SEVENTEEN

Despite the fact it had been a relatively slow night, the kitchen didn't close till about 10.30 p.m. What with all the cleaning and the prep for the next day, barked out under Femi's eagle-eyed supervision, we weren't allowed to set up video cameras and recorders till after 11 p.m. when the place was almost deserted but for a few core staff.

We had already installed the infrared equipment on the dining floor in the afternoon. Sam had attached motion sensors after the customers had left. We used the waiting staff to test that the equipment worked as they tidied and cleared the room. It did. It was pretty amazing. I was a little bit impressed.

Downstairs, Sam set up a thermal scanner, a thermal imaging camera and several normal video cameras on various tripods, which occupied most of the cellar floor space. Another digital stills camera was fixed on the wall and there were several audio recorders dotted around the room. He had also switched on the Spirit Box and EMF detector and was holding the latter in his hand doing a 'control' survey of the space, when I came down to check on him. He was miffed that Ray hadn't let him put talcum powder on the floor, to check for imprints/footprints, as he'd only just managed to get rid of what he had referred to as 'that bleedin' flour', a rather accurate though horribly evocative choice of words.

I thought it was fair enough, and I told Sam so. 'Talc is a nightmare to clean. My friend Cerise uses it sometimes.' I was playing with a bunch of leftover cable ties. We'd used them to secure some of the equipment in place. 'But even though she confines it to the bathroom, it gets everywhere. Ghostly footprints all over the hallway.' I shivered. 'Could complicate things in this case.' I didn't add that I had my new boots on and I didn't want them getting dusty either.

Sam put the EMF detector down on a nearby stool. I thought he was going to argue with me, but he didn't. 'So when am I going to meet this legendary Cerise?'

I narrowed my eyes. 'Why?' There's usually only one reason single men ask to meet your single friends.

'Oh, you know,' he said, and grinned. 'She sounds funny and a bit scary. Like you.'

I stopped twiddling with the cable ties and rammed them in the back of my jeans. His last words, you see, had really caught me. 'Like me? Why am I funny and scary?'

His eyes locked on to mine. I could tell he was building up to something: his lips twitched and he paused for a moment then, to my amazement, said, 'The way you make me feel sometimes – it's scary.'

Whoa, that was out of the blue.

For a moment it felt as if everything stopped. Except for my heart which began to accelerate. 'What do you mean?' I stuttered. 'Good scary or bad scary?'

His face opened, the smile deepened, amber flints in his eyes shone under the glare of the lights he had erected. 'You're funny, you're smart, you're beautiful.' He took a long breath. 'You hold my destiny in your hands.'

I couldn't help it – a smirk was out before my brain could snap to action and rein it back in. 'Your destiny!' It was just that Sam didn't usually use such florid language. My knee-jerk reaction was to poke fun. My knee-jerk reaction was dead wrong.

I saw his shoulders tense, then he took a step back, and said, 'The destiny of the Witch Museum is what I meant. Of course with my studies, I am inextricably bound to it for the next few years. Unless you sell.' But a blush was spreading across his cheeks. 'The future is scary.'

Damn and blast. Stupid me!

'That's what you meant, is it?' I said inching across the floor towards him. 'It's all about the museum?'

He didn't move although I could sense a faltering within. 'I, I …'

My god – I had caught him on the hop.

There was only a couple of feet between us now and I was conscious of some kind of window of opportunity closing. I didn't want it to shut. 'Sam,' I said, and reached for his hand.

I picked up the long, slender fingers. Cool and soft, the hands of an academic. They fluttered like ribbons around my hand then deftly closed over it.

We were holding hands! I could feel sparks where our flesh touched. It was stunning, it was breathtaking. It was weird.

'We should talk about this,' I said after a moment.

He brought his chin up and took in a long breath. Our eyes met and zinged as a bold frisson of energy passed between us.

Then a voice broke in from above. 'Hello? Rosie? You there?'

I jumped and looked around. Sam instantly opened his fingers, dropped my hand, then took a step back. Flustered, he ran the hand that had been holding mine through his hair and forced a smile. 'Perhaps not the time nor place. A fitting reminder,' he said croakily. Then he coughed and shouted up the stairs to where the voice had called, 'She'll be right up.'

I saw him gulp and straighten himself – he was slipping back behind the Mr Uptight persona.

The space between us widened.

I stepped back and looked into him, but everything had changed. We had gone back to how we were two minutes ago, like the hand thing had never happened. Normal service had clearly resumed. Not that I was happy about it.

Blimmin' heck. Whoever shouted down for me had better have a good bloody reason.

I muttered out a stroppy 'okay'. There was no point lingering.

Then I slunk upstairs.

It was Agatha, waiting outside the cellar door. A lot of the staff were refusing to go down into it now. Only the brave fetched cellar stock, and super quickly too. You couldn't really blame them, could you?

Behind Agatha. I spied Jarvino and Femi loading dirty dishcloths into a washing machine.

'Yes?' I said to the bartender, sounding marginally less irritated than I actually was.

She didn't seem to notice. 'I have Mr Henry Warren's details,' she said, and handed me a note.

'Who's he when he's at home?' I asked. Now my grumpiness was coming through.

Her features tied into a little knot that became the centre of her face. '*You* asked *me* for his number,' she chided. 'He's a regular. Big spender. You must treat him with courtesy and respect.'

It would be rude to do anything but agree, though I was ready for an argument just for the hell of it. I reminded myself that it wasn't Agatha's fault she'd interrupted something that I hadn't wanted interrupted. At all.

'Yes, of course,' I told her. 'Though I'm only going to ask him how he knew about the ghost.'

She seemed satisfied by this and pointed out she'd given me a landline and a mobile. 'Don't use the landline now. It is late. And the mobile, I suggest you only text.'

'Message received and understood,' I said.

Femi and Jarvino announced they were leaving and Agatha said she'd go with them so we all said our goodbyes, then when I heard the front door slam shut I went and took up position at a table by the hatch.

It was just as well I had set my kit up earlier for I was still rather distracted. There wasn't a huge amount to monitor compared to Sam's Aladdin's cave downstairs: a camera, which was battery-operated though rechargeable and of the 'quaint' variety. As the kitchen was a much bigger space than the cellar I'd had to find a high point for it to sit on so the lens could take in as much of the room as possible. Earlier I'd tried a stepladder, which was too rickety, so had ended up improvising with the cable ties and managed to fix the camera by its handle to an upper shelf. After securing it with at least fifteen of the plastic strips, I had been satisfied with the angle. Now I carried out a technical test to ensure that the equipment hadn't come loose – I poked it. When it didn't wobble, I pressed record.

Next, before I forgot, I texted Henry Warren and explained I had some questions for him regarding La Fleur. I requested, very politely, a convenient time to meet. Didn't get a reply but like I said it was quite late by then so it he was probably asleep. After that I downloaded an EMF app on to my phone, double-checking that it was fully charged.

Then I copied Sam and did a 'control' reading to work out what the various norms were in there. Walking round the perimeter of the room I listened to the fridges humming and singing in their own mechanical way. Above me pipes gurgled and coughed. I reckoned the plumbing was ancient. It was odd that the place looked so new and glossy out front, when behind the façade, the body of the building itself had to date back centuries. You could tell that from the pipes, which were, to my reckoning early 1920s, maybe even Victorian. They had been painted several times and some of the most recent paintwork was flaking away.

I gave up inspecting them and went and sat back down at the table and laid down my phone, EMF app on and speaker side to the room. Next to it I had a torch, spare tapes, some pens and a few sets of batteries.

Sam had allowed me a lamp. I had argued that ghosts wouldn't care if there were lights on or not. To which he had acceded, or possibly submitted. He intended to 'set an example' by going for the 'complete darkness' option himself. Though the cellar door was still open and a bit of my lamp-light illuminated the upper part of the stairs.

I didn't feel uncomfortable. Not really. I'd done stake-outs before. Inner-city London was never deserted or inactive. Up here in the kitchen, I could hear the low sounds of traffic in the distance, the muffled scream of a police siren tearing off to an emergency. Closer by came the irritating drip of a tap somewhere in the building.

Sam had told me to note anything that seemed out of the ordinary or which seemed very ordinary and to keep a register of the time. I wrote down *Midnight – nothing doing*. Then I waited.

My mind drifted back to what had taken place downstairs. It really was a bugger Agatha had called for me then. I wondered what might have happened if she'd been a couple of minutes later. I'd never know. However, I reflected, our interaction had certainly been intriguing. I could still feel a residue of excitement flitting around my body. Sam liked me, I was sure. But his reticence and caution spoke of someone who had considered the possibility of getting involved with his boss (of sorts) and thought better of it. That kind of thinking never got you anywhere, in my mind. Sam's, however, was of a completely different variety, I was aware. Well, he was right about one thing – this wasn't the right moment in our relationship to open that particular Pandora's box. We had things to do, ghosts to debunk.

Hopefully there would be more opportunities. Certainly if I kept the museum.

About forty-five minutes later I became aware of a faint rustling noise, down by the cabinets, as if an animal had got in and were exploring the room. I was probably quite wired because it also made me think of a woman in a crinoline skirt brushing against the walls. It had obviously come from Mary's descriptions, which must have wedged into my mind. I reminded myself it was more likely to be a rat. They had form here, so to speak. I turned on my torch and had a closer look at the skirting boards.

Nothing doing. Still.

Just to be on the safe side I cleared my throat loudly so if there was a rodent lurking it now knew there a human was present. Let's hope that would scare it away.

Sam called up from the cellar to see if I was okay. Bless him. He cared.

I told him I was and that I thought I heard an animal noise but that it had stopped.

I checked the EMF. Nothing.

I put it on the table next to where I sat.

I logged the sound in my book.

I kept vigil.

Time passed.

The clock on the wall ticked.

I became aware of the coming of the next tock and wondered if somehow it was getting louder.

I thought about the probability of that happening and then my mind returned to Sam. Of course it did. There was a bit of a problem, I thought, with me being the owner of the museum. If we did ever get it together (I shuddered slightly at the joy of the notion), if everything went well, it would be amazing. But if it didn't, if it went wrong, then it would be disastrous, awkward and we probably wouldn't be able to continue working together. If indeed that was what we were doing. Sam might even decide to leave the museum. Not only would that scupper the museum, what would he do about his book, his PhD he had spent so long on? He was only halfway through it. Maybe he'd have to pretend everything was okay, just to complete his thesis. Ew – that was a hideous notion. He wouldn't, would he?

Appalled, I started to understand Sam's reticence. Maybe it was better that we stayed like this, for the present. I mean, we didn't know each other terribly well. We needed to spend more time together, finding out what we were like, not rushing things, but taking it slow. And I thought about a gradual deepening of understanding, a friendship that turned into something hotter and sexier and passionate and sometime during this contemplation I must have dropped off to sleep. Because moments, minutes, maybe hours later my body jerked up, instantly rigid, conscious and alert.

Sitting on the edge of my chair, I appeared to be mid-action – lifting my head up from my chest where it had been resting.

All my senses had jangled to attention.

Which is why I think I heard it so clearly.

A hard *rat-a-tat-tat* against the window of the back door.

My face snapped to the sound.

From my position at the table I couldn't see anything beyond the glass there. No outline or form behind it.

I took a breath and decided to wait.

The EMF detector buzzed: interference in the magnetic field close by. The dial on the meter swayed hard to the right. The light on the table went out.

What the hell was going on?

I cocked my head into the kitchen.

The fridges gave a sigh then ceased humming.

I switched the lamp on and off.

Nothing.

Must be a power cut.

Of course. The light had gone out in the street earlier. Should have realised there was a fault. Probably generated by the workmen above.

That explained it. Didn't it?

I rubbed my eyes and hoped they'd adjust to the thick dimness.

The room became ominously silent, as if all the sounds had been sucked out of it. You didn't often get that in London. I was surprised by how unnerved I felt.

I was about to call out to Sam when the rapping came again. This time much harder against the window. Angry and impatient.

Oh, blimmin' hell. What was I meant to do about that?

It wasn't on the schedule.

Should I answer it?

When I was in the middle of an investigation?

Was that what you did?

Or perhaps I should go back to Plan A and call Sam?

I bit my lip. Summoning up menfolk to solve a situation was something I normally liked to avoid.

I was a big girl. I could deal with it on my own.

I moved towards the back door, my footsteps deliberately light, virtually inaudible.

As I approached, though it was dark out there, the view into the yard became more distinct.

There *was* someone lurking. But not close to the door. A little further back.

However, the late-night mist had clotted into what clichéd cockney TV characters might call a right 'pea-souper'. Dense and yellowish in colour. It obscured everything but the wavering outline of the person in the yard.

There was nothing else for it – I would simply have to pluck up courage and open the door. Maybe it was just a member of staff who'd forgotten their bag or keys. There was nothing spooky about someone knocking on a door was there? *Tsk*.

I heard Sam shout up from the cellar, 'Rosie, are you getting that?' I assumed he meant the door and yelled back into the house, 'Yes, no problem.' To my dismay, I saw the cellar door swing back on its hinges and slam shut. *How rude*, I thought. Typical of Sam, leaving me to deal with the 'interruption' so that he could continue his investigation unharassed.

'No, it's fine,' I muttered. 'You just leave it to me.' Then I stepped into the yard.

Bloody hell, it was freezing.

The dank smell of burning coke, lightly sulphuric, dusty and smoky, hung in the air. Could people be burning fires now? At this hour? I supposed we were in the heart of a hyperactive city that, like New York, never slept any more. Some people might still be up and stoking fires.

All the lights out back had gone out, but the round moon was trying to break through the fog. I could make out within it a strange twist. Something thin and dark was moving stutteringly, almost like a stop-motion cartoon. Humanoid in shape, it dipped and flickered like it was made up of a swarm of a thousand winged creatures.

That couldn't be right, I thought. I must have something in my eyes so rubbed them. I'd not long been awake, after all. The cold smog pushed against me. Moisture clung to my skin. I blinked and opened my lids even wider.

But no, it was still there.

Actually it wasn't an 'it'. It was a 'she'. At least I thought it was a she, for long dark and matted hair hung down over the shoulders, or where the shoulders should have been if I could see her properly. It was peculiar though. I was trying to get a fix on her but my vision was fragmenting as soon as it touched her form, sliding off as if she were somehow visually slippery.

I crept a few steps into the yard. 'Hello?'

A shape in the mess turned to me. I saw the semblance of a human face, dirty and smudged. Petite pinched features, eyes woefully sad, large open sores about her mouth. But around that, the perimeter of her face was less clear, merging with the shadows cast from her hair. Despite the fact it felt like I was viewing the girl through a smudged window, I knew that this wasn't one of the La Fleur staff. Her build didn't match and, also, I didn't think any of them got around in hessian sacks. Unless that was some new Hoxton trend. This girl certainly didn't look like a confident follower of fashion. She looked upset and disorientated. Though I noticed she sported a thick black choker, crafted from metal, about her neck as some kind of statement jewellery – a grungy industrial-goth fusion. Actually, I thought, she seemed really young. Not more than thirteen. Maybe a runaway? Terribly thin.

And she looked distraught.

I experienced a sudden sense of despair. Where had that come from? Was I feeling her pain? Perhaps I was detecting a nuance?

'Are you okay?' I stretched my hand towards her, only to realise I was still holding the torch. 'Are you lost? Have you forgotten something?'

Part of me thought she might recoil if I got closer. But she didn't.

About five feet away, she turned her fuzzy flitting face to the east and the adjoining yard.

'Vere,' I heard her say. 'Vover vere.'

As the words left the black hole of her mouth, I heard them as a vibration in my ears, a tickle, like an insect had flown into them and was beating its wings.

I put my hand to one and covered it. But the words wormed their way into my head and created meaning in themselves, echoing around until I heard them as 'over there over there over there ...'

I tried to shake them out and then, slightly dizzy, directed my gaze to where she was pointing.

'Over here?' I'd need to humour her till I'd worked out what to do, so began to walking very obediently and very slowly to a gap in the wall that separated La Fleur's yard from next door's. A dozen bricks had tumbled down months back and not been built up since. They formed a small hump of debris that blocked access either way.

'Vere,' she mumbled. There was something wrong with her tongue. Despite the lack of volume her voice was urgent. Forgetting my new boots, I clambered up on to the rubble and flicked on my torch.

There was nothing but the neighbour's yard and his place next door. Tall and thin, maybe four storeys high, it had clearly been built at the same time as La Fleur. Except its basement was slightly higher than La Fleur's. There was one barred glass window just above the ground. A flight of stone stairs led down from the main door. Everything was dark.

'There's no one there,' I said, and turned back to the girl.

A cloud crossed the moon. Only her face remained, oddly luminous yet a rusty red. Her shadowy eyes blinked then. A thick mucus-like liquid started to seep out of the right one.

Oh god, poor girl. She was injured. Perhaps she had taken a knock to the head.

I watched helplessly as another trickle cascaded from her left eye this time.

'Are you okay?' I asked. 'You look like you're bleeding. Your face …'

The two purple rivulets were turning into bloody streams that dribbled on to the ground in a viscous puddle and then … and then … dissolved. Before my eyes.

It must be some trick of the light.

I looked up to where her face had been.

It was empty of anything. No shape, no form, no weird luminescence, no ruddy darkness.

I began to stalk forwards to the patch of ground where the puddle slopped so briefly, searching beyond the yard for the girl but, as I did, something smashed behind me.

It had come from the neighbour's yard.

A prickle of fear ran down my spine.

I could either go forwards and see where the girl had vanished to or go back and examine the source of the noise.

What to do, what to do?

Maybe the girl had slipped past me, though God knows how, and broken something in the yard?

Could that be possible?

I wasn't honestly sure if she could be so lightning fast but I made a decision and spun round returning to the pile of rubble, shining my torch about the back of the building.

There was glass on the ground near the basement window.

Oh crap. Burglars, I thought, and another thrill of panic fired through my abdomen. Though even with my torch I couldn't see anyone else there.

'Please,' a thin weedy voice drifted up from the broken window.

It was slight, like a like gasp or a sigh.

Had the girl got into the house?

I directed my torch over.

The bluey-white circle of light shone through the bars and I saw, astonishingly, the pale features of a woman's emaciated face.

Another one.

Different to the girl in the yard.

This one was only slightly more rounded. Her eyes were deep black and bruised. Dirty fingers, showing torn and broken nails, gripped on to the iron bars across the window. Beyond them I could see where boarding, jagged strips of wood, had been prised apart.

This was totally weird.

I'm seeing things, I thought, and for a moment I was completely overawed by a kaleidoscope of emotions and options. Should I go back and call for Sam? Should I go and look for the other girl? Should I scream? Call out? Run? Take a deep breath? Panic?

I stood there, with my torch, and did nothing until the scraggy blackened hand reached out from the bars. 'Help me, please?'

The desperation in her voice rang an alarm bell within me, and this is what jerked me into rational thought. This was a plea, pure and simple. A cry for help.

Without consciously making a decision to do anything in particular, I ran at full speed to the window and knelt down.

The woman in the basement room was shivering violently. Her face was insipid, eyes weak and bleary, possibly drugged.

And she was wearing nothing but her underwear. Now I was that much nearer I could see some kind of metal manacle fastened on to her wrist.

'My name is Gloria,' she said, trying to keep heavy lids open. 'He is keeping us here. He will be back soon. Just gone out. The alarm,' she pointed at the back of the building. 'It is broken. Help us get out.'

I was breathing hard and finding it difficult to process what she was saying at first and replied, 'Can't you come out through the back door?'

With a remaining sliver of energy she raised her hand and clanked a chain that I now saw ran from her wrist manacle to an iron circle on the wall.

I rocked back on my heels as I realised what I was seeing. 'Oh shit. Don't worry,' I said. 'I'm phoning the police.'

I felt my jeans pocket, then, bugger almighty, realised I'd left it in electromagnetic detector mode on the table in the kitchen. 'One minute,' I told her. 'I need to get my phone. Stay there.' Which was a stupid thing to say all things considered but I wasn't thinking.

I heard her scream for me to stay and clank something hard against the iron bar but I knew this was the right thing to do so raced back into the kitchen. There was no way I could get the girl out on my own. Not with that chain.

In the kitchen, I shouted, 'Sam! Sam!' as calmly as I could, keeping out of my voice the hysteria that was starting to rise. 'Phone the police. Quick. Come here.'

I grabbed my mobile before he could reply and whipped back out into the yard again.

'I'm phoning them now. The police,' I yelled, hoping Gloria could hear me as I galloped back into the yard.

It was crossing my mind briefly that I might be getting into stuff I shouldn't poke my nose into. A sex game gone wrong? Kinky behaviour by consenting adults? This had almost floored me on my last adventure with the remains of the witch.

As my resolve began to waver my pace slowed too but then Gloria started to cry. And she was absolutely terrified. You could tell.

'Hang on in there,' I said as, at last, I got through to the emergency services. 'I'm reporting ...' I paused. What was I reporting? My not very expansive experience with the police suggested that they were overworked and understaffed which meant they had to prioritise jobs. 'There's a murder in progress,' I told the operator. 'With a bomb. Please get here as soon as you can.'

The gravel behind me crunched.

'What's going on?' Sam asked, as he caught up. He was a little on the breathless side. Me and him both.

I handed him the phone. 'Quickly!' I yelled, 'Give them our address.'

'Why?' he said.

'Just do it. Now! And after that, phone Monty. Just in case.'

Gloria's wails were becoming almost feeble Either the drugs were kicking in or her energy was running out.

'Stay with me,' I called. 'You're doing really well.'

I squatted down and looked at her through the bars. She

was swaying unsteadily but as I watched her suddenly she became rigid. Her eyes changed, now wider and rounder. Turning with a newly energised fervour she staggered to me and pressed her face hard against the iron. 'No, no, I can hear him,' she said. 'He's coming back.'

I felt for my phone in my back pocket, remembered Sam had it, but found my fingers enclosed on something else. Three stiff strips. The cable ties.

I pulled them out and looked at them. They were thin and made of plastic but strong. They'd have to do. 'Give me your hand,' I told her. It was all I could think of.

Scabby fingers poked through the bars. I grasped them and said, 'I'm going to wrap these around our wrists. Can you thread it and pull it tight on your side? He won't be able to take you, without taking me. All right?'

I didn't really know what I was talking about. I hadn't had time to wonder if the unknown man wanted to take her anywhere. I just knew that she wasn't happy or safe where she was and that I needed to do something to help.

Wordlessly Gloria obeyed slipping the strip round with her manacled hand. But her eyes were unfocused and unsteady. She was having trouble threading them through the catch.

'Hurry,' I told her, lashing one of the cable ties on to my own wrist, 'as quick as you can.' For I too could now hear the heavy tread of footsteps in a passage beyond.

As the door inside the shabby basement was thrown open I managed to link the ties and pull them tight. Gloria shrieked in weary pain.

Someone over by the doorway swore then a man entered

the shadows of the room. In the dimness I couldn't see much more than his outline. But I said, 'The game's up. We've called the police.'

There was a moment of inaction, then, abruptly, the lights came back on.

For a moment we stared at each other: me and this man.

I don't know who I had been expecting to see – someone from the restaurant perhaps.

But I didn't recognise him. He was a stranger.

Albeit a stranger who was livid. As he processed the sight, his eyes broadened and began to smoulder with outrageous fury.

If I could have shrunk back from Gloria right then, I'm ashamed to say I probably would have.

The poor girl whimpered and blinked against the fluorescent light that was still flickering on. I looked past her and saw the guy's eyes focus on me. They did not look good. It was like someone had flicked a switch and something demonic had channelled down. He curled his lips, and made a snorty noise. Bits of spit flew out of his mouth. His expression was full of something I can only describe as murderous, insane, depraved. His shoulders hunched. Indignation and fury funnelled up over him, transforming the hue of his skin from puce to purple.

Before I could prepare myself he had lunged at Gloria.

I heard her yelp in my ear and found the hand bound to her pull down sharply into the room. My whole body followed with it, hauled across the yard as far as it could till I smacked hard against the window bars.

Gloria panicked and let out a frantic wail. My arm was yanked around, though I couldn't see how: up to the shoulder it was inside the room.

Sam was scrambling around somewhere behind me. 'What's going on?'

But I couldn't speak because the man inside the room, who I could no longer see, was pinching and scratching the flesh on my forearm. I yelped as he dug his nails into the crook of my elbow, then he bawled out something obscene.

Underneath me bits of broken wood and glass were digging in through my clothes. I couldn't pull back, couldn't twist my head around.

Sam's hands wrapped round my shoulder and pulled back. But as someone on the other end of the phone started to speak, he became distracted and loosened his grip.

The pinches stopped and the heaviness the other side of the window relaxed. I took my chance and began to crawl back but again, my arm was grabbed, wrenched back into the room. Too fast for me to react, I collided with the bars once more. My head slammed into the bricks next to the window. Pain shot out across it and down into my chest, which convulsed with the involuntarily need to gag.

For a moment, I was aware only of a loud ringing in my ears, a red film over my vision and searing hotness on the right side of my head. Reflexively I tried to bring my hand up to touch it but found I still couldn't move it for it was stretched and extended into the room and had something wet attached to it that was sinking and taking me down with it.

A blackness around in the yard seemed to flow into my

mouth as I tried to draw in breath. I must have looked up because I remember seeing the stars in the sky swell and glow ever so, ever so bright and wondering absurdly if they might sing. Then a drift of honeysuckle swam to my nose. Another female presence here smelt strongly of roses. And right in the middle of this feminine essence I detected warmth and calm, a suckling sense of nurture. Then a voice I didn't recognise whispered softly, 'Come back.'

Swift strong hands reached down around my shoulders and began to prise me once more from the window into the yard. The pain in my head crowded back. Oh, it hurt. The resistance the other end had weakened and I felt my arm dragged again over the jagged broken glass and sharpness. Then I was fully conscious. Aware of Gloria slamming back against the bars with a horrific crack. She squealed. I whimpered. Sam continued to haul me back but Gloria's arm was making cracking noises – it could stretch no further.

This ridiculous see-saw wasn't going to work.

'Stop,' I gasped. 'Film it, Sam.'

Gloria's arm suddenly slacked. Despite the excruciating fire in my shoulder I found her hand and squeezed it. Then I rallied my senses and angled my face towards the room The man had let go of her and was just standing there. 'I'm filming this,' I told him.

To my amazement the words effected a change. For his posture altered. He looked up, then very dozily, like he was coming out of a dream, went to scratch his head.

As the sirens piled into the yard, he said, 'There's no need to get aggy. It was just a bit of fun. That's all.'

CHAPTER EIGHTEEN

But it wasn't just a bit of fun, we learnt. The man, or boy as he had seemed to me, Jackson, hadn't been having anything consensual down in that basement. He'd got himself involved with something much more sinister. Something, DS Edwards told us, other members of his constabulary had been looking into for quite some time.

You just don't think that slavery goes on under your nose. You just don't think that your neighbours could ever be involved. Ordinary, decent people. But greed, corruption, power, these can be the real demons and some become possessed.

Jackson Jova and two of his cousins were.

I couldn't quite believe it.

As I sat on the wall, hours later, DS Edwards reported an edited version of the Jackson guy's confession in the back of a panda car. He had contacted Gloria, and it turned out, another woman known only at present as 'Ruby', who was in the neighbouring basement room, luring them with the promise of work as waitresses at La Fleur. Somehow he had managed to hack into to the restaurant's Wi-Fi and was able to make a copycat email. It wasn't hard, apparently, if you knew how.

Gloria and her friend had been picked up at the airport and then transferred here. They hadn't worried about it, until they'd seen the living quarters. That's when the chains were strapped on. And, they'd been told, before they could leave they would have to earn the cost of their flight back. But not by waitressing.

No one minded when I was sick.

Everyone seemed to think it was a natural reaction. Including the paramedic getting the glass splinters out of my arm.

Though I insisted to DS Edwards, or rather Jason as I was allowed to call him now, that I usually didn't do such things.

'It's okay,' he said, and handed me a tissue. 'I'm hoping you don't run into sex trafficking regularly, do you?'

I was happy to concede the point.

Although happy wasn't one of the things that I was feeling there and then.

More like depressed, confused and disgusted. And knackered and in pain.

Sam had draped his jacket over my shoulders while the paramedics checked me out. I didn't want to go to hospital. I had a gash on my arm and maybe a little concussion, but I thought I could deal with that. It didn't seem right to divert attention from Gloria and her friend. They had, after all, been through so much more, it kind of felt indulgent to accompany them in the ambulance.

Jason pulled up a purple chair that had clearly come from La Fleur's dining room. 'It seems that Seth Johnson discovered what Jackson was up to. Took a sweetener to stay quiet.'

'Oh, really?' said Sam and shivered. He only had a T-shirt on. 'Is that how he paid off Pots Fischman's account?'

Jason frowned and eyed me. 'Who?'

'Oh yes, we kept meaning to tell you. We did our own bit of investigation. From a tip-off.'

'Fact is, I wish you had,' he said, and set his hands on his knees so he looked firm and substantial. 'Because we might have avoided this.'

I nodded. It hurt. Although I wasn't sure I believed him. 'Really?'

The DS stroked the sporadic stubble on his chin. I wondered if he always grew it like that. 'Well, there's this thing called a police force that comes in handy when tasked to investigate crime.'

'Funny,' I said.

He raised his slightly tweezered eyebrows, 'We're running several lines of enquiry and this information may have led to a breakthrough.'

I noted his use of conditional tense. From where I was sitting this looked like quite a major development.

'It wouldn't surprise me,' he continued, 'if Seth asked for more money, maybe blackmailed Jackson and his cousins, and that's what broke the camel's back.'

It was a theory. Could be credible. 'You mean Jackson might have killed him? Murdered Seth?' My words sounded slightly fuzzy – adrenalin was starting to recede and I was feeling dopey.

'He doesn't seem like a man of many scruples,' Jason rued. 'So it may have been something like that.'

'All right,' I said, and stifled a yawn. 'Doesn't explain the bonnet and lady and stuff. That's what Mary described.' But Sam had started talking to Jason so neither of them heard me.

I let them ramble on and took a moment to survey the yard. With the yard lights on now, I could see the area outside the restaurant was actually quite small. The girl in the sack dress must have been either just inside of the perimeter wall by the gates, or just outside of it. I couldn't work out how she had disappeared so quickly without me seeing her go. Though it was still foggy out here. Sprays of moisture licked around the lamp lights like watery flames. It had been thicker earlier. The perfect conditions for mirages and tricks of the eye.

I watched the police photographer take some final photos of the broken-down gap I had used to get through into Jackson's yard. When he finished that he shouted over to Jason that he was going inside.

Sam wandered over and stood close by. 'You should really go in too, Rosie.'

He was right. It was cold out here, despite the Sam's jacket and the blanket. My hair was wet, slicked with fog and about to start going frizzy. Plus, I wanted to get away from the smell of sick.

Jason looked over to Sam and said, 'I'll need to corroborate Rosie's statement about the woman who knocked on the door. The one in the yard. Do you think you could get me the tapes?'

And so Sam shuffled off into La Fleur to fetch them.

'Here, let me help you.' Jason put my good arm over his shoulders and tucked his hand around my waist.

He paused when he saw me flinch. 'Sore?'

'Sorry.' I could feel one side of my face was bigger than the other so didn't bother trying to smile. 'And, I'm not used to it. In my line of work, people don't usually touch you. In fact, the physical contact that does occur tends to be classified as common assault.'

'Ditto,' he said. 'Shall I or not?' He was holding his hands up and away from me.

'No, it's fine,' I said. 'As long as I know it's coming.' And actually it didn't feel bad at all. Plus, I was seriously enjoying his body warmth.

'Listen,' I told him as we began to hobble over the yard, 'she wasn't a woman. She was a girl. I'm pretty sure of it.'

The door was open and a single rectangle of light projected over the back steps. Jason helped me over them. 'Your description is quite vague, I've got to admit. But I think we should put out a search. She might be involved.'

'It's all on the tape,' I said.

He nodded and fell silent as we passed into the kitchen. I stretched my back, rubbed the side of my shoulder that had hit the wall, then, as he lowered me on to the chair by the table where I had earlier kept my vigil, I yawned very loudly again.

'Well.' The sky was lightening through the window. 'I should be off,' I told him. 'I've got work in the morning. Is that okay?'

He looked surprised. 'I thought this was your job? And that museum of black magic place.'

'It's not a museum of black magic,' I said, and reached

around for my phone. 'It's the Essex Witch Museum. You know most of the women who were charged with witchcraft, who were executed, were completely innocent? It's a classic miscarriage of justice. You should know all about that.'

'Is that so?' His mouth was pulled back into a smile and giving his cheeks dimples. 'And you've got to get back to it in the morning?'

'Oh no,' I said, and pushed my hair back then wobbled. I think I might have been looking like I was drunk. 'No, I've got a proper job. In Benefit Fraud. Public servant and that.'

Jason Edwards' eyes swivelled down from my hair to my boots. I looked at them too. They were scratched across the toe and some of the gold leather on the sides had been torn. Typical.

'I have enduring respect for public servants,' he said.

There was something in his voice that made me flush. He really was quite good-looking. So, I smiled and said, 'Me too.'

'Perhaps,' he said suddenly rather snuggly, 'we could have a chat about it over a glass of wine?'

Instinctively, I looked at the cellar door, wondering if Sam was there. But we were going to be friends now, weren't we? Maybe I should take Jason up on his offer. 'Well,' I said, making a decision, 'you're timing's not impeccable but I think I could find a slot in my diary for that.' I fiddled with my hair and felt an unexpected little flutter in my stomach. It didn't mean anything. I could maybe just have a drink, after all. I mean, it wasn't like I'd started something with the curator.

'I say! Not interrupting anything, am I?'

We both turned to see a tall man in a smart tailored suit waving a phone and walking boldly across the floor towards us.

'Oh, Monty,' I said. 'I forgot about you.' Of course, I had told Sam to phone him.

I stretched out my good hand to give him a hug. Though it hurt more than a little.

Monty smiled and reciprocated my gesture, although he was a little awkward about it. I think hugs weren't de rigueur in his social circle: I'd noted on previous occasions that he had perfected the gentlemanly handshake. I bet that had come with lots and lots of practice.

'And you are?' Jason eyed the stranger.

Monty's bearing was chipper. Although I'd never seen him anything other. This evening he was sporting formal dress, complete with black tie. He didn't look like he was going to explain why. I liked him. He had a pleasant though thin face, was maybe a few years older than me but always had this mischievous glint in his eyes and a sparky energy about his movements that combined to make him seem younger.

'MI6, MI5,' I explained to Jason's territorial confusion. 'Or something like that. I don't know really.'

Monty winked at him. 'She's an informant.'

Jason swung round and gaped at me with open surprise and said, 'Is she?' at the same time as I uttered, 'Am I?'

'Seems so,' said Monty and pointed at his phone. 'Need to talk to you in private, I fear.'

We both glanced at Jason, who was going with a stern

expression but still seemed rather miffed by this interruption. But in the end he said to me, 'Okay then. Rosie, send me your video footage please. As soon as you can,' and handed me his card. 'I've got your number,' he whispered then winked.

'And I've got yours,' I said, and waved it in the air.

As he withdrew into the building, I said to Monty. 'If this is going to take long, can we do it in the car? I've got five hours until my team meeting and I really need to be on time.'

'The pleasure is all mine,' he said. 'Your carriage awaits.' Then he ushered me back out the door.

We were halfway to Leytonstone when I realised I'd forgotten something – Sam.

Slightly embarrassing.

Monty detoured back to Fetter Lane and went and got him. The curator hadn't noticed I'd gone anyway. He'd been far more interested in reviewing what tapes Jason had left behind.

'You got a fantastic reading on the EMF detector,' he said as he swung into Monty's BMW. 'I managed to note it before that detective inspected your phone.'

'Which reminds me,' Monty piped up. 'Rosie, you really have to stop calling the police and telling them there's a bomb. I've tried to smooth it over, again, spinning the old informant line but in future, call me on this phone. My personal number is in there and a hotline which should come through 24/7. In case of emergencies.' There was a reprimand in his tone, though it was cordial as with all his communications.

'I know, I know,' I said. 'But I've had circumstances.'

'Yes, I'm aware,' he said after a pause. 'But you'll get investigated if you're not careful and that's not something any of us wants. Is it?' he said, and snuck me a pinch of grin. I was really just too tired to argue so I nodded and said, 'No.' Then added, 'But it's not me who has actually done anything wrong.' Then I thought I'd better be grateful so went, 'Thank you very much for your consideration,' and took the phone off him, surprised to see it was gleaming new and top of the range. 'Wow, thanks.'

'It's a pay-as-you-go. It's got £20 pounds in it to start you off then you ought to top up the rest yourself. Buy new SIM cards as frequently as possible.'

'Okay,' I said. 'Can I transfer my number on to it?'

'No, Rosie,' he cooed. 'That's the point.'

'But how will I call my friends?'

'On your own phone.'

'Oh, yeah,' I said. 'Well, I'll need Sam's number. Just in case.'

'You will indeed,' said a voice in the back seat. 'We're here.'

And we were. It only dawned on me later that I'd never told Monty my address.

We dropped Sam off. The sun was ascending over the low hills of Essex. I told him to make himself at home, which he already had done, and that I'd be back later in the afternoon. Then Monty kindly took me on to work. During the journey I tried to sum up the full extent of our involvement with Seth Johnson, Ray and Mary Boundersby, and La Fleur.

I had got to the tussle by the window when a memory revisited me – the cool and sweet presence of that unknown female. It halted my flow of speech and prompted a curious reflection. I could remember it with an amount of clarity that seemed improbable given I was in the throes of concussion at the time. I wasn't going to mention it at all, but this early in the morning my impulse control was pretty slack.

Breaking off from the main narrative, I asked Monty, 'Do you know anything about my grandmother's disappearance or who she was or what she did?' Several neurones that might not have connected the presence, or sense of presence, to my grandmother had fired off before I could check them sensibly. Though even as I said it, I knew that the experience had likely come from what Sam and Bronson had shared with me recently, that it had resurfaced to meet me in a moment of panic when my brain started triggering 'comfort' memories. I remembered the cottage in which she lived had been covered in honeysuckle. And the fragrance of roses that accompanied my hallucination or whatever it was – well, you just had to think about what's in a name. Mine and my grandmother's.

Monty, however, looked rather taken aback. 'What's this got to do with sex trafficking and ghosts?'

'I'll get back to that in a minute. Probably nothing. It's just if I don't ask you about Ethel-Rose now, I may well forget. I've got a lot of other things going on upstairs.' I tapped my head and winced.

His leather driving gloves gripped the wheel. 'I'll have to refresh myself with the case notes. But, if I recall, she was an alleged clairaudient. That much I do remember.'

One of his words stuck in my throat. 'Alleged?' I said.

He shrugged. 'Everyone's alleged until proven otherwise. I'll have a look at some point. Is it urgent?'

'God, no,' I said as my office loomed into view. It was nestled in the heart, or rather centre, of Margaret Thatcher House, a squat three-storey affair held up by scaffolding which was cold and hard and made of cranky inflexible materials that were largely redundant today. Or should be in a perfect world.

I switched views and sent Monty my most charming and wistful smile. 'I'd appreciate a quick squizz at the file, if I'm allowed to?'

'Absolutely not.' His firmness slightly stunned me. 'But I can give you a precis at some point. You know, we still haven't had dinner,' he said, and pulled up.

'I know,' I told him. I owed him a proper four-star chow down for a favour he had done Sam and I. 'I'll see what I can sort out at La Fleur. They've got to owe me a discount or two after this.'

'Your beauty is exceeded only by your generosity,' Monty said with a sardonic smile. I was never sure if this was his personal style just for me or if he flirted with everyone. 'Which,' he went on, 'is powerfully exceeded by your strong work ethic. Which, I also have to say is rather startling. But don't take that the wrong way, I think it's marvellous. Hope you make it through the day.'

'Yeah, well, flattery will get you everywhere,' I said with a painful wink and got out. 'I'll be in touch in the none too distant. Thanks for the lift and goodnight.'

That dinner would have to be organised pretty soon, I thought, as I swiped my card at the door and gave in to the biggest ever yawn. Sam had indicated that he thought my dad's attitude to the Witch Museum was tied up with whatever happened to his mum. If I wanted his approval to do with the museum as I wished then I'd need to sort that out and delve into the past. But discreetly so as not to draw attention and irritate his condition. Whatever that was.

Otherwise, if I couldn't, then there was no two ways about it: the Essex Witch Museum would simply have to be sold. The thought of it made me shudder.

Now that was a new one.

CHAPTER NINETEEN

'Good Christ. You look like you've been in a car crash.'
Derek's bony face loomed into focus. He was far too close
and breathing Weetabix fumes all over me.

For a moment I thought I was in bed and wondered if I had
got drunk last night and, no surely, I wouldn't ... No. That
would never happen, not if he was the last bloke on earth.

It took me about thirty seconds to recognise the false
ceiling and its square polyfibre tiles. Thank god for Margaret
Thatcher House. I'd never before been so grateful to see the
artificial suspended lights, the uniform slate-coloured carpet.
As I sat up the battleship filing cabinets swanned into view,
all chosen from the local authority's interior designers' swatch
set of various greys. Above them was Derek's sign: *You don't
have to be crazy to work here – but it helps*. It gave us all a
laugh – if you were sectioned then you couldn't work at all,
legitimately or otherwise.

'If you'd told me you were sick as a dog I would have never
asked you to come in.' Derek smiled and showed his yellow
teeth. 'What have you had? Someone should have been
eating those apples, shouldn't they?'

'What?'

'You need to keep the doctor away.' He retreated and perched his bottom on my desk. I didn't like it there but it was better than having him invade my personal space. He never looked particularly healthy because he had food allergies and seemed to exist off breakfast cereals, bacon, chips and oat milk. I'd suggested a nutritionist but he didn't apparently believe in 'other faiths'.

I shook myself as I woke up, becoming aware my body was aching all over. It took me a while but I tried flexing my shoulders and loosened them. The muscles on my right side were obviously in some state of disrepair for they set off sharp pains. Plus, my head was beginning to pound like a madman on an anvil with a big rubber joke hammer. 'Am I alive?' I asked Derek. 'I haven't died and gone to,' I surveyed the office suite, 'purgatory?'

Derek's big fat orange moustache quivered. He was very proud of it for it was bushy and thick. A complete contrast to the wheat-coloured strands that he combed over his pate to disguise the thinning of his hair. I had tried several times to persuade him to shave it all off declaring bald could be sexy these days. I mean, look at Billy Zane, Jason Statham, Vin Diesel. He didn't know any of them so I mentioned Duncan Goodhew and Ross Kemp but he wasn't convinced.

'Mmmm,' he said, peering closer. A strand of hair fell backwards off the top of his head and stuck out at a ninety-degree angle. 'You look awful peaky. I think perhaps you should go home.'

'No,' I told him. I'd willed myself here despite criminals, police, sex slaves, being whacked on the side of my head, vomiting in the yard and hardly sleeping at all. There was zero probability I was going to wuss out now like a lightweight. 'The team meeting's at 9.30, right?'

'True but under the circumstances I think it might be wiser if we continued without you, Rosie dear.'

'I'm not having an unauthorised absence,' I said, indignation growing. Not after all I'd been through.

'Well, yes, but no,' said Derek. 'I'll authorise it.'

'I'm here now, aren't I? Might as well get the meeting over and done with. I'll knock off early though if you don't mind.'

'You were snoring,' said a voice opposite. It was Charlie, my junior, who was a few years older than me. He wanted my job. 'Loudly,' he sniggered and smoothed his tie down over his shirt. It was navy with little anchors on it. His wife had bought it for him. She thought it was jaunty.

It wasn't jaunty. It was stupid.

'I'm fine, thank you very much,' I said, stood up and fell over. 'Just a bit fluey that's all.'

Derek righted me. 'All righty ho. Looks like she's in the right place, because this lady's not for turning.' He grinned and waited a second for a laugh.

None came.

Deflating only marginally, he clapped his hands together. 'Right, chop, chop suey, Charlie. Go and round the others up. Let's get this ole show on the road.'

The meeting went quickly in the blink of an eye. Possibly

several blinks and a micro-sleep. We trudged through the agenda. Things ticked over. Charlie queried his holiday leave. Marcia, who came in late, complained about her overtime rate. Stanley, who didn't even work in the department, started talking about the lack of vegetarian options on the in-house lunch menu, and Dennis, who was new and keen, asked about clarification on an urgent initiative that no one else had heard of.

Derek spluttered and prevaricated and eventually hurried us along till there was just one item left. A case about an eye injury on which we were collaborating with the Department of Work and Pensions. Someone needed to go and collect results from the designated optometric consultant. Optician in old money. I volunteered.

'All right,' said Derek. 'But if you still don't feel well afterwards may I suggest you go home.'

'I just might take you up on that,' I told him.

Doctor Roberts worked out of the hospital on Wednesdays. I was in the waiting room when my phone went. It was an unknown number though I recognised DS Edward's voice as soon as he said hello.

'Managed to get some shut-eye?'

'A little,' I told him.

'How's your head?'

'Still on my shoulders, thankfully.'

He chuckled then said, 'Listen, I just thought you should hear it from me.'

Intriguing.

'Well, we've reviewed your tape from the camera in the kitchen and ...' He paused as if collecting his thoughts.

'Yes?'

'We can clearly see you in the yard talking.'

'Uh-huh?'

'But it looks like there's no one else there.'

What exactly was he implying? 'You mean the girl is outside the field of vision?'

'Possibly. We should be able to see her feet though, if she was where you described her.'

'But?'

'We can't see any. It's not great quality, I admit, and the tape runs out seconds later.'

I thought this through. 'She must be further back then.'

There was silence for a beat, then he said, 'I thought this might be good news for you.'

How on earth did he work that one out? 'Why?'

'Might potentially be your ghost?'

I was flabbergasted. 'Of course it can't be. There are lots of explanations for the tape. I just need to find my way through them.' I was surprised that he, with his job, could countenance such a thing. Especially as the detectives seemed to have given Mary such a grilling about her account.

'Okay,' he said, sounding put out. 'Like I said, I thought I'd give you the heads-up. We're going to check around for more CCTV. There's a bit of a black spot at the rear of La Fleur. Mr Boundersby hadn't got round to installing surveillance cameras yet and QPC Technology who are practically opposite the back door had a faulty camera. Ironic really, given the nature of their business – security.' I heard him tut and imagined him shaking his head. 'We advised them to get it fixed but I'm not sure they've acted on recommendations as of yet. We'll look into further cameras but I'll need you to think back. See if you can remember more details about the girl. Height, clothes, hair, shoes, things like that.'

'Okay, I'll let you know,' I said, and hung up.

It wasn't the call I'd been hoping for.

The conversation, however, preyed on my mind while I was interviewing the doctor. I could hear her talking me through the results of the tests, concluding that the client's illness was genuine, but I was constantly thinking back over the flitting form of the yard girl. The one who pointed me to Gloria. I couldn't recall her exact height. She had seemed fragile, smaller than me and yet her face had, at times, been on a level with my own. I think. It was all a bit bleary.

Had she even been wearing shoes? I couldn't honestly remember. If I sent my mind back into the yard, if I tried to hold her image still, then I couldn't see anything but darkness beneath the knee. That was wrong.

But if I couldn't see anything did that mean the fault lay with me. Maybe I *had* seen something that wasn't there. Maybe my brain was playing tricks? Perhaps I'd caught something off Mary. Oh god. I remembered Sam telling me about the Salem witch-hunt. How girls had attested to seeing spectres. How more and more of them said they saw these crazy doppelgängers, even in court in front of sober judges. How the visions spread up to the ages. It was bizarre. Could you catch hysteria? I wondered.

Was I in fact succumbing to it?

Was it making me see things?

Doctor Roberts closed the file and pushed it across her desk to me.

'Believe me,' she finished, 'I've seen symptoms that are a lot more off the wall.'

I'd met Doctor Roberts several times before and she had always come across as a very erudite and helpful ophthalmic consultant. She was a bit older than me and had what I thought of as a very self-possessed chin.

I thanked her then I said, 'So Doctor Roberts, can I ask you a question, as a doctor?'

'Case-related?' she pushed her glasses over her long nose.

'No,' I told her. Honesty being the best policy on occasion.

'Okay, go ahead.'

I thought about how to phrase the question and came out with this: 'What would you say to a patient who told you they'd seen a ghost?'

'Have you?' Doctor Roberts folded her arms and regarded me with determined neutrality.

'It's someone I'm dealing with at the moment.'

'Well, I'd ask them to describe what they are seeing exactly – is it people or abstract things, shadows, colours or shapes? Feelings? Sounds? Movement that's not there?'

I thought about how Mary Boundersby had first described the apparition. 'What if they said they'd seen a woman ghost?'

Doctor Roberts didn't bat an eyelid. She kept her expression soft and friendly. 'Okay, then that would lead me more to think – is this something that's medically or physically wrong with the eye or is this a visual processing disorder?'

'Oh,' I said, feeling immensely calmed by her cool logic and total lack of excitement. 'What's visual processing?'

'A visual processing disorder occurs in the brain and hampers its ability to make sense of information taken in through the eyes. You know ninety per cent of vision is done in the brain?'

I shook my head, which still hurt and felt sorry for my own poor hampered brain. 'Didn't. No. But that makes sense.'

'Visual processing is different to issues with sight, clarity or sharpness of vision. It's more about how visual information is processed or interpreted by the brain. Or,' she paused, 'misinterpreted. People are usually *aware* that they are seeing things that aren't there or that there are shapes and flickers that they can't account for. It's a fascinating area. Sometimes patients see objects that get bigger or smaller. Micropsia or marcropsia are the proper names for that particular condition but it's also been called Alice in Wonderland syndrome.'

'Really?' This was amazing. The information emboldened me to go a step further and ask, 'What if they were seeing a woman in old-fashioned clothes?'

Again no frown or judgement passed over her face. Just consideration. 'Mmm. Well, there is a disorder, which has something to do with the degeneration of the macula, where symptoms involve sightings of people. Often in period costume.'

Whoa! A fuzz of excitement went off in my head and zipped down my neck. 'You're joking. Really?'

'Yes, you can look it up on the Internet. It's called Charles Bonnet syndrome. CBS for short.'

'Charles Bonnet?' I thought of Mary's description of the phantom with the bonnet. Was that a coincidence or a clue?

'That's right,' said Doctor Roberts. Behind her glasses grey eyes shone with sharp intelligence. 'Quite often patients will see things out the window – Victorian people walking around in their garden. Sometimes these strangers come up to the window and look through at them.'

I laughed, but she shook her head and said, 'No really. That's what they see. Can be quite alarming for the patient as you can imagine. It doesn't happen all the time, comes and goes. It's always in their central vision, not on the periphery. Because it's the macula that's effected with that condition and that's the part of the eye that's responsible for your fine vision. If it's impaired, it means you can't see detail. So that's when the brain decides to improvise.'

'I see,' I said without irony. What she was saying called to mind Mary's story about the woman walking past the window of her third-floor flat.

Doctor Roberts nodded at me. 'It's so interesting the way a person's brain does this when they start to lose their sight. It stumbles over the fact that it's not getting as much information as it used to so it fills in the gaps with fantasy patterns or images that it's stored. They're hallucinations of course. Nothing to do with dementia or mental health.'

'Hang on,' I said, and remembered Mary's large round

tortoiseshell glasses. Her prescription lenses were fairly thick, if I recalled. They made her eyes look bigger. 'But does this only happen when people are losing their sight? I mean, would they be aware that they were losing it?'

'No, not necessarily. Not at first. But if they are experiencing symptoms of Charles Bonnet's, then the degeneration would be noticeable.'

'Oh,' I said. Well, this might certainly help Mary's defence, if she still needed one now. I'd have to get on the blower to Ray. It was good news, I thought, then another question occurred. 'But can the patients recover?'

Doctor Roberts held my gaze, and answered without emotion, 'No, I'm afraid it's incurable. Blindness is inevitable.'

That was hard to hear.

Doctor Roberts was staring at my face. 'But it could be something else. There are plenty of options that could be explored to explain these sort of hallucinations: traumatic brain injury, or maybe a cerebrovascular accident.'

I didn't like the sound of the last one. 'A cerebellum accident?'

'A stroke.'

'Oh shit.' I had no great fondness for Mary Boundersby but one couldn't help feeling sympathetic: none of these sounded particularly good.

Doctor Roberts folded her arms carefully and leant across her desk. 'Listen, you should make an appointment really but I have got about thirty minutes. Hop up here.' She tapped the weird electric torture chair that all opticians have. 'And I'll do a preliminary exam.'

'Oh, it's not for me,' I protested. 'It really is for someone else I'm investigating on the side. Well, when I mean on the side, I mean not for the department. It's another matter. But I do think there might be something in what you're saying. Can I get her to give you a call?'

Doctor Roberts didn't look convinced. 'Rosie, you look dreadful. I think I should take a look at your right eye. Yes, I'll see your client but you've obviously been in some kind of fight yourself and I'm not letting your walk out of my surgery without checking you over first. No questions asked.'

'No, I'm okay, really.'

Her register didn't change as she continued to urge me. 'Would you like me to report your extracurricular activity to Derek? I have no qualms.'

The conviction in her voice made me hesitate.

'Sorry. I would be failing in my duties if I didn't look at that eye.' All resistance was futile: she was pulling on latex gloves. 'Now shut up and hop up,' she said. 'Please.'

CHAPTER TWENTY

I was asleep on the sofa when Sam got home. He tried to tiptoe around me but then started banging about in the kitchen and woke me up. I didn't mind. I was glad to see him. I wanted to talk about what I'd learnt today.

I turned on the lamps around the lounge area and kept the mood cosy. Then we sat down on the sofas with steaming piles of pasta. I was really hungry. And, to be honest, I was also glad to be spending some quality time with Sam. I felt like I had missed him today. Though we were going to be just friends, I liked the zippy feelings he gave me. I liked him. That was a good thing. Even if nothing happened. For the time being.

But we were both quite excited about talking to each other. Sam obviously had some interesting news to tell too. As ever, he was gentlemanly and let me go first.

I filled him in, between mouthfuls of tortellini, about the extraordinary conditions divulged by Doctor Roberts. He was similarly amazed by them and said 'Well, I'm blowed' several times and even made notes. The Charles Bonnet syndrome, he said, might explain a recurring visitation a man back in Adder's Fork had confided to him: an Edwardian gardener who peered through his French windows. I told him about the loss of sight and blindness thing and he said that unfortunately fitted.

I also informed Sam that I had phoned Ray Boundersby and relayed this information about these conditions to him. It was a difficult conversation to have, but I seemed to find time and time again that the right thing to do wasn't often the easiest option on hand.

As you can imagine, Ray wasn't over the moon about what I had to share but he promised to raise the subject with Mary and was grateful for Doctor Roberts's details, agreeing it was wise to book an appointment in the near future. I got the impression he was irritated with me or more likely with what I had to say. He probably had mixed feelings about everything. With good cause too. After all, the revelations of Jackson's repulsive activities must have taken the heat off Mary. The former was looking like a more likely contender for suspect number one in Seth's murder. Nevertheless, there were problems with Mary's credibility and this could explain them in a cool scientific way that courts would listen to with due care and diligence. Of course, it might mean that Mary lost her sight. Which was an unfair outcome, it was true. But whatever, she ought to be checked over. If it came to nothing then they would have just wasted an hour or two. If something was detected, then (hopefully) it could be treated and Mary would have a legal argument for her defence. He grudgingly conceded.

I had also, incidentally, been given a clean bill of health

with a notice to monitor myself for anything unusual and some strong prescription painkillers that had knocked me out as soon as I got home.

Sam had wisely spent most of the day in bed until he had been awoken by a call from DS Edwards checking he had all the tapes and who also ended up telling him about the absence of the yard girl on the ones his constables had already checked over. Sam agreed that she'd probably turn up on CCTV footage from some of the other concerns that backed on to the La Fleur yard. He expressed an interest in reviewing them, when they were recovered, and was politely surprised when DS Edwards agreed. 'He seems to have warmed up to us a bit,' he said, and smiled at me.

A flush of guilt spread through me. I muttered something about it being important to stay on the right side of the law and then fiddled with the tortellini.

'I know it looks like we may have got a measure on Seth's unfortunate demise,' he said. 'But I'm afraid it doesn't close the case as far as I'm concerned. There are a number of incidents that have yet to be explained. It's not only Mary who has seen the apparition, remember. MT has perceived it too.'

At the mention of her name, I relaxed a bit. Sam, after all, had a thing for MT and made no bones about hiding that. That meant it was okay for me to maybe have a thing with Jason. Made sense, didn't it? He might even get jealous and be spurred into action. Who could tell?

'As well as the many others who have attested to hearing it,' he was saying, leaning into the armchair, his feet up on one of my white stools. 'Then there's the writing on the wall. I'm still at a loss. I don't like being at a loss,' he said then, amazingly, popped open a bottle of wine and poured himself a glass. 'You're not having any on those painkillers,' he said, waving the bottle, and put it down close by his feet. Out of my reach.

I thought about protesting but couldn't be bothered. Plus, he was right. Booze would put me straight to sleep again.

'So,' he went on and took a long glug, the rotter. 'Once I'd finished talking to DS Edwards, I was awake. There was no point trying to go back to sleep. It was quite late in the afternoon but I decided to take myself off to the Metropolitan Archives to have a bit of a dig around in La Fleur's past. As I said, there are certain things that don't add up, and I'm interested in that daisy wheel, the demon trap. I'd quite like to date it. Anyway, the archives aren't far from La Fleur actually. Though I should have got started earlier really because I was just getting stuck in when they booted me out and closed. I'll go back first thing tomorrow.'

'Okay,' I said. 'So what did you find out?'

'Well, Femi was right when he said that bit of London is dark.' He put his hand under his chin and said almost to himself, 'Now, that's a thought! I wonder how much he knows,' and then appeared to drift off.

He became aware of me waiting for him and twitched his head. 'Yes, sorry, well, a few bits and bobs of what I learnt, if communicated to impressionable minds, could certainly encourage people to attribute negative meaning to random incidents they may have been witness to aurally or visually.'

I tried to translate. 'There's stuff gone on there that might give people the heebie-jeebies?'

'Yes, the place is crawling with death and nasties. Much worse than Essex. So much denser, probably because it's been intensely populated for such a long time. I mean, right on the corner of Fetter Lane and Fleet Street there was an execution site. That's literally a stone's throw from La Fleur. We've passed it several times. The Catholic priest and accused traitor Christopher Bales was hanged here in 1590. Some poor sod who only made a jerkin for Bales was executed up the road in Smithfield. Anthony Babbington, a plotter aiming to get Mary Queen of Scots on Elizabeth's throne, was executed at Lincoln's Inn Fields, right where the bandstand is now. This chap was hung then cut down from the gallows, still alive and conscious, and made to watch as the executioner hacked off his "privy parts".'

'Bloody hell.'

'Literally, I would say, for they were then flung on the fire. After this followed disembowelment and dismemberment.'

'What a way to go.'

'Indeed. The public outcry that followed this caused Elizabeth to insist his fellow conspirators, who were to expect the same, should be dead before the disembowelment and so forth.'

I shook my head slowly and shuddered. 'How kind. But this means they were gutted, right?'

'It does.'

'Like Seth?'

'But he wasn't hung or quartered.'

I thought about the blood in the cracks of the cellar and imagined the sight Mary would have seen if that had taken place. It made me giddy with revulsion. 'But he was hung up. To the hook.'

'And Newgate Prison was up the road too,' Sam continued, oblivious to my dry and silent retch. 'About two hundred and fifty metres from La Fleur. It was the main site of London's gallows after they were moved from Tyburn in 1783. The executions took place in public until 1868. In fact, if you draw a line between Lincoln's Inn, the Fetter Lane execution site and Newgate, they form a neat triangle of death.'

'Nice,' I said. 'And I bet you're going to tell me that La Fleur is right in the centre?'

'No, not in the centre but in it, yes. If you include Smithfield's too it's a kind of trapezium of death.'

'Not so catchy,' I murmured and grimaced.

'Quite so,' he nodded. 'And there's more. Can you cope?'

'Mmm.' I was feeling a bit queasy to be honest. 'All this stuff is a bit too Chamber of Horrors for me,' I said. 'I find it depressing. It makes me think of damp smells and the idea that there is dirt on the floor that can't be hoovered up. Do you know what I mean?' I asked Sam.

He scrunched his forehead up. 'Eh?'

I knew what I meant.

'Okay, well, this might cheer you up. Quite amusing, I thought. You know those rooms that you pointed out that stick out over Fleet Street? The Tudor-looking ones. Well, I discovered that they're called Prince Henry's Room, even though they are plural!'

'Crazy!' I said.

'Hang on, I'm coming to it. Well, it's one of the few buildings to survive the Great Fire of London, you know, though the site goes way back beyond that to property owned by the Knights Templars. But for a while in the eighteenth and nineteenth century the front part of the house featured a Mrs Salmon's Waxworks which were in fact, as you say, a Chamber of Horrors of sorts. Though these were diverting displays, really. There was apparently one of Boudicca, a Turkish harem, and an automated figure of Old Mother Shipton, a clairvoyant witch from Skipton. Quite famous. But there was one that sounds hilarious. That of Hermonia, a Roman noblewoman. Her father offended the emperor and was sentenced to be starved to death. He evaded the reaper by suckling at his own daughter's breast!'

I stared at him. For one of the first times in my life I was speechless.

'I thought you'd find that funny,' he pushed on.

'Jesus Christ. Sam! That's gross. And there was me thinking that the Witch Museum was tacky.'

'Now you're sounding like an American teenager.'

'Hey, you have completely lost any moral high ground you once had.' I folded my arms high.

Sam rubbed his hair and looked confused. 'Oh, all right. I thought you'd laugh. They also had a tableau depicting King Charles I upon the scaffold,' he offered by way of consolation.

'God,' I said. 'You're right, though. All of it's creepy. Femi, for all his weird path-of-the-righteous-man act, was totally on the ball. If he knew half of that, it would make the place appear to him as corrupt and grotesque. Seriously, I've gone off La Fleur big time. I was going to take Monty there, but, man, that place has got a dark and belligerent past.'

'Monty?' Sam's eyebrows rose.

'Yes, you remember. I said I'd buy him dinner after the work he did for us with the witch bones.'

'Am I invited?'

I squinted at him. 'If you want?'

He sent me a look I couldn't work out. It was either a 'get over yourself' expression or a 'cheeky cow' glance. I was going to ask him to clarify when he said, 'And present.'

'Eh?'

'La Fleur's sordid past taints the present too.'

'Oh,' I said, getting his point. 'You mean, last night?'

He nodded. 'The discovery of Gloria and Ruby I find supremely unsettling.' This was something, coming from the guru of the Essex Witch Museum with all its gruesome frights. 'I won't hide it – I've been feeling on edge and upset all day. How the girls are going to recover, I really don't know.'

His concern caused a well of deep affection to open within me. These soft moments of his were affecting and I just couldn't help appreciating him more. At the same time, I knew exactly how he felt. 'People are so horrible to each other. I'm amazed that kid Jackson was capable though. He didn't look more than mid-twenties to me.' And he'd been slight of build too, not tough-looking or macho. Just opportunistic. And clearly devoid of any moral compass. Terrifying.

'Matthew Hopkins, the self-appointed Witchfinder

General,' Sam said. 'He was probably around twenty-six when he died. Never underestimate people. Where there is a will there is a way.'

'Especially, if that will runs evil,' I said, and crossed my arms, feeling this time, that I did probably look like a teenager. 'I still can't quite believe it. That that was going on next door. What were they going to do with them? Gloria and Ruby? What would have happened if we hadn't found them when we did?'

'It's not worth thinking on.' Sam fell silent and took an urgent draught of the wine.

The shadow of unspoken horror had fallen over the room, subduing the atmosphere and making the pair of us twitch uncomfortably and avoid eye contact.

Hunching forward, I watched Sam's hair fall over his face in its familiar way. His lips, full yet tight and pale, were beginning to tinge Rioja-purple in the soft little wrinkles. He tapped his glass abruptly, put it down, sat back into his chair, then looked at me.

The darkness in his eyes remained. There was activity behind them. Memories, maybe, colliding. Flints sparking. A kaleidoscope of feelings seemed to flicker across his face but I couldn't tell what they were. The base note of it all was a sadness that radiated out of his body. I had felt it before, but couldn't discern detail or understand where it came from. The texture was singular and unique. I could feel it now, like a cold fire burning. 'At least they weren't children,' he said, and again I felt like there was more he had left unspoken.

Fleetingly I wondered how he had arrived at that thought, but I let that go too and only commented, 'What a horrific notion.'

'It happens you know,' Sam said, in a low, shaken voice. Breaking my gaze, he reached for the glass of wine, finished it in one gulp and filled it up again.

This was very un-Sam. This was a huge shift. There was indeed a little mystery there, which I would have to try to unpick. It occurred to me again, as it did on these rare occasions when he took me by surprise, that despite the feeling I had of knowing this man very well, to a certain extent he remained a stranger. I knew so little about his past and what he did. I should really make some more effort. We should definitely get to know each other more before anything progressed. When we wrapped up this case and went back to the museum I would cook him a meal and we could talk maybe a little bit about him. I didn't even know how he had met my grandfather or how Septimus had come to trust him so.

I was considering phrasing this into a suggestion, when he suddenly said, 'But to a certain extent it explains the phenomenon reported by Mary and the staff. Some of it at least.'

That threw me. I couldn't remember the 'it' to which he was referring.

He frowned at my blankness. 'The chains clanking, wailing and so on.' When I didn't register, his voice rose slightly. 'The phenomenon reported by staff at La Fleur? Much of it must be now attributed to the plight of Gloria and Ruby.'

I watched him shudder again and knock back more red. 'Jackson's uncle's cellar adjoins the restaurant's. DS Edwards told me that it looks like the girls had been pulling away some of the wall bricks. Trying to escape. It's quite possible that the sounds made by them could have carried through to La Fleur: scratches, moans, chains. Acoustics in old buildings are often unconventional.'

'Yes, you could be right.' I was glad the practicalities of the case were bringing him back from his dark place.

'And if these eye conditions explain Mary's visions we may be on the home straight to a certain extent.' The animation was back in his eyes. He was happy as long as he wasn't thinking about himself. 'Certainly the woman in the bonnet could be explained by that syndrome,' he went on. 'And yet, the woman Mary reported seeing in the cellar ...' He stopped momentarily and fixed me with a sharp look. 'Do you realise she's remarkably similar to the girl you attest to seeing in the yard? She said the same thing: "Vover vere," which you translated as "Over there" and then, allegedly, she pointed you in the direction of the captive women.'

I'd come to a conclusion about that this afternoon. 'Agreed. Which suggests to me that because Mary and I have seen something similar then the probability is that we've seen *someone*. A real woman. I concede that it's possible Mary's description might have influenced what I saw. Doctor Roberts was saying that the brain is responsible for interpreting the signals it gets from the eye. It was foggy last night so my brain might have been filling in details that were actually obscured by the mist. And then afterwards, when I gave my description, I was concussed, I think. I can't really remember the actual sight clearly now. Only my description of it. Is that weird?'

'Memories aren't reliable. You must know that. Given the similarities of both your descriptions – thin, pale, reddish – I would wonder if, whether conscious or not, you might have been trying to give credence to Mary's account.'

'It's possible.' I should check what I'd written down as Mary's description. 'Can you pass over my notebook please, Sam? I want to have a look at something.' It was on the coffee table next to my dirty plate.

I flipped through the pages. On the date we had interviewed Ray and Mary Boundersby I had helpfully written: *30th December. Not a rat. Vover vere. Funnel. Crazy. Toilets. MT. Toilets. Floater. Slutty. Potential fire hazard?* Underneath I'd drawn a picture of a stick woman with big hair sitting on a toilet. There was a big red cross over the top of her and lots of childish scribble. Marta Thompson.

'Anything?' said Sam. 'Can I see?'

'No,' I told him, and snapped it firmly shut. I really needed a more consistent approach to note-taking. Sometimes I was flakier than a 99.

'Well, no matter. There's a good book on London's murder houses that mentioned Fetter Lane,' he said, as if he were trying to cheer me up. 'It's in the archives.'

'Go on,' I said, hiding the notebook down the back of the sofa.

'Found it but didn't get to read it today. It was a reference book. They literally took it out of my hands.'

'Have you googled?'

He smiled, his lips pulling slightly to the left. Such a lovely genuine wonky smile. 'Of course. The Internet doesn't have the monopoly on information, as we're both well aware. Things slip through. Books still work.'

'Yep.' That had been so in a previous case, certainly. 'Early morning for you then tomorrow, Mr Stone. What time do the archives open?'

'Nine thirty sharp. What are you going to do?' he asked as my phone began to beep. 'Laze in bed?'

'Don't know.' It didn't sound like a bad idea. I pulled out my phone and clocked the text message that had just arrived. Another number I didn't recognise. I clicked on it and read: *Can do tomorrow. 2.30pm.*

'Actually, Sam,' I told him. 'It looks like I'll be visiting Mr Henry Warren.'

CHAPTER TWENTY-ONE

Warren's address was very close to Lincoln's Inn Fields. In fact, I had to pass over the bandstand on my way there and had a good old shudder about Mr Babbington's chopped-off privy parts.

The building where Henry Warren worked was grand and old like most of its tall, elegant neighbours. According to the website, the firm specialised in commercial disputes across corporate/chancery and offshore, whatever that meant. Something legal, I assumed, as it was referred to as a 'chambers'. The pompous title always made me think of bed-pans and Goosey Gander.

Warren, himself, turned out to be a bit of a Boris Johnson type of bloke. He'd gelled a splat of gingery-blond hair into submission by pressing it flat against his head in a 1920s schoolboy style. There was something about him that reminded me of Charlie back in the office. Both had a similar curve to their gut and a toothy, gappy grin. Red cheeks too. But while Charlie's made him look like he was on the verge of a heart attack, Henry Warren's gave the impression of frank health. The cut-glass accent was pronounced and he had a smothering, double-fisted handshake.

He told me to take a chair, braying like a donkey, then apologised for only sparing me a couple of minutes as something unforeseen had come up: he was waiting for a phone call that he would 'simply have to take'.

I thanked him for agreeing to see me, in spite of this, and promptly got down to business. No point messing with small talk.

'We have been investigating La Fleur,' I said. 'Some of the odd things that have been going on there.'

'Not sure I'd classify them as "odd". Outrageous perhaps.' He jerked a pink cuff out of his sleeve and straightened the cufflink. Gold, I noted.

'Indeed.' I bowed my head in acknowledgement. 'You're right. There have been some shocking revelations.'

'You can say that again. A brothel right next to old Boundersby's attempt at self-aggrandisement!' He let go a little smirk. 'So vulgar. Must be quite a blow to the poor fellow – he's tried so hard to distance himself from the gutter.' I reckon he would have been grinning broadly if I hadn't already announced I was working for Ray.

I decided he was a prick and had probably been a bully when younger. Big guys like Henry, rugger buggers, full of the superlative confidence that money and wealth bring, always seemed to end up in business, finance or law. Somewhere they could shout, harangue or argue for a living.

'Oh, it wasn't a brothel,' I said, keen to burst his bubble. 'They kidnapped girls and chained them up in the cellars.

Made them do sex acts. Raped them.' That's what happened. No point beating around the bush. Horror was horror. Warren should know what had really gone down. There were no jokes to be made about it or smirking to be done.

'Oh?' he said, eyes wide. Two even redder rashes appeared in the middles of his cheeks. 'I had no idea that sort of thing was …' He swallowed hard and broke eye contact.

For a moment I wondered if I had given too much away. DS Edwards had told me not to speak about the case.

'I mean, that's what I heard,' I added. 'It goes on, you know, that sort of thing. Everywhere. But actually despite the utter heinousness of that shit storm that's not what I'm here about. I wanted to ask you about La Fleur being haunted.'

'Oh yes?' he asked and crossed his legs under the desk. Monographed socks appeared over super-shiny lace-ups. Bet he didn't polish them himself.

I eyed him carefully ready to note his reaction. 'Where did you hear about it?'

'Me? Hear about it? Haunted?' His face was more relaxed now, full of rosy smile. Possibly he was relieved to be on safer ground: ghosts were easier to deal with than sex traffickers. I certainly knew which frightened me more.

He looked like he was waiting for me to clarify so I skimmed my notebook for some detail to hook on to. 'Did you tell anyone at the restaurant that it was haunted?'

'Me?' he said, then narrowed his eyes. 'Why?'

'Well, your name has been mentioned in this regard.'

Right on cue his phone started ringing.

'I'm sorry, Ms Strange,' Henry Warren gestured to his desk. 'One moment. I'll have to get this. Do you mind popping outside? Confidential. I'll see you presently.' He waited for me to leave.

I grabbed my bag and made towards the door.

'Denise will take care of you,' he called. Then he returned to the phone and I heard him say, 'Johnny, what's the problem …?'

Denise was at her desk. Neat and tidy and antique. Like the desk. She smiled with professional courtesy and asked if I'd like a coffee while I waited for Mr Warren. Might as well, I thought.

Indulging me in professional small talk the PA commented on the mildness of the day as she guided me to a sofa, asked how I took it, then went off to fetch refreshments.

A coffee table was piled with copies of *Country & Town House* magazine, the *Lady* and *Good Housekeeping*. I had no desire to read any of them so turned my attention to the olde worlde charm of the antechamber which was represented by lots of old pictures that covered the walls. Some were paintings others photographs, sepia-tinted. Above my head was a pencil sketch of Lincoln's Inn Fields as it had been maybe three hundred years ago, complete with horses and carriages. Beside it was an engraving of another building in the square that I had passed coming here – a magnificent portico built in the classical style with huge columns. The Royal College of Surgeons apparently. Right above this was another picture, which at first glance seemed of a different genre to the rest – a pencil drawing of a skeleton suspended in a curved arch. I had had an odd experience with a skeleton recently so it caught my eye. The cranium had been sketched in a stylised manner to give the impression the head was grinning. The eye sockets, though empty, were slanted to make the skull look angry. Underneath it a caption read, *The Skeleton of Elizabeth Brownrigg in Surgeon's Hall.*

'Ah-ha!' Denise offered me a matching ceramic cup and saucer. 'MT went straight for that too.' Her face was angled towards the picture. When she registered my slight bewilderment, she added, 'Sorry. I assumed you were a friend of Marta's. You're from La Fleur, aren't you? Henry mentioned your appointment ...'

'Oh yes,' I said vaguely, took the coffee from Denise and sipped it.

'That's her. The skeleton.' With her now free hand Denise pointed to another portrait above the grinning skull. 'When she was alive.'

For a moment, I was confused as to whether she was talking about MT but did as I was told and directed my gaze to the indicated picture. It comprised two sections. At the top was a plain portrait of a sneering woman, supposedly this Elizabeth Brownrigg, dressed in a corset dress, full skirt, shawl and wide-brimmed hat on top. Beneath her a scene had been sketched: a dingy room with stairs descending into a subterranean space. In there the Brownrigg woman was depicted arching her back, arm high, whip in hand about to beat a strangely familiar figure – that of a thin frail girl, dressed in sackcloth, long dark hair and sores around her mouth.

I gave a start as I took in the detail.

Oh god.

The stairs, the hook, the cellar. The dimensions of the room looked remarkably similar.

I swallowed and stepped back, my heart beginning to pound at a rate. 'My goodness.'

'MT had exactly the same reaction,' Denise said, and tactfully removed the trembling cup from my hands before I started spilling the coffee. 'It's all silly superstitions, I know. You can't help it sometimes can you, but I did wonder if it might account for some of the bad luck you've had at La Fleur,' she said. 'It being old Brownrigg's house.'

The effect her words had on me immediately alarmed Denise.

'Oh dear,' she said. 'You've gone quite pale, my dear. Let me get you a glass of water.'

I sat down heavily on the sofa.

And tried to slow my brain.

Had this Elizabeth Brownrigg murdered that girl?

That girl who was hooked up like Seth had been? Who looked shockingly like the girl in the yard?

No, I stopped myself. How friggin' stupid is that?

That was a coincidence, that's all. And anyway the spectre that had reportedly been seen in the yard was a woman with a wide-brimmed hat. A bonnet.

I turned my face slowly back to the portrait of Elizabeth Brownrigg. A woman whose description pretty much matched the spectre's.

But she was a symptom, surely, of Charles Bonnet syndrome.

But then hadn't MT seen this bonnet-clad spectre too?

And hadn't MT been here?

Yes, she had. Denise had just told me.

MT had been here and she had seen the picture of Elizabeth Brownrigg.

And yet the front-of-house hostess had not mentioned that to us.

In fact, she'd not told Mary or Ray or anyone else either. But the likeness of the apparition she'd seen bore a striking similarity to the ghost she'd described gliding past her in the toilet.

To the ghost, she had *said* she'd seen.

'Blimey,' I said, and slapped my forehead. Things were starting to become glaringly obvious.

'There you go,' said Denise and bent down with the glass of water. 'Have a sip. Are you all right?'

My breaths were still coming in short and fast. 'I didn't know about Brownrigg. That La Fleur was once her house.'

'I'm surprised,' she said, then qualified. 'I would have thought that MT would have—'

'Yes,' I said, interrupting. 'When did she see that? MT? Can you remember? Why was she here?'

'Oh,' Denise looked briefly uncertain of herself. 'She's been dating Mr Warren on and off for a few months now. I don't think it's serious. At least not on his part, but she seems keen.'

'Really? How long has she been seeing him? When did she notice this?' I gestured to the wall.

'Now, let me see,' said Denise. 'I remember that first time, she'd been rather upset about waiting for Mr Warren. I don't think she had a lot of time to spare. But he'd had a long meeting that went over. Now who was it with?' she muttered out loud and flitted back to her desk. 'If I can remember that, then I can find the date.' She unlocked her laptop and began to browse. 'Ah yes, Purkiss and West, that's right.'

My mind was clicking over so quickly that I wasn't paying full attention to the way I was speaking and my words were coming out a bit rushed and whiney. 'When was it? Can you find out please?' I grabbed my notebook and tried to trace through my notes to see when Mary and Ray had told us all the strangeness began.

'Here we go,' said Denise, bringing up Warren's diary. 'Yes, it was early in the new year.'

'When? Please? Exactly? Can you get me the date?' I asked, finding the right notebook entry.

Here it was: Mary had seen the first apparition in the cellar in December. The one that was all thin and bloody. I cast a glance at the engraving of the girl strung up to the hook. She had a chain round her neck too. Chained up like the girls next door. The past repeating itself. Shit. How awful. But that wasn't the issue here, was it?

Think, Rosie, I told myself. When did Mary tell the staff about the woman in the bonnet? I needed to know when she went public with her confession. I turned over a page and there it was.

According to my notes the sighting had taken place a week later on Friday 6 January. Then there was nothing until … I paused, flicked a few pages forward then took a breath … There was nothing else until MT saw that floater in the toilet.

'Here you go,' said Denise. 'I thought it was January but it wasn't. It was the beginning of February. The third.' She smiled triumphantly.

I looked at my notebook and read the date that MT had seen the apparition in the toilets. There was no way it was a coincidence. It was the following evening. The fourth.

'Jesus.' I said, and got to my feet. 'It's her! Got to be. She's fabricated the whole thing!'

I slipped my notebook into my bag and said hurried goodbyes to Denise.

'He won't be long now, Ms Strange, I'm sure,' she bleated apologetically.

'It's fine,' I said. 'He's been more than helpful. Please say goodbye from me.'

Outside on the steps I took out my phone. It began to ring in my hand as I held it to my ear.

'Hello?' It was Sam. 'Rosie, can you meet me at La Fleur in thirty minutes. I've got some important news.'

'Yes, on my way, but, oh god, Sam. I've just made a discovery – I think I know who killed Seth,' I jabbed down the phone.

'Me too,' he gabbled. Then before he hung up, he added, 'A real turn up though. I would never have suspected him.'

CHAPTER TWENTY-TWO

I sat in La Fleur drumming my fingers on the table and stared at MT preening in the mirror behind the bar. She couldn't see me where I was, in the shadows of the circular staircase. There was a glitzy standard lamp plugged into the wall but I hadn't turned it on, purely so I could stay here unobserved.

She flicked back her hair and bent her neck to the mirror, tilting her face to the light to check something on her cheek. Unmistakably though superficially attractive, I was trying to work out why she'd go to all this tremendous trouble. What was her motive? What did she want to achieve?

The glass door to the restaurant caught the light as it opened and Sam bustled in. His face was tight and he was biting his lip. I stood up and waved at him from the shadows.

As he got closer I was unable to contain myself and the words 'Oh my god oh my god oh my god' tumbled out of my mouth.

'Shh,' he said. 'Sit down.'

I darted a glance at the bar and noted that MT was watching both of us. But then Agatha came in with a bunch of clean glasses and said something and she turned round to speak to her.

Sam took my arm and bundled me back into the shadows.

'It's astonishing,' he said. 'I don't want to talk here. It's not safe. Let's go to the pub down the road.'

I gathered up my stuff and within fifteen minutes we were ensconced in a snug in the Leicester where we had first talked to Joel.

I leant back against the wood panelling and took a long slug of the cider Sam had bought me at the bar. I was thirsty and the drink took some of the nervous fizz out of me and calmed me down. A fire was roaring in the hearth. The place was cosy, dark, full of Victoriana, like something out of a Dickens novel. Someone had helped that impression along by lighting candles on each table. It felt like the right place for a secret powwow.

'Okay,' said Sam. He had bought a half of real ale so I knew he must be excited too. 'I went back to the archives today and checked out that book I told you about. And guess what?'

'La Fleur is built on a murder house.' The candle on our table flickered appropriately.

'That's right,' he said, and cracked a little half-smile. 'It was the site of a notorious and vicious murder committed by an intensely unpopular woman.'

'Elizabeth Brownrigg,' I finished.

'Oh.' That floored him. 'How did you …?' His mouth hung open a second longer.

'Go on, go on. I'll tell you in a minute. What was the crime? What happened there?'

'Brownrigg was a nasty piece of work. She was a practising midwife and therefore held a certain status in the community. Orphans from the Foundling Hospital up the road were sent to her, ostensibly as servants, housemaids, to be apprentices and trained up. But Brownrigg was a sadist. She punished them for the slightest thing, then at some point, she discovered she got a kick out of inflicting the punishments and it spilt over into torture. Things came to a head when she tortured a Mary Mitchell, a Mary Jones, then a Mary Clifford.'

'Oh,' I said, genuinely surprised. 'Three Marys. That's come up before, hasn't it?

'There's three Marys at La Fleur now.'

Some green wood in the fireplace hissed and popped. Sam and I and a man who was seated at the table opposite, looked over. A small coal fell out of the grate.

'Is it relevant?' I turned back to Sam. 'Coincidence?'

Sam drew away from the fireplace. His eyes were thoughtful. 'There is a possibility it may well have sown seeds for future events to flourish.'

'What do you mean?' I asked him. 'How can the incidence of three women with the same name affect anything at all? Other than create ridiculously shortened nicknames that sound American but aren't.'

'Precisely,' he said, and smoothed his fingers over the notebook he had taken out and laid next to his glass. 'It's an aside, however, worth stopping for a moment to consider – this alignment may have created the right conditions for something to stir, something that had lain dormant for a very long time perhaps. A theory exists that the numerous articulations of correct names can be used to invoke not only the dead but also demons.' He caught my gaze and shrugged. 'Not that I've had any direct experience myself.'

There was a jumble of words tumbling over themselves in my head, trying to sort themselves into some kind of order. Eventually I managed it, 'Are you suggesting demons have been at work at La Fleur?'

'I'm just throwing it into the ring.' He frowned over the rim of his glass.

Oh dear. Just when I thought we were doing so well.

'Yes, you might well look like that, Rosie,' he said, his tone reproachful, 'but I'll have you know your grandfather met several men and women on his travels who asserted they had witnessed demonic evocations.'

The man in the suit across the room looked over his newspaper and checked Sam out.

'Shh,' I said, and moved closer in. 'You're talking too loudly; people can hear. Anyway, we now know that medicine can explain any number of conditions. I'm thinking Charles Bonnet syndrome, I'm thinking epilepsy, I'm thinking that we are no longer living in the Dark Ages.'

Sam took that with good grace and bent to my ear. 'Septimus told me he once met a very interesting Icelandic shaman who summoned spirits by repeating their true name. In fact he also reported seeing a manifestation himself. Yes, your granddad, with his own eyes,' he asserted with triumph. 'Although he did remark the said shaman had first required him to partake of a peace pipe which contained something ritualistic that may or may not have been of the whacky baccy variety.'

I just sat there and stared at him for a moment. My granddad had smoked weed? Possibly? And knew Icelandic shamans. I should have known him better. What a guy.

'Anyway,' Sam said, reading something in my face. 'That aside, Mary and MT saw something. Whatever its origins. The uncanny woman they described was similar and specific.' Underneath the notebook he had an A4 plastic wallet, which he slid out. Presently, he removed a sheet of paper, which bore a line drawing of a woman sitting in a cell. She was wearing a wide-brimmed straw hat, a striped corset top, full skirt and a shawl. 'In terms of description,' Sam pointed at the bodice, 'the clothes certainly are remarkably similar to what both women attested to seeing.'

'Elizabeth Brownrigg,' I confirmed.

'Yes,' he said, loud again. 'I'm keen to know how you discovered this?'

'Later,' I said. 'What exactly did she do?'

Little narrow lines appeared above his eyebrows, bunching them together to make longer deeper ones. 'She subjected her charges to countless awful treatments: whipping, punching, kickings. She'd dip their heads into pails of water and laugh. But Mary Clifford,' he continued, 'gradually became the primary focus for Brownrigg's sadistic urges. She was young, only fourteen, and was frequently tied up to a hook in the kitchen ceiling, stripped naked and beaten with a hearth broom, a horsewhip or a cane till she was unconscious.' He looked at me and repeated, 'Tied to a hook and whipped.'

'Fuck.' I didn't need him to draw parallels between Seth's murder and this ancient atrocity. I'd seen it depicted on Warren's PA's wall.

'Right here, in the cellar of La Fleur, I presume?'

'Yes.' Sam shuddered and breathed out so heavily the candle flame almost went out.

'People were cruel,' I stated simplistically. 'Still are. So what happened? In the end?'

'I printed it out for you,' he said, and passed an A4 sheet over the table.

The text was narrow but legible. It was clear this was a section from a larger document. Sam had drawn a square round the relevant part. I read it:

In the course of this most inhuman treatment a jack-chain was fixed round her neck, the end of which was fastened to the yard door, and then it was pulled as tight as possible without strangling her. A day being passed in the practice of these savage barbarities, the girl was remanded to the coal-hole at night, her hands being tied behind her, and the chain still remaining about her neck.

The elder son one day directed Mary Clifford to put up a half-tester bedstead, but the poor girl was unable to do it; on which he beat her till she could no longer support his severity. Mrs Brownrigg would sometimes seize the poor girl by the cheeks and, forcing the skin down violently with her fingers, cause the blood to gush from her eyes.

The last clause was underlined several times. I read it out loud to Sam. 'Shit that's what it said on the wall right?'

His expression was grave. 'More or less the same words.'

'Uh-huh. I've really got to tell you what I found out at Henry Warren's. Just let me finish this.' I kept my mouth shut and read the next lines.

Mary Clifford, unable to bear these repeated severities, complained of her hard treatment to a French lady who lodged in the house; and she having represented the impropriety of such behaviour to Mrs Brownrigg, the inhuman monster flew at the girl and cut her tongue in two places with a pair of scissors.

Which meant, I thought as a cold chill broke through my pores, that she couldn't speak properly. Just like the girl in the yard. No, that wasn't possible though. This was a set-up. Had to be. I read on.

On the morning of the 13th of July this barbarous woman went into the kitchen and, after obliging Mary Clifford to strip to the skin, drew her up to the staple; and though her body was an entire sore, from former bruises, yet this wretch renewed her cruelties with her accustomed severity.

After whipping her till the blood streamed down her body she let her down, and made her wash herself in a tub of cold water, Mary Mitchell, the other poor girl, being present during this transaction. While Clifford was washing herself Mrs Brownrigg struck her on the shoulders, already sore with former bruises, with the butt-end of a whip; and she treated the child in this manner five times in the same day.

I threw it down unable to read any more. 'Five times a day. That poor child, those poor children.' They were stories lost in time. Now found again. 'I hope they got her? Brownrigg?' I asked Sam, not really sure if I wanted to know the answer.

'Eventually she was discovered,' Sam said. 'Mary Clifford's

stepmother came to see her. After some kerfuffle she and the neighbours were able to search the house. They found her stepdaughter in a very sorry state hidden in a cupboard and did rescue her but it was too late – she died from her multiple injuries. Brownrigg was tried and then hanged at Tyburn. She was absolutely reviled and became rather a bogeyman in later years.'

'Good,' I said. 'What a nasty piece of work. Those poor girls. Treated like trash. Like slaves.' Then I thought of Gloria and Ruby and, again, the girl in the yard who had pointed me to them. The thought, the parallel, was greatly troubling.

'You're right, Rosie: cruelty doesn't age,' Sam voiced my thoughts, though a little more fluently. 'It still flourishes where it can. A strange dirty nick in the human character, unchanged by either evolution or prosperity. One can only wonder why that is. But such questions we may put aside for now. We have a case to hand, to which this is of great and pressing relevance.' He tapped the table to get my attention back. 'I wanted to ensure I had as much detail as possible. I felt it imperative I didn't miss anything vital. So I returned to the enquiry desk and asked the young woman there, Anna, if she knew where I could find more information on this Elizabeth Brownrigg.'

I thought about asking him how he had got on first-name terms with the archivist but then decided not to give in to sulkiness and buttoned my mouth again.

'Now, as it turned out,' he said, voice low in storytelling mode. 'Anna hadn't been in yesterday. She had the day off for a doctor's appointment and the hair salon.'

'Is that relevant?' I asked, irritated. I would like to think I had been soured by thoughts of human brutality, but I knew myself too well, and it was more likely my motives were less noble. And hypocritical.

'Yes, it is,' Sam said softly although with emphasis. 'Because Anna hadn't been there when I asked about Brownrigg yesterday. Do you want to guess what she said when I asked about the murderess?'

'No. Tell me. Tell me now.' I was trying to suppress my pouty face.

Sam's eyes glittered. 'She said, "Oh, wow, she's popular."'

'Huh!' I said, and snorted. 'What a way to refer to such a vicious bitch.' That was slightly more emotive than intended.

'I made the same comment myself with less colourful language,' he tried to chuckle. 'Anna apologised, of course, but explained that no one had looked into Brownrigg for years until recently another young man had been asking about her. He was distinctive, she said, quite charming with curly black hair and very blue eyes. She looked up his name for me. It was Tom Limbert.'

'Oh no,' I cried, genuinely shocked and then absurdly moved. Not Tom. Dear god, I could just imagine poor Mary's distress when she learnt of the betrayal. Hadn't she been through enough already?

'I have to admit,' said Sam. 'I was quite surprised. It's not going to go down well, is it?'

I shook my head and thought of something. 'Didn't Tom say he knew MT before the restaurant?' It was starting to fit together.

'That's right,' said Sam. 'They were at university together. I checked them out. He read History and got a low 2.2. She took Business, 2.1.'

'Interesting,' I said thinking it over. 'It must be a bit of a blow to have ended up in the City, a glorified waitress.'

'Possibly, why?'

'She struck me as materialistic when I met her. Those heels, that coat. And,' I broke off a bit of candlewax and rolled it in my finger, 'MT is a social climber. She's been dating Henry Warren.'

'Ah yes, the customer who allegedly told MT or Seth that La Fleur was haunted. Not Tom then? She's not been dating him, at least?' Sam appeared as concerned for Mary as I felt. 'Where does this fit?'

'Okay.' My turn to spill. 'Henry never admitted to knowing about the ghost. But, while I was waiting for him to finish a phone call, I was in his secretary's room. There was a picture of Elizabeth Brownrigg's skeleton hanging in Surgeon's Hall and another of her beating her apprentice. She's described as the murderess of Fleur de Lis Court. Warren's secretary told me MT had seen it. But way back in February.'

'I see.' Sam rubbed his chin, the cogs behind his eyes gearing up and beginning to whirr. 'So what do we gather from this? Had Mary told her about her visions of the ghost at that point?'

I nodded vigorously. 'Yes. And the day after MT had been in Warren's office she then "saw" the "ghost" herself.'

'You doubt her veracity?' He went on before I could answer. 'And I hazard the description she gave was not only like Mary's but also very similar to that of Elizabeth Brownrigg. She was trying to anchor the apparition, to link it to the history of the house.'

'Which,' I picked up the thread of his conversation, 'she had also discovered was where La Fleur was situated. And that hook in the cellar, well, it could easily be the same one Brownrigg had used to string up the apprentices.'

Sam stifled a spasm of repulsion. 'So she would have been hoping someone would start researching into the history, to bring up the murder, no?'

'I'm guessing that was the plan. She may have even suggested it to Ray. I suppose she must have also roped Tom in at some point. Dispatched him to the archives to find out more details to point the way to Brownrigg. As a history graduate he'd know his way round the system. Such a shame though. What were they hoping might happen? What did they want to get out of it?'

'That we may never know,' said Sam and smoothed down the portrait of the grim murderess. He was giving the impression that he'd summed up and drawn a line under the business.

'And why did they kill Seth? And how?' There were lots of questions still bugging me.

'Ours not to reason why.' He touched his hand to his chest. 'Though actually the quote is "theirs". I assumed you wouldn't be familiar with the original Tennyson,' he added by way of opaque apology.

'What? What are you talking about?'

'Next steps,' he explained, evidently moving on. 'It's not

our place to question them about motive. Our way forward is clear. We type this into a report and send it to Ray and the police.'

'Don't be a spanner,' I said impatiently. 'That is a massive cop-out.'

'If I might comment at this point that it is commonly you, Ms Strange, who is the reluctant partner, unwilling to become involved in nonsense at any great depth.' He looked very smug indeed.

I refused to take the bait. 'Well, Sam, I'm surprised that you want to *give up* on the investigation so easily. To *surrender* your findings to the strong arm of the law, as fine a representative of such as Detective Edwards is.'

But he wasn't biting either. In fact, he grinned. 'Well, I do have a few questions of my own I'd like to pursue. But, Rosie, I'm not sure how we might go about continuing.'

Hmmm, he was right. I picked up another strand of candlewax and held it over the flame as I pondered possibilities. 'Well,' I said, after a couple of minutes, 'everyone thinks we're ghostbusters, don't they?'

He winced then agreed, 'I suppose.'

'Then why don't we try and bust that ghost?'

For a moment he was baffled. 'And how exactly do you propose we go about that?'

'I've got an idea,' I said, and reached for my phone. 'Buckle up your seatbelt, this may be a bumpy ride.'

CHAPTER TWENTY-THREE

Sometimes I am awed by the wonders of our modern age. For instance, how you can learn just about anything on the web. With a quick google, it's possible to discover how to make jam, lay lino, repair anything, design a website, trim nasal hair, develop computing skills, contour your face, learn a martial art, dance moves – the list is endless.

Most importantly, however, you can also find out how to host your own séance. A critical skill which can be executed in five easy steps.

Step One requires you to set the scene.

This was done effectively using all the candles in La Fleur. Ray Boundersby was most cooperative after we had explained what we wanted to do, though we didn't tell him everything we knew, and agreed to close the restaurant early Saturday night so we could get the place ready and commence the proceedings at the suitably creepy midnight hour. He also personally helped us dress it, reducing the size of our chosen area – we needed to keep it contained and intimate. La Fleur had black screens on rollers that they sometimes used to section off areas of the restaurant for private parties.

We pushed them around a large oval table and used some left-over purple curtains to cover the gaps in between. The screens only went up to about nine feet high so you could see over the top. But that was fine by us. In fact, it would work well. According to superknowhow.com the shape of the table was vital – either oval or circular – so all participants could hold hands and create a circle of 'protection and energy'. The writer of this particular entry also suggested we deck it with flowers and food to attract the spirits. Consequently I had raided La Fleur's cupboards and laid the table with white foods and rice crackers. The tablecloth was a snowy colour too, so everything kind of glowed. It was perfect.

At each end of the table Sam had positioned cameras on tripods ostensibly to capture any manifestations that may occur but really to record how people reacted. We were both hoping for something a little more concrete than a couple of dustballs in front of the lens.

Of course Mr Weirdopedia wanted to race back to the museum and consult his books but I didn't feel we had enough time. It wasn't going to be long before word got out about my visit to Henry Warren's chambers. Time was definitely of the essence.

Step Two instructed you invite people who believed in the spirit world, or at least who could do a good job of looking like they did. And they shouldn't be deeply afraid of ghosts or of a nervous disposition. This ruled out a few people instantly.

However after careful consideration we selected Femi (a definite believer), Joel (open-minded, thought Mary was innocent), Agatha (Catholic), Tim (didn't seem nervy), and MT. Then of course there was the boss who was not going to miss out on this, Ray Boundersby, his daughter, Mary, and her traitorous shit of a boyfriend. It was a real bummer, I thought as I seated the couple round the table, a pleasant grin frozen on to my chops. To all intents and purposes they appeared genuinely in love. Tom kept squeezing Mary's hand. She kept gazing back adoringly. Shame, shame, shame.

Sam and I had not divulged to the Boundersbys the entirety of what we'd learnt. We hoped we wouldn't have to be the messengers, because we all knew what happened to them. But we were anticipating that after tonight, it might fall to other people.

Sam and I brought the total round the table to ten. A good number apparently.

Sam was to assume the role of narrator and instructor, while I myself was going to be the medium, the conduit for the séance (Step Three).

I'd fished out an old turban from an *Abigail's Party* party I once went to and a flowing kaftan which I thought made me look spiritual but Sam had shaken his head from side to side and told me to put on something 'less provocative' (oio). I didn't think he really understood the power of clothes so we argued for a bit and in the end compromised on my scarlet velvet dress and dramatic gothy make-up. A sumptuous corsage of deep red roses, snatches of mauve heather with a big central lily was pinned over my right breast. I thought it added a certain pizzazz. My hair was piled up in an up-do and I fixed in some dangly crystal earrings. Sam muttered something rude about Gypsy Rose Lee and showed me a photo of this old bird called Doris Stokes. I told him he could sod that look for a game of soldiers so he gave up and left me to it. I knew I looked savvy and exotic so I kept my gear on. Tim appreciated it anyway and he was the fittest bloke at the party. I mean séance. Apart from Sam, himself.

My colleague was dressed in a dark suit and looked professional, in a funerary kind of way, a little bit *Reservoir Dogs* with a big dose of handsome. His eyes were dark, his face full of sharp-chiselled purpose. There was an authority about him too. It thrilled me when he was like that, and made me start thinking about other things which were inappropriate and shouldn't be consuming me so. At least not right now.

When we were ready, he boomed out, 'Welcome,' and all eyes turned to him. He was positioned at the table beneath one of the cameras to my right. 'Thank you for agreeing to help us tonight,' he said very seriously. 'As you are all aware, La Fleur has been the location for a number of awful things, including, unfortunately the recent killing of your colleague Seth Johnson.'

The gathered heads nodded and murmured.

'So,' Sam went on, 'investigations have not reaped rewards. Or not as profusely as we anticipated which is why we are gathered tonight in an attempt to contact the earthbound spirits who abide here and who may help us bring peace and learn who or what is behind the horrors of La Fleur.'

He sat himself down and gestured over to me. 'I am privileged enough to be able to work alongside one of the most powerful clairvoyants of our time. Rosie Strange is descended from a line of gifted mediums able to penetrate the veil and communicate with the spirit world.'

Joel, next to me, sniggered at the reference to penetration. Beside him, Agatha tutted.

Sam continued, 'We are very lucky to have her on board tonight, guiding us.'

I bowed my head and tried to look in tune with the spirit world by pouting and flaring my nostrils at the same time.

'Tonight,' Sam said quickly so the eyes swivelled back to him, 'we will attempt to make contact with those who have passed from this world on to the next plane of existence.' He paused for effect. 'To establish initial communication, we shall be using the old and sacred art of spirit rapping. Do not be afraid if you hear knocking noises around you. We are in capable hands.' He took a moment to let his lighthouse smile beam over everyone.

'Our medium, Rosie, will ask a question. Traditionally a single rap in response means yes. Two raps a no. Sometimes during this method the table may tilt, you may feel the cold brush of a hand or gust of air – it is vital that you remain calm. Under no circumstances should you break the circle. This is imperative.' He eyeballed everybody individually. A long moment of silence rolled out before he continued. 'Sometimes the spirit may use telekinesis to move things on the table. Do not be alarmed if this happens. I repeat again, it is important that once you have joined hands you continue to do so whatever happens. So,' he said taking the hands of Tom and Agatha, who were his neighbours at the table. Everyone else, including me, followed his lead. 'Let us join hands while Rosie says a prayer for us.' He looked over.

What? This was news to me. Sam hadn't mentioned anything about prayers when we were planning this. My family weren't religious. I didn't know any prayers. But everyone was staring at me.

'For what we are about to receive,' I said as mystically as I was able, 'may the Lord make us truly grateful.'

Sam grimaced. Ray glowered and Tim laughed but managed to turn it into a fairly convincing cough.

It was the best I could do.

'Amen,' I finished and everybody echoed. Then I made my voice low and husky, and quite sexy, even if I do say so myself. 'I would like everyone to take a minute to close your eyes and reflect in silence upon what we are about to do. If you have anyone who has passed into the spirit world, then you may wish to think of them.'

I looked around the circle and noted the expressions on the gathered faces. Agatha was concentrating madly, her face screwed up into lines, her hands gripping hard on to Joel, who might have been asleep for all the expression on his face. Femi had his eyes shut firmly and fervently and held my hand in a hard grip. Tim, up the end, looked wry but obedient. Ray was surprisingly the most unlined and thoughtful that I'd seen so far. He'd lost the usual bulldog demeanour and appeared, for a moment, more Siamese for the first time since I'd known him. Mary next to him looked ever so sad and watery. Tom was clearly shitting himself. Sweat had broken out down the ridge of his nose and across his cheeks. MT, at the other end of the table opposite Sam, looked unruffled and beatific and pretty. She had a glittery eyeshadow that was eye-catching and yet subtle at the same time. I hated her a lot. Sam's eyes, however, were open and fixed on mine. He nodded fractionally, a signal we'd predesignated. I bent my head on to my chest and pressed down with my chin until I felt the button on the air-conditioning remote depress. It was concealed beneath the elaborate corsage. Within minutes the place was going to start to feel a hell of a lot colder.

The corner of Sam's mouth tugged slightly to the left. *So cute*, I thought briefly and was about to respond with a grin when I saw Agatha's eyes snap open. Instead I breathed out loudly and said, 'Thank you. I can feel a change in the air. Let us begin.'

The blackness around us seemed to thicken in anticipation.

I cleared my throat and asked lowly, 'If there is anyone from the spirit world with us, I would ask you to make yourselves known with a single knock.'

Everybody, including me and Sam, held their breath. Even Tim appeared less lackadaisical then a couple of minutes ago. Nobody moved.

Nothing happened.

I waited a moment more then asked, 'Is there anybody there?'

Femi looked about him from side to side. Agatha shivered. MT maintained her composure.

A single knock resounded from somewhere nearby.

A visible ripple of surprise spread through the circle.

'Thank you,' I said into the darkness and paused

dramatically. 'We have contact.' I let that sink in for a bit then asked, 'Spirit of the hereafter, tell me please, are you attached to this building, La Fleur? One knock for yes, two for no.'

We all waited. Nothing. I opened my mouth to clarify my request as we heard another knock.

Agatha drew in a sharp intake of breath and said, 'It's moving closer!'

'Stay where you are please,' I called to the table. We didn't want anybody freaking out and breaking up the party. We had important stuff to do.

'Spirit, may I ask you if you are responsible for some of the phenomena these people have witnessed?' I was aware of MT tensing to my right.

We waited. For one long minute nobody breathed, the only sound the air conditioning droning. Goosebumps rashed down my arms.

Sam shot me a subtle look: go on.

'The spirit does not answer,' I began as there came a series of long hard loud bangs, like something rolling and crashing to the floor. It was quite impressive.

Mary gasped and let out a little whimper. Tom, next to her, looked petrified and began darting glances around.

'Mad,' said Femi in a low voice. 'The spirits feel fury.'

MT's usually lineless face had a hard angry nick in the middle of her forehead. It made her look a bit Klingon-like. Which was pleasing. 'That's a yes, then,' she said resolutely, although her voice cracked on the last word.

'I sense confusion.' I murmured and closed my eyes. 'Spirit, are you responsible for the murder of Seth Johnson?'

Immediately two raps resounded across our séance space.

'A firm no.' I kept my eyes shut. 'If you didn't do it, oh spirit, then do you know who did?'

Silence.

I let it roll out uninterrupted till, suddenly, all of us heard a solid rap, which seemed to echo throughout the restaurant.

'Yes,' I said. 'You do know who. I see.'

Tom raised his hand to rub his face taking Mary's hand with it. He breathed out loudly. His girlfriend shot him a worried glance.

MT muttered, 'This is ridiculous.'

'Who?' I asked the invisible presence. 'Who, spirit, who is responsible?'

Everyone tensed up.

A *sh-sh-sh* whispery sort of noise seemed to descend from above. I opened my eyes wide. 'I can hear her. Inside my head. She is trying to speak. Trying to communicate. With me! Yes, yes, spirit,' I closed my eyes and let my head roll from side to side. 'She has seen them.' My eyes flew open.

Opposite me Mary was swallowing hard.

'She has seen those who committed the atrocity.' I paused and surveyed the faces. 'She is describing them.'

Now MT was looking visibly scared.

The candles on the table flickered.

I felt a cold blast of air pass over my neck and shivered. Something weird had started going on behind my right ear. A change in air pressure, as if someone had stepped close to me.

Then a voice, really, really close, began to whisper. I couldn't hear them first, not properly, but then as I focused my attention and tuned in to the noise I began to distinguish words. 'Not mean to,' I fathomed, as if it was halfway into a sentence. 'Not all the way.' It was a man's voice, shipped into a uniform London accent with personality added by way of lost consonants à la East End gentrification. At the same time it had a hollow quality to it that I wasn't expecting. Like the bloke was speaking down a wooden tube.

We hadn't planned for this, but I was a professional, happy to go with the flow. Maybe there had been a change of plan. Perhaps Jason Edwards was improvising.

'Wait!' I said, and would have held my hand up if I hadn't banged on about everyone keeping the circle tight. 'I hear something. Someone else is trying to reach us. A man.'

The voice went on pleadingly, nagging. 'Tell them, tell … bit of a laugh, take Ray down a peg or two. Him and his daughter. "Why should Mary have it all?" she said. "Didn't deserve it," she said. "All bought on ill-gotten gains, she said."'

I straightened up, playing my part. 'I hear you spirit. He's saying initially it was a joke. Designed to take Ray down a peg or two.'

The whispering faded as crackling and air gushed into my ear. 'Don't go, spirit,' I appealed. After a moment it came back again, but was rather distracted and stuttering. This was not very impressive. I would have to feed this back to Jason when it came to our debrief. I sighed to convey my annoyance and called out pointedly, 'Spirit, can you speak more clearly please?'

Sam darted me a face full of raised eyebrows.

My plea, however, had no effect – the mumbling continued.

I managed to catch only snatches of sentences this time – "'lose money," she said, "hand over fist,"' *mutter, mutter, crackle crackle*, "'an investor lined up,"' *sounds of static like an early Internet connection*, "'step in and buy La Fleur,"' *words inaudible*, 'she said, she said – "had him lined up,"' *hissing sigh*, "'run the restaurant by themselves."'

The candles flickered energetically.

Those gathered about me seemed genuinely engaged.

I caught Sam's face, wrinkled like a perplexed prune, and Ray's which wore an expression of disdain. Tom had shrunk down into his chair.

I voiced what I was hearing. 'He says it was too much,' I said lingering over the vowels. 'Something about food poisoning – that night before the argument.' The words became higher, shriller, more sibilant, slightly painful. "'She put it in the food – four different dishes – all compromised – that couldn't have been one ingredient. It was her."' A violent and cold sigh filled my eardrum and made me shiver. 'Look like his fault – compromised his integrity, reputation. Too much. He's saying something about reputation being everything.'

The chill in my ear was spreading down my throat. I wanted desperately to turn around and gesture to the guy he should stand back a bit, but I couldn't; all eyes were upon me. I could only repeat his words. 'He was out. The whole deal was over. It was too much. Too far. But she said he was in too deep. They argued, in the cellar, he was going to phone Ray. He'd had enough and told her so. She wouldn't have it. MT, she wouldn't have it, said he was in for the duration.

He'd committed. But he started to dial Ray's number and then – crack – on the head and now he is, he is …' the voice faded again as though confusion had entered it; as if, he, the speaker, the policeman, or whoever it was had come up against a blank. His script had run out.

But there was movement going on down the far end of the table. MT was wriggling out of her neighbours' grip, throwing their hands down on to the table.

'Do not break the circle,' Sam shouted. His voice had an edge of something I couldn't really work out but was still authoritative. It made MT stop.

'This is bullshit,' she said angrily, but she was white as a sheet behind the bronzer. Hard lines and snakelike wrinkles appeared over her face. Her make-up suddenly seemed overdone, drag-queen style, crude like a ventriloquist's dummy. She stood up.

However, we had foreseen this scenario occurring – the drawing out. I drew myself up and delivered the cue.

'Spirit reveal yourself,' I commanded as grandly as possible.

There was a single ring of a bronze bell, followed by the clash of a cymbal. An unexpected cackle of laughter stopped both me and MT in our tracks.

All eyes swivelled up over the tops of the screens to the mezzanine where a ghostly white spectre appeared to be floating. Dressed in a full skirt, corset and bonnet, the apparition was strangely luminous. In one bony white hand she held a horse whip, which she held up and cracked. We heard it slice the air.

MT whimpered.

With her other bony arm the apparition stretched out. Long fingers uncurled and pointed towards MT.

'Elizabeth Brownrigg,' I said, voice shaking and trying to concentrate on the script, despite the fact the officer had come back to continue whingeing in my ear. 'Murderess. Killer of Mary Clifford. Did you, spectre, did you murder Seth Johnson?'

The bonnet swivelled from side to side and she appeared to float down towards us, a melancholy embodiment of evil.

'Who did?' I called. 'Tell us, if it wasn't you – who killed the chef?'

The other bony hand reached towards Tom, who was rising up from his chair clutching Mary's and Sam's hands to his chest and making a weird noise that sounded like *glok glok glok*. He wobbled his head feverishly in response. 'No,' he began, his voice on the brink of a howl. 'It's not true. I had nothing to do with Seth, she did it on her own. She's crazy,' he blurted. 'She wouldn't stop.'

MT threw down Tim's and Femi's hands once more. 'Shut up, Tom, shut up. Can't you see what they're doing?'

But Tom wasn't listening. Push had come to shove. He was totally absorbed in saving his neck. 'MT asked me to research her – Brownrigg.' He pointed at the apparition fearfully. 'I helped her spray the writing on the wall and tipped over the bloody water. She let the rats out. I thought it was a prank. Not serious. I didn't kill Seth. I had no part of that. And I didn't know that Mary would end up a suspect. I was going to come clean. I was just waiting for—'

Mary let out a whimper and pulled away from Tom.

'I didn't mean to,' he said, and tried to reach for her. But she squirmed away and put her hands over her eyes.

'Oh, he did at first,' MT said, and all our eyes snapped to her. 'He only went with you, Mary, because I suggested it,' she gloated. 'He did anything I asked. Used to follow me round like a lovesick puppy.'

'But then it changed,' Tom whined. All eyes flitted up the other end of the table. 'I fell in love ... with you Mary.'

MT laughed nastily, 'He's weak. But he's as much a part of it as me.'

Femi stirred to my left. 'The ghost, she has gone.'

For a moment everyone stopped and looked up to where she had been. Nothing was there.

The voice in my ear took the opportunity to amplify and curse. 'Tell Ray sorry,' it said.

Personally I couldn't see how this was going to lead to a conviction so I ignored the officer.

'Tell him,' it said again.

'He's sorry,' I said.

'Seth,' said the voice in my ear.

'Seth,' I said.

'Well, I'm not,' MT piped up. Her hands were on her hips but she was moving her torso as if she was gearing up for a run. 'Seth was collateral damage.' She said it so calmly that Tim and Femi both gasped and shrank away from her. 'You people, though,' she said in Ray and Mary's direction. 'You make me sick. I've worked bloody hard, gone to university, got a degree and for what? To play second, third, fourth fiddle to a common thief, a conman who thinks he can buy class and breeding, and his fat lump of a daughter. You don't deserve this ... you're nothing but a pair of criminals—'

I was contemplating the irony of this when Ray, who had been sitting stoically, jumped to his feet. I had never seen the barrel-like body move so fast. His face was like thunder, his fists clenched.

Within seconds he had leapt at the maître d' and wrapped his fingers round her throat.

Now this was development was strictly off-piste.

I sent a helpless look at Sam who was just standing there looking stunned.

'Forgive me,' said the voice in my ear with an insistence I wasn't expecting either. Couldn't he see what was going on?

Ray raised his fist.

MT began to hit his chest.

Tom got to his feet.

Mary burst into tears.

'Forgive me,' urged the voice in my ear. The words needled into my head growing louder still. I needed my ears syringed, I thought as they started echoing in my brain, accumulating volume internally. 'Forgive me forgive me forgive me ...'

It was so annoying and I was so confused that I shouted out, 'Oh, for god's sake, shut up. You're forgiven.'

For a brief moment there was silence, internally and out.

My random outburst had produced an unexpected pattern breaker.

Everyone looked at me shocked.

Ray turned obviously relaxing his grip, allowing MT

to push him away. She fumbled in her jacket pocket and brought out something that caught the candlelight and glinted.

A powerful burst of wind exploded into the room. It carried a roar with it. All the candles blew out plunging us into darkness.

There were sounds of scrambling on the table. Metal. Clothes brushing. People gasping. Then a brief flash of yellow. The smell of sulphur. A smatter of dust descended on us. I had seen this before, and the last time it happened I had got into a fight that wasn't mine and come off with a few injuries and a fat lip which meant I couldn't wear lipstick for a whole three days.

I decided to stay put and root down in the mayhem.

Something was knocked over opposite. Someone shouted, 'Argh!' There was the sounds of footsteps, another crash. A gurgling noise. Someone else, a woman, screamed. A shock of white flew across the space.

To my left I heard Femi's voice. 'The evil one,' he screamed. 'She walks.'

Then a familiar voice rang out, 'No, Ray, no.'

Someone switched all the lights on.

The chandelier and recess lights flooded the space.

I blinked.

Joel was standing up beside me. 'Shit the bed,' he muttered.

Across the room was a tumble of limbs and groans and huffs. I made out MT's slim legs, which had lost their shoes, and astride her the black mop of Tom's hair, his face in profile, lips drawn back in a lupine snarl. He was bleeding somewhere on his left arm. Though he seemed not to notice, for his right hand had curled into a fist. It was raised, pulled back, ready to punch into MT's snarling face, but was held back from release by none other than Ray. He in turn was being held back by the white-clad bony arms of the phantom Brownrigg, aka Auntie Babs.

'You've done enough, love,' she was saying to Boundersby. 'Leave it to the fuzz now. You need to look after Mary. Can't do that in the nick.'

And then our séance was inundated with a surge of black uniforms. Jason Edwards' men arriving just a little late, if you asked me.

CHAPTER TWENTY-FOUR

Now that Auntie Babs had removed her hat and white wig she looked a bit more like her familiar self, despite her attempt at an eighteenth-century costume: a disconcertingly well-worn Anne Summers white(ish) basque worn over a long 1950s net petticoat. She kept the glistening ivory shawl draped around her shoulders though. It was still rather bracing as no one had yet adjusted the air con.

'Thanks,' I said to her, as she began the long job of cleaning off her luminous make-up. 'You did a good thing there, with Ray.'

'Some mug had to step in, didn't they? I tell you, my old blister wouldn't be too happy 'bout it though, would she?' She sent me an accusing look and shook her head vigorously. A tumble of extensions unloosed themselves and dropped down about her shoulders. She'd had them on top of her head, as was the fashion in Brownrigg's time.

'Still,' she winked a heavily extended eyelid at me. 'A friend in need, as they say. Poor Ray's had such a lot of trouble and strife since he lost his wife.'

Auntie Babs rolled her eyes and dabbed at her arms while

I contemplated the pile up of clichés and rhyming slang and waited for her to refer to Mary as a bin lid.

'From what you've told me, this ghost business ain't helped neither. Can't have him going down, can we? Not with his girl to sort out.' Bin lid a stretch too far then, I thought. 'If Mary's seeing things like what you reckon then he's got to get her to the quack's pronto, ain't he?'

I nodded. 'Yeah. I reckon he's going to do that now the heat's been turned down a bit.'

'Family matters,' sniffed Auntie Babs and gave me a funny look. Well, at least I thought it might she might be trying to communicate meaning. It was difficult to tell as her false eyelashes on the left eye had unpeeled themselves and were dangling over her cheek.

'Fine words, madam,' said Femi, setting down a teapot and mugs and some brandy glasses for the remaining séance participants. Joel, Agatha, Tim, Babs and I had all come off relatively unscathed.

'Oh lovely, Mr Femi,' Babs purred and reached out for a mug. The eyelashes finally suicided off into the dark folds of her cleavage.

Ray and Mary were in the kitchen with DS Edwards and a female officer, who might have been Victim Support. Sam was on the mezzanine making copies of the tapes before he handed them over as evidence.

Tom, under arrest, by the great glass door, was cuffed and being seen to by a paramedic. From time to time, he looked over and called, 'Tell her I'm sorry. I love her.' I noted it made Joel cringe.

Over the by the bar MT was sullen. Every so often she'd answer Tom's wail with an insult. The glamorous façade, which had been oh-so-enticing and exquisitely constructed had pretty much come apart in the fight with Ray and Tom. She looked dishevelled, thin and sharp-edged. And rather unhinged. Her hair extensions were falling out, the nice nude lipstick had come off and she was bearing her teeth like an animal. The dazzling blue eyes that had once seemed so bright and full of intelligence now had taken on a crazed demonic aspect, which put me in mind of Jackson next door. Those eyes now flicked about the room as if tracking an invisible fly. A man in a green jumpsuit was binding her hand in a bandage while a nearby officer kept a steady watch.

'Let me, Mrs Boundersby,' said Joel, who took Babs's mug and, having appointed himself 'mother', poured what he remarked was a proper cup of tea.

'Oh, I'm not Ray's missus,' Auntie Babs simpered, yet the thought clearly warmed her cockles.

'She's my aunt,' I told him. 'Drafted in at the last minute to flush out the evidence.'

'Oh yeah, I can see the resemblance,' he grinned. 'The nose, complexion and general luminous beau-tay.'

I regarded my aunt's nut-brown wrinkly skin and extensions. She was much thinner than me, and privately, though she strongly resembled my mum, I could never spot any shared features. Bit sad really, as she wasn't a terrible looker for an old girl.

Auntie Babs patted the back of her hair and giggled. 'Thank you,' she said, and sent Joel a wide toothy smile. Her two fleshy boobs, hoisted up inside the basque, quivered with delight.

Joel averted his eyes and tried to look unperturbed. 'So, Rosie, do you think that you've got enough to send down MT?' he said.

'That's not up to us,' I said. 'We were filming it all. She more or less admitted to everything. So I reckon it will hang together okay. The police have got enough to go on, surely, and anyway DS Edwards says he might have picked her up on the CCTV on Holborn after Seth's murder. Or an accomplice that looks just like her with very dusty clothes.'

From the doorway Tom yelled something incomprehensible before he was finally evicted from the building and thrown into a waiting panda car.

By the bar MT let rip with a suitably maniacal cackle.

Agatha crossed herself. Tim turned his chair towards us so that he had his back to the bar. I handed him a brandy, which he necked.

'Still can't believe Tom dun all of that behind Mary's back,' Joel said sadly. 'And MT – well, you just never know people, do you?'

'True thing said there, young man,' Babs piped up. 'You're very wise for your years.'

'Thank you, Rosie's auntie.'

'Babs,' said Babs and uncurled her taloned hand and held it out.

Joel shook it hastily, then backed away and changed the subject. 'What was with that whole flour thing anyway?'

'I think it was spur of the moment,' I said. I'd thought

this one through. 'In fact, the whole murder was. I don't reckon MT was expecting to kill Seth, but when she did, she thought if she hoisted him up and made it look like Mary Clifford, Brownrigg's victim, then there was a chance the haunting spirit might be blamed. She'd read everything that Tom had dug up for her about the way Brownrigg murdered her charges. They were kids,' I told them. 'Mary Clifford was only fourteen.' Joel, Auntie Babs and Tim flinched collectively. 'This was the Brownrigg's home. La Fleur.'

Tim shuddered and began looking around. Joel regained his composure, but Babs said, 'Disgusting,' and crossed her arms.

'Of course,' I went on, 'MT knew the police wouldn't buy the ghost theory. But then something fortuitous happened – she realised it was Mary who was upstairs. She knew Mary thought she was seeing ghosts. I'm guessing that MT might have googled conditions or just conjectured correctly that something was going on with her eyesight. So she took her chance to escape and burst the sack of flour either accidentally or to spread it all over the crime scene to clog up evidence or simply for the sack, because it was this that she twisted over her head to resemble a bonnet. It wouldn't have looked convincing to anyone else, but to Mary who was having problems with her visual processing, it did the trick. Whatever her brain interpreted that night, in the dark, it processed it imperfectly, filling in details that weren't there. Mary "saw" the ghost she suspected was already haunting the premises, complete with her trademark bonnet.'

'How did she get Seth up there? On the hook?' Agatha tutted. 'She's so scrawny.'

'Joel told me that her dad was an engineer on Tower 42. Pulley mechanics are very simple. They enable someone to hoist something much heavier than themselves. There's a pulley in the basement. Wouldn't have taken much time or effort. Thing is, Seth wasn't quite dead. His moans alerted Mary, who was upstairs.'

Joel took a moment to process this. I noticed that everybody else had stopped talking so they could listen in.

Tim stroked his beard. 'But what I don't understand is why she decided to do it in the first place?'

'Well, it was the police officer whispering in my ear who suggested there had been some kind of set-up with Seth, some agreement to run down the restaurant, maybe so that MT could come in with her "investor".'

I nodded at Sam who had come over with his suitcase full of tricks and put two tapes on the table.

'That might be Henry Warren,' I said to him as he slid the case along the table. Then explained to Tim, 'She's been dating him.'

'Do you think Henry Warren knew what she was up to?' Sam asked.

I shook my head. 'Doubt it. He's a bit of a hooray, but he's also a legal eagle. Doubt he'd get his hands dirty. Too much to lose. He's got a nice situation over in Lincoln's Inn. I wouldn't be surprised if MT was still working on him. Or if it was all in her head. She's obviously a bit deranged.'

We all paused and glanced over to the bar, where the now

fully bandaged maître d' was being read her rights. And cuffed too by the looks of it.

Femi shook his head. 'Get thee behind me, Satan, for it is written.' Agatha crossed herself yet again. Auntie Babs and Joel simultaneously sucked their teeth then smiled at each other.

'Such a waste,' Joel muttered sadly, looking back at MT. 'Did she really see a ghost too?'

'I doubt it,' I said. 'I think she realised she could make something of Mary's sightings. I mean, everyone trusted what the boss's daughter had seen. Why wouldn't they? Certainly no one suspected Miss Boundersby to have a malicious agenda. And so if MT said she'd seen a similar sight, it was sure to be accepted too. Especially as it would reinforce Mary's evidence.'

Tim shook his head. 'However mankind changes outwardly, we still cling tenaciously to the old beliefs.'

I smiled, more than a little impressed.

'Sounds like a lot of effort,' said Joel and yawned.

The kitchen doors swung open and in came DS Edwards with Ray and Mary.

Ray looked across the room and saw MT being forced up. He stopped stock-still. Mary put her hand out protectively to restrain her dad if necessary. DS Edwards slipped in front of him, blocking his path to his former employee.

The officer bundling the hostess forwards began to forcibly navigate her through the tables towards the door.

As she passed us by, Femi shouted out, 'You will atone for your sins. May God forgive you.'

Agatha mouthed, 'Amen.'

For a moment MT managed to wriggle out of the police-man's grasp. 'Oh, shut your mouths. Bunch of low-rent losers. You can't blame me for trying. I have ambitions.' Her lips were pulled back, showing those artificially white teeth. The canines looked very sharp indeed. 'And I was getting there too. Handling the outcome perfectly well, *perfectly*.' She drew out the last word, drawing everyone's attention. 'Till *When Harry Met Sally* here showed up.' She nodded her head towards me and Sam.

As final lines went it was a slight improvement on pesky kids.

'I don't think that's true,' said Jason Edwards, who had come up to needle her on. I wasn't sure which of MT's state-ments he disagreed with.

He set his face into a standard-issue expression of Metropolitan Police determination; then with a squeal, a clatter of heels and some localised restraining procedures executed by several more long arms of the law, Marta Thompson, chef-killer, femme fatale and scheming psychopath, was whisked right out of there.

Agatha shouted, 'Hurrah.' Femi snorted. Joel made a sucking noise with his teeth.

'Thank Christ for that,' said Tim, unexpectedly.

'Good riddance to bad rubbish is what I say,' said Auntie Babs.

'What's *Harry Met Sally*?' asked Sam.

I felt myself suppress a cringe, then had no choice but to surrender to it when Auntie Babs gave me a theatrical nudge and said, 'Oo-er, Rosie. I got the DVD at home but you can stream it online for cheap, love. Do you know what I reckon?' she turned to a bewildered Mr Stone. 'I'd say it's time you two went back to the witch house and got a cosy night in with the telly.' Then she winked at him. Twice.

CHAPTER TWENTY-FIVE

'Well,' said Sam bouncing up and down on the bed. 'It's bigger than the one in the spare room. I thought we could put it in there, if that's okay. And maybe turn this into a library.'

We were on the first floor of the Witch Museum in an area that I hadn't spent much time in at all. It was at the front of the building, whereas the main living quarters – Septimus's bedroom and the lounge – were located at the rear.

The room was full of shadow, fairly large, maybe fifteen feet by fourteen or so, and led off a very wide landing. This landing, which was behind me, was brighter, illuminated by two windows that faced west. Currently though, dark clouds were gathering, letting the sun shine only intermittently. I wondered if a storm was coming and checked the windows were firmly shut. These were the 'eyes' in the museum's skull-like façade. Made of leaded lights and arch-shaped, they stood sentry over the muddy car park at the front.

A sudden gust of wind howled against them, causing the curtains to stir in the draught. The hairs on my arms prickled and I moved away, further into the bedroom and promptly sneezed. The air in here was full of dust motes dislodged by the curator's bottom. According to Sam it had once been my dad's. Somewhere in the dark caves of my mind there was a place that must recall it to be so because this news didn't come as a surprise.

As I surveyed the room I noted brighter rectangles on the wallpaper where posters had once hung. Around them the paper pattern was faded. It covered a wall at the back of the room where the bed was and featured a vintage superman in all manner of manly poses. I must have definitely seen it before, if not in person then certainly in a photo, because I could remember planes hanging from the ceiling. In fact, I could clearly picture teen Ted in here at his desk, hunched over his Airfix models, tongue poking out of his mouth, concentrating hard on matching the right numbers on the fuselage to the correct enamel paint.

So normal.

And yet, so at odds with the strange displays only yards beneath his feet.

No wonder he had got out of here as soon as he could. The man had never ever expressed a spiritual or esoteric opinion in his life that I was aware, other than to rubbish what foolish people said of course. It was probably a reaction to or a rebellion against his childhood spent growing up in here. And really who could blame him? It wasn't the ideal place to bring up kids. I thought briefly about Auntie Celeste and wondered what she had made of it and how she might have turned out had her life not been cut short by the accident.

I guessed you could go one way or the other. Reject it or embrace it.

Sam had ventured that a great deal of Dad's aversion to the museum was down to his mother's disappearance. That figured – Septimus had himself created it as a reaction to the event. With best intentions of course. But still, I could see how a mother's disappearance and then the following upheaval – the transfer to the museum – might sour a child to their surroundings.

And Septimus would have had to concentrate on setting up the museum, launching it too, which would consume a great deal of energy, so who, I wondered, had looked after the kids? Maybe they looked after themselves. Maybe Dad looked after Celeste. Or one of the grandparents or aunties.

I was beginning to think that Dad's rejection of all things supernatural and prophetic, and of the museum, actually presented a denunciation of his mother. After all, from what Sam had told me, Ethel-Rose had believed herself to be clairvoyant or clairaudient or whatever. Her final ill-fated demonstration of these 'gifts' appeared to have been, if not the cause, then certainly the catalyst for her strange vanishing. That would have to generate some serious issues. Resentment. Bewilderment. And yes, I could also see how the angry dismissal of the whole caboodle might fix into a character trait.

It would be far easier to deal with that way.

Poor Dad. No wonder he didn't like me hanging around the place. It would present a constant reminder to him of the mother that he had lost. And of the pain and rage that had followed.

I imagined him sitting on the bed in his sailor suit, as he was depicted in the family portrait, swinging his feet back and forth and scowling at me. He wanted me to go home, I felt sure. Back to the comfortable superficiality of my steady job. Back to safety.

The only thing was, I didn't think I was going to. Not just yet.

There was stuff to do down here.

In a weird way, I was starting to feel a certain obligation to my dead grandparents and had been thinking about a few things. Sam had already mentioned one – why had Septimus left me the museum? Especially if he knew Dad's feelings about the place? And what really happened to Ethel-Rose?

'So,' said the breathless curator finishing his bed-bouncing routine, 'if we knocked through this wall we could have a rather magnificent open space which would make a beautiful study-cum-library.' The place darkened as clouds swarmed over the sun. 'We're running out of room downstairs in the office so I could relocate the books. We could have shelves from floor to ceiling on three sides. It would help. What do you think?'

I thought that I liked the way he said 'we'. Though I also thought he was making assumptions. Like I said, despite the fact I was not about to put the place straight on the market as I had thought I might do a month ago, I wasn't stupid enough to think about spending big money on renovations. If Dad's condition worsened and I couldn't talk him round, then the museum would simply have to go. I really didn't want my actions to contribute to his sickness. At the same time I didn't really want to upset Sam either. He was becoming a friend. Something more than a friend, if I was being totally honest.

Plus, the place wasn't actually running at a loss and the odd little parcel of cash kept falling into our laps. The odd but *well-deserved* little parcel of cash, I might add. The latest instalment from Boundersby I had agreed, after expenses, could be used to enhance the place cosmetically in the meantime. To put the Witch Museum back on the map, if it had ever been on one, and maybe encourage it to be a tourist destination that might produce an effective income. Just for a little while.

I could even consider a sabbatical, take it on as a project maybe. I was secretly desperate to get my hands on the car park and vacant green outside. I'd thought about using some of the recent income to create a memorial garden to the witches and was visualising a section full of herbs that some of the cunning women might have used. Plus, pretty flower beds with hardy perennials and bloomers that might coincide with half-term, Easter and the summer holidays. These might even coax the phantom flower-bomber out. It was a thought worth thinking on. But anyway, I was sure we could stretch to a few picnic benches to woo schools and more families to make a day of it at the museum. Maybe a climbing frame and swings where children could play while parents relaxed. That wouldn't break the bank.

And I needed a new pair of boots. To replace my luscious gold beauties that were scratched and now slightly forlorn-looking after the tangle with the slave trader. He should be made to compensate me really, the nasty bastard. Maybe there was insurance or something I could claim them on. I'd have to check it out.

And I was also contemplating something else a little more personal – a rose garden to commemorate my grandmother. Bronson could dig up some of the grass round the front without causing too much trouble. A few of those gorgeous Ethel-Rose roses could probably be begged or borrowed from one of the villagers. I'd get Bronson to put out the feelers. It certainly wouldn't cost a lot and it might well soften Dad. On the other hand, he might blow a fuse and flip out altogether. I wasn't sure how to play it yet – but a plan was forming. I intended to do some of my own metaphorical digging around to see if I could shed any light on what happened back in 1953.

So, collecting my thoughts, I replied to Sam, 'Why don't you start with the landing? Get Bronson to put some shelves in across the back and bring a table up that can be used as a desk. You said there's two storage rooms that have got loads of stuff in them – one outside and one in the attic, right? Let's look at them and see if we can furnish it cheaply. I quite like having this as a spare room. Just in case anyone comes to see us. But if you want a larger bed, swap this double with the one in your room.'

He smiled, the left side of his mouth pulling sharply up, making him look a little goofy and very adorable. A sudden rectangle of sunlight shone through the window framing him where he stood, picking out the ochres and russets in his hair, the flecks of amber in his eyes, which looked for a second, full of mischief. 'You said "your room".'

'Yeah, I did.' I smiled back and lingered on his shoulders. Sometimes I could feel my arms moving as if they had a mind of their own – wanting to reach out. I could quite easily imagine the fabric of his green sweatshirt under my palm, the ribs beneath it. Stop that, Ms Strange.

Sam's smile widened and kinked to the left as was its habit. 'Does that mean I can stay?'

His eyes became rounder, looking so momentarily big and hopeful, I couldn't help but laugh. 'Sure, for as long as I've got the place.'

'Great,' he said, and beamed. 'Because I've already moved in. Hope you don't mind. Had to give notice on my studio flat in Litchenfield.'

Huh! I thought. *Cheeky tart.* Still, I let it go. 'I didn't even know you had one.'

'Well, I used to.' He shrugged and looked away. The sunlight died and the room dimmed again. 'Splendid. I'll remove the dummies to the downstairs storage,' and he started talking about the size of that ground-floor area and the fact I hadn't seen it yet either and how it might make a nice summer sitting room.

I watched him get up and pad across the floorboards into the middle of the room. He was still talking, his face animated, legs smooth and long and graceful.

The light from the eye windows was rapidly diminishing behind me. Clouds were coming in from the south and gathering. Night would be about us soon. I wasn't sure if I was looking forward to the evening with Sam or not. Which was unusual. A shadow had been cast by the news that he'd reviewed the séance video tapes and wanted to go over them with me. I intuited this wasn't going to be straightforward, because he also committed to streaming a new comedy with a predominantly female cast. He hated comedy unless it was black. It did not bode well at all.

You might think this pre-emptive but I'd already taken the initiative and lined up a shrink. Mostly because DS Edwards had phoned in the week to let me know that none of his officers were owning up to impersonating the dead chef. He went on to state that although practical jokes weren't uncommon in the day-to-day life of the average London plod, he thought it highly unlikely that someone would muck around like that on a murder investigation. It could compromise the case and get them all referred to the Independent Police Complaints Commission, for which none of them had an appetite.

So, if it hadn't been a wayward copper feeding me infor-mation, then who the bloody hell was it? Who could know that much detail, most of which had now been confirmed, about the murder? These were the most pressing questions on Jason Edwards' lips. Luckily, he'd informed me, none of my DNA had shown up at the crime scene so I wasn't seriously considered a suspect. Plus, I had an alibi – Sam and several traffic cameras which put me (speeding) on the A12 heading out of London towards Adder's Fork on that fateful Saturday.

So then who?

Who exactly had whispered in my shell-like?

The detective had let a full minute scroll out on the phone

while I thought about what to say, finally shrugging, which of course he couldn't hear. So I added a sigh.

'You know,' he said. 'I'm getting the sense you may well be a sceptical sort of ghostbuster? You should meet my mum.'

I wasn't sure how to respond to either of those statements, but in the end I said, 'My knee-jerk reaction is to suggest that one of your team might just be covering up because they went off-script and mucked things up. Given that you believe what they say, however, I will revise this. Which leaves me with a question mark.'

'That makes another one,' he said after a pause. 'Because, we've still not got to the bottom of the girl in the yard.'

'She was, I'll admit it now, comparable to the description that Mary gave of the original apparition.'

'The one that looks like Elizabeth Brownrigg's victim, Mary Clifford?'

'How did you know that?' I was surprised.

'Sam sent me a reproduction of the illustration in Henry Warren's office.'

'Oh,' I said, and petered out.

'We've also looked at the Newgate Calendar illustration and yes there are similarities. Although we're still working on Marta Thompson. She's fessed up to killing Seth. Quite proud of it too. But I'm still wondering about her antics at La Fleur. The whole haunting thing. I wonder if she might have shown a picture to Mary and thus influenced her description. Or Tom may have done without realising. I think there's more to come out of those two. We are now looking at the possibility that they were also aware of the situation going on next door with the girls. Certainly we know Seth Johnson was. And he was part of the La Fleur plot. He might have confided in his co-conspirators. We think Thompson may have even orchestrated Mary's first sighting. To cover up the girls' screaming. We're pursuing the matter.'

'Not sure that the timeline works though,' I muttered more to myself than Jason. 'What I really wanted to do is go back and have another chat with Mary.'

'Might be problematic,' he said. 'I understand from Mr Boundersby she's undergoing medical tests right now.'

I sighed again. It would have to wait a bit then. 'Do you know how that's going?'

'Not really. But Mr Boundersby sounded positive, if that's any consolation?' Yes, that was unusual enough to be a good omen.

Jason cleared his throat and moved on. 'So regarding the details that you came up with. During the séance?' I could hear him attaching verbal quotation marks around the last word.

'Yes,' I said. 'It's odd, isn't it? Normally I incline to scepticism. However, lately I've started to realise it can be just as blinding as faith. I don't think we have all the answers yet. Probably best to keep an open mind about it till I talk to Sam.'

'I don't think I'll be able to write that into my report,' he moaned.

'Tell them I'm telepathic,' I said.

There was a pause down the other end, then, 'Are you?'

'No,' I told him flatly. 'At least I don't think so.'

No doubt Sam would have a theory lined up and ready to expound when we watched the tapes. I was really glad I had *Bitchfest* to look forwards to at the end of it though. *When Harry Met Sally* might have prompted a few too many questions about the current state of play and while, on one hand, I was not averse to the idea of a bit of love action, on the other I'd decided not to rush things.

There was too much going on.

Although we'd sorted out La Fleur, mostly, and had a healthy balance on the Witch Museum bank account, Dad was still undergoing tests and needed calm. No changes or surprises, Mum had said. I thought any kind of sexual liaison with the curator of the Witch Museum might be a bit of an unpalatable shock given his feelings on the subject. Plus, I had a fuller debrief with the Met lined up over dinner in a few days' time. Wasn't sure if his mum was coming too. Might prove something of a problem if DS Edwards wanted to take down my particulars. Which I was also not averse to. The Sam stuff, if it was ever going to happen, should grow organically. I reckoned he'd run a mile if I ever made the first move or forced it.

'Rosie?' He was looking at me intently, waiting.

'Sorry, what?'

He tutted. 'I said, "Hecate's talking to you."' He pointed to his feet where the majestic feline was sitting, regarding me coolly through large green eyes.

'Greetings, Hecate,' I replied.

She made a humming noise, twitched her head and then looked up at Sam and meowed again.

He considered her for a moment then nodded. 'Good

idea.' He grinned back at me. 'Perhaps now it's time for you to see the girls' room. Well, where your grandmother and Celeste's belongings are stored?'

Sometimes Sam was the paragon of scepticism and rationale thought. Then there were other times …

'Why not?' I said, as rain began to spatter against the windows.

He turned on his heel and followed the cat across the landing. Outside the sky had turned black.

I, who also used to be so rational, dutifully trailed the pair of them down the corridor scuffing my heels on the uneven parquet.

When he reached Septimus's living quarters, they both stopped. Hecate yawned and twitched her head towards the living room. Sam opened the door and let her in but didn't enter the room. Instead he bent over and pressed something down by the skirting board. There was the sound of metal clanking, then a door that had been hidden by wooden panelling revealed itself and sprang open.

'Oh my god!' I said, as dust spiralled down from above. 'I never realised that was here.' I must have passed it at least thirty times and not noticed.

Sam chortled to himself. 'Your grandfather built lots of these into the museum. I don't know whether or not it was to enhance the mystery or for practical reasons. The kids loved them though apparently.'

'Oh,' I said, wondering if the plural extended to my dad. If so, they were the first positive words I'd heard in relation to his childhood home.

Dull light was coming in from a window at the top, barely illuminating a flight of stairs. I followed Sam as he ascended through the cobwebs and soon came out into a very large attic room. It seemed to have also been, at one time, used as a bedroom. By a female of the species. There were dormer windows in the roof that sloped to the rear and overlooked the land behind the museum. In front of them, a large dressing table that had probably once been white was gathering a layer of dust. Despite the window there wasn't much natural light in the room. The sky outside looked dramatic and ready to burst. I groped at the wall and found a light switch, which I fiddled with until it clicked. The light bulb in the middle of the room came on then fused with a small bang.

'Bugger,' I said.

'Hang on.' Sam called. 'I think I left a torch the last time I was up here. It's down by your feet, I think. Go on, have a feel around.'

I bent down and soon located a thin cylindrical object, which I switched on. It wasn't very strong but certainly helped visibility. Now I could see over in the corner a smaller window, which was circular, and a French-style bed with a lilac eiderdown. Opposite it was a big white armoire, slightly open. I caught a glimpse of pink taffeta peeping out of the door. It looked like the same dress Ethel-Rose had worn in the family portrait downstairs. Wouldn't it be fab if it fitted?

In the distance thunder rumbled.

'Storm,' said Sam. 'Hope the Cadence wing holds. This will be the new roof's first test.'

'I'm sure it'll be fine,' I said. 'But we'll go and get the buckets ready after this, just in case.'

I wasn't ready to rush down yet, though. The torchlight had fallen over waist-high bookshelves and a coffee table with a Dansette record player. It seemed to be a listening/ reading corner complete with nylon bean bags. There was junk piled up on every inch of available floor space. It looked like a hoarder's paradise: stacks of old magazines teetered on armchairs and stools. A telescope pointed out the window beside two mannequins, one wearing a frilly dress, another laden with a dozen mesh hats and silk flowers. There were a bunch of lampshades, a chaise longue with the stuffing coming out, two single bed frames. A dresser had been shoved in front of the fireplace and was covered with fortune-telling paraphernalia: phrenology heads, a crystal ball, palmistry hands, teacups, some weird-looking Morph creature that Sam said was a 'golem'. At one end, rectangular parcels of black velvet were laid out on tins – tarot cards apparently. Several paintings and pictures were propped against the wall, beside a miniature puppet theatre and a whole heap of cardboard boxes piled in towers. There were more books, of course, but in the far corner, next to the armoire, a tall box-like shape loomed beneath a dust sheet.

'Here,' said Sam. Somehow he had got behind me. I flashed the light on him. 'We could move this desk downstairs to start with.' He was pointing at a slim wooden table that still bore signs of study – a full pen pot and several jotters.

'Was that Celeste's?' I coughed. It was so dusty up here.

Actually, it was dusty everywhere in the museum. I should get a cleaner in.

'Looks like it, doesn't it? Do you mind?'

''Course not. This was her room, wasn't it?'

'Yes, but as you can see there a lot of Ethel-Rose's personal effects in here too.'

It felt peculiar. Almost intrusive. Some bits and bobs looked like they had not been touched since Celeste walked out the door on her last day of life.

There was a strong sense of both women – the faded scent of rose petals, baby powder; an open *Cosmopolitan* on the bed, cut-glass perfume bottles half full set beside a hand mirror and brush that had a couple of long black hairs still in it.

Until now, they had been only characters in the story of my family but in this room, among their things, I was confronted by the reality that they had been living and breathing and here. And, for the first time, I was touched by a spasm of grief. My own, for them, having never been acquainted, combined with an acute almost painful wave of sympathy for Septimus and his great loss. A wife and a daughter. How agonising. Dad too had suffered the trauma of a losing a mother and a sister. Quite unexpectedly, I felt myself well up.

Hiding my face from Sam, I turned away into the dimness. 'What's this then?' I said, to distract him from my emotion. 'Under the sheet?' and shone my light on the big object in the middle of the room.

In the distance thunder rumbled.

Sam replied with a grin in his voice, 'Why don't you see? Take the covering off, go on.'

I did as instructed and whipped it away, dropping the cloth at my feet. A sheet of lightning lit up the windows and illuminated a fortune-teller machine.

'Whoa,' I said, stepping back. Not what I expected at all. It was the kind of thing you see on piers and in amusement arcades: a large box made of glass and wood that was decorated to resemble the velveteen interior of a gypsy caravan. Across the top was a wooden sign in a circus-type script that read *Madam Zelda*. Beneath it, the upper half of an automaton bent over a crystal ball. It was dressed in a bodice with long flowing sleeves and a large gold-link necklace. Black hair fell down beneath a fringed headscarf. Her eyes were heavily lined, her lips ruby red. Attractive, as far as dolls went.

Lightning struck something outside, a couple of miles away, and again the room blazed white.

I laughed with delight as a light came on above the gypsy's head and flickered.

Something clicked noisily.

Zelda's eyes flashed green and opened as she whirred into life.

The head rotated clunkily towards me, her hand juddering over the crystal ball now illuminated. Big hoop earrings jangled. Her chest moved as if she was breathing and a voice rang out of the speakers, female, layered with an 'exotic' Eastern European accent.

'A dangerous coupling,' she trilled, 'that is not resolved, leads to fatal decisions. Beware. Be astute in your judgement of people you encounter. They may not be all they seem,' she finished. The lights darkened.

I turned and looked at Sam with a sardonic nip on my lips. 'Pfft,' I said. 'Very well planned. How did you do that? Remote control? Tripwire?'

In the torchlight I could see his face was kind of frozen. After a long moment, he looked at me and grimaced and said, 'I didn't do that.'

'Kidding?' I returned.

He shook his head.

I copied his movement and said in a lightly mocking tone, 'This place, honestly. If I didn't know better I would say it was trying to tell me something.' Then I waited for a disparaging comment.

We spent the next few seconds in silence, for on this occasion Sam said nothing.

Eventually he pointed at the floor near my feet. When I shone the torch at the space I saw the plug lying there.

'Oh,' I said. 'Really not you then? But if it's not plugged in, it can't get electricity, so ...'

'I realise that,' Sam said at last.

I took a long hard look at him, then had to turn back again.

In her fortune-teller's cabinet, Zelda had started to laugh.

Thunder rattled the casements.

AUTHOR'S NOTE

Elizabeth Brownrigg did indeed carry out the crimes outlined in this book. She was a midwife for the Saint Dunstan's Parish and, as such a professional, was given custody of several girls as domestic servants who came from the nearby Foundling Hospital. I'm sad to say that she was not the only abusive adult who exploited vulnerable children and young women. She became a pariah in the popular press and was executed at Tyburn on 14 September 1767, after being found guilty of torturing her female apprentice, Mary Clifford, to death. The house where she lived and where these crimes took place was in Fleur de Lis Court, also known as Flower-de-Luce. This was situated to the east of Fetter Lane and north of Fleet Street but was absorbed into Fetter Lane between 1848 and 1851.

It's very easy to relegate these incidents to the past or treat them as an unfortunate episode of our history, however, we know that human slavery exists today. Young women and girls are at present subject to a worrying pan-global phenomenon which sees them kidnapped, raped, groomed and trafficked, and at worst murdered. Much of this goes undiscussed, the victims forced into silence for fear of retribution. We have to start speaking out and stating clearly that we value girls just as much as we value boys. And so too must we challenge any prejudice we come across, regularly, no matter how small or allegedly 'jocular' it may seem. There are, of course, many charities and groups trying to address this problem, but by raising these issues and talking about them openly, in this small way we can effect change by ourselves. I think that's how we make a better world for everyone.

21 May 2017

For more information, check out:
Act for Girls – https://plan-uk.org/act-for-girls/
Anti-slavery – www.antislavery.org/slavery-today/slavery-uk/
DINNødhjælp (Your Help Needed) – http://dinnoedhjaelp.dk/
Safe Child Africa – www.safechildafrica.org/
Women's Equality Party – www.womensequality.org.uk/

ACKNOWLEDGEMENTS

As always, multiple thanks go to Sean and Riley without whose support my books would be impossible to write. The magic beans *will* grow!

My editor, Jenny Parrott, is THE BUSINESS! Where would I be without her astute judgement, boundless energy and irrepressible spirit? Not here, for sure. She is an absolute peach. More Oneworld notable mentions must include Margot Weale for her brilliant campaign for *Strange Magic*. Here's to the next two, Margot, and lots more Essex Girl cocktails. Thanhmai Bui-Van walks a great and rather sassy walk with the sales malarkey. Ilona Chavasse does strange occult things with rights and everything associated therewith. Cailin Neal and Mark Rusher talk the marketing talk with grace and zeal. Paul Nash, James Magniac and James Jones are responsible for turning the manuscript into a physical thing – and those gorgeous covers too. Emma Grundy Haigh gets her hands dirty with the copy-edit and makes the words work. Becky Kraemer does all of this all over again in the US. Thanks also to Juliet Mabey and Novin Doostdar.

I must also thank Robert Longhurst for his most invaluable

help and advice regarding all things optometric and for the detail on visual processing disorders. It was our initial conversation, while I was having my eyes tested, that led to a discussion about Charles Bonnet syndrome which partly inspired *Strange Sight*.

John Gurel gave me a lot of advice with respect to occupational hazards and habits which was so insightful. While paranormal investigator and author Richard Estep got me through some of the very technical bits. Thanks to Twitter buddy Julie Haves, for introducing us. For a sceptical take on ghost-hunting you could do no worse than visit Hayley Stevens website www.hayleyisaghost.co.uk.

Friends in the Fourth Estate who have been incredibly supportive of my bursts into publishing deserve a thank you too – Kelly Buckley, Darryl Webber, Louise Howeson, Emma Rice, Chris Hatton, Steve Neale, Sasha James. And I have some great literary supporters to whom I am also very grateful – the Essex Book Festival, the Forum in Southend, Sarah Perry, Cathi Unsworth and Travis Elborough, Jo Good, thepool.co.uk, Bluebookballoon, Crimesquad.com, thecrimewarp, TheQuietKnitter, Gateway, Lucy V. Hay.

Thanks to everyone at Metal. A great bunch of people who are very understanding around publication and kind and nice and just amazing colleagues. A special shout out goes to Nicky Bettell in particular, for the Sandra face. She doesn't have one, but she entertained me for a hysterical half hour describing it and let me insert the phrase into Rosie's vernacular.

I wrote parts of this book in Australia and have to thank

my Oz kin for their interest and encouragement – Des and Kath, Simon and Jo, Xave and Genevieve. Darren and Wendy too. And also my lovely Australian friends Jo Todd and Justin Le Gouilon, without whom my life would have gone in an entirely different direction. Can I also point out to Gabrielle and John that I did rise to the challenge of getting both *Gabrielle* and a *donkey* in the same paragraph, thank you very much.

Thanks as always to Mum and Dad, Pauline and Ernie, and my family and friends who are great. Too many to mention but you know who you are. Kate Bradley and Steph Roche, however, get special mentions as they have done so much for me with my literary efforts.

And thanks to you the reader. You make it happen.

'*Strange Magic* is that rarest of things: a book which sets out unashamedly to entertain, and does so with wit, style, and erudition. I gleefully submitted to a tale of witchcraft, feminism, mysterious strangers, historical atrocities, plucky heroines and ghastly apparitions – and came away more proud than ever to be an Essex girl.'
Sarah Perry, author of *The Essex Serpent*

Book 1 in the Essex Witch Museum Series

STRANGE MAGIC

Syd Moore

Rosie Strange doesn't believe in witches. No, not at all. It's no surprise therefore when she inherits the ramshackle Essex Witch Museum, her first thought is to take the money and run. Still, the museum exerts a curious pull. There's the eccentric academic who demands Rosie hunt for old bones, those of the notorious Ursula Cadence, a witch long since put to death. And there's curator Sam Stone, a man Rosie can't decide if he's tiresomely annoying or extremely captivating. Her plans to sell the museum might need to be delayed, just for a while.

Finding herself and Sam embroiled in a centuries-old mystery, Rosie is quickly expelled from her comfort zone, where to her horror, the secrets of the past come with their own real, and all too present danger, as a strange magic threatens to envelope them all.